GEOFFREY WOLFF'S
THE FINAL CLUB

"Wolff brilliantly explores the idioms and idiosyncrasies of class...
A complicated novel that celebrates youth while paying tribute to
experience...ultimately it is a story about grace—the kind that
springs, spontaneously and mysteriously, from the depths of the
human heart." —*Detroit Free Press*

"Deeply compassionate and heartfelt...The blue blood that flows
through the book is cauterized by a shocking, bizarre opening and a
searing blast of reality at the end. Steeped in wisdom and framed in
anguish...*The Final Club* is unforgettable—and enormously
entertaining." —*San Diego Tribune*

"His prose style—a mix of nabob and nowhere-man dictions—
sings, at turns both fancy and funky.... His appetite for telling
detail and his ability to register its nuances in muscular, telegraphic
prose charges *The Final Club* in bracing moments.... Wolff does
what Waugh did for Oxbridge—imparts a sense of real drama to the
social rites of young men and women." —*Village Voice Literary Supplement*

"Wolff has constructed a Princeton-based universe that far surpasses
any sentimental vision of the golden years. By focusing on the elite
facade and inner sanctum of the class of '60, *The Final Club* exquisitely captures the wider world within its shadowy but hallowed
walls.... beautifully handled...a strong and delicate novel." —*Boston Globe*

THE FINAL CLUB

THE
FINAL CLUB

GEOFFREY WOLFF

VINTAGE CONTEMPORARIES

VINTAGE BOOKS

A DIVISION OF RANDOM HOUSE, INC.

NEW YORK

First Vintage Contemporaries Edition, November 1991

All rights reserved under International and Pan-American Copyright
Conventions. Published in the United States by Vintage Books, a
division of Random House, Inc., New York, and simultaneously in
Canada by Random House of Canada Limited, Toronto. Originally published
in hardcover by Alfred A. Knopf, Inc., New York, in 1990.

A portion of this work was originally published in *Esquire*.

Library of Congress Cataloging-in-Publication Data
Wolff, Geoffrey, 1937–
The final club / Geoffrey Wolff. — 1st Vintage contemporaries ed.
p.   cm. — (Vintage contemporaries)
Originally published: New York : Knopf, 1990.
"A portion of this work was originally published in Esquire" — T.p. verso
ISBN 0-679-73592-5 (pbk.)
I. Title.
PS3573.O53F56   1991
813'.54—dc20   91-50016
CIP

Manufactured in the United States of America
10 9 8 7 6 5 4 3 2 1

To Walt Litz
and in memory of
Richard Blackmur
Larry Holland
Bill Ward

Author's Note

While the campus of my Princeton is Princeton's Princeton, while some of her legendary personages are invoked, while the institution of Bicker is too perversely odd for my fancy to have fabricated—I have taken liberties. My entire purpose has been to take liberties: I've staffed my Princeton's faculty, rigged the outcome of athletic contests, and taken charge of the Office of Admissions, welcoming an imagined student body, excluding from my Princeton those substantial souls who believed themselves to be my characters' college-mates. Those who move through *The Final Club*, wherever in the world they may travel, are inventions, believe me.

Contents

PART ONE

THE CLASS
OF '60

One

The Empire Builder
and the Dinky

Winter term of Nathaniel's eleventh-grade year, sometime between midnight and dawn, his mother woke him from untroubled sleep. She appeared anguished. This night her distress was urgent to a third, fifth, nth power beyond the low-boiling domestic dismay to which she seemed to have accustomed herself. Dragged up from sleep, the boy thought fire, saw in his mind's eye the wrecked Jag, emergency room . . .

"Mom?"

"Come downstairs."

"What's the matter?"

"Come down *now*!"

His mother kept her hair neat, swept back in a bun. Tonight it was undone, wild. She moved herky-jerky; this was different. She smelled odd, like sour cream. Nathaniel had a master's nose for his dad's off odors, the disguising mint, revealing tonic, alien perfume. But till tonight his mother had smelled scrubbed, till now reliably fresh.

Nathaniel followed his mother down from his attic room; he glanced through the open door of his father's bedroom at the damned firepole. He passed the shut door of his mother's bedroom, followed her downstairs into the cold kitchen. By the light at the end of the dock out there, lit all winter— why?—he saw sleet falling, heard it sweeping off Lake

3

Washington, driving against the window, rattling the panes. Drops struck the fire's dying embers, and the woodstove smoked and hissed. Nathaniel's father was a volunteer fireman; trouble was his hobby. He kept his ears on for sirens, had installed an alarm above his four-poster's headboard. His black oilskin slicker and sou'wester, his Wellington boots, were in place, dry, beside the back door. Nathaniel's father was drunk.

"Dad?"

"Hey, swee'pea! Give your pa a hug."

"Sit down!" What was this? Nathaniel's mother had a soft voice, so you had to tune in to make out her meaning. She normally had a gentle, quick laugh. She never shouted, till tonight. "Sit in that chair, beside your father, right now!"

"She's a little upset," his father said. "It got a little tipsy out, and some got on me. Listen, honey—"

"Shut up! You . . . shut your face! I hate your face. Hate you!"

"I've been fooling around," Nathaniel's father explained to his son. "Darlin'—" he had turned to his wife, seemed to blink her into fuzzy focus—"Jesus H. Kee-rist! What did you think all these years? What're you thinking?" Then, seductively, "Penny for your thoughts, lovebug."

It was then that Nathaniel saw what he might have seen at once had he been looking for it: his mother was leaning against the firepole anchored in the middle of the kitchen, the controversial firepole that had required bravura saber-sawing to cut that difficult-to-explain-to-schoolfriends hole through the kitchen ceiling to his father's bedroom. A truth came to Nathaniel that night in that kitchen: what a person didn't notice could kill a person; he had been taught to take his life's unremarkability on faith. Now, resolving to stay wide awake and on watch, Nathaniel saw his mother's unaccountably soiled nightgown was unaccountably unfastened, and that thing there was a government-issue Colt .45 automatic, huge in his mom's delicate left hand.

"Baby," Nathaniel's father said. "Sweetheart."

"Shut up! I want Nathaniel to select. In five minutes I'm going to shoot your father, or myself. One or the other. You say which. Believe me. You pick the survivor. Your mother, or your father and his new—his newer, newest—cunt. And his silver flasks. And his sports car. Choose. One. Pick which."

She held the automatic to her face, put the muzzle in her mouth. Nathaniel tasted the oil against her tongue, like old pennies, electric.

"I don't need this," Nathaniel said. "I've got a chem test in the morning and a hockey game tomorrow afternoon. Goodnight, folks."

Nathaniel climbed the stairs to his room; he waited to hear the thud, or not. Years later he'd ask himself how he conceived to say it. He'd wonder if he'd been smart or dumb, brave or yellow. His mother had decided he was just cold, but she was wrong there. His father had laughed, but then he had always laughed.

Now, a year and a half later, Nathaniel's father was dead and his mother sick; her people were sending Nathaniel east from Seattle to Princeton. The redcap had finished stowing the boy's bags in his roomette; the redcap gave a grave little bow and touched the bill of his cap when he saw what Nathaniel's grandfather had slipped into his palm. Nathaniel's grandfather, in the convention of grandparents, was called by a pet name, Gander, after baby Nathaniel's mishearing and misspeaking of "grander" ("I'm grander than any father," the short, slight, tidy man had said); Gander did not look like a man with a nickname. He wore gray: flannel suit nipped at the waist, deep-pleated trousers that broke not quite foppishly on the uppers of his dainty Lobb cap-toe shoes; gray tie tight at his starched collar; gray homburg; gray hair cut short, just so; gray brush-cut mustache, fastidiously trimmed. When William Faulkner had showed up seven years ago on the front page of the *Post-Intelligencer* with his Nobel in literature, Nathaniel's grandmother had said, "Look, that man has stolen his good looks from my husband."

The redcap noticed Gander's lapel buttons, American flag on the left and on the right, just north of a linen handkerchief folded with calculated nonchalance, *I Like Ike Again*. The redcap told Nathaniel that he was almost tempted to switch from Stevenson and put the general back in the White House another term if this generous gentleman was representative of Ike's champions.

"Don't you dare," Nathaniel's grandmother said. "This man is a dinosaur. We"—showing Adlai and Estes on her own lapel—"need every vote."

Nathaniel's grandfather rolled his eyes, shook his head, said, "Hatsie Hatsie Hatsie, leave this poor man in peace." He took the redcap's hand, said, "Harriet'll soapbox your ears off, better hightail it while you've still got 'em."

This meant: *Leave us alone*.

When the kin were to themselves, they stood at the train window, regarding the platform bustle, anxious little dramas of leavetaking and prospect. For a few minutes the three stood in easy silence.

"We're proud of you," his grandfather said.

"You mustn't fret about your mother," her mother said. "You can't do a thing for her except be happy."

"It wasn't your father's fault," Gander said, almost as though he believed this.

"It wasn't really his fault," Nathaniel's grandmother said, and then she began to weep a little, and this flushed her face. Her cheeks were pink as polished apples, and her fine white hair had yellow in it, like aged paper.

"He was a charmer," Gander said.

"I guess," Nathaniel said, on guard. He thought he had never heard a person speak of his father without invoking charm. Charm had come to seem a disagreeable quality, a hypnotist's trick with a snake, a bauble fixed haphazardly to a jangly bracelet, meretricious. "I guess he had charm okay."

"We have something for you," Gander said, "for the trip. To keep you busy at night."

"During the day look out the windows," his grandmother Harriet said. "There are great sights out there, west of the Badlands."

"Chicago's quite a place, too," Gander said.

His wife gave him a look, and shrugged.

"I'm going to phone them," Nathaniel said.

"Of course," Gander said.

"As you wish," his grandmother said.

"I love you," Nathaniel told his grandmother.

"I know," she said, stuffing greenbacks in his jacket pocket.

"You too," he said to Gander.

"That's ironic," said Gander; "I've just cut you out of my will."

Gander's wife gave her husband's hand a little slap, and they winked at each other, and Nathaniel winked at both of them, and they were winking at him to beat the band. Nathaniel was pleased to understand that his family's common genetic signature was this chipper neural tic, this voluntary, learned response to solemnity.

The "All aboard!"'s had begun, and the pace on the platform quickened. Nathaniel was obliged to account for his checkbook, cash, tickets, medical report. Then Gander pressed the package on Nathaniel, and Nathaniel's grandmother put her dry cheek against the cheek of her only child's only child.

"Be a good boy," she said.

"Goodness gracious," Gander said. "How good, for goodness' sake, should he be? Here's some good advice: ride a train far enough and something will happen to you. Take my word. Be ready, be open, that's the best advice I can give you."

"That's more advice than he needs," his wife said, and there they went again, winking at one another in a rondo of irony.

And then Nathaniel's grandparents swung down from the train, and arm in arm walked purposefully down the platform and disappeared into the steam sweating from hidden works beneath the cars. And then the train gave a little shudder, the couplings groaned, the whistle blasted, and the Great Northern's Empire Builder began to roll east, putting on speed, away from home.

As soon as the courtly porter had taught Nathaniel the ways of his compartment—a trick with the sink, how to lower the berth, where the iced water was kept—Nathaniel went forward to the Vista Dome car. All that power up there. The great transcontinental locomotives were called Big Boys, and they were. At the train's first stop Nathaniel felt the weight of the Empire Builder, saw with what gravity people gathered along the tracks to watch it come in, go off.

East of Snohomish they rocked and thundered into wild country, a fog-hung forest of hemlock and Douglas fir; Weyerhaeuser had slashed and ruined all that could be sacked and sold, and the loggers were at it now. Moving north, at a right angle to the Empire Builder, a monster steam engine was dragging a train of huge, fresh-cut fir trunks across a gorge, rolling along a trestle of bizarre complexity that had itself used up a felled virgin forest.

Up there to the left? That must have been Mount Baker, in the Cascades. Down right, Mount Rainier, its snowy hump sunlit violet, solitary. As far back as he could remember wanting to see anything, Nathaniel had looked first thing every morning and last thing at sunset for that mountain. To see it was good: clear weather, daytime, reference point for south and east, measure for beauty and standing. Not to see it was to wonder if the bad weather would ever break, whether the mountain was still, after all, there. Nathaniel recalled a spring vacation ski trip at Mount Rainier with friends back in seventh grade. He had loved a girl with gray eyes and yellow hair, Judy. Judy loved a pretty boy—was it a Bobby or a Billy whose dad sold the Olympic Hotel and took his money and family to Santa Barbara?—who loved Caryl. Caryl didn't love anybody. For a time the epidemic unrequited love was pure pain, reliable as toothache. Nathaniel would come in from skiing alone to sit in front of Paradise Inn's fieldstone fireplace, and the hum of conversation among his classmates would break off. He'd sit apart blushing from dim, unlocated shame, pounding with want, trying to think of something to say; he'd pretend finally to have important business in his room, and no sooner was his back turned than giggling began. And then . . . and then the assertive beauty of Mount Rainier after a great dump of new snow, alight beneath a halo of cirrus, the sweet fragrance of red cedar, the abrupt flash of sunstruck iced aspen branches, the good times of good turns on steep slopes . . . all this beat back the hurt, what was so perfectly called a "crush," and directed devotion from Judy and Whosis and Caryl to that place at that time. Nathaniel liked remembering how they'd got together one night after dinner in the inn's cardroom to discuss how they felt, how they'd actually talked it out, spilled their guts, admitting to feelings they thought they'd never admit to. (Nathaniel didn't tell every last thing, perhaps; perhaps he didn't explain how he fell for Judy in Latin class, at just that moment when she raised her bare-shouldered left arm to adjust her hair and Nathaniel, two rows back, a couple of seats to her left, was set on fire by the hidden pocket under her arm, the almost imperceptible curve of her almost imperceptible breast.) It was an intimate occa-

sion, remarkable, and they felt tender, protective of one another, grown up. And then, beginning the next morning,
with bright sun on new snow, they had all let passion loose on
the mountain rather than the awful abyss of self, and they had
let themselves be a gang of kids, a sweet club of giggling
playmates. Nathaniel knew he'd never forget what happened
there, with Judy, Caryl and What's-His-Name.

Now, having traversed the Columbia, the Empire Builder's
great locomotive laid a plume of smoke down its back and
highballed horning stridently through central and eastern
Washington's wheat fields baking under the September sun.

They crossed into Idaho north of Coeur d'Alene as the sun
fell, and the porter told Nathaniel that this might be a useful
time to eat dinner, that there was a young lady in the dining
car who would perhaps agree to make room for Nathaniel at
her table. Nathaniel expected the porter to wink, but he
didn't. Nathaniel winked; the porter, impassive, showed no
response to the young man's gesture of complicity.

It was so: she sat at a table on the south side facing east, and
a waiter, who seemed to have expected Nathaniel, led him to
a seat across from her. This was happening too fast, Nathaniel
thought. She was pretty, beautiful, handsome; she was . . . oh
my! his age, maybe older. He thought he knew her face:
magazine cover? movie? Gander had promised Nathaniel an
event on this journey, and here it was, too soon, the most
common thing and the least foreseen, a girl. She wore a dark
red velvet dress, with little spaghetti straps loose on her bare,
pale shoulders. The dress was cut lower than dresses Seattle
girls wore. Before he could introduce himself, she leaned across
the table with an unlit cigarette between her soft, pouty lips,
looking frankly into Nathaniel's eyes.

"Light," she said.

"I'm sorry," Nathaniel said, "I don't smoke. I mean I don't
have a lighter."

The pretty girl pointed to a book of matches nearer her than him. The matchbook bore the Great Northern's feisty logo, a mountain goat, and taking it in hand Nathaniel felt raffish to be aboard, a pioneer. He lit her cigarette, and she held his eyes.

"I know you," she said. "You know the Pierces. You're the one with the speedboat."

"It was my father's boat—"

"You go to Yale," she said.

"Princeton," he said.

"I knew it," she said. "I knew I knew you."

"I haven't started Princeton yet."

"Do you know Hugh Tedder?" the pretty girl asked.

"From Seattle?"

"No! Princeton! All the Tedders went to Princeton. They live in Tuxedo."

Nathaniel said he didn't know Hugh Tedder, or any Tedder. "My name's Nathaniel," he said. "I wouldn't know anything about any Tuxedo."

"Tuxedo *Park.* Nathaniel what?" the pretty girl asked.

"Clay," he said.

"Well, Mister Clay, my name is Carr. My first name is spelled 'D-i-a-n-a,' and we pronounce it 'Dee-ah-nah'; we think Dye-anna sounds tacky, not to mention Dye-an, with its awful unsounded final syllable."

"Huh?" said Nathaniel. "Pardon?"

Dee-ah-nah stared at her dinner partner, shook her head as though waking herself from a nap, looked down at her menu and said, "What wine shall we order?" And then, as though bored by her question, asked another: "What does your father do?"

"He'd retired," Nathaniel said.

"Uh-huh. What did he do before he retired?"

"Well," Nathaniel said, "he died."

"Sorry," Diana said.

He understood what she meant by "sorry": not sorry he's dead, but sorry I asked, sorry to get such an unfun answer.

Way ahead and off to the south a warm orange glow bloomed on the skyline. Last night Nathaniel's grandfather had traced the Empire Builder's route across an often-folded, hand-drawn map framed in the old man's library. Gander had told his grandson this document had belonged to Jim Hill, who dealt and grabbed and bullied and cheated and blasted the Great Northern from Chicago to Seattle. The Empire Builder, named for that old mountain goat and for what he built, took the High Line east, bearing north toward Whitefish, along the edge of Glacier National Park, into the Blackfeet Reservation. That illumination down on the world's rim must be Butte, an infernal blaze of smelting furnace, a hill of evil glitter. Or maybe it was Anaconda, spewing copper fumes from the Tallest Stack on Earth. "I don't want to send you east on the low line," Gander had said. "I'm a capitalist, and that's a fact, but I don't believe in open pit mines, and I especially don't believe in Anaconda. Anaconda's named for a snake, you know; wraps around its victim and squeezes the life out of it. You'll like the High Line better. It's a better kind of wild."

The waiter stood waiting. He said those were fires out there, forests were burning north and south, they were heading for a bad blaze up in Glacier.

"Are we in danger?"

"No, ma'am."

Nathaniel asked if the fires were under control, if they'd done much damage.

The waiter shrugged.

Diana wanted to know: "Will there be a delay? I have to be on time in Chicago. Lake Forest, actually. For a party, actually, a dance. A coming-out party. Actually."

The waiter said he couldn't imagine a forest fire would slow the Empire Builder's progress.

"We'll have the '49 Pichon-Longueville," Diana said. The waiter nodded, smiled.

"That's good," Nathaniel said.

"Uh-huh," Diana said. "I speak French perfectly. I don't have an accent. I mean an American accent. Of course I have a French accent."

"I meant the wine. It sounds good."

"Uh-huh. Do you think I have a perfect French accent?"

"I think you have a beautiful voice," Nathaniel said, disbelieving he had said it.

She leaned forward for another light. An almost invisible network of exquisite veins laced her throat and breasts. He imagined he could see her pale breasts pump to her heart's sexy beat. He could feel his heart pound, imagined he could hear it above the click of wheels against rails. The train rocked. Or was the world rocking? He could see their whole train, curving visible up there around the bend, climbing, hugging the western slope of the Continental Divide. How did someone get so beautiful? Diana was instructing Nathaniel in the ins and outs of Seattle, where the best people lived. She herself was from Connecticut, Darien, but she'd been obliged to visit her cousin Ann Pierce, this "absolute homesteader." Nathaniel knew Ann Pierce. His father had sailed and played backgammon with Mr. Pierce. "I mean she's so homespun. Such a hick. So provincial." Ann Pierce was a good swimmer, a friendly girl who wore pigtails and liked to water-ski behind Nathaniel's Chris-Craft Riviera when he came to visit. "I mean she got into Briarcliff and she's not even going. She's going to some godforsaken place she calls the U. of W."

"University of Washington," Nathaniel said. His mom's parents had studied there. Who could not know what was the U. of W.? What it was like growing up near Husky stadium, watching the great Don Heinrich pass against California and Stanford, seeing the heavyweight Husky crew move an eight-oared Pocock shell—built in Seattle!—slowly away from the boathouse ramp on Portage Bay, enter Lake Washington, pick up the stroke, row full bore past the Clays' dock? Nathaniel said, "I like Ann."

"Uh-huh." Diana looked at Nathaniel quizzically, tilting her head. She exhaled a little sigh—*let's get to it*—and sipped her wine. Now her pouty lips were blood red. She was using her tongue on a bit of cigarette paper stuck to her lower lip. Nathaniel stared at her. There was a spot of lipstick on her tooth. She smelled of perfume. Her cheeks blushed. A strand of hair had fallen across her face. It was hot and close in the dining car, and the hair was stuck to her face at the corner of her mouth.

He adjusted the starched white napkin covering his lap. The tablecloth too was white and starched stiff, now spotted with drips of wine from the bottle she poured from before she'd emptied her glass. The silver was substantial, heavy, polished, worn, well used.

The Empire Builder lumbered through the Cabinet Mountains and crossed western Montana's turbulent Kootenai River, boiling white down there in the ambient light of the train. Diana ate voraciously; he picked at his food.

"You've got a wolf in your stomach," he said.

"Huh?" she said.

"Just a saying," he said. "Something my mom says. Sometimes."

"Uh-huh," she said.

Now she invoked where the Pierces lived on Lake Washington—Mercer Island—as a kind of talisman, dropping the unmusical proper noun into her opinions. "They have a charming little boathouse at the end of their dock on *Mercer Island*. . . . Mr. Pierce keeps a seaplane in front of their house on *Mercer Island*. . . . Dixie Gilbert came over to *Mercer Island* from her family's tedious *faux*-Tudor manoir in Laurelhurst . . . her father practically runs Boeings—"

"I live in Laurelhurst," Nathaniel said.

"Uh-huh," Diana said.

"It's 'Boeing,' " Nathaniel said.

"What is?"

"It's not 'Boeings,' " Nathaniel said. "Lots of people make that mistake." He poured himself some wine.

Diana poured herself the last of the wine. "When you get angry, your eyes flash," she said.

"Angry?" he said.

"You have such elegant eyelashes," she said. "Oh, look. He blushes." She chose a wildflower from the bud vase and threaded it dripping into the buttonhole of his tweed jacket. Nathaniel glanced at his sleeves: they were too long; his grandmother had insisted he leave growing room. Still, the tweed had gained some ground on his high-school wardrobe: loafers with a blinding plastic sheen, suntans, skinny belt, chlorine rayon shirt with top button done up, Lord Jeff V-neck lamb's-wool sweater. Yellow. Neat. Diana was staring at him, and Nathaniel blushed. "You look dashing," she said. "You may come to my compartment."

Nothing like this had ever happened to Nathaniel, taking into account that nothing—properly speaking—was happening now. Oh, that's crazy; of course something was happening. They had kissed, she had kissed him, as soon as the compartment door was shut. The little room—chaotic with Diana's clothes, intimate clothes, too—was heavy with perfume and tobacco. She lay on her berth, and drew him down to her, and put—she put—his hand on her breast. He was thinking wildly ahead, and the train whistle blasted, and the train rocked and his head was bursting, and she seemed to be

moaning, and then she stiffened at his one particular explora-
tion, and said, "Stop!"

Nathaniel stopped. She rolled away from his pounding
chest, and put her back to him, and stared out the window,
looking north and east. He moved as circumspectly as a
tracker, and adjusted his fit to her, and with evident casualness
draped his arm across her hip, and smelled her hair. Where
had he learned this?

She opened her lips, and stuck out her tongue at the window's fogged pane. Erotic, shocking. Was she connecting with
something out there in the fire-glowing, wild dark? With
Nathaniel, looking at him in the glass? With her reflected
image, with herself?

"Never betray me," Diana said.

Nathaniel said nothing. He didn't know what to say. He
looked out the window and saw more orange and yellow up
there on the horizon, as though the whole world to the north
was ablaze.

"Look," he said. "It's like a city on a hill, lit up."

"Never touch me wrong," she said. "I shouldn't trust any
Princeton boy. Don't take advantage of me."

"I'd never—"

"I can't control myself if you take advantage of me."

"What?" He couldn't quite make her out, he thought,
above the muffled chatter of steel on steel.

"Don't you know? I'm wet."

"You're?"

"Don't talk," she said. "Let's be still and look outside; if I
fall asleep from the wine . . . Wine goes to my head. If I fall
asleep, you must leave me. I shall trust you."

Nathaniel dared say nothing. He wanted this to go on, just
this bewildering way, forever. He pulled away slightly from
her back, to help her trust him. He could see her face reflected
in the window. She seemed not to look out there but to be

focused near, on her reflected image. Her red velvet skirt had ridden up her thighs, and he could see the top edge of her silk stockings, her white garter belt. She moved just a bit, adjusting her clothes, and now he saw more, a flash of white panties.

"May I ask you something?" she said.

"Of course."

"I don't even know where you went to school."

"Laurelhurst."

"Laurelhurst?"

"Uh-huh."

"Is that a day school?"

"Uh-huh."

"Private?"

"Unh-uh."

"Oh."

He awoke from a shallow sleep as they grated to a stop. Feeble mustard light seeped in on them, and he saw they were beside a rural station, on a siding. He heard a hum of voices and then he saw the men slouch-shouldered beside their gear, wearing face masks, like outlaws, train robbers. For a moment, smelling the smoke, seeing the smoke smudge the sky, watching a steady fallout of ash leaking from the sulphur clouds, hearing the explosions off in the distance, Nathaniel thought the final war had begun. Now, he thought, it was already too late to have this beautiful girl he by now loved. It had happened too fast, and it had happened too late. Nothing Nathaniel had seen in war movies could have prepared him for the menacing faces of those soldiers, smoke-black where the bandannas across their mouths and noses hadn't covered. The exhausted soldiers looked like West Virginia miners he had seen in a book of photographs his grandmother admired.

"Gross!" Diana said. "They can see us."

"They're firefighters," Nathaniel said, understanding now. "The woods are on fire." The gunfire pops he heard way off were explosions of pine. "They're smoke jumpers, Diana. My father told me about them. He loved fires. I mean he loved fighting fires. He was a fireman, sort of."

"He sounds like some *law* enforcement officer, some *sheriff* or something."

"Nothing so glamorous. He was just a volunteer."

"Uh-huh," said Diana.

"They're coming aboard," Nathaniel said. "Riding to the next place they'll try to hold the line. Look, they're Indians." The Empire Builder was somewhere in the Blackfeet Reservation. They must have had a gathering of the tribes to make a few bucks off the disastrous outcome of some camper's wienie roast. Nathaniel's father had told him about these big fires, how Indians sometimes gave nature a helping hand in her wish to provide a wage for all her children, setting a little fire a valley or two over from their valley to make work for themselves.

Nathaniel fumbled uselessly with the window shade. "The porter showed me how to work it," he said. "I guess I wasn't paying attention."

A couple of Indians stood on the embankment a yard from Diana's face, staring at her. Nathaniel wondered how much they could see of the dark compartment, and what they thought of what they saw. They were talking. One of them punched his friend in the shoulder, and laughed.

"Gross," Diana said. "I didn't want anyone to know we're alone in here together. If you're so interested in forest fires, go talk to them. I want you to leave now. I don't even know you. I've never heard of where you went to school."

He stared at her. She was biting her lower lip. Sulky. Angry. He said, "Diana, darling"; he said the five syllables with a soap-operatic unfelt emphasis that astounded him.

"Dee-ah-nah, dah-ling." He had meant to call her "sweet-heart." Where had his new voice come from?

"You're all such *boys*," said the girl, now smiling prettily. "All right, all right! You can escort me to Dido's tedious extravaganza in Lake Forest tomorrow night. Go, you naughty boy. We'll have breakfast."

And so Nathaniel—too befuddled to tell all the complications of train scheduling and haberdashery that made his attendance at a Lake Forest extravaganza unlikely—nodded, and left.

He wanted to ask the firefighters what was happening, but he didn't. They were beat—not party-till-dawn beat, or pull-an-all-nighter-before-the-midterm beat—but burnt out. When the coach seats were taken, the rest of the firefighters squatted in the Empire Builder's aisles, or huddled in the cold, clamorous vestibules between the coaches, talking in hushed, modest voices, gently. No dining car for these Blackfeet; no Vista Dome for these Flathead or Nez Percé. Now Nathaniel was weary, after his own fashion. He felt shame to feel tired from what had worn him out. He looked at those smoke-blackened young men, most of them near his age, and he thought about his compartment, its iced water, sink, soft towels, clean sheets. The firefighters were restricted to coaches; he brushed past them going to his sleeping car. There and here, classes divided as soon as the first train rolled along the first set of rails, the way of the world.

He couldn't sleep. Fires sparked the sky north and south. It had been an arid summer, hard on farmers out here. Near Havre, electrically aglow with its own meager business, the firefighters climbed down. This was a railhead for branch lines that could carry the Crow and Cheyenne back home. The Nez Percé were at the end of their line. Near here, in Chinook, Chief Joseph had surrendered his Nez Percé, given up resisting. Nathaniel blushed to remember learning about Chief Joseph in the ninth grade at Laurelhurst, how he had burst out during History of the Wild West: "Why don't we give it back? It's theirs! We have no right to it." How Mr. Vannek had said, hamming it up the way he did, that wouldn't really be practical, would it? Perhaps the Black Hills should be returned to Sitting Bull's descendants, and all those mineral rights too, not to mention Mount Rushmore? Nathaniel's teacher was warming to his work; he was on a tear: How exactly did Nathaniel propose to make the exchange, assuming of course that Chief Joseph, dead in the ground according to Mr. Vannek's understanding, could be brought back to sign the appropriate contracts? Mr. Vannek knew he was hilarious. As funny as a rubber crutch. But despite Mr. Vannek, Nathaniel had learned something. He had learned about Indians' instinct for connection and loyalty, their easy way of naming someone in the tribe—anyone at all—"cousin" or "sister," claiming kin as though there were nothing to it at all, as though it were the most natural word there was—brother, sister. Nathaniel thought History of the Wild West had taught him this, that this was good to have learned, that he could use this.

Before first light the Empire Builder slowed, passing yardmen at their switches lit by glowing oil pots. That was sere, forlorn Malta. Nathaniel saw this country as alien and hostile, unmeshed with his own, wherever was his own. He wanted to belong to some society beyond the community he had left on the margin of Puget Sound. Nathaniel wanted to be the wide world's neighbor. He didn't know how to articulate this want, but he knew there should be a place for him out there, east of here; he wanted to have begun an adventure. He imagined the beautiful girl he had kissed, touched, smelled; he hoped she felt some of the feelings he felt.

The stationmaster stood in the door of the Malta depot, staring balefully at Nathaniel as the Empire Builder resumed its eastern way. The windswept little shacks seemed to Nathaniel hopeless. What would it be like to wake up in such a place as Malta, to make it through the day to dark, to lie down there knowing you would wake there, unbroken cycle, no more to be expected than what you already knew? And not just the poverty of the place. The prison of it. To be stuck anywhere. Seattle, lakeside, in a pretty house. To *know* that tomorrow would be no more than today.

From his train window Nathaniel watched a ribby mongrel hound chase a cat from the dog's dusty yard. The dog pursued the cat to the edge of a sidewalk and gave up the hunt. Before the Empire Builder moved out of sight, the cat was already nearing the dog again, testing. The dog was asleep now.

The college-bound boy opened the package his grandfather had pressed on him. A book and a leather-back, handwritten journal, Gander's father's log of his enterprises during his journey from Chicago to Seattle soon after the Civil War. Gander had attached a note to the journal. Nathaniel smiled to see the heavy five-by-seven folio writing paper, ecru (he'd been told the beige color was called), with gray letterhead. "Beyond every hinterland," his grandfather advised, "is always more hinterland."

The book was published by Charles Scribner's Sons, bound in dark green cloth, without a dust jacket: *The Great Gatsby.* It had been inscribed by his father in New York a few days after Nathaniel got good news from Princeton, a few days before his father died: "I hear this has the dope on Tigertown. That's more than I have, even though I think I went there. I'm not positioned to offer much advice, except maybe what that old fart Polonius told his boy, not to borrow money, tell the truth to yourself, red with meat, white with fish, whiskey on beer, nothing to fear."

His father was mistaken, of course. Nathaniel knew enough about Fitzgerald to know his father had confused one novel with another: *This Side of Paradise?* Never mind. The sleepy boy began to read, and by Wolf Point, on the northern edge of the Missouri River, Nathaniel was with Nick and Daisy and Tom and pretty Jordan, in West Egg, at a pretty party, where people's voices sounded like money.

Diana came to the dining car after North Dakota, too late for breakfast, but got them to cook for her and serve her. "God, I'm so hung!" She looked better than fine, as though she'd just come from the shower after a few sets of tennis, flushed and excited. She said she didn't remember a single thing after dinner. She said this so assuredly that Nathaniel might have believed her, were he only a moron. It hurt him to hear, but he recognized that their relationship was complex.

She fished for a cigarette, and Nathaniel had the match alight before she had it in her mouth. She seemed to be taking her time leaning toward him; he burned his fingers, and immediately lit another match, and she leaned toward him. She wore a cotton sundress, he thought it was called, a pale blue print. It did not have a high neck. She wore a coral necklace, and his heart was broken by a silver-and-tortoiseshell barrette holding back that dark hair above her gorgeous ears.

"Pathetic!" she said. "Sauk Centre! Sinclair Lewis grew up here. Look at those Babbitts on the platform, what yokels! What a dump! God, no wonder he was a drunk."

"You know your American literature," Nathaniel said. He had read *Arrowsmith* in tenth grade, and for a while wanted to be a doctor. Gander had led him to *Main Street,* Gopher Prairie, Zenith.

"I know my Yale," Diana said. "Lewis went to Yale. My

grandfather says he didn't know him there. Thank heavens, my grandmother says."

Now the Empire Builder was slowing for St. Paul, where Jim Hill had begun his imperial push west to the Pacific. The railroad station revealed a Minnesota universe at the antipodes from Sauk Centre; this was Scott Fitzgerald country. Here was Nathaniel's first sight of a gathered tribe of boys and girls sent east to become gentlemen and ladies, bond salesmen and post-debutantes. They were being seen off by clots of tanned moms and bluff, red-faced men wearing (like their sons) pink-soled white bucks or saddle shoes, and Brooks Brothers blue button-downs, white button-downs, yellow button-downs, pink button-downs. No pockets, a roll to the front of the ample collar. Nathaniel didn't note (then) the specifics of these shirts, but he should have: this had been his father's button-down of choice.

A couple of girls coming aboard wore beaver coats. It was a comfortably warm late afternoon, but Nathaniel was not so innocent that the fur coats puzzled him. Was that Diana on the platform, kissing the short curly-haired golden-haired boy on the cheek? Laughing with him as though they were best friends? The sight struck a blow over Nathaniel's heart. He had just had a glimpse, he realized, how this older world, so new for him, made its intricate orbits.

Alone in his compartment he read. He was at the end now, and Nick Carraway was recollecting where he'd come from, and how it felt to go back. It was difficult for Nathaniel, rolling east, to share Nick's nostalgia for a reverse journey in a contrary season, the other half of a round-trip Nathaniel felt no eagerness to experience, on those parallel tracks yonder. Fitzgerald's Nick recalled the scene in Chicago's "old dim Union Station at six o'clock of a December evening":

> . . . I remember the fur coats of the girls returning from
> Miss This-or-That's and the chatter of frozen breath and the
> hands waving overhead as we caught sight of old acquain-
> tances, and the matchings of invitations: "Are you going to
> the Ordways'? the Herseys'? the Schultzes'?" and the long
> green tickets clasped tight in our gloved hands. And last
> the murky yellow cars of the Chicago, Milwaukee & St.
> Paul railroad looking cheerful as Christmas itself on the
> tracks beside the gate.

The Empire Builder rocked explosively as a long-haul pas-
senger train blew past, shaking the windows. It was a shock to
feel this opposing rush. Nathaniel looked up from the pulpy
pages of *The Great Gatsby* into the other train's windows. He
saw flashes of faces hurtling west into the burning forests,
toward the ash- and cinder-spoiled once-green breasts of the
no-longer-new world.

> When we pulled out into the winter night and the real
> snow, our snow, began to stretch out beside us and twinkle
> against the windows, and the dim lights of small Wisconsin
> stations moved by, a sharp wild brace came suddenly into
> the air. We drew in deep breaths of it as we walked back
> from dinner through the cold vestibules, unutterably aware
> of our identity with this country for one strange hour,
> before we melted indistinguishably into it again.

Nathaniel read on to the end, and found to his surprise that
he was weeping. Not for Gatsby's death or for what became of
the New World when it grew middle-aged or for the impost-
er's broken dreams and pathetic green light. Nathaniel was
weeping for love of beauty, and in particular for a beautiful
girl it seemed Fitzgerald had known before that girl existed.
Nathaniel was weeping old, old tears, the tears shed when a

drunk put a nickel in a jukebox and heard a song sung to him alone, about *his* sweet baby, his broken heart; such tears had dropped in Babylon and the Fertile Crescent, Troy and Provence, Rome and the Seattle-Tacoma metropolitan area. . . .

He wanted to see her. He made his way forward through the vestibule into a blast of hot, menacing air.

They were in the club car, drinking gin and tonic. Diana was using a cigarette holder. As little as Nathaniel knew about eastern proprieties, he knew right was on the side of his wish that Diana were not using a cigarette holder. He sat alone at a table across from the group of four, hoping Diana would want to introduce him to her friends, a couple of boys and a cheerful girl. She did, said who was who, said where each of her friends lived, and they all lived in the same place, Wayzata.

The tiny towhead she had embraced on the platform said, "Diane—"

"Dee-ah-nah," Diana said.

"Whatever. She says you're a Princeton man."

"Well," Nathaniel said.

"If you're a Princeton man, I should know you. Do I know you?"

The other boy smirked; the girl said, "Come on, Jamie."

"Well," Nathaniel said, "I'm just a freshman."

"Oh, then in point of fact you really aren't a Princeton man, as Diana believed." The curly-haired blond peewee got her name right.

The cheerful girl said, "For cripe's sake, Jamie." Then she said to Nathaniel, "Don't mind my brother. He can be such a pain."

Nathaniel said to the runt goldilocks, "I guess you have a point. I guess I'm not really a Princeton man." He thought this exchange was good-natured, and he smiled: "Maybe I can call myself a Princeton *boy*. And if I'm not that, what am I?"

"You tell me," the boy named Jamie said.

"Let's eat," Jamie's sister said. "I'm starved. Nathaniel, you sit with me, okay?"

In the dining car the towhead ordered fried chicken, and Diana said, "Good choice!" When Nathaniel ordered fried chicken, the blond boy glared and Diana shot Nathaniel a look as though he couldn't have made a worse selection if he'd asked the waiter to soft-boil him a one-minute egg.

Another thing. Diana wouldn't shut up about what fabulous jazz piano the blond boy played. How Wilbur De Paris had let him sit in once at Jimmy Ryan's . . .

"More than once," the curly-haired Jamie said.

"Well, I heard you once," Diana said. "He's the best piano player! I don't think there's a better jazz piano player alive."

After Diana said this several—half a dozen—times, Nathaniel said to the towhead Art Tatum, *My girlfriend uses the present tense. But in point of fact, my dear contraction, you aren't actually playing the piano just now, are you?* The blond vest-pocket Oscar Peterson agreed this was so. *In point of fact,* Nathaniel said, *you are a very ordinary piano player, are you not? You're just two teensy clumsy hands bristling with ten fucking thumbs. I mean, to be precise about the matter.*

Or that was what Nathaniel said to his mind's ear, much later, when he finally realized he had been in a seedy little joust with the Thelonious Sphere Monk of Wayzata, Minnesota. In point of fact Nathaniel said, "I'd love to hear you play sometime."

Diana gently bit her lower lip and looked to be reconsidering something.

The next morning, in Union Station, he knew what she had reconsidered. He had not been able to get her alone again on the train, even though he had whispered to her in the dining car that he had to talk with her. "Why?" she had asked.

Now, standing below the station's huge departure board, softly illuminated as though in a cathedral by pale beams of dusty brass light, Diana said that something had come up, that to invite Nathaniel to Dido's tedious Lake Forest extravaganza would be . . . would be . . . *uncomfortable*. Nathaniel said, "Well, okay." The Wayzatans stood not quite out of earshot, with their steamer trunks, hailing a redcap. "I'll probably catch the Twentieth Century tonight," Nathaniel said.

Diana looked hard at Nathaniel's—Nathaniel's father's—English calf suitcases, dark as walnut, battered and saddle-soaped, with heavy, burnished bronze clasps. "Have you got a light?"

Nathaniel shook his head.

"You are a tiresome boy," she said. "Why do I . . . care for you?"

"I'm falling in love with you," Nathaniel said, wondering as he said it how one word "love" could describe what he felt when he took leave of Gander and Granma, and what he felt now.

"Uh-huh." Diana cocked her head. "You're sweet, Nathaniel."

He realized this was the first time she had used his name. He wondered if she liked his name.

"Do you know anyone in Lake Forest?" she asked.

Nathaniel said maybe, perhaps, possibly, why?

Diana said she could, perhaps, find a way to be alone with him if he could find a place to stay in Lake Forest. She gave Nathaniel a name where she was staying. He asked her to write the name down, and the telephone number.

"It's in the studbook," she said. "Gotta fly. Phone me."

Nathaniel was perplexed by much that had just happened, but most consequentially by the conundrum: what was a studbook?

The Union Station dispatcher announced the coming and going of trains in a sepulchral Walter Winchellish cadence, assertive and urgent. Nathaniel had to shout into the phone to be heard above the din, but he managed to convey to the Filipino houseboy in Lake Forest that he wished to speak to Mr. Clay, that he was indeed himself a Clay.

The old gentleman came on the line wary. Who was this? Oh, I see: well, speaking from where? Which station? Central? Dearborn? La Salle Street? Oh, Union, of course, from Seattle, that would be Union. Well, what brought you to Chicago? Oh, en route to Princeton, of course. Well, he surely wished it were possible to lend a hand with the educational expenses but he didn't see how he could possibly undertake—

"Grandfather. That's fine. I'm just calling to say hello. I'm here, and I wondered . . . I just want to say hello."

Well, fine, his grandfather said. He was glad Nathaniel had had a few minutes to call. Well, good luck at Princeton, by the way. Many a Clay a Princeton man. Surely hoped Nathaniel would give a commendable account of himself there. Many a Clay before him had done quite a commendable job at that college. It was really quite a commendable aspect of the family record.

"Yes," Nathaniel said.

"In fact," his grandfather said, "my son, your father, went to . . . was at . . . spent time at . . . Princeton University."

"I know," Nathaniel told his grandfather. "I'm sorry . . . the funeral. They wouldn't let me . . . I couldn't . . . ."

"Funeral?"

"Dad's."

"Oh. Well. We didn't go. Better that way."

"Oh. Well, what I wondered, I wondered . . . I'm here, I wondered if I might come out to Lake Forest to see you both."

After a beat of silence, another beat or two, half a dozen

more, Mr. Clay cleared his throat. Well, this was rather unexpected. Well, Nathaniel had best speak to his grandmother
about that one. The household schedule was her department.
Well, it certainly had been a pleasure talking about Princeton
with Nathaniel. Well, here was his grandmother.

"Nathaniel? From Seattle?"

"Grandmother, yes, this is Nathaniel. I'd like to catch a
train out to Lake Forest and see you both, maybe stay the
night?"

"Oh. Let me give you to your grandfather."

"He said you'd want to talk with me."

"Why ever did he say that? I mean, of course I want to talk
with you. The thing is, the trouble is . . . I don't feel well."

"Is it serious?" Nathaniel asked.

"Temporary," his grandmother said. "A discomfort of the
moment, you might say."

"I'm sorry," Nathaniel said.

"Don't be. You go to the Ambassador East. There's also an
Ambassador West, but you're to understand we will have a
room put aside for you at the Ambassador East. For tonight.
I assume you will continue your trip tomorrow?"

Nathaniel assured her that was so. He hoped she felt better
soon. She assured Nathaniel she would feel better soon, would
probably feel fine sometime tomorrow.

The Ambassador East expected him. Nathaniel was handled with exemplary courtesy, escorted by the assistant manager to a suite of rooms overlooking Lake Michigan. It was
all quite grand. Flowers. A basket of fruit. A note with the
flowers: "With the compliments of Mr. and Mrs. Clay, who
wish you to enjoy your brief visit." A ticket to the Cubs
game that afternoon with the Cardinals, last of the season.
Nathaniel thought he wouldn't use that ticket. Instead,
what he thought he'd do, he thought he'd track down Di-

ana, tell her about the suite, ask her to come see him in his commendable suite of rooms with their commendable view of Lake Michigan. He put the assistant manager on this case, said the people he was trying to reach were in the studbook, and this was their name. The assistant manager assured Nathaniel he would have a *Social Register* sent up right away, no trouble at all.

Nathaniel phoned and left a message. He phoned again, an hour later. And again. He dared not take a bath, dared not sit for a shitting lest she return his call when he was beyond second-ring reach of the telephone. During his fourth call, the woman with whom he spoke said, "This is absurd. Diana, take this call!" She did not know how to pronounce his Diana's name.

Diana said she had not been given his messages, it was a madhouse, there was a party before the party, swimming and so forth, an absolute mob of Williams boys, Dido's brother was at Williams, had been at Hotchkiss.

Nathaniel thought this was the most musical voice he had ever heard. He wondered if this was the kind of voice Jordan Baker was meant to have. He explained that he had a suite, that the suite had quite a view, that he hoped she'd come see him. Maybe she'd leave the coming-out party early. Or after the party, he'd like to see her then. Or for breakfast. Maybe they could go east together on the Twentieth Century Limited?

Diana said the proposal sounded sexy. She said Nathaniel was a wicked boy, that he should be ashamed, that she'd think of something imaginative, that he should stay right by the phone, that she'd get back to him in a couple of minutes, what was his room number?

A couple of hours later Nathaniel caught a cab to Wrigley Field just in time for the seventh-inning stretch. He had a box seat behind first base. His first major-league game. Years later he couldn't have said who won. In fact, ten minutes after the final out he couldn't have.

Back at the hotel he sat in his room, watching darkness come down over the beautiful lake. He waited. He told the front desk he expected a call, maybe a visitor. The front desk told him, "We know, we know, you told us." Well, Nathaniel said, he thought he'd mention it again, he'd be in the Pump Room, at a table for two, in case his guest came during dinner. The Pump Room was like a palace, or a museum. Seattle didn't have restaurants that resembled the Pump Room. Nathaniel drank a rye and ginger in the Pump Room, and watched the headwaiter dressed in a fancy military costume set food on fire. The table was set for two, but after an hour a busboy removed one of the place settings, and Nathaniel ate food that burned pretty well: a grapefruit, meat, a mighty blaze of dessert.

That night, into the next morning, he waited for a phone that wouldn't ring to change its mind. He passed time reading the handwritten diary Gander had given him in Seattle. At first—sensible boy, after all—he recognized what Diana had done to him, made resolutions provoked by his perception. The log, his great-grandfather's journal, was a rambling narrative in a hasty hand, telling of adventures—triumphs and reversals in the fur trade, cutting and selling timber, selling right-of-way to the Great Northern. The freebooter's progress was erratically westward, his decisions got made *ad hoc,* his reach was ambitious. As Nathaniel read more, noting that the financial accounts interspersing his great-grandfather's anecdotal narrative were detailed, exact, fussily inscribed, the solitary young man began to read with what he fancied were Diana's eyes.

Mayer of Wayzata razed hot fires of hell with Jim Hill, Jas. Jerome Hill, the Little Giant. Sed the dam train barels past the Gleason House (mayer owns the dam hotel), in fron a the hotel porch and behin Lake Minnetonka. Dam fancies from St. Louis pised and holered we cant sleep. Dam train makes such a dam raket at night we cant sleep. We come to rest and see the dam lake. Swells got to cross the tracks to get to the dam lake. Mayer got a injunction plus a pismire fine against the GN. So Jim says pis up a rope why dont you and tears down the dam Wayzata depoe and puts a depoe up in Holdridge insted and sens his dam trains stormin past Wayzata like the red fires of hell, ringin ther dam bells and blowin the whistle and throwin smoke and cinder over every dam thing includin the Gleason House fron porch and the dam water tower that burned to the dam ground last night. Dam. Wish I had owned that Holdridge land.

He wished Diana were here, imagined she might enjoy, might even be impressed by, his ancestor's rough-and-ready history among Injuns and bad men and pioneers and prospectors. This was a new sensation for Nathaniel, blood pride. How could he have imagined, waiting by a black telephone, that to learn blood pride is to risk blood shame? Now he began to account to himself reasonable good-willed explanations for the telephone's dumb silence. He believed Diana cared for him. He knew this. She had looked at him just so. She had offered opinions about his eyes, his eye*lashes*. High opinions! He looked up from the old diary, into the mirror. Squinted his eyes, gauged his lashes. She had called him . . . what? *Dashing*. She was his good luck. Now began his new life. He had found Diana. He was a Princeton Tiger, a man of parts. Look. There was the sun. The lake. Was he or was he not the luckiest man alive?

He rode east alone on the Twentieth Century Limited. Not alone alone, but alone without Diana. He counseled himself in

patience, what was right would be. He had much to look
forward to. He felt supercharged by the fast forward motion of
the great train. What names. Super Chief . . . City of New
Orleans . . . Orange Blossom Special . . . Dixie Flyer . . .
Empire Builder . . . Twentieth Century Limited. Unlimited!

In New York, during the afternoon commute, he caught
the Pennsy south. After the easy elegance of two great trains,
the coach seemed hectic, hot, what Diana would call "gross."
Not that the passengers—many got up in seersucker suits and
panama hats, here and there a flat-brimmed straw boater, as
though this cattle car were the Thames, Newark Henley—
were proles. He was hefting his own sturdy baggage was it.
The air-conditioning was on the blink was all.

Nathaniel took a seat on the aisle beside a young man
more or less his own age who stared resolutely out the window. Nathaniel wondered what out there in the theatrically
awful Jersey Flats could have the fellow's undivided interest.
Across the aisle, at a window, sat another young man,
rangy, wearing blue jeans, black high-top sneaks and a clean
white T-shirt. This young black man had a newspaper folded
across his lap, the classified section, with want-ads boldly
circled. The aisle seat beside him was empty, and as passengers moved down the car—looking for friends?—the
young job-hunter would smile at them. He couldn't have
been seventeen yet, and Nathaniel remarked to himself how
bright his smile seemed. Improbably enough, Nathaniel
thought of his own great-grandfather, moving from opportunity to opportunity. As passengers seeking a free seat kept
coming, kept going, the boy's smile in small degrees
dimmed, guttered, and by New Brunswick had died. He
glanced covertly behind him, and saw what Nathaniel had
already seen, passengers standing uncomfortably in the hot
aisles, jostled by a hard ride on a bad roadbed. Nathaniel
watched the friendly boy get the picture. How must it have

felt to get the picture, hear the nickel drop? What would a person do with the rest of his life, with his smile and circled want-ads, once he got the picture? And the gentlemen wearing straw skimmers, who had just drawn this boy a picture of his future? They'd do well to look sharp, keep eyes in the backs of their heads. Nathaniel caught the boy's eye, and smiled at him, and the boy did not smile back. Nathaniel took the seat beside him, and the boy stared out the window at the New Jersey wasteland. Nathaniel sat perfectly still, flushed and sweating, blood pounding at his temples. He waited for one of those straw-hatted, linen-jacketed, bow-tied shitweasels to take the seat he had vacated. No one took the seat; it wasn't quite so simple as that.

At Princeton Junction he changed trains for the last time, to the P. J. & B., Princeton Junction & Back, what he would learn to call the Dinky. Meeting trains from the squalor of the greater world, the two-car trolley chugged cutely five minutes along a spur line, grinding charmingly to a halt with a surprised squeal of brakes at a slate-roofed depot with copper drainpipes and ivy crawling its fieldstone façade. And this was just the railroad station. Too perfect. It made Nathaniel, still alert to nuance after his ride down beside the young black job-hunter, think of the terminal Gander had told him was at Treblinka, with its trompe-l'oeil clock (ten past noon or midnight), a perverse stage set. Whoa! *He* was perverse. No fair: the end of the Dinky's line was just a sweet little mock-Gothic college edifice. And on the station platform huddled frosh in spanky new linen or madras jackets, kids like Nathaniel, excited, confused, scared, proud, hopeful. One of these young gentlemen, standing beside his own baggage, tall and skinny, his long legs cased in white flannel, his hair shorter than fashion invited, looked directly at Nathaniel. He smiled; Nathaniel smiled back.

"Hi," Nathaniel said. "Hi."

"My name is Pownall Hamm," the young gentleman said, pointing with one hand, holding out the other. "There it is," he said, and so it was, a late-summer garden of a campus, green, smelling of fruit and blossom. This was the place.

Two

The Fresh Man

Sept. 23, 1956
Pyne Hall
Princeton University
Princeton, N.J.

Dear Granma and Gander,

I hope you're not sore at me. I've started many a
letter but as soon as I tell you about my life here,
something new happens and the letter is outdated.
That's a crummy excuse for why you haven't had an
answer to your great letters (and thanks for the money,
Granma!); they've meant a lot to me, because sometimes I can't help feeling homesick.

Not that I'm unhappy. Gander, remember when you
bought the Chris-Craft for Dad, and you pretended it
was really for me? I said that nothing could ever make
me as happy as getting to use that beautiful boat, and
nothing did make me that happy, until I got into
Princeton last year. And then I said nothing could ever
make me that happy again, but I was wrong again,
because I met this girl Diana Carr I told you about in
my postcard from The Ambassador East, where Dad's
parents were kind enough to put me up while they
were out of town.

Now a new something else has made me happy. I'm
a Princeton man. Let me tell you what that means,
and why I'm so proud and excited. First of all I'm surrounded by truly excellent young men from all walks
of life. At the first meeting of our freshman class in
Alexander Hall, President Harold Dodd told us we
were the smartest and most excellent class ever to enter
Princeton University. It made me feel pretty humble
to hear how many of the men in that room were football captains and class presidents and valedictorians.
Sitting in that room with me were men from great
boarding schools who had chosen Princeton above every
other college. There were men from every state in the
Union (I don't know why I never met the boy from
Seattle before. Maybe because he went to a school
called Exeter, back east. Have you ever met the owner
of a Chinese restaurant called Wang Wu's? That's
Willie Wu's dad.)

President Dodd told us about Princeton's Honor
Code. As a Princeton man I am to write on my examination blue books "I pledge my honor as a gentleman
that, during this examination, I have neither given nor
received assistance." Can you imagine how honored I
am to be at a place where the professor hands out an
exam, and then hangs around a few minutes to answer
questions, and then leaves the room till the exam ends?
I've already written my Honor Pledge on an essay
about Prince Hal and Falstaff (they're characters in
William Shakespeare's *Henry Fourth Part Two*), and I
felt so trusted. I wouldn't say this to anyone else, because it sounds boastful, but I think it's going to be
easy for me to tell the truth because of the way I was
brought up by my grandparents. I hope I don't sound
sappy saying this. I can hear Gander saying "shush

with that," see him waving his hand, like what I've
said is a bug molesting him. The drawback to the
Honor Code is that I would have to turn in a student I
saw cheating, and this would be hard as the dickens,
but I don't think it will come up because the students
I've met are such fine fellows.

Anyone caught cheating at Princeton has to leave
Princeton, and is left by Princeton; a guy down the
hall says that if this happens it's as though you never
went here. You disappear from Princeton's records,
as though it never happened, as though *you* never
happened.

I'll tell you, it would be awful to be deep-sixed from
this place. The flowers, Granma, I just wish you could
see them. You'd go ape. I wish I knew what they're
named, but you know me and Latin. And the trees are
so old and big, it's as if they've been here forever.
"Old" is Princeton's middle name. The buildings belong in the Middle Ages. My room in Pyne overlooks
the little railroad depot, and even it looks older than
any building in Seattle. This guy down the hall, the
one I mentioned before, Pownall Hamm, says that the
illusion of antiquity is just a slick trick here at Princeton. He says all it takes is a shipload of old English
brick from some country house someone couldn't afford
to keep up, an understanding of the climbing properties of ivy, and there you are: an ancient railroad station. Pownall says the dished foot-treads were
sandblasted into the steps of McCosh Hall (where I
take Shakespeare) before the building's concrete foot-
ings had set up. Pownall's a sharp customer; you have
to get up pretty early in the morning to steal a march
on Pownall Hamm. You'd love him, Gander. He's sure
been friendly to me. Well, I've got to go to the libe. I

have a paper to write for Introductory Logic. Here's the question: If God can do anything, can He make a stone so heavy He can't lift it? I know you're not God's greatest fans, but you might try this one out on the Friday Night Bunch, and see what they come up with.

Before I say goodnight, thanks. Not just for sending me to this beautiful, wonderful, inspiring University, but for teaching me every good thing I know. (Gander: I wish I'd known your dad. There's so much I want to ask him about the old days, and how America treated him.) I hope you'll tell Mom I miss her. Do you think she understands where I am? Do you think she thinks about me? Does she ever talk about me? Should I write her a letter? I love you.

> October 25, 1956
> Pyne Hall
> Princeton University
> Princeton, New Jersey

Dear G & G,

Granma: I just can't agree with your opinion about Prince Hal and Falstaff. In my opinion Prince Hal had no choice: he had to turn his back on Falstaff, even if this hurt Falstaff's feelings. Prince Hal, who was in training to become King Henry V, owed it to England not to hang around with a fool, even if that fool was a friend and fun to be with. You might like to read Niccolò Machiavelli's *The Prince,* or Baldassare Castiglione's *The Book of the Courtier.* These are what are called "treatises" on politics and manners. We are reading them in Italian Renaissance 202, and they throw a good deal of light on Prince Hal's responsibilities and the dilemma Falstaff put him in.

Gander: now I have to disagree with you! I don't think Antony was "just a darned strumpet's fool" to forfeit all for Cleopatra. You have to remember what an amazingly beautiful woman she was. Remember how Enobarbus said she "beggar'd all description"? I feel that way about the Briarcliff girl I told you about, the one I met on the Empire Builder. Remember how Enobarbus tells about her boat, some kind of barge? (It must have been a pretty fancy barge! Not one of our Lake Union houseboats, I guess.) "Purple the sails, and so perfumed, that / The winds were love-sick with them." When our Shakespeare professor reads these passages he really gets into them. He saws the air, and cries out, and does all those things Hamlet taught the players not to do. Most of the fellows in Shakespeare think the professor's pretty corny, but I have to admit I like his acting. As a matter of fact there was a moment when he read some lines by Ophelia that made me cry the way Granma cries at movies. I guess you know who I was thinking of.

Tell her I love her too. (Did she really mention me, Gander? I'm not doubting your word. You're the most Honorable man I ever met! But still.)

I'm sorry I disagree with you about these two plays. But I guess that's why you're sending me here, to make up my own mind. I love you.

P.S. I got a "2" on my God Lifts a Big Stone essay. Grades here go from "1" (A) to "7" (Flagrant Neglect). So I got a B. I agree: it was a pretty stupid question. It was just about words, I guess.

P.P.S. You ask about my roommate. He's a bruiser
from New Orleans, and he's a football player. He
wears a nightcap to bed. I thought this was to keep his
head warm, but he says it makes his hair behave. He
talks to a snapshot of his girlfriend, even when I'm
trying to study. I guess he misses her. I guess he's
homesick. I guess I'll room with someone else next
year.

Fall of freshman year, oh had Nathaniel written Diana letters. Opened his veins to her. Couldn't stint. Tried to find
words to send to Briarcliff to say how it was watching that
black kid on the train coming south to Princeton Junction.
Tried to describe the moment when the kid was still confused
why no one had taken the seat beside him, was just about to
be unconfused, still couldn't quite believe what seemed to be
happening . . . how the black kid had scrunched himself
against the window, to leave free space aplenty for any lady or
gentleman willing to share a little journey with him. How
when Nathaniel sat beside him the kid pushed so remorselessly
against the window he seemed to be trying to break through
the skin of the car. Diana hadn't responded to that letter, and
Nathaniel wondered whether she could sense an unfelt sentiment in his disingenuously liberal speculations about the boy:
"Who could he have been: a boy like any other coming to
Princeton for an admissions interview? Coming to Princeton to
look for work in an eating club kitchen? Coming to visit his
granddad, who works in an eating club kitchen? Coming to
visit his granddad, who is a professor of anthropology?"

Nathaniel warmed to his rhetoric in those unanswered letters, refined as they were manipulated through many drafts.
God knows he couldn't call the one-way messages "correspon-
dence." That autumn it was hard to say what was what right
down the line: he felt such contrary attractions and repulsions,

resenting and prizing the sardonic laughter and the quick, graceful, wised-up boys from great eastern schools while he worked up a full head of empathetic steam in response to the Budapest uprising and its suppression (*crushing,* he called it).

Oh, Diana, sometimes I feel so *tired.* As a citizen of the Second Imperium of Dwight David (Caesar) Eisenhower I feel like a man hunched under the blast of a factory whistle. Have you seen Bergman's *Seventh Seal?* He's pictured it exactly, the terror of our modern Plague Years. We call it Brinksmanship, but it's the same now as then, darkness and imminent death. I don't know. I'd love to hear how you feel in these awful times.

Have you read *The Ginger Man?* It's banned over here, but a friend in my entry of Pyne, Booth Tarkington Griggs—I don't think you know him, according to him—loaned me the copy he brought back from Paris, where he bought it at one of these bookstalls they have along the Seine River. It's an Olympia Press book. Olympia usually publishes dirty books, but I wouldn't recommend *The Ginger Man* if I didn't think it was an *important literary document*! (It certainly isn't as dirty as that *Peyton Place* our countrymen are so busy reading when they aren't keeping Negroes in the back of the bus.) Anyway, this character in *The Ginger Man,* Sebastian Dangerfield, says "I think we are the natural aristocrats of the race. Come before our time. Born to be abused by them out there with the eyes and the mouths."

Isn't that perfect! I thought of you when I read it, because you are such a natural aristocrat, and I know how you feel about coarse people. Oh, I don't know, Diana! Sometimes I think I should go to Cuba, and

head back into the mountains with that Fidel Castro.
He is an Outlaw, what the great writer Albert Ca-
mus calls a "Rebel," which I prefer to translate
"Outsider." By the way, have you heard this song,
"Folsom Prison Blues"? It perfectly defines what I'm
struggling to convey.

So why go on, you must be asking, in a world
where contraceptives and nuclear fission usurp each
other as negative functions? I can only say that in
the ruined warrens are pockets of beautiful life. Take
Princeton, for example. I know you've been here (you
probably know the place better than I know it), but
I can't tell you how exciting it is to make friends
with people unlike people I ever met or heard of.
We sit around in what we call "bull sessions," sometimes all night, arguing about religion and philosophy and politics. It's so great to have my own room!
It's nifty. Overlooks the train station. I think sometimes how it would be if you came in on the Dinky,
and we went to dinner at Lahiere's, and came back
here together. I've got Jackson Pollock and Saint
Vincent Van Gogh (have you seen *Lust for Life*? It's
too Hollywood for words, of course, but Kirk Douglas still made me want to know Van Gogh!) on my
walls. I've got wind chimes! My classes are taught by
some of the most brilliant men I have ever known!
There's a poet named Richard Blackmur, for example. You'd love him! He doesn't even have a high
school diploma. And Professor Hyde: he smokes ciga-
rettes exactly the way you smoke them, holding them
on the little-finger side of his middle finger, left-
handed, just like you, even though he's right-handed,
like you. When I listen to him speculate about Aes-
thetics, which I guess you know means the philoso-

phy of beauty, I can't help thinking about you.
Especially when he's smoking.

Nathaniel unaccountably found himself, for the first time in
his short life, doubting his honor. One moment he wanted to
belong, the next to stand apart (and of course above). At times
he wanted both together, and of all people to burden with his
whipsawing wants he had had to choose Diana Carr. What was
her response to Khrushchev saying "History is on our side; we
will bury you"? Did it signal the close of The American Generation? Did Great Britain sacrifice honor to Suez? Would she
be his date at the Yale game? Did she know how it felt to
glimpse her across Palmer Stadium next to a sophomore at the
Yale game? Did she? Could she? Would she? Might she? He
was in love; what more could be said?

Not much was said. Thanksgiving came, and no word re-
bounded from Briarcliff. He flew home for Christmas, saw his
mother in the hospital. He knew at once he wouldn't tell
Diana about his mother's brittle laughter and determined good
cheer in the hospital, so he finally quit writing to the girl
frozen in his memory in her red velvet dress, with a wisp of
damp hair at her lips. Then, of course, she wrote to him. How
she knew to write to him *just then* or lose him was an old and
uninteresting story, but the letter worked, presto chango.
Such letters always worked.

Love-blind as he was, Nathaniel wasn't so dim he didn't
note the irony: She scolded him. "Why don't you ever tell me
what you've been *doing*? Haven't you *gone* anywhere? Who have
you *met*?"

Nathaniel was beginning to comprehend. The next time he
wrote, he told Diana the names of the boys he'd met and where
they came from and where they'd gone to school. Oh, and
some gossip about their families. And then he didn't mail the
letter. He couldn't have put a name to the thing that made

him not mail the name-dropping letter to the girl with delicate veins laced along the pale skin of her throat. Probity
wasn't the word, integrity wasn't. Shame was in the neighborhood, self-contempt in the ballpark. But so was uncertainty. Suppose he dropped the name of a friend who wasn't a
friend? Suppose he dropped a name she'd never heard? Suppose
he dropped a name she had heard and didn't care to hear again?

February 10, 1957
Pyne Hall
Princeton University
Princeton, New Jersey

Dear Grandparents,

Your letter feeds my guilt. Have I really let all this
time pass since Christmas? Your telephone calls and
letters have been a tonic all year. I have told you on
the phone how appreciative I am for all you did for me
at Christmas—the ticket home and back here (yes, I'm
afraid the return east was as uneventful as my return
west)—and for your generous gifts of books. I haven't
had a chance to get to *Portrait of the Artist as a Young
Man,* but I fell head over heels for *Dubliners.* Remember how you used to tease me, Granma, for walking
everywhere with my skates and hockey stick, just in
case a pond froze? Now my Princeton friends tease me
for my habit of walking around the campus with my
nose in an open book. Believe it or not I have found a
way (patent pending) to read while I walk between
classes in the rain. This would be a useful device in
Seattle, and perhaps Gander could arrange to market it
in the Accessories Department at the store. If I can
trust you with my secret: I have cut a hole in my clipboard, and through this hole I have slipped a narrow-

handled umbrella; thus, using right hand to hold
contraption and left to turn pages, head and book
(clipped to clipboard) are kept dry in all weathers. I
read the close of "The Dead" walking between my
dorm and Baker Rink, with snow falling faintly,
faintly falling thick through the New Jersey dusk.

Gander: I wasn't conscious I made so many references during Christmas vacation to my friends' boarding schools. Since you ask why they're so interesting
I'll try to tell you: the men from those schools seem
armor-plated, impervious to hurt or perhaps indifferent to pain. (Although I've heard from Booth and
Pownall, the fellows I talked about so much at
Christmas, that some graduates of the very top
schools were pretty disappointed by the outcome of
Bicker, which is the name Princeton gives its club
selection process. Think of clubs as fraternities, and
Bicker as "rush." I know you and Granma didn't
join such institutions, but here pretty much everyone
joins an Eating Club. I know I will.)

Anyway, about boarding schools. The best I can
learn is that Hotchkiss, Choate and Taft specialize in
the sons of New York merchant-princes and the Connecticut gentry; they feed Yale. Groton and St. Marks
prefer old money, and feed Harvard. So it is that
Princeton fellows from those schools seem specially
marked, sent to Princeton by a Princeton father, or
otherwise powerfully drawn to the place, and no wonder! The most popular fellows with other boarding
school graduates are the Exeter students. They seem
dazzlingly smart, they aren't snobs and they're terrifi-
cally witty. I guess you'd call them "sardonic," world-
weary. Deerfield boys are wholesome straight-arrows,
no nonsense, fine athletes. Andover men are self-

assured, with year-round sun-tans, mighty arrogant, in my opinion. My friends Pownall Hamm and Booth Tarkington Griggs were roommates at St. Paul's School, in Concord, New Hampshire. Before that they were roommates at Fessenden, a boarding school for little kids. This first thing you'd notice about Paulies is . . .

Why am I telling you this stuff? I don't even know what I'm talking about. You asked if I felt disadvantaged by my public school education, and the answer is, of course not! My grades show that I'm keeping up. Remember, I learned a lot from you and Granma, and from Mom, before she went away. As a matter of fact I've begun to wonder whether those fancy educations weren't a little wasted on some of these guys. Last week in the dining hall I sat beside someone I know slightly from Shakespeare last semester, and asked who's more interesting, Iago or Othello? "How should I know?" he said. "I hate wopera."

I don't want you to think I'm disappointed in the intellectual life of Princeton. Or that I'm not grateful to be here. I just get confused is all. Because sometimes men (never my professors!) treat me as though I must be ashamed not to have gone (like Dad) to a school like Choate. Nothing could be further from the truth. Believe me!

Gander, thanks for the job offer. I'm going to take you up on it. I agree that I should work my way up. I know I've got to start at the bottom. Not that a job in Sporting Goods is the bottom! I know it's a privilege to have a job in the store. Besides, I miss you both so much, and I want to come home to you this summer. (No Granma: I'm not homesick. And I am keeping

warm. And Princeton has its own laundry service, and
I use it faithfully. And I was just kidding about Mystery Meat being green.) I'll stay on campus during
spring vacation, though as I said before, I wish I had
the moxie to go to Cuba.

Tell Mom I'm okay?

Nathaniel envied the passion that sent dozens of classmates
south for their spring break, to join Castro in the Sierra Mae-
stre. The cry was "*¡Fidel sí, Batista no!*" But then the boys
returned tanned and sheepish, from Fort Lauderdale and Del-
ray Beach. It turned out, they said, to be a real pain in the
ass to get to Cuba. It was dawning on Nathaniel that a pain
in the ass was more pain than his comrades-in-books cared to
tolerate.

In April the campus blossomed. The place was fresh, sweet-
scented, noisy with song, budding. A children's Paradise,
Princeton went over the edge into childish riot. Later, after a
half-dozen students were expelled, solemn people tried to un-
riddle what had happened, what series of bad choices and
accidental intersections had provoked the silly disgrace that
The New York Times and *Newsweek* and *Life* titled "The Bob
Butter Riot."

There was general agreement that the fiasco began when a
Dartmouth freshman stood on the green outside Cuyler Hall
insistently calling for his Princeton freshman friend: "Bob
Butter? Where's Bob Butter? Does anyone know Bob Butter?
I need Bob Butter!"

Soon the cry was joined: "We need Butter too!" The cry for
Bob Butter spread, and soon the elusive fellow, hunkered
down oblivious on B Floor of Firestone Library, was sought in
every corner of campus and village. "WE WANT BUTTER!"
Damage was extensive; the riot was well reported. Granma
wrote an alarmed letter; Nathaniel explained that the boys

hadn't really meant to break Nassau Street shopwindows and destroy Prospect Gardens, they were just letting off a little steam, they were good fellows with maybe a few rotten apples among them, basically fine kids. Princeton students were famous for boyish energy, Nathaniel explained: they liked practical jokes, and teasing, and dares. Just the other night a fellow Nathaniel knew well—Booth Griggs—had scaled Nassau Hall to steal the bell-clapper. This was a fine adventure. Couldn't Gander and Granma understand?

Booth Tarkington Griggs. The second Princeton boy Nathaniel had met, Booth did nothing to diminish the vision of Princeton that Nathaniel had carried east from the Cascades. Nathaniel first spied him sitting on the ledge of his second-story window, dangling white-flanneled legs, laughing at a couple of other freshmen playing grab-ass in the courtyard, his wheat hair lit by late-afternoon sun. Pownall hailed Booth ("Lend a hand with these grips, Griggsie"), and Booth swung from the sill to the thick branch of a Chinese chestnut, and climbed down. This seemed to Nathaniel at the time quite the most audacious stunt he had seen someone of his age perform; later he learned that many a Pyne dweller used the chestnut as entrance or egress, but to Nathaniel it was thereafter Booth's tree, Booth's feat. Pownall introduced Nathaniel as though he'd never not known him, announcing him to be an immigrant from the land of Lutheranism, rain forests, rockchucks, Populist ideals, salmon, and good, rural Norwegian stock. Somehow, placed in just this teasing way and at just that anxious moment of arrival, Nathaniel was made glad to have come here from where he had come.

Booth shook Nathaniel's hand languidly, as had the tow-headed shrimp from Wayzata back there on the Empire Builder . . . when? Two days ago? More like two hundred years.

Booth wore his maroon SPS sweater inside out, so the letters only faintly showed through, but of course they did show, but of course Nathaniel had no notion what they stood for, which was just as Booth preferred it.

Booth was affable, but he kept a boundary, an inviolable segregation between him and the dozens of classmates who believed him to be their best friend. Booth maintained the moat, calculated its width, could pull up the drawbridge just like that—*go away*. Pownall, by contrast, was without self-consciousness or guile. Captain of St. Paul's crew, he hadn't thought to equip himself with a letter sweater to wear inside out. He was a quick laugher, mostly at himself, but he carried with him—despite his goofy, gangly slouch—a menacing reck-lessness, a destructive indifference to outcome. Students (excepting young Hamm himself) believed Pownall to be the pattern of offhand ease. Pownall seemed to be a boy with a mor-dant secret, despite his sweet disposition, and Nathaniel came sometimes to feel his new comrade's smile as too knowing.

But that came later. The first weeks of college, the three shared a couple of classes, ate dinner together in Upper or Lower Eagle. In those cavernous dining halls called collectively Commons, friendships were formed, oddballs were sometimes celebrated, more often not, and these boys—still children, if they knew it—banged their forks against their plates like convicts when the mystery meat was especially noxious. Pownall and Booth sometimes asked Nathaniel to their room to listen to jazz, or play Monopoly; now and then the three drank of an evening at the Peacock Inn. But when Booth asked Nathaniel—a few days after the Bob Butter riot—if he might be willing to room sophomore year with him and Pownall, Nathaniel looked this way and that around Pyne Court, to see if his famously graceful classmate might be addressing another.

"You'd be doing us a favor, really. We've found a pee-whistler of a room in Holder, but it's a suite, room enough for three, we need a third. We both thought right away of you, but Pownall said you'd have been spoken for by now."

"No, I'd like to live with you. I'd like that a lot."

"Pownall's a slob, filthy habits. He gambles, I'm afraid. Offsetting his vices, I don't fart. In fact I never *have* farted. In fact I can only guess, through literature and vulgar rumor, what a fart is."

Nathaniel felt wonderful. How had this happened, this election?

"By the way," Booth said, "my ma knows your auntie, and knew your father."

"I wouldn't want a family connection to—"

"My father knew your father. Here, I guess, among the spires and gargoyles. My father . . . we have this in common . . ." Nathaniel had never heard Booth stumble for words. "My father is dead, in fact. Like yours."

"How did your father die?"

Booth looked astounded, as though it had never occurred to him there was more than one way a father might die. "In the war. Shot down."

"My father died differently," Nathaniel said.

"Oh," Booth said.

Three

Under the Clock

First night of his sophomore Christmas vacation Nathaniel was in New York, where he had hoped to spend Christmas with his father's sister; that estimable lady had written him as though he were a deprived kid and she was the Fresh Air Fund, promising to give him a nice Christmas holiday. But something had come up, she had to go to Hobe Sound, she was sorry, maybe next year, she wished they had *room* in Hobe Sound, Nathaniel wouldn't like it there, it was such a *fussy* place. He had never met his aunt; Nathaniel wondered how she knew how he wouldn't take to the Jupiter Island Club.

Nathaniel was now to spend the Christmas–New Year week skiing at Stowe with Pownall and Dr. and Mrs. Hamm. It had been difficult to explain to Granma and Gander why he preferred to stay east; in fact it had been difficult for Nathaniel to explain to Nathaniel why he didn't want to go home now, if "home" was what he'd call Seattle.

But tonight he knew why he was where he was: in town, at the Biltmore, Saturday before Christmas, a year into Ike's second term. He'd timed his arrival to the barbershop's hours. He'd brought fifty dollars from Princeton, and he took himself with his money to the Biltmore Hotel barbershop. In that tiled, scented, gleaming, knowing cavern he'd given his instructions: shampoo, light trim with shears, singe, shine, shave. Oh, and a manicure. Did he want some sun? Sure. Do it: the lamp was an inspired notion.

Now, with twenty dollars and change, newly tanned, he was Under the Clock for the gathering of the tribes. Here were kilted Smithies, Vassar radicals, Briarcliff junior collegians with perfect teeth, apprentice co-eds from Farmington, Ethel Walker's, Foxcroft, Garrison Forest . . . Black dresses (Saks), kid gloves (black or navy), pearls, tweed skirts (Peck & Peck), cashmere cardigans (the Bermuda Shop). Also: herringboned phalanxes of J.-Pressed Yalies, guys from Trinity wearing Yale neckties, crew-cut Deerfield boys, Sons of Old Nassau greeting or getting met, anxious, cranked on holiday.

One reached the Palm Court from the Biltmore lobby by passing Under the Clock, running a gauntlet of edgy students waiting on facing benches for their dates, firing up Chesterfields, giving lights. Nathaniel fingered the lighter in his jacket pocket. Dunhill. He'd had to choose between an olde model—fussy and clunky with flint wheels and miniature tubing—and this Art Deco thing in his pocket, a slim ribbed rectangle of streamlined sterling, substantial. He could have gone for silver plate, but this was for Diana, engraved "DC" (he didn't know her middle name, remembered too late he might have looked it up in the—what did she call it?—studbook). Cost him a month's allowance. This too would have been difficult to explain to Gander. Now he touched it, till he realized he was slicking it with sweat. Suppose she'd quit smoking?

The Clock. Seven-thirty. Rumbling through a light snow toward Grand Central (tunneled beneath this very hotel), New York, New Haven & Hartford trains bore a heavy cargo of privilege to their apprehensive escorts. Much fantasy had been invested in these cross-gender collisions. Nathaniel wondered if those others here, looking superficially Nathanielish, Dianaesque (except not so arrestingly lovely, of course), had as much riding on what happened after they met under this trifling, legendary clock.

Almost a year after he had given up hoping for her interest, had quit sending his dreams and fears by unanswered post, had almost quit thinking about the girl who once brought him to her sleeping compartment, once kissed him, once said to him things he could not credit having properly heard, after he found himself getting through whole hours without thinking about Diana Carr, there came this casual question: Pownall Hamm asked did anyone want a couple of tickets to *West Side Story*? They were good seats, but he couldn't use them, was obliged to be "some boring where else." Neither could Booth use them. That Saturday night was spoken for.

"Nathaniel?" Pownall asked.

"I don't know. Sure. Sure. Thanks. But I'll need only one."

"Come on, buckaroo. You don't want to go alone to the theater." Booth liked to call Nathaniel "buckaroo." He called everybody west of Louisville and Cincinnati buckaroo. He called people who lived on Manhattan's West Side ("Say this for it," he said of the West Side: "it's convenient to Europe.") buckaroo. Nathaniel wished he'd quit calling him buckaroo.

"I think I do. Want to go alone."

Pownall asked, "What about that pretty you used to tell about, the Briarcliff scholar?"

"Out of the picture," Nathaniel said.

"Draw a new picture," Booth said.

"She's not interested," Nathaniel said.

"Get her interested," Pownall said. "Tickets open the path to an uninterested heart. *West Side Story*'s a hard ticket. You need a ticket to ride, Nathaniel; harder the ticket, easier the ride. She'll be tempted. She'll be flattered. This musical's a love story, Romeo and his gal, ethnic pileup, collision of two worlds, very deep stuff, plus she'll leave humming the tunes, plus she'll thread her arm through yours and, flushed by the noisy, melodic uplift, ask you to take her dancing, and in the Checker cab, with its leathery aroma, so metropolitan that smell, so New York, you'll tilt her face to your own, look into her eyes—"

"Jesus," Booth said, "give it a rest! Now you've got me wanting those tickets. Nathaniel, what's the girl's phone number?"

So Nathaniel called Diana's dormitory from a bank of pay booths in Chancellor Green Student Center, the Monday after Thanksgiving. His heart was pounding so hard he couldn't catch his breath. Her voice! They traded small talk. She seemed distracted, kept talking above his voice to someone, or several someones, near her phone.

"Try oxbow," she said.

"What?" Nathaniel said.

"Five letters for a crooked stream. Meander is too many letters," she said.

"I'm sorry," Nathaniel said.

"Madora is doing a crossword," she said. "Tell him hi for me!" Diana shouted at someone. "Tell him he's an enemy for life if he doesn't waltz with me at the Black and Silver. Tell him," she told somebody, "I won't make a baby with him if he doesn't at least Charleston with me at the Junior Assemblies. *Ciao!*" Then she said, to Nathaniel, "Sorry."

So he asked: might she be interested . . . could he tempt her . . . he'd love to . . . to share . . . with her . . . he'd understand if she was busy, of course. She deliberated and the appointment—under the clock—was arranged.

Agony not to check the watch again, not to steal a glance at the clock. She was forty-two minutes late. Please come. Booth wouldn't wait five minutes for a date; Nathaniel knew it. Booth would say, *What the hell! Sucking pipe? From a Briarcliff girl?* Booth would make a move, maybe on that

Bennington/Sarah Lawrence artiste waiting on the narrow-upholstered bench, biting her fingernails, jiggling her silk-stockinged legs. But how to move? How did Booth and his friends pull it off, chat someone up, ask for a smoke, offer a light? Wait! No need. Here Diana came, up the steps from Vanderbilt Avenue, snow in her hair, snow on the shoulders of her fur coat, wasn't this the greatest time in the best world? Wasn't it? A peck on the cheek. ("That *damned* train," she said.) Her flushed cheek was warm, hair damp. She smelled wonderful. Yes, she said, of course the Palm Court. God, she was *dying* for a drink.

"Diana, what will it be?"

"Pernod, *mais oui*." (She had told on the phone she planned to "study" in Paris, Reid Hall.)

"Waiter, Pernod, and make me a whiskey sour."

Why was the waiter staring at him as if he were some freak? "We have no Pernod," the waiter said.

"Rye and ginger," she said. "The morons never have Pernod," she said, approximately to Nathaniel. "Or maybe they can't pronounce it."

She told him about a boy from Harvard ("crazy about me, for some obscure reason") who had seen a runty little freshman in blinding-new white bucks give an order at Cronin's, "Waiter, make me a whiskey sour," whereupon the waiter had folded his arms and said to the boy, in much the tone this waiter had just used on Nathaniel, "Poof, you're a whiskey sour!"

"Ha-ha," Nathaniel said. (Ha-ha was not his customary laugh—too guarded; its circumspect sound alarmed him, brought a hot blush of anger to his cheeks. But anger at what? At whom? Maybe at waiters? This waiter?) When the drinks appeared, this young man not from Harvard but for some obscure reason crazy about Diana said, "Waiter, make me a whiskey sour." The waiter stared at him, perhaps insolently. "*Another* whiskey sour. I'll be ready. And waiter, who's playing tonight at Ryan's?" But the waiter had already turned his back. "At Jimmy Ryan's," he called to his back.

"Oh God," she said, "I'm so *bored* with Ryan's. And Condon's."

Nathaniel had wanted to take her to a jazz club. His favorite was Eddie Condon's, downtown in the Village, where the musicians had dissolute faces and wore double-breasted pinstripe suits stained with cigarette ash and slicked their hair straight back and drank black highballs while their friends blew a solo chorus of "How Come You Do Me Like You Do?" He had wanted to take Diana to Condon's, but he reckoned it was too far downtown for her taste, so he had thought he would take her to Jimmy Ryan's, a Dixieland club just west of "21" on Fifty-second Street. He wanted to sit in the dark, and hold her hand and admire the sweet music, "I've Got a Crush on You." To have their picture taken. To put that picture on his wall at school. But Diana was *bored* with Ryan's, *bored* with Condon's. "Well," Nathaniel said, "would you like to go dancing after the theater?"

"Where? You're not dressed for the Stork. Don't you love the Stork Club? It's . . . heaven. Heavenly. The Stork Club is," Diana continued, "pure . . . *heaven*!" She stared at Nathaniel: "I like your jacket. But the sleeves are too short. You should show a little cuff, not the whole wrist! Brooks?"

"I don't know," Nathaniel lied. "I guess Auerbach's."

"Maybe the St. Regis Roof will let you in. That would be okay. We could have dinner." Nathaniel released the Dunhill lighter he was fingering while she talked, and touched the money clip in the same pocket with the expensive gift. The money clip had slipped off his folded bills, and no wonder: they made a thin sheaf. The St. Regis Roof was not the restaurant of choice for bargain-hunting young lovers. Diana said, "The food's awful, of course, but if we're there, we may as well eat."

Hilarity at the table to Nathaniel's right, U. Va. rowdies. To his left a crowd of Choate boys, theatrically urbane and mature, disapproving of the childish, noisy collegians. He wondered if he'd ever see anyone from Seattle in this place or in a place like this.

Diana watched the Choate boys, and talked: "You didn't hear about it? God! This perfectly dis*traught* girl, in town with her daddy from Denver or Grosse Pointe or some *distant* place, well Santa Barbara, actually Montecito, and her father was right here in this room having tea, waiting for her. My sister's roommate's cousin's best friend saw it, it might have been at *this table*! And here came his daughter, late, as usual. Glass everywhere. Right through that"—she looked up and so did he, through the grimy panes; he saw the dim dirty-gold glow of room lights, way up, or was it the moon, filtered through snow?—"skylight. It goes to show: never book an inside room. My God, that's Pownall Hamm, I can't believe it, and *look* at the costume!" Diana spoke with uncharacteristic discretion, so low that it could only just be heard at the Choate table, above the din: "Pownall's at Princeton." Then, uncertainly: "You *do* know him?"

"He's my roommate."

Diana studied Nathaniel.

"Who's with Pownall?"

"I don't know her," Nathaniel said.

"Not *her,* silly! The dreamboat."

"Booth."

"Booth who?"

"Griggs."

"Does he go to Princeton?"

Nathaniel nodded.

"Do you know *him*?"

"Roommate."

"Well, where are your manners? Call them over. How did *they* come to room with *you*?"

Or did Nathaniel, his most primitive defense mechanisms on full alert, presume the emphasis? Hers was a question, after all, he had sometimes asked himself.

"Nathaniel," Diana said. "Did you hear me? Get them over here!"

"Please."

"Please what?"

"I'd prefer you say 'please.' "

She looked at him. Adjusted her face. What a smile! "Smart" defined her face exactly. High cheekbones: they seemed an attribute of intelligence. Full lips? High intelligence quota, blockbuster Stanford-Binet. Perfect white teeth, as regular as a Fairfield County white picket fence: brain power. "Nathaniel Clay, you've grown on me!"

He misunderstood, of course. Melted, of course. "Thank you," he said softly, from his heart.

"Not that way, silly goose! I mean grown up. You're so much taller."

"I guess," Nathaniel said.

"Pretty please, Nathaniel. Invite your dreamboat roommate to have a drink with us."

"I think they're busy."

"Pownall! Pownall!" Diana made herself heard. Nathaniel studied her preposterously perfectly wrought features, the blade of her nose, her pouty lips, her rich hair; Nathaniel wondered how one thing went with another, such a creature with such a voice.

There weren't enough chairs; *tout le monde,* as Diana had remarked, was here at the Biltmore. Nathaniel offered his seat to Pownall's date, Beth, who said—direct and friendly—she wasn't tired. Pownall was got up in his grandfather's soup and fish, with black brogans on his feet and a frayed white button-down. A cowlick stood like ferns at the crown of his head, and he wore a Band-Aid where he had cut himself shaving.

Booth wore the dress uniform of a Royal Air Force officer; Nathaniel knew this was foolishness honestly come by. Booth Tarkington Griggs was not a fellow to buy an Eton tie at J. Press just because he favored that shade of blue. Neither was he a fellow to stand beside a table merely because there seemed to be no chairs. There soon *were* chairs, removed from the Choaties, who had been saving them for latecomers but gave them up after a few whispered words from Booth Tarkington Griggs, who smiled while he explained that he wanted the chairs.

They drank. Pownall and his date drank glass after glass of gin, straight up. Diana asked Pownall's date if she *liked* gin, and the question puzzled Beth. "Doesn't everybody?" she said.

Booth ordered a bottle of Muscadet and held court. He lived year-round in Newport, but seemed to know the social geography of everywhere. So many boys and girls came to Booth— to tell him a joke, ask advice, confide a secret, touch his shoulder, kiss his cheek—that Diana gave up asking who they all were, where they had gone to school, where they were at college. The courtiers were tricked out in variations on formal fancy dress, mostly military, hired from theatrical costumers and fancy-dress-ball masqueraders. British uniforms were preferred, and three undergraduates within view of Nathaniel's table were got up in the scarlet tunic with black facing, the red-plumed brass helmet of officers of the King's own Second Dragoon Guards.

Diana wanted an explanation.

"Guards' Ball," Pownall told her. "The Dubs."

"Dubs?" Diana asked.

"Dubutante Cotillion."

"Oh," said Diana, "the Dubutante *Cotillion*! I was asked to come out at this cotillion."

"Well," said Pownall, "it's sort of a guys' thing."

Some guys! This year a Cartier, a Lamont, a Lippincott, a Mellon, a Rockefeller, an Ansell, a Gifford, a Weld. Escorting them and about forty others were the Misses Auchincloss, de Claireville, du Pont, Pell, Pennoyer, Van Riper, the Cole sisters (Gussy and Sally) . . . is the picture clear? The sophomore chevaliers attended colleges across the entire educational spectrum: big Harvard, medium Yale and little Princeton. Fifteen from each. (Fourteen from Princeton, after a whole-grain-cereal magnate's only son's midterm run-in with the honor code.) The college boys, not laughing at themselves as heartily as they believed they were laughing at themselves, seemed already to be feeling at home in the kilts of the Argyll and Sutherland Highlanders, the great popinjay busby of the Royal Fusiliers. To Nathaniel's eyes, his contemporaries belonged in their cocked hats, that bearskin shako. Armor, he thought, would have been a little too much, but no one wore armor to the Dubutante Cotillion, Guards' Ball. Rather, the uniformed collegians wandered the Palm Court looking doomed and resigned, as though it were the eve of Blenheim, the dawn of Balaklava, and not a fancy-dress party at which Lester Lanin would play in the Grand Ballroom at eleven, chicken in the basket to be served at two, after the Dubs were toasted with beer in champagne glasses, when they became, at midnight, tongues in cheek, Men of the World. From where he sat, Nathaniel decided it would be nice to be a Man of the World, but not as nice as being out on the town with Diana Carr.

"Why," Diana asked Nathaniel (who had felt the question edging toward him two drinks ago, who felt across the network of his synapses the full-alert defense mechanisms of an animal in peril, who imagined his nose to twitch, his ears to prick up, his rattles to shake; if he were a bobcat he'd hiss, call him grizzly and his head would swing from side to side), "aren't you" (was she actually going to ask *him*?) "a Dub?"

Nathaniel sighed.

"Well," Diana said, "why aren't we . . . why aren't you"—and she threw her arms out, as though embracing the uniformed dandies—"part of all this?"

Now she'd caught Pownall's attention. Pownall regarded Diana, regarded his date, regarded Nathaniel, cocked his eyebrow, stared long and frankly at Diana, finished his gin, told the waiter no, thanks, he'd had enough, had to run.

"Take care," he told Nathaniel. "Take care of yourself."

Pownall's date, standing, couldn't stand; she fell back in her chair. "Oopsy daisy," she said.

"Not to fear, Hamm is here." Pownall Hamm helped his date stand, and helped her walk away, but not before he helped her finish her tumbler of warm gin.

Now Booth was staring at Diana. She was waiting for an answer: how could it be that she was at a table with three Princeton fellows, all roommates, and two of them were *debutantes*, d*u*butantes, whatever, and the third, *her date*, was *not*? An explanation was owed.

"We couldn't persuade Nathaniel to join our tomfoolery," Booth said. "He managed to snag a couple of ducats to that Broadway show he's treating you to." Nathaniel wished he'd called them "ducats," and then wished he'd wished no such wish.

"I wasn't invited," Nathaniel said.

"Uh-huh," Diana said. "Oh," Diana said. "I see," she saw.

"Where do you . . . study?" Booth asked. Diana said Briarcliff. "Oh," said Booth. "I see. And where *did* you study, before Bennett?" *Briarcliff*, Diana reminded, and before at St. Meg's. "St. Meg's? What school is the saint nicknamed for? I know no St. Meg's."

"St. Margaret," Diana explained.

"St. *Margaret*? Now I've heard of St. Mark and I've heard of St. Paul—"

"Those are boys' schools," Diana explained.

"By George, you're right! Oh, and let us not forget St. George's, self-important little school with a great big chapel in my neighborhood—"

"You're from Newport," Diana told Booth.

"I guess you have me there. I guess I *am* from Newport! But St. George's is a boys' school, too. Isn't it?"

"Of course." Now Diana was wary.

"Of *course* it is! Now St. Tim's has gals, no?"

"St. Tim's is in Maryland, the Green Spring Valley. I could have gone there. My mother's roommate her first year in college went to St. Tim's. St. Margaret's is a Connecticut school, in Waterbury."

"Ah-ha!" Booth said. "*That* St. Maggie's."

"Meg's," Diana said.

"Well," Booth said, slapping his forehead with his palm, "call me out to lunch but I've never heard of the place."

"I'm surprised," Diana said, sounding surprised.

"But I've heard of it now, and I'll never forget St. . . . Molly's, is it?" Diana sought to correct him, but he fended her off with a raised palm. "Whatever," Booth said, "I'll never forget your school or you. What is your name?" Diana told him she'd already told him, and told him again. "I hope you'll write it on a little scrap of paper," Booth said, "because I want to be confident I never forget your name."

"Okay," Diana said, and blushed. "Have you got a pen?" she asked Nathaniel.

"I do not," Nathaniel said.

Diana called the waiter, who reluctantly gave her a pencil and watched while she fastidiously wrote on the Princeton-sealed envelope of a Princeton-sealed letter from Nathaniel, a letter confirming this meeting at the Biltmore, under the clock; she added to her name and address written in Nathaniel's hand her phone number at Briarcliff, at home, at her father's New York office.

"What use could I make of your father's telephone number?"

"In case you can't find me at the other numbers."

"What does your father do?" asked Booth.

"He's in business of some kind."

"How interesting!"

"He likes it. I think."

"But of course he does!"

"We have to leave," Nathaniel said. "We've stayed too long. You've got a dance waiting for you."

"I'll be sure to remember your name," Booth told Diana. "There are consorts to be selected next year, and if your name comes up on any list of ladies, I want certainly to remember it, and put in my two cents' worth."

"I'd love to be a Dub's consort," Diana said.

"Would you?" Booth said. "I'll remember that," Booth said. "Nathaniel, please remind me if I forget."

"Jesus, Booth," Nathaniel said.

"Jesus yourself, buckaroo. You're taking the hosepipe from this little gal."

"Booth—" It was a riddle, how Booth behaved. He despised discourtesy, would forgive a slight directed at himself— in fact relished a slight directed at himself—but in the face of unkindness was ruthlessly unkind. If this was chivalry, it didn't exactly add up for Nathaniel.

"Oh-oh," Booth said, "now he's pissed off! The buckaroo is cross with old Griggsie." Booth helped Nathaniel to his feet, led him to the spurious privacy of the Choate boys' table. What must those prepsters have thought hearing Booth's speech? "Listen, Nathaniel, this has gone on too long. You have no business with this girl. She doesn't mean you well. You're above this. This is not a nice girl. You don't want to be pussy-whipped. Heart-bruised." Nathaniel returned to Diana's table, and Booth followed him.

"Don't fret about invitations," Booth said. "When has a rectangle of fake-engraved cream cardboard kept a friend off a dance floor? Come to my room. I've taken a room here. In that room I've got a dinner jacket from last night. It may even be clean. Wear it. Come play. Come with me. Come."

"I don't know, Booth . . ."

"Come on," Booth said. "Pownall made me promise I'd bring you. I don't care myself, but Pownall made me promise."

"I'm not properly dressed," Diana said.

"You're right," Booth said, looking her over. "You're not. Are you coming?" he asked his roommate.

Nathaniel looked at Diana. How did someone get made so beautiful? She was using her tongue on a bit of cigarette paper annealed to her lower lip. He'd seen her use that tongue that way before, plenty. There was a spot of lipstick on her tooth. Her pouty lower lip was wet. He'd seen the sight. She smelled of perfume and tobacco, and her cheeks blushed. A strand of hair had fallen across her face; it was hot in the Palm Court, and the hair was stuck to her face at the corner of her mouth. Old movie. She was looking at Nathaniel, puzzled, wide-eyed. He fingered the Dunhill in his jacket pocket, wished he hadn't sprung for the damned engraving.

"Let's go," Nathaniel said. To his roomie.

"But what about me?" Diana said.

Booth put a fifty on the table, much too much for the drinks, even counting Pownall's gins. Fifty dollars was what a bravo paid for an all-nighter.

"What about me?"

"I'll never forget you," Booth said.

"Nathaniel!" Diana whispered. "What do you think you're

doing? Where are you going? We've got *theater* tickets! What are you doing?"

Nathaniel was past answering Diana's questions. She had asked at least one question too many. But he'd never forget the way she smelled, and years later he'd ask the snit behind the perfume counter at Bendel's to spray his palm with this scent and that scent, hoping to find that smell, and give it to the woman he was about to marry, so that his wife would smell just as Diana smelled tonight, Under the Clock. Diana smelled . . . complicated. She was why they had that word, "smart." It was the right word. It had also just become the right word for him. He was smart now, wised up, could see Diana through Pownall's eyes, and Booth's, and couldn't see her fresh again, couldn't see what love had lit up. He wished he could be glad to know better than he knew on the Empire Builder, to see with Booth's educated eyes the common girl got up in such an uncommon face. He wasn't glad about any of it. He felt cheap—diminished and diminishing. Led by Booth through the merrymakers, he was almost beyond earshot.

Diana had the last words, and they were clamorous. People under the clock heard; people in the lobby heard; Nathaniel heard. "Who do you think you are? You goddamned weenie. You Hundred Percenter!"

Got up in Booth's black tie, Nathaniel waited with his roommate by the elevator bank where they were joined by Pownall, who had emerged from an adjoining room.

"Beth?" Booth asked.

Pownall shrugged. "A tad poorly. She ate a bum olive."

"No olives in those gins," Booth said.

"Really! That must be the cause! Mustn't drink on an empty stomach." Pownall smiled at Nathaniel. "Where are you bound?"

"Booth talked me into crashing the Guards' Ball."

Pownall gave Booth a look. "You know," he said to Nathaniel, "there isn't a dumber way to put in hours than to watch a crew of self-important tots, in Halloween suits, pretend to make fun of themselves. I'd rather go to a show. Or to sleep. Booth, is this an easy one to crash? On a scale of one to ten, what's the degree of difficulty here?"

"I wouldn't know," Booth began, "I've never—"

"—crashed a party," Pownall finished. "Why then do you encourage our roommate to crash a party?"

Booth said, "Butt out, Hamm. You're loaded."

"I guess I am all of that. Have you gentlemen called for the elevator? Because I'd like to get a bet down on one of them, any of the three, to reach us before the other elevators." He spoke deliberately, and held his head still, and breathed deeply.

"I don't care which elevator comes first," Booth said.

"I know you don't, but indulge me. And Nathaniel, *you* join the fun, don't let me think you have a teensy set on you, pick an elevator. If it's the quickest elevator, or if it's merely quicker than mine, you can have my Guards' Ball invitation. You can be, as it were, Pownall Hamm, and better luck with the name than I've had."

Contracts were made; Booth chose; Nathaniel chose; Pownall got what was left. Elevators docked in turn at the tenth floor.

"Oh my," Pownall said, reaching into the vasty deeps of his trouser pockets, producing twenty dollars for Booth, an invitation for Nathaniel, who wondered what a gentleman should do, who wondered if his father would have known what he should do and at what moment he would have forgotten or ceased to care what properly to do. What Nathaniel did, he refunded to Pownall the *West Side Story* tickets that Pownall hadn't needed because he had been asked to be a Guard at the Dubutantes' Ball. Nathaniel saw by his watch that the curtain was long ago up at *West Side Story*. Nathaniel didn't feel like a man who'd gambled and won.

Leaving Pownall, smiling, by the elevators, Nathaniel asked Booth: "What if he had won? I think he doesn't approve of me crashing—"

"Pownall never wins. Always bets, never wins, always pays. That's the way it is, has been, will be. A sportsman with a simply awful won-lost record."

So why did Nathaniel, noticing for the first time he was now taller than his roommates, feel so sharply cut, as though *he* had been pruned, had lost, was lost?

Sailed in. Surrendered P. Hamm's brevet to a bosomy professional list-examiner and credentials-checker. Booth and Nathaniel followed a cocksure, imperial squirt who breezed right past, muttering that if he wasn't on the list he should have been. Nathaniel knew this diminutive junior, this virtuoso of reputation, this sighted George Shearing. The woman checking names gave Booth a look, and he returned a rueful grin. She waved him toward the ballroom without checking her guest book, but Booth said he could wait; he had time aplenty. He knew she had a job, and he would not for the world make that job difficult for her. The woman radiated gratitude. Booth draped an arm around Nathaniel, who wondered how people came to know what Booth seemed to know: exactly the right thing to do, the perfectly unexpected appropriate word to say.

"I know your mother," the woman told Booth, who nodded; of course she knew his mother. "Your mother, too."

"I beg your pardon?" Nathaniel said.

"I know your mother," the gatekeeping lady repeated.

"I don't think so," Nathaniel said before he felt Booth's hand tighten on the back of his neck. It was an excessively forceful gesture, Nathaniel thought. Hurtful.

"Of course you do," Booth said, "Mrs. Hamm—"

"*Dr.* Hamm's wife," the gatekeeper completed, beaming at her power of recall.

"Exactly!" Booth said. "Exactly!"

"Enjoy yourselves, boys. Have a *lovely* evening."

Lester Lanin played "Manhattan," and Lester Lanin played "I Get a Kick Out of You." Lester Lanin played "A Fine Romance," played "East of the Sun," written by a Princeton man for the Triangle Show, or so Booth said, and Booth would know. At midnight, after monkey business with swords, the Dubutantes were made Men of the World by their escorts, and Lester Lanin played "Land of Hope and Glory." Booth, dead center of a line of costumed Big Three sophomores, smiled thinly. The ceremony reminded Nathaniel of the initiation rite for a club the neighborhood kids in Laurelhurst had put together in sixth grade. They'd called themselves The Desperados, and they'd dubbed themselves with wooden swords, because his tame gang members had no appetite to mingle blood. Now the photographer was giving orders, and the bosomy gatekeeper was counting heads, and Nathaniel noticed her brief look of bewilderment.

"We need Pownall Hamm," she said.

The St. Paul's boys huzzahed at Pownall's name, ditto Fessenden boys, and boys and girls from Philadelphia, and boys and girls who summered at Northeast Harbor. "Where's Pownall? We want Pownall!"

The bosomy gatekeeper was staring at Nathaniel, and he met her gaze. Okay, red-handed. He made a gesture of surrender. She began to speak, and when Nathaniel shook his head *no, please,* she held her tongue. He thought she was kind; he mistook her priorities. Nathaniel walked to her, and said he was sorry, he shouldn't have . . . *tricked* her, he'd leave, of course.

"Don't think of it," the lady said. "If this gathering of friends is so attractive to you that you'd *gate-crash* it, stay, mingle with the young ladies and gentlemen. I won't ask your name, because I presume you won't tell me the truth."

"Nathaniel Clay," Nathaniel said to her pale, fleshy back, less for her benefit than for his. He too wondered who he was, and to say his name was a stab at learning who he was. "I'm Nathaniel Clay."

After the self-conscious gaiety of the mock coming-out party had dissipated in giggles, after the Dubs were toasted with beer in champagne glasses, the Guards' Ball was a pretty good dance. Lester Lanin played "Fine and Dandy." At two in the morning the skylarkers ate chicken in the basket, and Lester Lanin played a set of Dixieland, and invited the Thelonious micro-Monk of Lake Minnetonka, Minnesota, wearing the dress uniform of Her Majesty's Life Guards, to sit in on "Ja-Da Ja-Da (Ja-Da Ja-Da Jing Jing Jing)." He was pretty good.

Later, Nathaniel danced when there was no danger of a waltz. It seemed to him he was cut in on with notable ferocity by a Yale Dub, but he was still uneducated in eastern decorums. He could not fail to notice that after he had been cut in on, his lank, bony, milky-skinned, honey-haired former partner failed to return his smile from the sideline, refused even to meet his eyes. He knew he was not a good dancer, but still . . .

Maybe Booth had noticed this little drama, because he cut in on the lank, bony, milky-skinned, honey-haired dancer. He smiled at her, whispered something in her ear; she laughed, and now Booth scowled; he seemed to be having a bad time even before he'd had a chance to have a bad time.

Most of the Guards seemed to be having a great time. Nathaniel admired their easy way with fun. He admired their fine hair and pale eyes. He admired their languid pace when they moved, as though whatever they moved toward would by God wait for them to get to it. How pleased were the Guards with their steps. Lester Lanin played "It's De-Lovely." How pleased with life these Big Three Ivy Leaguers. How delightedly—"I'm de-lovely, I'm delicious, I'm de-wonderful"—these gala-goers sang into their dates' ears. Out at the perimeter of the floor Nathaniel stood aping the costumed revelers, standing with one hand on his hip, affecting a squint, casually furrowed brow, *how curious, how boring,* looking beyond the present festival to some distant and superior memory or prospect, abruptly affecting an inquisitive glance, *say,* that's *odd.* Lester Lanin played "Shiny Stockings," and Nathaniel watched the festive couples spin and twirl and dip, while the Dubs blasted hard off-key jazz harmonies—Tigertone stuff—at their partners. There was the Minnesotan with his nibshit nickname—Jamie—wearing a monocle attached by a black silk ribbon to his waistcoat. When a pretty girl would pass near the bantling, he'd go wide-eyed with admiration, dropping the monocle plop into his champagne glass, fishing it out nonchalantly by its black silk cord. This antic caused pretty girls to laugh, to kiss the pismire's cheeks. Nathaniel wondered what the pretty girls saw when they noticed Nathaniel. He found his reflection in a ballroom mirror placed to return to the celebrants their pleasing likenesses, and he recoiled from his image as though from an enemy, and stood still, solemn, his hands at his sides.

He saw Booth arguing with friends, who gestured at Nathaniel, who wanted to get the hell out of that place. He fathomed he had made a mistake. He imagined Booth might want to open some distance between himself and Nathaniel, but Nathaniel was wrong to imagine this. Toward the end Booth stuck like a bodyguard with Nathaniel, and when Nathaniel suggested he leave (Lester Lanin played "Anything Goes"), Booth said: "Don't consider it! Why care what they think?"

The Princeton Tigertones sang "Teasin' " and "Ain't Misbehavin' " and "Mavourneen" and a song about desperate warriors that declared in a close harmonic crescendo: "We are brave and gal-lant Ban-do-laaaay-rose; we'll conquer or diiiie!" The Yale Whiffenpoofs sang "Tear It Down," "Bermuda Buggy Ride," "My Daddy Is a Yale Man." The Harvards sent no triple quartet to warble at the Dubutante Cotillion. The Big Three had, after all, singularities.

Standing beside Nathaniel with *his* hand on *his* hip, Booth explained which was which, and not for the first time. How Harvard was apart, head and snoot in the clouds. Nathaniel nodded, fighting to pay attention even as those whiskey sours took him by the throat. Booth said regard Yale. Calvin and Commerce, partners in enterprise. It was the '50s place, Yale, ubiquitous. Everybody's girlfriend left him for The Guy from Yale, sturdy and clear-eyed, able, sobersided, in great physical shape.

"Has your girlfriend left you for The Guy from Yale?"

"Which girlfriend?" Booth said.

"Any girlfriend."

"No," Booth said. "About the Big Three," Booth said. "Take clubs. At Harvard they have waiting clubs and final clubs. The waiting are where you have a drink while you wait to get in a final club."

"What are you talking about?" Nathaniel asked.

"Harvard's final clubs, my friend, Yale's secret societies, Princeton's eating clubs. Very important institutions."

Nathaniel had heard of final clubs and secret societies, and he sort of knew that last year's dubutantes, dubbing this year's Men of the World, had already made the cut at Harvard into A.D., Porcellian, Fly. The new Yalie Dubs were sweating Tap Day, pretending not to fret about getting their tickets punched by Bones, Wolf's Head, Scroll and Key. "Why?" Nathaniel asked.

"Why what?" Booth said.

"Why are they very important institutions?"

"Because if you don't get in, you're out. Because if you're

out . . ." Booth made a nasty slashing motion at his throat. "You don't want to be out, buckaroo, unless you choose out. That's why they're important institutions. That's why these gentlemen are so anxious to be in."

"They don't seem anxious to me," Booth.

"You're not looking with smart eyes, buckaroo."

Maybe, but Nathaniel looked with the dreamy eyes he had been given, the eyes with which he wished to see. He saw gallant young officers smoothly swirling their lovestruck and beloved partners around the polished dance floor of a great city's great hotel's ballroom. He saw glamour. He saw young and graceful men of his age, men he wished to have—was desperate to have—as friends, to join as comrades, fellow-scholars, family. Being a clubmate—why, that was merely incidental. "Maybe, Booth, they want to join those clubs because they simply like one another."

"What?" Booth asked, swimming up to the here and now from wherever he had been.

The costumes worn at the Guards' Ball were not for nothing called uniforms. The boys playacting officers and knights-errant, showing the colors, were superficially distinct, but fundamentally uniform. Stripped of pomp, of identifying facings and plumes, they would have been expelled into the grim chaos of a battlefield whose combatants wandered in mufti, unable to distinguish friend from foe. Farfetched? What's a club tie for? What's the value of an engraved invitation with the name Pownall Hamm on it? Had Nathaniel's social ganglia been better evolved, he might have felt in the air that self-consciously festive night the jittery insolent brass of soldiers on the eve of battle, preparing for a great shaking out at which most here would go over the top and make it, and some few—some unhappy, unhappy few—would not.

"What's the big deal about clubs?" Nathaniel said. "Maybe clubs are just a bunch of guys who want to hang out together."

In fact, clubs weren't the least bit on Nathaniel's mind just now. He fingered the cigarette lighter in his pocket. Diana was on his mind. He was ashamed to have acted badly, and he was ashamed that she had acted badly, and he was ashamed to love her, and he was ashamed to be ashamed to love her.

"No! No! You don't understand," Booth said. "Let me tell you how it is!"

And he told how it was. Taught the Iron Law of Clubmanship that holds: many are outside looking in, a few are inside looking . . . in. This Darwinian model of the feral world requires fewer us's than thems, or why be an us? Up or out: the elevation to be mounted was not a greasy pole but a slick pyramid, with scant room at the apex—ninety Yale seniors, say, of a class of a thousand. At Harvard and Yale so few made the final club, the secret society, that the many thems at least had the solace of their own great society.

"But Princeton's different!" Nathaniel said.

"Oh, puh-leeze!" Booth said.

"What's a Hundred Percenter?"

Booth made a dismissing gesture. "Nothing you need to worry about."

Nathaniel stared at Booth. No one knew what another needed to worry about. And if Booth had said not to worry without believing what he had said, what then? "Let me have the room key, Booth. Please. I'm about out of gas."

"Don't go," Booth said. "I want you to meet some people."

None of this was what he had expected. Nathaniel felt his skin tightening dry from his cheap, expensive, barbershop sunburn. "I think I'd like to go to bed," he said.

Booth gave him the room key. "I hate to think of you up there alone," Booth said. "This is a lousy night, first night of Christmas vacation, to be alone. Come back down if you feel lonely. Okay? I'm going to miss you. Okay? You all right?"

Nathaniel, taking the key, nodded. Walking toward the

grand staircase to the lobby, he saw the bosomy gatekeeper, and approached her to apologize, but she turned her back on him. And then, directly under his nose, he spotted the lanky blonde with whom he had had such an uneventful dance. She was sitting eating scrambled eggs and bacon with several boys in uniform, among them Minnesota's response to the piano artistry of Earl Fatha Hines. Nathaniel stood above her, reaching into his pocket. "I'd like you to have this," he said.

She looked at him; she looked at it. "It's a cigarette lighter," she said. Nathaniel nodded; it was indeed a cigarette lighter. "I don't smoke," she said.

"Maybe in the future you'll smoke," he said.

"It's got your initials on it," she said.

"Those aren't my initials."

"I don't even know you," she said.

"That's okay. I'm not sure I know me. Goodnight, everyone. Have a ball."

Walking away, he heard the lanky blonde laugh a high musical laugh.

Nathaniel half heard a boy say, "He's just blotto."

Nathaniel was too far gone to hear the ivory-tickler say, "He stole the damned thing."

"Who is he?" the lanky blonde said.

"Nobody," Jamie Hill said.

Four

Bicker

. . . ground glass folding-doors divided my premises into two parts, one of which was occupied by my scriveners, the other by myself. According to my humour I threw open these doors, or closed them. I resolved to assign Bartleby a corner by the folding-doors, but on my side of them, so as to have this quiet man within easy call, in case any trifling thing was to be done. I placed his desk close up to a small side-window in that part of the room, a window which originally had afforded a lateral view of certain grimy back-yards and bricks, but which, owing to subsequent erections, commanded at present no view at all, though it gave some light. Within three feet of the panes was a wall, and the light came down from far above, between two lofty buildings, as from a very small opening in a dome. Still further to a satisfactory arrangement, I procured a high green folding screen, which might entirely isolate Bartleby from my sight, though not remove him from my voice. And thus, in a manner, privacy and society were conjoined.

—Herman Melville, "Bartleby the Scrivener."

"I would prefer not to."
—Ibid., Bartleby speaking.

Friday, a month after the Guards' Ball, Princeton University, McCosh 50, America's Best, MWF 9 a.m., John Hyde was professing to a packed lecture hall. Topic: point of view. Method: a focused reading of Melville's text, that smug, purse-proud, self-justifying biography of the forlorn Bartleby—a human copy machine—told by his employer, a Wall Street lawyer whose book-length briefs Bartleby finally prefers not to transcribe and proofread. Three hundred and more undergraduates sprawled, sat bolt upright, dozed; a few transcribed every word John Hyde uttered—beginning with "Good morning"—as faithfully as Wall Street's most obedient scrivener. Others wandered in late, this one with pajamas visible beneath his coonskin coat, that one—delivered by the last train from Penn Station—wearing patent-leather dancing pumps and a dinner jacket.

Professor Hyde seemed to register nothing of the students' motley. His voice was pitched high, singsong, ceremonial. It seemed to Nathaniel, who felt alone with Professor Hyde in the tiered lecture theater, that his teacher spoke directly to him, and as Hyde moved through Melville's odd story, Nathaniel fell out of himself and into the bewildered lawyer and adamant Bartleby. It dizzied Nathaniel to be transported by Professor Hyde to a past time, another place, alien dreams and chimeras; he fought his vertigo with fierce attention, trying with Professor Hyde's guidance to see with the homiletic lawyer's eyes his naysaying employee, to see with Bartleby's eyes the imperious employer.

"You must look where they look," Professor Hyde said. "This is a tale of blank walls, partial point of view, blindness, uncertain vision by sunlight and candlelight, dead-wall reveries, a man extending to his servant, without meeting his servant's eyes, without glancing up at his young servant, a bouquet of pages to be copied and proofread. . . ."

(*Young* servant? Nathaniel had missed that. Bartleby seemed weary, was alienated: how could he be "young"? Ah, sure enough, there he was, the morning he was hired: ". . . a motionless young man . . . pallidly neat, pitiably respectable, incurably forlorn! It was Bartleby." How had he missed that?)

Professor Hyde's subject was the failure of the lawyer's sight as a failure of fellow-feeling. Nathaniel was stirred. Professor Hyde dimmed the lights, showed Breughel's "Fall of Icarus," tapping with his outsized pointer a pair of pinkish legs scissoring awkwardly into a placid inlet while a ship sails off on a fair tide, while a shepherd looks to the sky, elsewhere, while the shepherd's dog looks at the shepherd looking, while an angler casts his line more or less in the direction of the legs of the boy who fell from the sky. "The fisherman's thinking fish," Professor Hyde said. "He's thinking dinner."

"What the fuck's the slide show about?" a scholar asked, in the dark behind Nathaniel. "Is this America's Best or what? Is this art history? What am I supposed to be looking at?"

Professor Hyde read from Auden's "Musée des Beaux Arts" in a keening monotone:

"In Breughel's *Icarus,* for instance: how everything turns away
Quite leisurely from the disaster; the plowman may
Have heard the splash, the forsaken cry,
But for him it was not an important failure; the sun shone
As it had to on the white legs disappearing into the green
Water; and the expensive delicate ship that must have seen
Something amazing, a boy falling out of the sky,
Had somewhere to get to and sailed calmly on."

Like all great stories, Professor Hyde said, Melville's "Bartleby" is heated by friction, collision, one man's gimme versus another's hands-off. The lecture-hall lights came up. "But look into your hearts," Professor Hyde preached, "and see if you find there the lawyer's heart, his blank-wall, walled-street, blind indifference." Nathaniel looked into his heart and felt not the lawyer's indifference but his own sentimental empathy. " 'Man's inhumanity to man / Makes countless thousands mourn!' Robert Burns," Professor Hyde said, "echoing Pliny, anticipating Wordsworth: 'Have I not reason to lament / What man has made of man?' " Nathaniel was at once cast down by the sentiment and elevated by its expression. "Bleakly, perhaps blindly, Melville's lawyer finds his senses at the story's end in New York's Tombs, where his failure of brotherhood has sent Bartleby to die, walled up. Listen to a partial account of their final meeting, see what the narrator sees: 'I saw the wasted Bartleby. But nothing stirred. I paused; then went close up to him; stooped over, and saw that his dim eyes were open; otherwise he seemed profoundly sleeping. Something prompted me to touch him. I felt his hand, when a tingling shiver ran up my arm and down my spine to my feet.' *There*," Professor Hyde said, "the lawyer at last connects. *That* is how one shock of recognition runs the whole circle round. Touch. Only connect."

Nathaniel felt kinship, but not with the student who told his seatmate across the aisle, not quite out of earshot, "The guy would have saved himself a mess of trouble if he'd shit-canned the bolshie pinko clerk on page 6." Nathaniel felt joined in a common enterprise with future lawyers and legislators and investment bankers and—yes, scholars doing the university's universal duty—who would see with their brothers' eyes, widen their points of view, reach out, connect.

"Next time," Professor Hyde said, "Stephen Crane's 'Open Boat.' A story of shipwreck, a view of the nature of things from a bathtub of a lifeboat. Four men sink or swim together, row together against their fate. And together they're alone out there, off the Florida coast. The desperate men see sightseers on a beach, and wave for help. The sightseers wave back, have a nice day on the water! 'In the wan light,' Crane writes, 'the faces of the men must have been gray. Their eyes must have glinted in strange ways as they gazed steadily astern. Viewed from a balcony the whole thing would, doubtless, have been weirdly picturesque. But the men in the boat had no time to see it. . . .' Will you see it? Will you look down from your imaginary balcony at those little creatures bobbing in that little boat? Will you look with some interest, or with none? Or perhaps you won't look at all. Or, looking, can't see. We shall see what we will see. But not for a fortnight. Today we close down this shop for two weeks. Bicker, gentlemen, begins tomorrow. 'Ah Bartleby! Ah humanity!' Fourteen days of—what did our attorney call it?—'fraternal melancholy.' "

Princeton called a two-week recess to its educational mission for upperclassmen to select attractive and agreeable sophomore meal-partners. Nathaniel found it difficult to take seriously a process called Bicker: the word suggested an enterprise petty and contentious. He liked better Preferential, which he could have looked up in the glossary of an institutional booklet—*Now That You're Ready for Bicker*—bearing the seal of Princeton University, had not Booth already explained the word's meaning. A Preferential was a tight congregation of roommates or friends who professed a preference to join the same eating club, who would together be visited and interviewed, wooed and winnowed afternoon and evening, by junior and senior members of twenty or so clubs. Of these, five—in ascending appeal Tiger Inn, Cap and Gown, Colonial, Cottage and Ivy—seemed to weigh in Booth's and Pownall's preferences.

The boys were uniform in Brooks white button-downs. Tweeded up: Pownall's jacket was out-at-elbows herringbone, a nice fit when he got it fourth-form year, two inches ago, at six feet. Booth's houndstooth, cut for his father on Savile Row by Huntsman during the Battle of Britain, was pinched at the waist; the boy rescued his presentation from foppery with a black knit tie and faded blue canvas Top-Sider sneakers, spattered by specks of bronze boat-bottom paint. Nathaniel was remarkably unremarkable in Harris tweed, a paisley tie either dark green or brown (the light was bad), Bass Weejuns, which he called "penny loafers," an expression Booth seemed relieved never before to have heard.

Now, waiting to be judged, Pownall reclined on the boys' St. Matthew's Opportunity & Thrift Shop leather sofa, musing: "There are worse fates than to be disliked."

"Trust Hamm to leave no homily unorated. Besides, the banality is unso," Booth said.

"Is it?" Pownall asked. He seemed interested. "Is it really, for you? Booth?"

Booth shrugged. "Clubs have their place. Associations are useful."

"Do you mean *connections*?" Pownall asked his old friend.

"Well, I wouldn't put it quite that roughly. Lay off. Don't be cynical. Cynicism is cheap."

Nathaniel said, "I feel shrunk by Bicker. I feel, I don't know—"

"Soiled?" Pownall said.

"That would be 'sullied,' " Booth said. "The Sea Lion insisted on 'sullied.' "

"Just so," Pownall said.

Nathaniel asked who was the Sea Lion.

"Rhetoric teacher, St. Paul's," Pownall said. "Named for his general sleekness, waddly snoot-up carriage, pinhead, massive and liquid middle."

"The Sea Lion was a large-framed rhetorician," Booth said; "Pownall is unjust to him."

"That's quite a march of *un*-words, Griggs. *Un*orated, *un*so, *un*just."

"Nego's all the cry this year," Booth said. "Ask any Exeter boy. Ask yourself." ("Nego," Nathaniel knew, was "negative," Club Row's boss honorific, antonym of "keen." The

Street's boss malediction. Keen boys were pushers, the horror, the horror.)

Pownall, slumped in a red leather chair, shoeless feet on an ottoman, asked Nathaniel: "Have you noticed our idiom? How clubbable is our discourse, how frothy and light, like mimosas at brunch? Were you to judge, would you not say we were bright as pennies?"

"Oooo," said Booth, "the subjunctive mood. How feathery!"

"You sound like strangers. Like actors playing phonies," Nathaniel said.

"Phonies in Seattle, buckaroo," Booth said, "but on Prospect, on The Street, clubmen. Cap and Gowners."

"Get serious," Pownall said. "Cap's gravid, wall-to-wall strivers and worthies, belt-and-suspenders boys, double rubbers. Colonial's just our cup of tea, quick on its toes."

Booth said, "Talk about double rubbers, Colonial's a gang of *bridge players,* for God's sake. Colonial chaps ride to hounds in the Green Spring Valley."

"What's wrong with horses?" Nathaniel asked. "You're crazy about horses."

"Not about horses," Booth said, "about buggies. I don't bounce on the heaving backs of sweaty beasts; I am drawn by rather than to them."

"Do us a favor?" Pownall asked. "Since we've submitted ourselves to the estimation of our seniors and putative betters, since we're meant I suppose to please our assessors, will you leave Old Dobbin—oats, tack, the whip's snap—home in his stable and out of our Preferential?"

"The *Now That You're Ready for Bicker* booklet says, right here, page 5, following a list of ten reasons why the club selection process mimics the real world of choice and consequence, of 'discrimination, in its most benign sense'—"

"Cut it out," Nathaniel said.

"It says right here," Booth went on: " 'Above all, Be Yourself.' "

"And if that doesn't work—" Pownall said.

"Be somebody else," Booth said. *"Dogma summa."*

From the day Nathaniel set first foot on Princeton's campus, conversations with the Sons of Old Nassau had turned in time, more often inferentially than directly, to clubs. Clubbing and being clubbed wasn't an incidental activity here; it was thought to be a consummation.

"Do we really have to do this?" Nathaniel said.

Booth stared at him. "I beg your pardon?"

Nathaniel wanted to figure out how this thing worked. With will and patience, Nathaniel believed, any process could be understood. Maybe even mastered. He knew he didn't *have* to join an eating club middle of sophomore year, but Nathaniel also understood that everyone joined a club. Tried to. You joined an eating club or you didn't eat, unless you'd call it "eating" to push a tray down the public chow line of the Balt, a shower room of a greezy spoon, hard fluorescent lights bouncing off its tiled floors and walls.

If feeding your face was your whole purpose, you were not obliged in January of sophomore year to submit your manners, bona fides, bloodline and livery to the scrutiny of post-adolescents a year or two your senior, but feeding his face was not Nathaniel's whole purpose. Nathaniel's whole purpose, modest enough, was to be among the many us's rather than the few thems. The system had begun in 1879 as an arrangement whereby ten boys, affronted by a food fight in the dining halls well-called Commons, established the Ivy Club, and with it a process of selection whereby ten boys rejected two thousand; this had evolved into an evil (Nathaniel wouldn't have used "evil" yet) whereby two thousand excluded ten.

To join the community of Us, a Princeton sophomore bent

to the guillotine, tied his own noose, adjusted its fit. A young gentleman knelt to Bicker, like a boy giving a blow-job. He sat in this room, made himself available afternoon and evening to the whim of visitors. How enter the tournament, went the logic, without taking the field?

"How soon," Pownall asked Nathaniel, "the fateful tread on the stair, the life-changing knuckle on the door?"

"Seven and a half minutes, more or less."

During the final countdown to 7 p.m., Nathaniel recollected last night's Architectural Tour, the first time that sophomores were welcomed inside the clubs to look them over, to be looked over. The scrubbed and shiny boys got just a feel, a little taste to motivate the underclass aspirants—glance at the hand-rubbed butternut paneling in Tiger Inn's billiard room, sightsee the busy television lounge at Colonial where wits and wags gave the business to Bret Maverick and the American Bandstanders, get a once-over of Ivy's library of rare books and dark-wood carrels, rubberneck Cottage's legendary taproom where Scott Fitzgerald Himself—time out of mind—fell down drunk. Cottage was seductive: wild parties with Meyer Davis playing this weekend, a Mississippi Delta blues singer next weekend, Wild Bill Davison the weekend after. And, always, the *best*-looking Smithies, *best*-dressed boys, *funniest* jokes, most elegant appointments. If one were to *Consumer Report* the clubs, Cottage would have to get Highest Rating for the categories Atmosphere of Prosperity, Buildings and Grounds, Self-Satisfaction.

Nathaniel knew Cottage on good authority. He had journeyed with Pownall to the brick Georgian clubhouse (McKim, Mead & White) next door to Ivy and dwarfing that older club. They had been greeted at Cottage by a Virginian who spoke to Nathaniel with studied courtesy. This Virginian was captain of the golf team, and the first thing he asked Pownall, whom he seemed to know, was why did Pownall row.

"Why do I row, why?" Pownall asked.

"Ah'm eagah to find oot wah a puhsun would *choose* to sit on his ass, gettin' wet, goin' back-wuhd."

"But the view ahead," Pownall said, "the finish line, the eighteenth hole, as it were, is so bleak."

The Virginian might have smiled; it was difficult in the subtle, golden light to be certain. He asked Nathaniel which of the club's rooms would most interest him to see. By now the sophomores knew the drill, having practiced their Architectural Tour tactics on lesser clubs. . . . Nathaniel was on the point of asking to see the dining room, which seemed to him, after all, the goal of this peculiar ritual of courtship and rejection, ground zero of an eating club, when Pownall asked if he and Nathaniel might see the cellar.

"Muh's the pity," the Virginian said, "we have laid down no wine."

"No," Pownall said, "I had reference to the *cellar* cellar, where the furnace lives."

And so it came to pass that Nathaniel, with sinking heart and rising comprehension, was shown Cottage Club's hotwater heater(s), copper pipes, radiators, structural supports, circuit box. And so it was that at the end of this tour a lanky Philadelphia sophomore told a diminutive Richmond senior, with conspicuous feeling, "The place seems sound, and well maintained; I'll buy it."

Nathaniel knew how to read the tight smile that answered his roommate's jape, the Virginian's considered response: "That's mahty good, Pownall, boys. Ah've never hud that one befo-ah. One way to suhvive these hahd days ahead is just your way, fri-vo-lous-ly. Ah'm suhtin we *all* take these clubs too ser-i-ous-ly. Gud evenin', genamen."

"So much for Cottage," Nathaniel said.

"Oh, do you think?" Pownall seemed surprised. "I shouldn't fret if I were you."

Nathaniel thought then how odd the conditional and subjunctive seemed in that context. Later he'd understand how imperfectly Pownall had imagined what "if I were you" meant.

Tonight of course that first knock on the door was mighty Cottage. Charm, tailoring, the very pictures of what Fitzgerald had written of his clubmates: "brilliant adventurers and well-dressed philanderers." Hair parted, like Fitzgerald's, down the middle. But then these boys had read Fitzgerald, as who in that place at that time had not? Was it possible, was there the outsidemost chance, that Cottage clubmen had read *This Side of Paradise* and *then* parted their hair down the middle?

Maybe this was worth considering as Nathaniel was grilled by a Cottage junior, one of three visitors, a visitor apiece for each in the Preferential. Nathaniel looked at this fellow with black hair parted down the middle and saw "brilliant adventurer and well-dressed philanderer," just what he who was seen wished seen.

Nathaniel stole a glance at Booth. He noticed Pownall, and was prepared to see the awful consequences of Pownall's impolitic joke at the Virginian's expense. He saw no such thing but, rather, a brilliant adventurer seizing Pownall fondly by the elbow, a well-dressed philanderer taking no notice that Pownall recoiled from the clubman's touch. Why, Pownall, already, with Bicker only ten minutes old, was being *courted*. ("Club reps are salesmen," Pownall had explained. "Never mind, look at the bright side: to endure Bicker is never after to buy life insurance from a stranger.")

Nathaniel's own experience was puzzling. The first words he heard during Bicker were not those he had been warned he would hear—"Have you got a glass of water?"—to which the response was most definitely to be "You bet. I sure do!" Nathaniel's brilliant philanderer asked, reading from a card: "What's your favorite kitchen utensil?"

The well-dressed adventurer couldn't be serious? Imagine he was. Imagine that this philandering adventurer holding Nathaniel's jewels in his hand had once heard his daddy say that his daddy's squash partner at Merion Cricket Club had read in *Newsweek* that that Rickover fellow (quite a guy, even if he was a, you know. . .) interviewed would-be submariners by inviting them to sit on polished chairs whose front legs were shorter than their rear legs, or by inviting them to smoke but offering no ashtray, or by asking, maybe, "What's your favorite kitchen utensil?"

Now a sophomore who wanted to eat next year with his friends (with silver utensils, off fresh linen, by candlelight) would want to say something memorable, but something that would not excessively thrust. Bicker's rules of decorum were as runic as the rules of court tennis, as Booth had tried to explain both. The scoring was Byzantine. There was nothing so brutally evident in this room as an accent in London, syntax in Paris, a dueling scar in Heidelberg. All was inference. What did a decision of style signal? Three days ago Nathaniel was laboring to decode metaphysical poetry, Donne's "Second Anniversary." Now he was laboring to comprehend was the SPS crew sweater worn inside out to hide an achievement or to draw the beholder's eye to it? Not for nothing was this young man a member of the *University* Cottage Club. Nathaniel already, this first night, understood that Princeton put a value on Bicker's calculations: good-better-best and fair-poor-worst mattered to an institution that titled an honored course America's Best. But how, electing to study this alien idiom, to parse the dense grammar of acceptance and disfavor? Well, a sophomore didn't want, in the phrase Fitzgerald used for these things, to "run it out." "Running it out" was not good. Running it out was weeping or saying something too hilarious during a solemn love movie at the Garden or the Playhouse. Running it out was having opinions about politics, art, culture. Running it out was the nonstop pace of Pownall and Booth, getting come-hithered and goo-goo-eyed by Cottage Club.

"My favorite kitchen utensil?"

"Indeed," said the adventurously dressed philanderer, brilliantly. "Of course, if you haven't one . . . ."

A fellow wouldn't mind being noticed, just the right amount. A corkscrew was too lah-di-dah. A beer-can opener would be too Cannon Club for words (but perhaps just right for Tiger Inn). A knife, Nathaniel decided, was counterproductively hostile.

"I've always thought I'd like to own a Waring Blender." That should have been the correct answer, though whether it would please by implying frozen daiquiri or chocolate malted, who could say? Who, in fact, could know that it *had* pleased?

It had not pleased. "Why not an Osterizer?"

"I never thought of an Osterizer."

"Well, you're entitled to your own priorities," said the handsome Bickerer, jotting something on the blue, tissue-thin page of a slim leather notebook.

It wasn't always that bad. An unfashionably togged crew-cut trio came calling from Quadrangle Club. The fellow chatting up Nathaniel had spent a year in Seattle when he was fourteen, and he and Nathaniel became excited celebrating the merits of Ivar's Acre of Clams chowder. Nathaniel's new acquaintance had shopped at Auerbach's, and had a high opinion of the store. Nathaniel was enjoying the visit, but his roommates were not. Across the room four young men stared long at their shoes, at the ends of their fingers, again at their shoes.

"Well," said Nathaniel's interviewer, "we'd better roll. A lot of territory to cover tonight."

"Oh," Nathaniel said, "please don't rush off! Let's talk some more. I'm enjoying this."

The two strangers across the room glanced at each other, and one made a face. Nathaniel's new friend was hurrying into his overcoat. "Say hi to Seattle for me," he said.

The Griggs-Hamm Preferential never saw Quadrangle Club again. They'd been cut from the bottom, as the phrase went. Too fancy for their own good and for Quadrangle's. Clay got cut with them; that was how the system worked, except when it worked another way.

Not that Nathaniel was sunk, yet. Campus Club sent a delegation of high-spirited boys, two of whom had been cheerleaders at their Pennsylvania public high schools. One reference led to another, and visitors and visited found themselves laughing, and the two Campus Clubbers each did a *sis-boom-bah*, with appropriate gymnastics; then Pownall and Booth had to put a chill on the occasion by singing the St. Paul's school hymn, and Nathaniel, deaf to the now discordant music, showed a trick he'd learned from his father and stood on his head, and when that failed to entertain he showed a trick he'd learned from Gander and walked on his hands, and it was thus—upside down—that he saw Campus Club exit his room, forever.

Something was wrong. The more time passed, the more clearly something was off. It was always Nathaniel on this side of the room, Pownall and Booth on that side. That side did better. That side got the laughter and intimate huddles, Nathaniel got "Do you believe in God?" (Cap and Gown) and "What's your major?" (Tower, and Elm).

"I haven't decided. I'm still a sophomore."

"Well, what *will* be your major?" (Tower.)

A Colonial Clubman, glass of fashion and mold of form, sat across from Nathaniel. "Well, tell me all about yourself." The dandy was touching the shoulder of Nathaniel's tweed jacket. "Say, that jacket's badly dimpled!"

"Say what?" Nathaniel said.

"Dimpled! Do you use *wire* hangers?"

"I guess so, yes, yes, in fact I do."

"There it is, then. Damned sin against a fine tweed sport coat. Didn't anyone at home advise you?"

"Advise me? I'm sorry . . ."

"Wooden hangers are *de rigueur*. Curved to the lie of the shoulder."

"I never knew."

"Jesus! Guys," the Colonial Club macaroni said to his fellow-Bickerers, "this guy doesn't know how to care for a tweed jacket."

His clubmates stared at Nathaniel, who made a gesture of surrender.

"We've got to head on down the road," said the clothes-care evangelist, rising, jotting notes to himself. "Never forget: *curved wood hangers*!"

Waiting to be courted or humiliated, depending on one's point of view, one told horror stories of bad club luck. Or Pownall and Booth told; Nathaniel listened. His friends must have wished him to realize he had company in the misery he had almost guessed was his: the sophomore who last year at Piping Rock had bird-dogged the date of an Ivy man with terrible acne and a sweet character; the Ivy man loved this girl the hapless soph had snagged with his smooth dips and spinning steps. Take the hosepipe, Parlor Snake. Dread curse: *dine elsewhere*. It wasn't fair, sometimes. Pity the luckless sophomore, dressed just fine, neither too much nor too little, quick to laugh, modest and able, affable, right on track for one of the Big Three until . . . until he opened, without knocking, an unlocked bathroom door at the Princeton Inn and revealed to about a hundred moms, dads, sisters and dates the Tiger Inn Veep vigorously moving his bowels.

And another, unlucky in drink at the Columbia game, roused from blackout at Palmer Stadium by a Cap and Gown senior screaming: "You're *sorry?* Sorry! You piss on my date's raccoon coat and silk hose and advise me you're sorry? Oh, you'll know sorry, sir. We'll show you sorry. You'll eat the next two years out of tin *cans.* Remember me."

Throwing up could cash in some awful chips. Laughing too loudly, or at the wrong time. Telling an ethnic joke, if it wasn't funny, or failing to laugh at an ethnic joke that was. (*What's eating that joker?*) Raising a hand in a seminar one time too many (which in a *Faerie Queene* class might be one time only) could stretch you out tits up, Bickerwise. It was nothing at all to go wrong, you just had to take your eye off the ball for an instant. If, mighty *if,* you were the *wrong guy.* If you were not, say, Booth Griggs, or Pownall Hamm. If, say, you were someone who had been encouraged to tell the gatekeeper at the Guards' Ball you were the Dubutante Pownall Hamm when you weren't. If you were, say, from Seattle. If you had drawn the notice of a Cottage Clubman named Jamie from Wayzata. If you were a—say—Nathaniel.

By the third night most clubs had dropped the three roommates. They'd been cut from the bottom by clubs who imagined, having been dazzled by Booth and Pownall, that the Holder Preferential was Ivy- or Cottage-bound, so why waste bids on three prepsters who considered themselves too well positioned for lesser clubs? To those who had cut the boys from the bottom, the Holder Preferential was monolithic, but for those who continued to visit and woo—Cottage, Colonial, Tiger Inn, Ivy and Prospect (a club so profoundly at the bottom of the food chain that it cut *nobody*)—the three did not appear monolithic. The Big Three sent five ambassadors: two hotshots each for Pownall and Booth and a small-talk specialist, called a "dump-artist," for Pownall's and Booth's friend.

Take this little rooster from Cottage, sitting knee to knee with Nathaniel. This would be Jamie, from Wayzata, full name James Hill. How could it be? Had the real James Hill torn an empire out of Eden, laid track across Paradise so his offsprings' half-pint offspring could study at Princeton shod in white bucks and know by heart the comings and goings of a two-car, five-mile, tin-whistle railroad called the Dinky? And was Nathaniel hearing aright, this smirking youngling interrogating him?

"So how did your father pass away?"

Nathaniel recalled in his mind's eye the little boneyard set on a hill above Zermatt, beside the Episcopal chapel. Soon after it happened, he'd journeyed there with Gander and his grandmother; he had stood alone reading the high-sentiment inscriptions on the gravestones set above those young gentlemen lying low, in the shadow of the Matterhorn's Hörnli Ridge, Latin tags cut in the granite, *per ardua ad astra,* exertion, valor, pure aspiration.

"He fell," Nathaniel said, and so saying seemed to wish to say no more.

That was Night Three. After the banty inquisitor made his exit, Pownall and Booth tried—pretty manfully, all things considered—to take Nathaniel across Nassau Street to the cavernous tile-floored, tile-walled Balt: "Let's chow," Pownall said. "I'll pay for no more than nine cheeseburgers, and no fewer than three cheeseburgers each."

"Tonight I'll pass," Nathaniel said. "I may soon be a regular at the Balt."

"That's not amusing, buckaroo."

"I know, Booth. I know."

When his roommates took their melancholy leave, Nathaniel listened carefully. What he thought he'd hear once they were beyond earshot—a joke, a laugh, a change of subject—he didn't hear. Alone, he sat in the chair Jamie Hill had used, reading his great-grandfather's journal:

They buy what I sell if they think its cheep and sell what I buy if they think they robin me and they sure say sure when I say drink up boys Im buyin. But the dam skonks got no use for me and I know it. Furriner. I am a furriner. Glad to be one. I been in a coffee house in Wien, Austria, gabbin with sidekicks, arguin whats in the papers and whats in are heds. We had stuff in are heds that wasnt timber and railrodes and credit at interst. Big idees. I miss Wien. Not enuff to go back. Heres the place. America. Buncha savages but Gott sei dank a man can come and go like he plezes and Im comin, by Gott Im comin. Look out America! Make way fer Herr Auerbach, buyin what I want, sellin what I got and liftin whats not nailed down. And when Im done they can shit in their hats, the dam skonks laff at how I talk. Jas. Jerome Hill got no accent like I got but he kin say the worth of a feller, furriner or not. Took his trezure and spent it sendin his pups back east to skool. Had to fork over plenty to bild the skooltechers a buncha bildins. Tole me he spent most of his life lernin to add but that Prinsten back east lerned him to subtrak.

It came to pass for Nathaniel on Night Four that a Tiger Inner asked the Seattle boy what flower he would like most to be were he to be a flower, while the clubman's friends, four of them, double-teamed Pownall and Booth with a full-court-press snow-job.

Nathaniel said, "I don't know, a pansy."

Minutes later, in the hall outside, frank laughter. Pownall and Booth at first mistook the sound for friendly laughter, a collegial appreciation of a good joke. Nathaniel knew better.

And heard, not so muffled as one might have hoped: "That guy is a wombat." And then heard the crackle of static, his recent interrogator saying into a walkie-talkie: "Preston to T. I. Preston to T. I. Do you read me, Tiger Inn?" They must have read him back at Prospect Avenue Base Command, because the radioman had something to add: "Cut Clay, that's Clay, Nathaniel, Seventh Entry of Holder, b-o-r-i-n-g!"

If that were the whole of it—popinjays and small-talkers and clotheshorses and cruel hard little boys—Nathaniel might have quit as soon as he began. But there was more to this experience than being rejected by his inferiors. He had met in his room these past few days and nights strangers he liked, strangers he hoped would like him. People he'd like to join for dinner. Not just "attractive" and "useful" guys. People quick to laugh, one or two athletes legendary in the small world of Nathaniel's University, men who'd read the books Nathaniel had read. But why should this surprise Nathaniel? Nathaniel loved Princeton, and Princeton prized Bicker. If it seemed trivial, Princeton said it was important. Princeton had chosen Nathaniel two years ago and now it instructed Nathaniel to put down his books and lay his ass on the line, and get himself chosen again. We chose you to be chosen again, America's Best, now Princeton's Best. Or not. We believe in this. This matters.

And what did those boys so preferentially bound now say to one another?

Little. Nathaniel would return to his room from a solitary walk down to Lake Carnegie or along the borders of the campus to Cleveland Tower, or he'd come back frozen stiff, red-eyed from the cold (but how could Pownall and Booth know the wind had teared their roommate's eyes?), and talk would end.

Nathaniel wanted his mother. He wanted his mommy. He wanted to say, *It hurts. Kiss it and make it better.* He wrote to Seattle:

Dear Granma and Gander,

You ask what am I learning. I'm not sure what to tell you. I've learned a lot, but not what I came here to learn. Princeton has shut shop for two weeks to let Bicker rule. I told you about Bicker last year, but I didn't know a thing about it. To inspire Princeton upperclassmen to concentrate exclusively on the distinction between sophomore weenies and sophomore non-weenies (guess which I am), Princeton locks its classroom doors, empties the library, cancels office hours.

In the service of precision I should say that the deans' doors are wide open; the deans stay in business doing the paperwork on tight-lipped, red-eyed sophs who want to transfer out, or go home to their moms and dads. But Renaissance Art has shut down, Philosophy of Science shut down, Probability Theory shut down, Atomic Physics and Quantum Theory shut down, The Literary Tradition shut down, Systematic Ethics shut down. I want this to end. Will it ever end?

It would end. A week into it Nathaniel found himself vis-à-vis the Secretary of Ivy Club. ("Detached and breathlessly aristocratic"—Fitzgerald.) Nathaniel knew all about Ivy from Booth, before he quit talking to Nathaniel about the place. Ivy skimmed the cream from every category: jocks, nobs, smarties. Its members rose when a woman entered the clubhouse, an understated, handsome, deep-red old-brick building at 43 Prospect Avenue, predictably stained-glass-windowed, furnished with leather, hunting-printed, paneled with carved—oh, you know.

Ivy men were not rowdies; their parties were resolutely unexceptional; the principled members' notion of hijinx was to slide downstairs on pillows. It was a place, the Ivy members' book told, where "congenial people" might get together "over good food." But the food was notoriously mediocre, running in the Yankee way to overcooked vegetables served with overdone roasts. Mutton was a staple.

But how to assure fellowship? How to select? You couldn't let just anyone wear the green-and-yellow tie. Blue blood alone didn't get the job done, not at Ivy. One infamous year during World War II the seniors and juniors of the club accepted only three sophomores. Graduate members were dismayed, of course, pointing out that even Christ chose twelve. But election to Ivy, alone among the clubs, must be unanimous: one blackball dropped in the walnut ballot box was a world too many blackballs.

Now the Secretary of Ivy said: "Well, how do you do? I noticed you last month, over Christmas hols, Guards' Ball. Wasn't there a confusion over what you call yourself? You're not Pownall Hamm, it seems. So, what will it be? Nathaniel? Nat?"

"I call myself Nate."

"You've got yourself wrong, I'm afraid. *Nate* is for Nathan."

"My mom calls me Nate."

"Oh. Truly?"

Back at Ivy, during the evening's soul-searching club meeting to discuss would-be members, at which meeting solemnity ruled (leave the wise-ass to Cottage, Colonial, Tiger Inn), the club Secretary, whose father was in surgical practice with

Pownall's father, opined that young Clay was a "curious fellow. Can't decide what name to use on himself, Nat or Nate."

Many an Ivy Clubman rubbed his chin hearing this news. It explained a great deal.

That same night, over at Court, a club hostile to the Bicker process, a club friendly to pariahs, the question was similar: "Is he a Nate, or what?"

Nathaniel was visited the following afternoon by a plain-talking farm boy from Wisconsin, Sam somebody, a hockey wizard, amusingly robust to his brothers at Charter Club, an approximate simulacrum of Ivy, a dump for boulevardiers. (Already, within days, Nathaniel had learned the lingo, "dump for boulevardiers." A quick learner, Nathaniel, good listener; if he'd talked as smoothly as he listened carefully, he might have been damned near Bickerable.)

"Clay, are you by any mischance, well, *smart?*"

"How, smart?"

The club detective rubbed his nose. "You know."

Nathaniel, despite himself, smiled: "Oh. Sure. I guess. Sure. Why?"

The upwardly mobile hewer of wood and drawer of water, despite himself, scowled: "Why? Why!"

Booth, across the room, sat up straight: "That's enough now!"

"Jewish religion or race?" Nathaniel asked, still grinning.

"Just . . . you know. Don't make me spell it out."

"My mother's name was Auerbach."

"She changed it?"

Nathaniel could not hear for the surfy din in his ears, the blood—his mother's, his father's blood—pounding through his heart's chamber to his temples. He thought of this boy whose moronic face, six inches from his own, was screwed into a show of bewilderment, this Sam, in the future, taking an evil hit in blue chips, begetting a son who steals his club tie tack, and sells it. . . .

"Well, yes she did, to *Clay*. When she married my dad."

"Oh," said the puck-sliding husbandman.

"You want to know whether I'm a gentleman or a Jew?"

"You're giving me a hard time here," said the divertingly bluff, goal-scoring ex-rustic.

"How so?" Nathaniel asked, against all reason curious.

"You're making it hard for me to like myself. Look, they sent me to ask, it wasn't my idea, what do I care?"

(Nathaniel imagined Sam coming home from Wall Street to be met by his pretty, charming wife, who has recently met a handsome, charming guy more her own type; in fact, what *could* she have been thinking senior year?

"Samuel, we'd better talk."

"*Samuel* is it? This sounds serious, hon."

"It is serious. I don't want to be married another day to a man with a seat on the Stock Exchange."

"Wha . . . Whoa! Your daddy *gave* me that seat! What the deuce, I'll sell it."

"No. You're perfectly fit for that seat. . . .")

"Be nice to yourself," Nathaniel said. "Sam, don't be so tough on yourself. I'm sorry to have been coy. Put down 'kike.' "

Diana's prophecy came out right on the money: Hundred Percenter. One with wonks and straight-arrows, gamblers who welched on bets, wombats and lunch meat, going to and fro on the earth with some despised Little Jesus, taking it in the shorts with the coxcomb said at a Bicker meeting to have been "hatched from a madras egg." Outcast. Not, definitely not, a B.M.O.C. Not an ace. Hosed. Sucker of maximum pipe. A certified banana. Didn't pack the gear, didn't please. Unclubbable. *Déraciné.* Call Nathaniel *persona non grata;* call him Nate, the Wandering Jew.

"Why me?" Nathaniel asked. "Because of my middle name? My mom's maiden name?"

"There's no good reason," Pownall said.

"Of course there's no good reason. But still: why?"

"Maybe because you crashed that damned dance over Christmas," Booth said. Pownall gave Booth a look. "Maybe because you stood on your head, walked on your hands. That was a silly stunt."

Nathaniel gave Booth a look. "It's because of my middle name."

"Maybe it's because you begged those Quadrangle guys not to leave. I have to admit, that sounded pretty desperate. That was a story that got around," Booth said.

"Middle name," Pownall said.

"It isn't that you're Jewish," Booth explained. "For some it's because you're *not* a Jew, I'm told. Others think you're pretending not to be. A Jew. For others it's that . . . they say . . . they say you *look* Jewish."

"Fuck you," said Nathaniel.

"How about fuck them?" Pownall asked.

After the great winnowing was done, and the boy cut by Colonial because he didn't know to unbutton the bottom button of his waistcoat had been nevertheless bid by Key and Seal, and the boy thought by Cannon Club to have too many "effeminate artworks" in his room had found a home at Terrace, and the boy cut by Cottage because he'd never heard of jai-alai had joined the brotherhood of Tower, after all the flits and cavemen had been accommodated there were twenty-three Princeton sophomores with whom no Princeton juniors or seniors wished to break bread.

Eighteen of these pariahs—or "rejects," as they were called—were Jews. This circumstance drew the attention of *The New York Times,* and it was from a reporter on that newspaper that Nathaniel Clay learned by telephone that he was bidless. The reporter had been given a list.

"Your name is on the list," the reporter told Nathaniel. "Don't ask where I got it," the reporter said, "because I won't tell you. . . . Hey, are you there? I'm on deadline."

"I'm here," said Nathaniel, who felt already gone from this place, already turned toward home, wherever home might be—say, back where the sun set. He had been called to a public phone on the ground floor of the Seventh Entry of Holder Hall. Sophomores stood clustered around him, slapping one another on the back, cheering, whispering. A few, moving through the drizzle toward Lower Eagle for dinner, trudged ahead with their heads bowed, in thanks, maybe, or to hide tears.

"I can't hear you. Are you there?"

"What do you want?" Nathaniel asked.

"Well, it's like this. Most of your classmates who got rejected are Jewish. It's pretty clear-cut. They have Jewish names. Thing of it is, you're named Clay," the reporter reported to Nathaniel Clay, "but the other thing of it is, my source says you're a Jew—"

"Who *are* you?" Nathaniel asked.

"Look, this is a difficult story, but it's a good story. I mean, this could nail those self-important donkeys. I need your help—"

"Is this what you do for a living? Tell people they've been blackballed by clubs? Is this your—"

"Beat?"

"Yes. Is your beat rejection?"

"Look, if it makes it any easier for you, I'm a Jew, too."

"I'm not."

"Well, my source said you were."

"Your source is mistaken."

"My source was pretty certain on this point."

"I've got to go to dinner."

"But not at an eating club . . . Hey, are you still there? Clay?"

"Sure."

"Have you got anything to say? I'd like to quote you."

"I've got to go now."

"Nothing to say? Are you still there? Listen, I'm sorry. It's not the end of the world, I guess, but I'm sorry."

Maybe he should have told *The New York Times* he was a Jew. Maybe he had done the wrong thing? Had he ever. Or maybe the wrong thing had happened to him. Climbing the stairs from the phone to his room, he remembered a distinction Professor Hyde had made—when? ten days ago? a lifetime ago?—between the phenomenal and the exemplary. In Melville's "Bartleby," the lawyer was "thunderstruck" when he realized he and Bartleby, for better or worse, were fated to share the world together. How did it go? Nathaniel, alone in his room, reached for *The Piazza Tales,* opened to the text:

> For an instant I stood like the man who, pipe in mouth, was killed one cloudless afternoon long ago in Virginia, by summer lightning; at his own warm open window he was killed, and remained leaning out there upon the dreamy afternoon, till someone touched him and he fell.

Professor Hyde said these words described a "mere" phenomenon, a freak accident. Professor Hyde said the deepest tragedies are exemplary, the result of volition, habitual action. Surely, in these terms, Bicker was no tragedy. Surely it was as phenomenal as summer lightning, a freak accident. Surely its cruelty wasn't exemplary? Surely it wasn't organic to this Princeton he had so recently so loved? Then why did Nathaniel feel gut-shot? Why had Bartleby said no? It was such a little thing the lawyer had asked Bartleby to do. Copy a document, grease the gears, serve the machine's dismaying purposes. The worst of this was Nathaniel's part in it. Coming out bottom dog in Bicker was not something that just happened to him, like having his pocket picked at the Dartmouth game, or getting rained on, or falling downstairs, or being struck by summer lightning. It was an injury he had seemed to invite so that now, trying to puzzle it out, shame overcame anger.

Another irony—there was no bottom to the benighted ironies—nobody, *nobody* felt worse about this than the President of the Interclub Council, principal apologist for the selective system, President of Ivy, owner of the most immediately recognizable capitalist surname in America. How cruel that Bicker's sweet system was misperceived by the world to have caused pain. Blackest irony of all, Hundred Percenters got their name from their failure to satisfy the dream of the Interclub Council, a Hundred Percent Bicker, every misshaped cog fit or forced into the machine's misbegotten works. "Hundred Percenters" were just those geeks who shaved the statistical dream short of one hundred percent selection: call them three-point-three percenters, call them Ishmaels.

As soon as the blackguard *Times* had done its devil's work, 1958's Bicker went to hell in a handbasket and would be known thereafter and forever as Dirty Bicker. Some Jews among the excluded collectively deplored and accused, petitioning, in the *Times,* an end to the abuse of club selection. Nathaniel was asked to sign this doleful letter and would not. His injury was private . . . no, there was more than stoic reticence to account for his refusal to add his signature to the aliens' lamentation. Truth was, he didn't like those signers of the letter; he had met a few. Truth was, *he* didn't want to eat dinner with most of them.

But think of it from the gentlemen's vantage. Dirty Bicker! To be tarred with that brush. To carry one's name into the future with "Dirty Bicker" clinging like ivy to it, clinging like some damned weedy vine. Look, think of Bicker as anti-toxic, not so much instruction in the techniques of discrimination as preparation for the hurly-burly out there. But try explaining this to twenty-three killjoy Sons of Old Nassau with no place to forage, no companions with whom to refresh the inner man. The blot on Ivy's good name was intolerable. Something must be done.

The happy solution was a slave market, what golfers call a Calcutta, an auction of the doomed, not unlike what happens when mean little kids choose up sides—shirts 'n' skins—and the last taken are elected in bunches: you swallow these left-overs and I'll swallow those, sissies and fatties and crybabies and four-eyes in undifferentiated clumps.

The horse-trading, the dealing went down the very night of Open House, when the lucky many walked as equals among those who had chosen them, making merry, banging a brandy concoction special to Colonial, Flames Over New Jersey, laughing and singing, studying how to *crave* expensive cigars, learning to stand at the club urinal pissing noisily, head thrown back recklessly, Havana Heater clenched between the teeth. Who could stop such a run of luck?

While outside in the fucking rain, stumbling in the dark behind the back entrance of Ivy Club, a dozen and more still in the game presented their pathetic selves to the estimation of the Interclub Council. Those worthies felt for those "in trouble." They consoled. This might seem like tough darts tonight—hell, they could understand that it must sting like the dickens—but there was more to Princeton, more to club life, in fact, than a single night's disappointment. Hell, no one's perfect; we'll do what can—in good conscience—be done.

So, in the rain, who still wanted in? To ask was mere formality. Who would be there, nosing the hindquarters of the Ivy Club, dressed in a poncho, who didn't want in? The question was, er, where? The outcasts had no voice in this, it was explained. The clubs would "divvy" up the "remaining" aspirants, according to the size of their sophomore sections, the wishes of the members, other considerations. *Everyone would have a place to eat. Bicker would be One Hundred Percent successful.* The President of Ivy Club, out there on his back stoop, promised this would be so. To prove he meant business, his club, Ivy, had already selected—just now, before midnight—one among the, uh, remaining sophomores.

Nathaniel, first of the unchosen to be chosen. Cream of the Hundred Percenters. Now why was Nathaniel Clay out there in the rain, huddled among the misfits, supping on charity's scraps? Why was his ticket west on the Empire Builder not already in his pocket? How could he? Was he not a Judas goat?

It was complicated. He told himself then it was perplexing, and years later he told himself it was intricate. Who was he to say they were all wrong about him? He'd wanted so dearly to study here, to wear the orange and black, to be a Princeton Man, to have been a Princeton Man. His father had thrown all this away. Even that wet night, hearing all around him the huzzahs of celebration, Nathaniel wanted to be part of it, to send a son to this place. He knew this on the instant of reading a telegram from Gander: "WE LOVE YOU STOP COME HOME WHERE YOURE WANTED STOP STOP STOP." They had it wrong. He'd had it wrong, and now they had it wrong. There was more to this than . . . this.

But how could that be? Well, look back a few hours to a stroll through the campus with Pownall and Booth. The disconsolate boys had made their way, as though on autopilot, toward Lake Carnegie. They didn't follow the obvious route— past 1879 Hall, The Street on the left, along Washington Road. Instead, dripped on by leafless maples, they cut along narrow paths, through sere fields that would flower in spring— oh, who could believe the palette? Princeton's gardens. The confederates were bound for the boathouse, designed by Pennington Satterthwaite, '93, Booth Tarkington's class. For Booth T. Griggs and Pownall Hamm the boathouse was sanctuary, a haven of uncomplication where merit alone weighed.

The boathouse was locked, but Pownall knew the way in. He found a light, and the three roommates sat on the decked floor and passed around a battered metal thermos of stingers.

"You know," Pownall said, "I love all this." He was looking around the hangar-like room, at the plaques and group photographs, the crew-cut oarsmen looking from year to year like interchangeable types, though of course they weren't. Some of those healthy young men got up in short pants, black T-shirts with orange slashes, some of them would go to fat, and whine at their wives, and go fast off the mark in the tool-and-die trade, and slip a beat, and blow out, and rail at their children, and wonder what happened, was it want of will, too many hits of loudmouth soup, kismet? On the other hand, number three starboard oar might become a pediatrician and row a scull alone on the Charles and win the Senior Championship when he turned sixty, and grow bushy white eyebrows, and become the most attractive grandfather on the Schuylkill River. What they all had in common, Nathaniel recognized, was Bicker. These mostly brave young men, who might, without being found out, pull not quite so painfully hard as they could, who nevertheless did not do this, who knew the right thing to do and did it, who relished the honest pain of crazy effort on a wind-whipped lake in early spring, these decent young men had all submitted themselves to the judgment of clubmen, had then in their turn as clubmen said "yea" and more commonly "nay" when asked if they were willing to eat with a fellow-student.

"What became of them?" Nathaniel asked, passing Booth the stingers. "Where are they?"

"Where are they? Ah, the trophies," said Booth. "Yes. Dillon Gym. Have you ever noticed the gargoyles peering down from Dillon's gutters? They wear helmets. They're footballers. You know, my grandfather remembers contracting for the stonecutters who carved those gargoyles. Italians. Back home they cut monumental figures for Italian gravestones. Mausoleums. Would that be 'mausolea'? Master craftsmen to the dead. Business was bound always to be good, wouldn't you think? Anyway, the University, through my grandfather's law firm, drafted the arrangements to bring them over here. Princeton promised to care for their families unto the fourth generation. I wonder if Princeton honored its promise? I rather suspect she did, don't you think? Anyway, we were discussing trophies. Silver, you know. You can't keep trophies unsecured. There's a . . . boatload of them. Grace Kelly's brother's Diamond Sculls. The Queen's Challenge Cup. Carnegie Cup. Rowe Cup. Child's Cup. Maybe Harvard has a weightier collection of sterling, Harvard even has bowls—"

"Nathaniel meant our ancestors," Pownall said. "Our teammates of yore, our crew."

"Yes," Nathaniel said.

"They came," Pownall said, "they conquered—by their lights. They left. The lucky ones. Left. Booth, give a chum a taste." Pownall tipped the thermos, and Nathaniel noticed how deeply his roommate drank. "The unlucky ones never left. Keep coming back, haunting." Pownall stood, and walked beyond the rim of dim light. "Look at these beauties. Nathaniel? Have you ever seen one up close? Come here, let me show you."

Beneath oars hung in rows against the walls were rack on rack of delicate shells, Pococks assembled from paper-thin wood, with hi-tech outriggers for the sweeps. The dim light shone orange off their glossy curves, and the air was sweet with varnish, shellac, linseed.

Pownall rubbed the chine of an eight-man shell. "Look at that. My father made me memorize all the material components. Let's say it was a surgeon's boy's first anatomy lesson: red-cedar skin, Indiana ash ribs . . ." Pownall was talking to himself now, as though reaching way back for a poem, or the words to a prayer: "Wild-cherry rudder, Idaho white-pine seats, Australian ironbark roller tracks—"

"They're built in Seattle," Booth said.

"I know," Nathaniel said. "Lake Union. I used to watch the Husky crews row past our dock. I'd wave at rowers, when I was a kid, but of course they couldn't wave back."

"Of course not," Booth said.

"I used to think rowing was something I could do. How hard could it be? I used to think. Now I think I know better."

"It comes easy to some people," Booth said.

"It came easy to you," Pownall said. "Say, someone seems to have drunk up our beverage. Is there another thermos?"

"No," Booth said.

"How unforeseeing of you," Pownall said. "Not to worry. Dr. Hamm has a little dividend upstairs in his locker. Quart of Mount Gay. Unbroken seal."

"Pownall," Booth said, "ease up. We've got a busy night ahead."

But Pownall, climbing the stairs to the locker room, seemed not to hear or to listen. Nathaniel and Booth were alone. Nathaniel thought, listening to the silence of the cavernous boathouse, how seldom he had been alone with his roommate, how seldom at Princeton he had been alone with anyone, how resolutely Booth sought tight knots of friends.

He was, finally, a clubman. No, that wasn't fair. That was sour.

"If you quit, they win, without even knowing they went up against you. They made a mistake. Join."

"I would prefer not to."

"How can you think of leaving?" Booth said.

"I haven't talked about leaving."

"Come on! We live with you. I do. You're about to take off, run home."

"Home? That's another, longer story."

"How can you care? It's nothing! It's a club is all."

"Twenty-some clubs."

"Twenty, forty. So what? Clubs were invented to keep bores off the streets. Come on! We're talking about one club. Aren't we?"

"I thought this was a family. I wanted, I don't know, to belong."

"Oh Jesus Christ. *Family?* He wanted, he doesn't know, to belong. You get asked to join, what do you get? It's like the guy who wins the pie-eating contest: he wins all the pie he can eat. Nathaniel. Let me be blunt. Who are these people? Face men, Cottage is a magnet for face men, comely he-boys who can hire out to pose for dust-jacket photographs, plead a case, front for a mortgage. Not just the Cottage trogs, either. The whole lot who call themselves 'gentlemen.' Who ever heard of an authentic courtier, a Castiglione Prince, calling *Don Giovanni* a 'wopera,' saying 'Jews'll stab you in the back every time'? These bozos aren't chevaliers, they're plebes. Their fathers and mothers both thought they had married up, and both had. These people don't matter."

"Then who matters?"

"We do. I only want to say this once, and I have to say it when Pownall is upstairs doing what Pownall does. I don't like saying it at all, but I'll say it as often as you decide you need to hear it: I'm your friend."

"Why?"

"Why what?"

"Why are we friends?"

Booth ran his hand gently along the inverted bottom of a double scull. He looked at Nathaniel, and his gray eyes didn't blink: "We're survivors. We're little orphan boys," but he said "orphing," mocking himself; he couldn't say it straight. "Well, maybe not orphings, exactly. Ma's much alive, thank you." Booth moved from the gleaming shells into a halo of electric light trained on the rowing tanks, two troughs of water split by two rails, along which slid seats in a rough likeness of an eight-oared boat, enough water on either side of both rails to allow the sweep of full-length blades. Booth positioned himself in number eight seat, stroke. He balanced a blade along its outrigger. "What about your mother?" he asked.

Nathaniel turned his back on his roommate and stared through the window toward Lake Carnegie, black out there. "It's a long story," he said, and then said nothing.

Booth sounded irritated: "How can you be ashamed of your own? Who cares if her name was Auerbach?"

Nathaniel turned, stared down at the fellow he so admired for his wit, speed of mind. "*Is* Auerbach. Why should I be ashamed of my mother's name? Her parents are Jews. So what? I don't know what I am, but if it's a Jew, that's Jake by me. I'm one guy—Nathaniel Clay—not a whole damned tribe."

"Then why so tetchy? Why so mum about family?"

Nathaniel's response didn't come right away, but when it came it had precise articulation, good volume: "I'm ashamed."

"So tell me."

Nathaniel processed his roommate's command, did a full exegesis on those three words, tested them for an excessively summary imperative mood, analyzed them for offhandedness, investigated them for hard-heartedness. Gossip was moot. Booth did not gossip. "My mother's off her nut."

"Oh, Nathaniel, oh boy, don't slang her that way. That's not right."

Then, trusting Booth Tarkington Griggs, trusting that dandy as he trusted no one except his grandmother, trusting him to understand what his grandmother could not understand, Nathaniel opened the door wide and went right through it. His words fell like tears on his roommate, who didn't interrupt, who poised still on his bizarre perch, balancing the long sweep as though to move were to capsize, to drown them both in about eighteen inches of the rowing tank's stagnant water.

He began with his father, born to a radio tycoon. Remember the Atwater Kent? Hell of a piece of work, right? Well, as Atwater Kent was a quantum superior to Zenith, the Clay was ditto to Atwater Kent. The Clay was the best radio receiver, finest-finished cabinet, most cherished possession, town pump, family hearth, the indispensable accouterment. As long as ladies and gentlemen had ears, ladies and gentlemen would wish to own a Clay console radio. Why, given such a certitude, pinch pennies? Why not give the heir his head, let him indulge himself? Cars and clothes and adventures and foreign travel and mahogany speedboats and roulette gave Nathaniel's father such pleasure. Why shouldn't he enjoy them while he was young?

American television was first broadcast when Nathaniel was two. Who could take it seriously? Let Zenith branch out; Clay would hold the high ground. By 1951 there were ten million television sets in the United States. Who cared? Then the Senate's McCarthy hearings gave a responsible excuse for people of good civic judgment to buy the toys: by tonight, as Nathaniel told his roommate an old American story, TV dinners were being eaten, citizens owned fifty million tubes, the eyes had it, Clay Radio Corporation had had it, was down the tubes, history, the family business broken into several bankrupt bits.

But Nathaniel's father was a never-was even before Clay Radio went has-been. The gambling debts mounted in his freshman year at Princeton, crushing his reputation. During the second semester of his first year, he accumulated five 7s, the abhorrent "Flagrant Neglect," fleg-neg, a full turn of the dial down from 6, mere "Failure." His record was so awful as to have rescued it from disgrace, elevated it to legend. So Nathaniel said, without approval, and Booth, who admired expressions of insouciance in the academic realm, did not find the earlier Clay's transcript attractive.

Let's say Nathaniel's father was controversial. Gentle. Generous. An enthusiastic hobbyist. He enjoyed fires and firemen almost as much as he enjoyed alcohol and fun-loving women—"popsies," he called them.

How did his mother come to marry this fellow? She met him in Chicago. He had come home to Lake Forest where his mother and father waited for him to decide what to do next, where to study, or—God forbid—work. Nathaniel's grandparents waited a long time for their only child to reveal his decision: his life's plan was to take it easy. Nathaniel's mother, Sarah, was at the University of Chicago. What *did* she study? Good question. Nathaniel didn't recall that she ever said, that he had ever asked. Anyway, Nathaniel's father was charming, everyone was clear on that point. Nathaniel could attest to his father's charm. Great laugher. Coined phrases, "fux deluxe," that kind of thing. Good tipper. The help adored him. Seemed attentive. Knew how to ask an interested-sounding question despite zero curiosity. Okay, maybe Nathaniel was being too hard on his father; how could one penetrate what another cared about?

The roommates heard Pownall banging around upstairs. He had begun to sing an Irish ballad in a sweet, keening tenor: "Have you ever been across the sea to I-yer-land—"

Booth said, "So your mother married him for charm. Why did he marry her?"

Nathaniel feared he knew what the question meant. *Why would a gentleman marry a Jewess?* But if the question meant such a thing, this nice boy couldn't be his friend anymore. Then what? After all, was it not fair to ask why (putting love aside) anyone married anyone? Wasn't that always a legitimate question?

"—and can see the moon go down on Gal-way Bay."

"Bravo, Pownall!" Nathaniel shouted.

Booth laid a finger across his lips. "Hush. Let him be, for a moment. Why did your father marry your mother? For money? Nothing to hang your head about, oldest story there is, everyone marries everyone for money. Or I guess that doesn't scan, fiduciarily, does it? I guess those books don't balance. Anyway, vows for money's an old, *old* story. Ask my mummy."

"Well. I guess not for money. I mean he used her money, later. Her money was all the money they had, her parents' money. They own a department store, nice store, Auerbach's. Heard of it?"

Booth shrugged no.

"It's a nice place. Not quite up to Nordstrom's or Frederick & Nelson, but nice. I mean think of someone like my dad, with all those appetites: a whole department store to browse. Six floors. This tweed jacket came from Auerbach's."

"Yes," Booth said. "I heard you tell the hangerman from Colonial the provenance of your sport jacket."

Nathaniel looked hard at his roommate, to learn what Booth meant this recollection to serve. He liked what he saw in Booth's smile, and laughed, and soon they were laughing together.

"I don't know. My Seattle grandparents were crazy about my dad. They knew he was a ne'er-do-well, called him a ne'er-do-well to his face. They're . . . principled. Upright. Jesus, good people. Cultured, I guess you'd call them. The family had come from Vienna a hundred years ago—"

"Just yesterday," Booth said.

"—some trouble after the uprisings under the Emperor Ferdinand. Actually, my grandmother was from Budapest. She said it 'pesht.' I said Buda-*pesht* once and my mother said, 'Don't put on airs.' My grandparents had this reading club, the Friday Night Bunch, and they'd get together with friends—some Jews, some regular people—and talk about the books they'd read, or listen to chamber music, or talk about paintings. My mom and dad and I would visit; we liked to visit; my grandparents liked us to visit. My grandparents lived next door in the big house. We lived in the guest house. Anyway, Friday nights the Packard dealer'd tease the bejabbers out of the Studebaker dealer. This doctor friend would tell my grandmother he could see something ailing in her droopy eyelids, and diagnose made-up maladies, and she'd never not fall for it. One of the Friday Night Bunch was a wrestling promoter, the gentlest of all of them. I'd ask if the matches were faked and he'd look at me like I was questioning Newton's Law of Universal Gravitation. 'You *doubt* us?' he'd ask. My grandparents had a grand time with their chums, but they didn't laugh enough. *They* said they didn't laugh enough; my dad made them laugh. He'd have some outrageous theory—how the sun revolved around the earth after all, they'd had it right the first time—and he'd back it up with statistics and citations, always from *The New York Times:* 'It's a true fact. You can go to the bank on it. I know whereof I speak. You could look it up.'

"He'd come asking for some plaything he 'needed.' A Jag XK-120, maybe, or a billiard table, or a Holland & Holland grouse gun. He'd beg one thing at a time, no lump-sum bequests, no thought of an allowance or trust fund. Toys. He always had a good reason, good story. They loved his stories, loved his fuck-ups. Said he had a great heart. I think sometimes they made my mother want to marry him. Whatever he did, they explained away. I mean, they forgave him. My mother, her brother, their parents played as a string quartet. They were good, really. Dad would come to dinner, right up to the curtain-closer, when Mother went off the deep end, and play jazz piano. He had a gift. He bought some Joe Venuti records for my grandparents—you know, with Eddie Lang? 'Beatin' the Cat' and 'Kickin' the Dog'? He got my grandmother doing jazz licks on her fiddle. My uncle hated my father."

Nathaniel tried to tell his friend how it had felt to watch people have contempt for his father. How his dad would come to hockey games at school to watch his boy, and Nathaniel could see the dandy with no job and a sports car and a bespoke sport jacket through the eyes of his schoolteachers, notice their arched blond eyebrows and thin Scandinavian smiles, their blinked eyes when they caught a whiff of gin from the charmer. Oh, long before Bicker, Nathaniel knew a snub. He knew a snub. You don't forget a snub. His mother, too, had a long, long memory.

Nathaniel's mother had always been "sensitive." That was the word everyone used. Sensitive and "thin-skinned." These hadn't seemed to Nathaniel like words that described a vice. "I was nuts about my mother."

Booth laughed. Nathaniel thought about Booth laughing at the word "nuts," and Nathaniel wished he too could laugh at his choice of words.

Booth said "Rubber room?"

"Academy of laughter. When Dad died. Before, really, when Dad talked some kid, some backpacking blonde bartender into love."

"Don't be snotty," Booth said. "You sound like someone who'd prefer not to be in an eating club with a person who once worked as a servant. Tell me something, Nathaniel . . ."

Nathaniel knew what question was coming, and he didn't want to answer it. Not now. So he asked, "How did *your* father die?"

"Oh," Booth said. "You want to talk about my father. Did you know your father?"

Nathaniel said, "Where's Pownall? Don't we need a drink?"

"No," Booth said.

"Yes, I knew him. Sure. We were close. If you can get close to a ghost, a drunk ghost. But sure, he was warm. Yeah, close. We were. I'd say we were . . . tight. Were you? With your dad? Tight?"

"My father died in '40," Booth said, "Battle of Britain. That would have been a year before the fateful year of the first American network telecast. Anyway, Pa was in 601, Eagle Squadron, the Millionaires' Squadron. I guess that goes almost without saying. Much about my father went almost without saying. Anyway, I was two. So I never knew him the least bit. I hear stories. Do I hear stories. Legends. You know his name was Hobart? Called after Hobey Baker, a first cousin, *another* first cousin, Lafayette Escadrille in Double-you Double-you One, fiery plunge to chilly Styx in same; he also did a star turn in this place. Hockey. Ditto Daddy. Ivy. Ditto. So I'm a legacy. Here and at Ivy. You might say I'm a hundred percent legacy. Strangers tell me, 'Oh, you should have known your father!' What am I supposed to say to that? He took a gorgeous picture, was most photogenic."

"Booth," Nathaniel said. "Go easy. This is not a time to be hard."

"No! He would have talked just this way if his father had died young. He talked this way about Hobey Baker. It's all casual grace at home, the light touch, understatement, well-timed shrugs. My grandparents would joke, while I searched for the punch line, that their son Hobart Baker Griggs III was in reality I-V, the *fourth,* micro-seconds short of the Bronze, fourth on the starting three-man hockey line, just out of the money with the fourth fastest time ever on the Cresta Run in Saynt Mór-itz, fourth American to be shot down flying for England. Do you believe in numerology?"

"Booth. I don't know what to say."

"Say how your father died," Booth said.

"Jamie Hill asked me that question during Bicker."

"Ah, Jamie. Little story about Jamie: seems he wasn't invited last month to Lilly du Pont's coming-out party. The infamy! The scandal of being uninvited! Insupportable! So he entrained to banal Wilmington—this was how he spent some of his holiday!—and hired a taxi to Brandywine where the party (which wasn't very pleasurable, I must report) was to take place—"

"Why?"

"To mail Christmas cards postmarked Brandywine to his similarly uninvited friends in St. Paul and to his similarly uninvited clubmates. Pure Cottage Club. So how did you answer Jamie's request for a death report on your dad?"

"I said he died falling."

"Sort of like my dad," Booth said.

"Off a mountain. Good mountain. Matterhorn. Only the best for Bicker, right?"

"Why did you answer the asshole?"

"Thing is," Nathaniel said, "he didn't fall off a mountain."

"Oh. My. Oh. I don't know what to say," Booth said.

"Say what?" asked Pownall Hamm, materializing, holding a quart bottle of Mount Gay down to the last swallow or two.

"I thought you said," said Booth, "the seal was unbroken."

"It was," said Pownall, weaving, fastidious in his motions, speaking deliberately.

"My father died reaching for one of those," Nathaniel said. "Not rum, in fact. Gin. Gilbey's. Or so they said. Probably because it makes a better story to say the brand. I guess I could have said Booth's. To make a good story, I mean. It was in New York. When Mother kicked him out of her house he didn't tarry, got right out of town. Oh, he thought to leave me a letter, more a note, I guess: *Come see me anytime you're east, and take care of your mother.* He was somebody's guest at the Knickerbocker Club. They'd been at Choate together. They drank till the club bar closed, and pestered the bartender to hang around and hear more stories and serve more drinks. The bartender went home. Can't imagine why he'd want to leave. My dad's friend was drunk. Most of his friends were, most of the time. This particular friend, exhausted by the struggle of remembering where was the coatroom in the men's club where he had spent every afternoon and night of his post-graduate life, forgot he had brought my father to that place. They found Dad next morning. He'd bled to death. Tried to reach across the bar to steal a bottle—Gilbey's, as I think I said. Fell overreaching. Broke some Waterford-crystal highball glasses falling on them, and they cut his neck. Funny what they tell you. The kind of crystal, I mean. Funny what you remember. Cut his throat, too."

Pownall passed his friend what was left of the Mount Gay, and Nathaniel drank it.

"We knew how your father died," Pownall said.

"Yes," Booth said, "we did. It's a story one hears."

Years later Nathaniel would pump his memory to recollect how it felt that night in the boathouse to learn this, just as he would try to remember *exactly* how it had felt to hear his wild mother command him to choose a choice that night in Seattle. Memory wouldn't deliver. All he'd ever know for sure about the night he disobeyed his mom, the night he didn't choose, was what had triggered her wildness. With another outcome it might have been just another narrative about his damnfool father, a yarn to dine out on. His father had met a fellow in a Tacoma roadhouse who stripped furniture for a living. They got along well, and when the roadhouse shut, Nathaniel's father had invited the fellow home to listen to Bix on the victrola. The fellow was grateful to be treated like a gent by a gent. Offered to strip and refinish every door in the house. This had seemed like a sterling opportunity to Nathaniel's father. How pleasing for Sarah. So the two new pals had removed—that very night and dawn—every door, and the stripper had trucked them away. So a week later, when Nathaniel's father was entertaining—in his firepole-equipped bedroom—a blonde, backpacking, bartending popsie recently met at a downtown steakhouse, he disremembered the absent door, and what had for so long been deduced by Nathaniel's mom was at last witnessed.

Pownall proposed a trial of endurance. He proposed that Booth and Nathaniel take up oars against each other, row up-tempo in the tank until one could row no more, the loser to pay the winner fifty dollars. Pownall would call the stroke. He himself had a hundred American dollars on Nathaniel, riding against his old crewmate. Booth cocked his head at Pownall, and took the bet. Pownall's roommates, in street clothes, saw the wisdom of Pownall's scheme. Booth strapped his feet to the rail, and took up a blade, and Nathaniel followed his lead. Booth stroked, and Nathaniel sat in seven seat, and Pownall held the Mount Gay bottle like a megaphone, and asked if they were ready. *"Êtes-vous prêts?"* He shouted *"Partez!"* and began to call out the beat, "Sta-roke . . . sta-roke . . . pull through, boys . . . sta-roke, play up, lads, play up, play the game, give me a power ten, bring it up, sta-roke . . ."

And in this childish tournament, this game of make-believe,

beating the water with oars, splashing one another, taking themselves right out past the limit till Booth could row no more, could give no more, the young men, let's-pretend adults, *children* after all, were in their own eyes ennobled.

And then Pownall said, "You have won a place in this crew. An oarsman earns a seat in the boat or does not. You pulled through. Now let's take you uptown to Ivy, where you belong."

And Nathaniel, breathless, said, without a stumble, "Sure thing. You bet."

That was how he came to stand at the back door of Ivy, waiting the call from the President of the Interclub Council to break the shameful logjam of Dirty Bicker, to mend the boo-boo. It was to be years before Nathaniel would realize that Booth had thrown their race that night down at the boathouse. Booth had said he couldn't go on, but had he wished he could have rowed forever. And on the drunkest day of his life Pownall Hamm, collecting on a hundred-dollar bet from his friend Booth, would have known this, would have known that Booth went in the tank to show Nathaniel that the race was not always, after all, to the swift.

Five

Boys Without Women

As a novice rower that sophomore spring, Nathaniel was favored with unremarkable virtues: long arms, long legs, strong back, stamina. The friendship of Pownall Hamm and Booth Tarkington Griggs counted for nothing, except that it weighed marginally in Nathaniel's favor that he understood without being taught that his friendship with two port oarsmen in the second heavyweight boat counted for nothing.

He learned to pull a sweep indoors, in the fetid tank, while ice veneered Lake Carnegie. It was rude, graceless labor to manhandle the heavy oars with his fellow oafish beginners in the overheated din-bin of the Class of 1887 Boathouse. He felt himself to be part of the team only during land training, when the crew ran up and down the steps of the football stadium to build their muscles and endurance, every aisle of Palmer Stadium, hauling ass up and down as fast as the young men could pump their legs. One circuit of the horseshoe was a *tour de stade;* one stade was required; Booth, who regarded such training as brutish, deigned do one stade; Nathaniel joined Pownall for an extra.

It hurt. Running stades hurt, pulling the sweep hurt, blisters hurt. Rowing hurt. When the ice melted, and the greenhorns rowed what were accurately called barges, insultingly homely galleys that were like shells only to the degree that training barges floated (sort of) and moved (it was claimed) by the motive power of oars stabbed strenuously, artlessly, willy-nilly in the water, everything hurt. Calves, thighs, shoulders burned; back cramped. Jesus, wrists ached! To be splashed with cold water by the fellow behind him digging in, and the fellow ahead working fecklessly to feather during the recovery stroke—this too Nathaniel sensed to be disagreeable. Nathaniel soon came to hate where he found himself every afternoon, to despise what he was doing there, to loathe the coaches who asked him to do it and never said, *Good show, old sport, well done, thanks.*

The ranks of hopefuls thinned. Muscles tore, blisters ulcerated, backs went out, trick knees played tricks, hearts were discovered to murmur, parents forbade, academic advisers discouraged, family doctors said nix. Nathaniel rowed. He rowed, and then he rowed, and when he was done rowing, he rowed. He also pulled an oar, swept a sweep, helped plow a training barge through the water. Sometimes the cox, irritated by Nathaniel's composure, would jump on him to pull harder. Unlike the coaches, the cox was new to this fun and didn't know how to read a face as impassive as Nathaniel's. It was privately held but conventional wisdom among experienced coaches that he who grimaced most pulled least. They read Nathaniel's unsquinted eyes and uncurled lips for outward signs of concentration so absolute, resolve so fierce, that the oarsman had no surplus energy to lavish on manifestations of agony. The only other oarsman as theatrically placid was Booth Tarkington Griggs, because Booth's whole purpose was to convey a false perception of effortless grace, casual arrogance, superiority. Superiority in a boat race was, simply, superior speed. But Booth didn't row just for speed or merely to win; Booth rowed because to pass fast under the Washington Road fieldstone bridge, past the lily pads and weeping willows, catching the beat, feeling the Pocock surge, hitting the swing with his fellows, hearing the water puddle and whirl as eight oars dug in together, *now, here,* thirty-two strokes per minute, *hit it!*—why, this was beautiful, no?

For a coach, beauty was incidental. Speed alone counted, to have your boys row two thousand meters just that micro-second faster than John Harvard and Eli Yale and the Wisconsin Badgers and Cornell and the University of Washington Huskies and Navy's Middies and Penn's Quakers (how peace-lovingly gentle, boiling down the course on your starboard!) and whoever else came to take your silver from a showcase in Dillon Gym and the shirt off your back. To have speed required those long arms, and long legs, those strong backs, that stamina. It required character, and traits uncommonly found in company with such ardor for beauty as Booth displayed: to row fast and to win required ferocity, purposeful rage.

This was what the coaches believed they recognized in Nathaniel's composed face. By mid-April, after Nathaniel had been moved up to a real McCoy shell, after he'd been taught and trusted to step into a thin-skinned Pocock without sinking it or stepping through it, the coaches put their hunch to the only conclusive test they knew of character and will, the trial of seat racing. Seat racing was a controlled experiment in which two boats—Nathaniel's fourth heavyweight and the third heavyweight shell—would race. If the race was close (it was), if Nathaniel's boat won (it did), the boats would race again, with one change: the huge shells would draw close, and be pulled alongside each other and Nathaniel, rowing in seat five, would switch seats with the number five man in the boat he had just beaten. If Nathaniel's boat won again (it did), the coaches believed Darwinian logic had taught them something.

It went like this: the fifth man in a boat rated above Nathaniel's materialized before practice beside Nathaniel on the launching dock. "I didn't know you rowed," the Ivy Club senior said.

"I didn't," Nathaniel said, "then."

"Oh," the veteran oarsman said. "See you on the water, right?"

Nathaniel shrugged.

And then Nathaniel, by George, saw that proud and experienced oarsman on the water. The coaches started it like a full-dress race, got the shells formed up square to the line, did the query in French (*"Êtes-vous prêts?"*), waited for the coxes' hands to fall, sent them off: *Partez!* And the crews dug in, flew off the mark at forty strokes a minute, settled down, and the putatively better boat took the lead, predictably. At twelve hundred meters, halfway down the course, Nathaniel's cox yelled, "We've got their rudder; we're coming up; we're rowing through them; give me a power ten!" Nathaniel's boat moved up, its bow oar overlapped their opponents' stroke; soon the boats were abreast, and Nathaniel indulged himself with a glance to the side, and heard a grunt of bewilderment from the guy in his seat, the proud and experienced sportsman and Ivy Club senior over there. Something went slack in the enemy boat, and Nathaniel's crew blasted off into a different time zone, and the cox crowed the blessed cry "Wane off!" It was done.

What the coaches didn't know, because the coaches didn't care: Nathaniel adored seat racing. Seat racing was bliss. Nathaniel had the hots for seat racing. During the Hundred Percenter's sophomore spring, it was *douceur de vivre* to go seat to seat against that Ivy senior who had three months ago—in Nathaniel's own room, sitting in Nathaniel's chair—judged him wanting; it was sunshine and felicity to hammer yonder Colonial Club junior who had cut Nathaniel dead some ninety days back. Talk about cut: move down a boat, asshole, make way for Nate! Nathaniel rowed right through those gay blades, and when he was in the third boat, making a move on the second, he did a horizon job on his opponent.

Not that Nathaniel confused these contests with wars. Maybe now and then he let himself imagine jousts, medieval tournaments; for the most part he knew what he was doing, rowing in a boat race. Not even. A heat. Tryout. And though Nathaniel never knew it, he had help in this enterprise from a couple of oarsmen in the second heavyweight eight, Mr. Pownall Hamm, seated number two, and Mr. Booth Tarkington Griggs, stroking. Let's say these gamesmen put her in more vigorous overdrive when Nathaniel was in their boat than when he was not. Let's say again: the race is not always to the swift.

Let it be recorded that friendship has limits. Let it be noted that at that time at Princeton University strokes rowed on the port side; thus, all port oarsmen were potential strokes, potential protagonists among the crew of eight, potential candidates for notice by name in *Sports Illustrated* and *The New York Times* and in boathouses in English-speaking countries on both sides of the Atlantic and at dinner dances and during job interviews. Booth stroked smooth on the same side of his boat as Pownall rowed hard; Booth, with an eye on no one but his cox and the competitors they rowed away from, had good reason to believe that Pownall kept an eye on him. Nathaniel, rowing in the middle of the laboring gang, in the engine room, rowed starboard. *Welcome aboard*, said Pownall; *Welcome aboard*, said Booth.

That spring the second boat went undefeated. After the races, having taken as trophies the shirts of the vanquished, having heaved the loudmouthed cox ("I want . . . gimme . . . get a wiggle on . . . take it down . . . bring it up . . .") into Cayuga's waters or the unpronounceable Schuylkill or the murky soup of the Charles, the crew would put a celebration in Pownall's capable control. Did Pownall love a celebration! Was this what Andrew Carnegie, harkening a loch in the auld country, had had in mind when he opened his moneybags to dam the Millstone River and make a lake, whereupon young Princeton gentlemen might tonically exercise away temptation, deter dissipation? Now the oarsmen would dive into the punchbowl of Bourbon Fogs or Moscow Mules or French 75s, and the hangdog crew of Princeton's repeatedly defeated first boat would look balefully at their nominal inferiors, and Booth, like Hermes lounging after battle in unbuckled armor, five or six satin-sashed, sweat-soaked opponents' shirts hung casually over his shoulder, would stare distractedly into the middle distance, out at the Harlem River or the Severn, wondering perhaps why he was stroking a Princeton boat that was not Princeton Boat Number One.

But more than getting the electric charge of winning seat races, more even than having the sturdy and private satisfaction of managing not to have failed his crewmates down the stretch, Nathaniel took his pleasure from the arduous practices, sometimes relieved by a joke or a tease or a word of encouragement from the fellow watching his back. And after: Nathaniel liked to hoist the Pocock, sixty feet, long as a yacht—"All together, boys!" the cox would cry—and invert it, and feel water drip cool down his sweaty back, and maneuver the shell (sweet name), eight moving as one, to its rack. Nathaniel might, if no one was watching, pat the pretty thing, its skin as delicate as a petal. (He might notice someone had taped a "For Sale" sign on the First Boat: someone seemed to think that an inferior hull was building a losing streak; someone was showing bad form.) And then Nathaniel would enter the dank showers, and face the wall, and make himself alone with himself so he could remember clearly—stroke by stroke—how it had felt not to fold, not to fake it. He could remember too how it had felt to bring the stroke up together, to feel the blades bite in together, to feel the crew's concerted motion smooth and swinging, no oarsman laboring to stand apart, or alien, or excluded. Nathaniel knew this: he had pulled his weight and more that day. Nathaniel knew this, too: he would pull his weight and more tomorrow, and on Saturday. He gave, he knew, One Hundred Percent.

Climbing from the boathouse along Washington Road with Booth and Pownall, past the theatrical forsythia, flushed, breathing easy, Nathaniel would nod to chattering classmates; the boys would hang a right at Prospect and with dusk coming down just make the last seating for dinner. The club steward, who liked to spend free time watching his employers' handsome boats fly up Lake Carnegie, would have put aside a trencherman's banquet for his boys, for *all* his rowers. Billiard balls clicked within earshot. Nathaniel ate listening to the snap of playing cards, the irregular beat of a ping-pong ball bouncing. In the alley between Ivy and Cottage a bicycle crunched gravel, and back of the terrace a power mower droned, hedge clippers snicked reassuringly, keeping the grounds in first-class order.

(Well, Nathaniel might have objected to the fundamental blindness of the end of the previous sentence, the imprecise subject of a couple of its predicates, implying that hedge clippers snick because that is their nature, not because someone labors to make them snick. Princeton's groundskeepers were like air, everywhere and unapparent. Unobservable? Of course not: unobserved. Ditto the slaveys picking up and providing in the dorms and dining halls. And if "slaveys" seems gratuitously flip, note that one of Princeton's dormitories— lore had it too appropriately and obviously Brown Hall—had been built ante bellum to put up southern boys' slaves. Several summers ago Nathaniel had cut lawns and pulled weeds on Mercer Island for a Japanese landscaper. Nathaniel was fifteen, and he commuted to work in his family's Chris-Craft Riviera. He'd slide up to his great-uncle's dock, change into overalls, transfer his lunch to a paper bag from the wicker basket his grandmother left every morning on his doorstep, sneak behind his great-uncle's hedges so that gentle and generous man wouldn't spot him and press on Nathaniel *a little something for his pocket,* the gift of a day's wage and more. The Japanese landscaper would stop his pickup at the end of the great-uncle's driveway and Nathaniel would climb aboard and the Japanese man would blitz Nathaniel with perfectly incomprehensible advice about horse-race handicapping and Over the Counter common stocks. They'd drive to a large house and go to work. Not infrequently this would be a house Nathaniel had visited as a guest at a birthday party or swimming party or tennis party. Not infrequently a gang of kids his age, kids he sort of knew, would be hanging around giggling or sulking on the lawn he mowed. Very infrequently—say, once that summer—one of those kids recognized him, and then only because Nathaniel asked the girl by name if he might have a glass of water. "Nathaniel?" she'd said. "Nathaniel Clay? What are you doing here?" When he'd said, "Mowing your lawn," she'd said, "Oh. I'll have to ask my mom about the water." As to the mower out back of Ivy, the hedge clippers, their motive power was not invisible to Nathaniel.)

How was Ivy for Nathaniel? Fine, okay, nothing special. *Nothing special* was the best of it. He was just another guy, and so were they all, just a bunch of guys. After all that fuss, nothing special. Everyone was perfectly nice to him, almost— but mercifully not—nicer than nice. That was the problem. If eating in his company was easy as pie, why had they put him through what he had gone through? If it didn't matter, why had it mattered? No member made him feel unwelcomed. So who dropped the blackball through the hole in the walnut box? That one across the table, asking Nathaniel when their Modern Poetry was due? Him with the wire-rimmed specs, wondering if Nathaniel knows what's playing at the Pit? Don't ask who—or how many—had said *negatory on Clay.* Just don't ask. A gent wouldn't ask. Anyway, Nathaniel didn't feel much like wrapping an Ivy tie around his neck. On the other hand he would eat there, hungrily. This was the purpose of the place, wasn't it? To feed?

The University had a grander design than to race rowboats and set a table to sustain rowboat racers, and Nathaniel, ardent to have a share in what the community proposed, had plunged head-first into that purpose.

Discrimination. Again. Critical judgment, taste, the great kiss-off, judging that this was better than that, and why. The work and play of sorting out, ranking, honoring, cutting, weeding. Nathaniel made no connection between this (refined?) process and the coarse procedure that had weeded him the year before. Nathaniel had come to Princeton meaning, like Fitzgerald, to major in literature. He never wavered from this ambition, never fretted about such a study's applicability to the world of getting and spending, never gave half a thought to how he someday might get, or on what spend. The study of books was a calling, and he thought of his professors as wizards, their lecture halls and seminar rooms his novitiate. About this relationship Nathaniel was without irony; this was a solemn bond, as Nathaniel understood it, with loyalty all one-way, coming from him to The Word, to those who lived by The Word, to those who taught the secrets of those who lived by The Word. No light touch here.

Not that his professors were such forehead-furrowing, beard-pulling pedagogues and pundits. Did they not have taste, proportion, a love of play, more than sufficient irony? On the departmental bulletin board, second entry of McCosh Hall, clippings from the egregious media were displayed:

DIAMONDS ARE FOREVER!

MORE PROFOUND THAN WORDS: DIAMONDS!

WINSTON TASTES GOOD, LIKE A CIGARETTE SHOULD.

Solecisms, Nathaniel learned they were called. Howlers. And hanging on the board were other insults to diction, examples of words we didn't use: "carpet" and "drapes" and "chaise lounge." Princeton taught Nathaniel to sweat rather than perspire, and after the summer before junior year he would reflexively flinch when he heard someone call a house a home: "Oh, what a nice home you have." (The error of this usage had been adumbrated for Nathaniel in Newport, Rhode Island, in the foyer of a very large house, the *home* of Booth Tarkington Griggs and his widowed mother.)

Now, fall term of junior year, he sat in Professor Hyde's office, looking through open windows at the abundantly leafed upper branches of a mighty sycamore. Below, midway between McCosh and the University Chapel, seniors were lounging near the Mather Sun Dial.

"See the pelican atop the dial?" Professor Hyde asked.

"Sir?"

"You're looking past my shoulder, out my window. I suspect you must have a line of sight on the pelican."

"Yes, sir; I can see it. I'm sorry, I was listening, sir, it's just such a dreamy afternoon."

"Yes it is, Mr. Clay; a remarkable afternoon. We should be glad to have it."

"Yes, sir."

"But we were discussing the pelican."

"Yes, sir."

"Do you know why it's there?"

"No, sir."

"Of course my question is unjust. Were you to demand of me, 'Hyde, why do the gargoyles adorning the buttresses of this building wear helmets and quilted cement football pants?'—I'd reply, 'Damned if I know.' But the pelican. Were I to tell you that the sundial out there is a replica—remarkably faithful, in fact—of Turnbull sundial, circa"—Professor Hyde pronounced this with a hard "c"; next time Nathaniel used circa he wouldn't begin the word soft, like "circus"—"1551, Oxford University, Corpus Christi College, what would you say?"

"I don't know, sir."

"You don't know, sir? You might know something to say. You might know to say that Princeton University is a damned dump heap of collegiate Gothic, an omnium-gatherum of Ancient Seats of Great Learning. You might say that you are ashamed to be associated with an institution so hell-bent on aping its betters."

"But I love the look of Princeton. Sir."

"Of course you do. Of course you do. Good for you. But the pelican. *Corpus Christi,* Mr. Clay! Hint-hint!"

"I'm sorry, sir."

"No classics? Less than little Greek and no Latin? No classics? Let me translate. Body of Christ. There you go, now you have it!"

"The pelican, sir?"

"Of course the pelican! Symbol of Christ's body! No hold on the sacraments? Art history mere rumor? Christian iconography *tabula rasa*? For shame! Well, let's roll up our sleeves, Mr. Clay. What do you want me to do for you?"

"I'd like to write an independent paper on F. Scott Fitzgerald."

"Dreiser beneath you, Mr. Clay?"

"Not at all. I'm a fan of *A Place in the Sun*."

"Oh, Mr. Clay! The novel written to give Miss Elizabeth Taylor an opportunity to give Mr. Montgomery Clift a speedboat ride is titled, less musically but more bluntly, *An American Tragedy*."

Nathaniel heard through the open windows the steady buzz of lazy talk, a sudden bark of unrepressed laughter. Outside Murray-Dodge the Tigertones were rehearsing; "I Talk to the

Trees" drifted in on a velvet breeze. Of course, of course: easy to snicker. Difficult not to. But still . . . Learning to love Princeton was like learning to love one's parents. Nathaniel had a binocular view of the place, and now, today, such a day out there, so green and easy and sweet: not so bad. . . . In here Professor Hyde, right-handed, held his cigarette wrong-handed on the wrong side of his middle finger, famously, between his second and third fingers. His preferred way was not the common way. He mumbled almost too softly to be heard, so that listening to him utter enigmatic "thou shalts" and "thou shalt nots" Nathaniel was obliged to lean toward him.

"I'd like, as I say, sir, to write about Fitzgerald."

"Actually, I should hate to read a student's sentences about Dreiser's jake-legged sentences. I don't suppose James would interest you? If manners have caught your attention? You could do worse than to read James. Ah, poor Henry. The boys don't like to read you. Are you an athlete, Mr. Clay?"

"I row, sir."

"Ah! Oarsmen, in my experience, especially don't like to read dear Henry. I know! Just the ticket. Miss Wharton! Manners! Miss Wharton's your game. I'd say Miss Austen, but she's another time in another country, and besides, the bitch is dead."

"Wench, sir. The wench is dead. Ernest Hemingway. *A Farewell to Arms,* I think."

"Think again. Punny trace in *Sun Also Rises.* Story title, 'In Another Country.' Your best think would be 'Portrait of a Lady.' "

"*James,* sir?"

"Another portrait, another lady. Eliot's. Borrowed, Mr. Clay. Marlowe. *Jew of Malta,* first scene of the fourth act. Barabas, responding to Friar Barnadine's charge." Professor Hyde put his heart in the delivery of the lines: "The Friar accuses: 'Thou hast committed—' Barabas answers: 'Fornication—but that was in another country; / And besides, the wench is dead.' "

"So is Miss Wharton, sir. I think."

Scholars were playing touch football outside. The game sounded vigorous and rough. Downwind the Tigertones were overwhelmed by a radio ballad, "Volare." It was difficult to be with Professor Hyde within earshot of "Volare," listening to a Texas accent thunder, "I touched your bony ass, pussy!"

"So is Miss Wharton what, Mr. Clay?"

"Dead."

"You're a quick study, Mr. Clay."

"No, sir. If you'd prefer not to advise me—"

"What else am I doing, Mr. Clay, if not advising you? You may write about Fitzgerald, and I will do what I can to encourage you to write well about him. Fitzgerald had an encounter with Miss Wharton, in Paris."

"Yes, sir. I read about that. It went badly. He was drunk."

"Drunk was not the heart of his problem, Mr. Clay. He was a social climber. That was the heart of his problem. His problem of personality, of character. Miss Wharton was not easy to climb."

"She humiliated him, didn't she?"

"Yes," said Professor Hyde. "He tried to shock the lady, and failed. His judgment of the experience at tea, drunk as he was, had precision. 'They beat me,' he cried. He pounded his fists on a café table: 'They beat me! They beat me! They *beat* me.' "

"You don't have a high opinion of Fitzgerald, Professor Hyde?"

"Of Fitzgerald? No, I don't have a high opinion of Fitzgerald. Don't be so solemn, Mr. Clay. Literature is not solemn; it is serious. Sometimes seriously grave, sometimes seriously playful. Have some fun, young man. Your Fitzgerald had great fun. Here, at least. Later, less fun. You're not a Cottage boy." Professor Hyde fingered his Colonial Club bow tie. "Are you?"

"No," said Nathaniel.

"Was there . . . trouble? With a club?"

"We were talking about Fitzgerald, Professor Hyde. Your opinion of him."

"My opinion of Scott Fitzgerald is low. He had a skewed notion of time. I am not a young man, but when I was a young man, Scott Fitzgerald would have thought me an old man. His temporal gauge was out of register. Worshipped youth, life after twenty-five merely a pre-mortem interlude; believed he was a goner at thirty and, believing this, was a goner at thirty. Travesty. Moreover, inconsistent notion of time. For a fellow so terrified of the future he had an odd priority: what did he say? 'It was always the becoming he dreamed of, never the being.' Something like that."

"But Professor Hyde, with all due respect—"

Professor Hyde held up his hand, like a traffic cop. "Look at him plain, Mr. Clay. Look at him plain! Forever gate-crashing the country club, creeping to the terrace to peek through the clubhouse windows at the dancers in there. Pathetic."

"But *The Great Gatsby*—"

"You requested, Mr. Clay, my opinion of F. Scott Fitzgerald. My opinion of *The Great Gatsby* is another opinion. It is wholeheartedly high. I share your enthusiasm. My enthusiasm is provoked by text, not by celebrity gossip about who beat whom in what Paris salon or prize ring."

The reproach battered Nathaniel. He felt an inkling of the pain he imagined Fitzgerald felt being estimated, a fly in a bottle, by Edith Wharton. Oh my: *text,* yes! *celebrity gossip,* no! What was *text* for? Had Nathaniel come to this garden of learning to unlearn moral precept?

"But Jay Gatz, sir. If you have difficulty with Fitzgerald, I have difficulty with Jay Gatz."

"He called himself *Gatsby*, Mr. Clay. So did Nick Carraway call him Gatsby; so did Fitzgerald. Gatsby is the word. You may call him Gatsby."

"But why? He repudiated who he was. Changed his name. Denied his father. Made himself up."

"The art of making people up, Mr. Clay, is what you have come to Princeton to study, and I to profess."

Professor Hyde was no snob. If his student's name closed with a sounded vowel—Merino, let's say—so much the merrier. There'd be no "Mur-eye-no"; he'd pronounce it accurately, and without fuss, without unfit emphasis, but musically: "May-ree-no," nicest name in the world. To have John Hyde's admiration one had merely to love books, or at least read them, or perhaps give ten dollars to the Firestone Library Fund. Or, if all else failed, leave Grandpa's library to the Rare Book Room. Every student in Professor Hyde's orbit came (privately) to believe he was Professor Hyde's favorite. Teases, encouraging nods, respectful candor. He'd pay a boy the courtesy of telling him a thing was foolishly thought or carelessly expressed. No pushover when grades were given: "May you be rewarded in Heaven, if not at the Registrar's Office."

John Hyde was a virtuoso of the preceptorial, "precept," a weekly seminar of seven or eight students bearing down hard on a piece of the week's required work. He worked by tact, beginning the colloquy in a hallway outside his seminar room with topical small talk, carrying it seamlessly into the business of the hour, beginning with an intimate monologue, free-form (as Nathaniel learned to comprehend) by scrupulous calculation, expatiating on Molly Bloom's resonant fart, or his discovery of a citation in the O.E.D. of an erroneous use of "twat" in Robert Browning's "Pippa Passes" that demonstrated (if further evidence were required) the poet's innocence: he thought the thing was integral to a nun's habit. This was play, foreplay.

"The real world is soft, gross and oozy as quicksand. In here," he said, "in *here*"—tapping *Absalom, Absalom!*—"the world is ordered, and symphonic."

The mission of the precept was not *ex cathedra* soliloquy but give-and-take, a trial of comprehension and articulation. Sometimes shouts could be heard through the open windows (winter, too) of Professor Hyde's seminar room, and shouts were fine by him. Not fine was the fine Princetonian art of *'ceptmanship,* wherein the husk of a con*cept* would be removed from an unread book by a callow boy, and this micro-con*cept* would be traded, by the *'cept*man in the pre*cept,* presumably for a low honor grade. ("In my opinion, sir, Quentin Compson is deeply depressed. Or so it seems to me.") Yet from this too—from loutish idiocy (or, rather, John Hyde's response to the sage baloney of 'ceptmanship)—Nathaniel learned. He learned not to horse around with what might, given luck, make a difference in his life. Not that Professor Hyde's precepts were a damned church service, of course. One especially arctic afternoon back in Nathaniel's sophomore year, a silent boy had spoken.

The text was "Bartleby," the matter under exegetical scrutiny the narrator's rhetoric, particularly as it applied to his hapless employee: "I think," the student said, "you're too hard on the law-law-law-law-law-law-law-yer!" The stutterer grinned; he had tendered his opinion, by gum, he had spat it out. Now he was ready to add filigree to his estimation: "I think he fu-fu-fu-fu-fu-fu-fu-eels for Bart-Bart-Bart-Bart—"

An eager beaver was waving his hand. Professor Hyde ignored the hand, and studied the stutterer. He had all the time—eternity could be arranged—the stutterer wished him to have.

Above the struggling scholar's "Bart-Bart-Bart-Bart"'s the eager-beaver 'ceptman with the hand was opinion-making with accelerating intensity loud and contrary opinions: "I couldn't disagree more utterly. Surely you can see that the Master in Chancery—you miscall him a lawyer, to be precise about the matter—is deeply, *deeply* implicated in—"

"Shu-shu-shu-shu-shut up or I'll bu-bu-beat the shu-shu-shu-shu-shu-shu—"

"*Shit?*" wondered Professor Hyde.

"Yuh-yuh-yuh-yuh—"

"He would like you to shu-shu-shush," Professor Hyde said to the boy with his hand waving. "And to put your hand in your lap." He digressed, as though reminding himself of something: "I like to have in my precepts at least one westerner, for the frontier point of view. And a southerner, for the music of stump oratory. And inevitably I am destined to have a boy with more answers than there are questions. . . ." He looked toward the boy with his hands in his lap, and smiled sweetly. "I have never before now had the good fortune to have a stutterer in here, and now that I have one, I would like to listen to him." And then, looking at the stutterer: "Please continue." And the boy continued and, at length, said a thing or two almost worth hearing.

Nathaniel continued a habit begun Freshman Week, walking the campus reading. He read in texts he'd been led toward by Professor Hyde, an opener of books, a goader. Eliot, the metaphysical poets, Jane Austen, Bunyan, Keats, Johnson, Pope, one tailing helter-skelter into another. Other English professors took notice of Nathaniel and called out to him by name in Prospect Gardens or Chancellor Green, and this made the young scholar happy to be where he was, doing what he did. In those buttoned-down days of strident indifference, what a young Princeton politics professor would call in a notorious book of cool student self-description *The Silent Generation,* heat made a statement, passion got noticed. Princeton's greatest teachers were the least remote of men; they were avid to be exploited; take an inch, they'd give a mile.

Soon Nathaniel and a few other interested undergraduates were routinely invited by Richard Blackmur to the Christian Gauss seminars he arranged. There, in Whig Hall (a replica—all those replicas!—of a temple from the isle of Teos), forty or so from Princeton's larger community of teachers and deep thinkers at the Institute for Advanced Study, and Nathaniel Clay, would listen to greats and comers try out ideas—"conversations with Richard," as they were informally titled. Edmund Wilson explored patriotic gore, and Eric Bentley Brecht, and George Steiner tragedy, and Francis Fergusson rhetoric. What Nathaniel had briefly dreamed Diana would become for him, teachers became. Sitting among the critics he took to be personages seemed to Nathaniel such a privilege—*was* such a privilege—that the white noise of his silent gee-whizzing (Am I really *here?* Am I *really* here? Am *I* really here?) drowned the notions he had come to attend. Blackmur would sit during these seminars with a fiercely impassive demeanor, his hand guarding his tiny mustached mouth. He might flinch, just visibly, at a run of ungainly syntax or a banality (once Nathaniel heard Blackmur utter, just audibly, "Bushwah"), and the reflex would red-alert Nathaniel's senses, and the young man's shoulders would tense as though the cox's hands were about to come down just before the starter yelled *Partez!* And Blackmur seemed to know the authority his least gesture exercised on such a youngling, because when he caught Nathaniel's eye he'd smile complicitly. Not that this enterprise was for Blackmur, or anyone else there, a charade, a promenade of hunches on stilts. Blackmur

could be as self-deprecating ("Criticism, I take it, is the formal discourse of an amateur") as his friend John Hyde
("There are no statues built to honor literary critics"). But
the marketplace of literary study was not a carnival. Not that
the aftermath of a visitor's presentation wasn't boisterous.
Oh, what a hullabaloo of surely-you-meant-to-says and you-
couldn't-possibly-means . . .

And the seminars were just for openers. After came the
parties. It would be a stretch to say Nathaniel hobnobbed with
Delmore Schwartz (who would have shot the breeze with such
a good listener) or Edmund Wilson (who wouldn't have) or
J. Robert Oppenheimer (who for sure wouldn't have) or
George Kennan or Saul Bellow or Allen Tate. . . . (In the
years just before Nathaniel's years, Princeton's great immi-
grants might have come to the parties: maybe not Einstein
himself, but John von Neumann—hadn't Nathaniel heard
John Hyde refer to him as *Johnny* von N.?—and Hermann
Broch and Erich Auerbach. Erwin Panofsky and Erich Kahler
still showed up. Oh, and Thomas Mann!) He shared a room
with them, stood elbow to elbow with them in Professor
Hyde's Library Place brick Georgian, in *John* Hyde's living
room. Nathaniel joined the bohemian women down from New
York in songs around Johnny Hyde's piano, "Chattanooga
Choo-Choo," "Lazy Bones," high-school football fight songs.
He sat on a Persian rug beside an older woman of almost thirty
(black turtleneck, sandals, pigtails, long cigarette holder putting distance between her unpainted lips and those loose-rolled
Gitanes), listening to W. H. Auden do limericks ("The mathematician named Hall" and "The nasty old Bey of Algiers");
then a Bollingen Prize winner did "Eskimo Nell" and "The
Highland Tinker," quibbling with his audience about variant
lines. Nathaniel listened to jokes, puns, obiter dicta, hearsay.
Disputes! They argued about everything; nothing was settled:
the Yankees versus the Red Sox, the Yankees versus the Dodg-

ers, whether it was Eddie Fisher or Tony Curtis who played the Black Prince ("Yondah lies the kessel of my foddah," Delmore Schwartz remembered). The next morning, writing to Gander, he'd pass on the intelligence that John Berryman had fainted dead away from envy when he got word of Randall Jarrell's (or was it Cal Lowell's?) Guggenheim. Nathaniel wasn't dropping names, he thought; Nathaniel didn't imply a cruel judgment of Berryman (Berryman had told the story, pouring John Hyde's gin): to have been there was important to Nathaniel, and his grandfather—*that* grandfather—would want to know that.

At length the great men would take their great ideas home to bed, and Nathaniel would visit Professor Hyde's bathroom less from necessity than for the graffiti Professor Hyde and his friends wrote on its walls:

KUBLA KHAN; IMMANUEL KANT

and:

EURIPIDES PANTS? EUMENIDES PANTS!

and:

PLANCK IS INCONSTANT

HEISENBERG IS UNCERTAIN

NIELS IS BOHRING

and:

NIETZSCHE IS PIETZSCHE

and:

GOD IS DEAD—Nietzsche

NIETZSCHE IS DEAD—God

and:

ME + ANYONE

Photographs, too. Unframed, thumbtacked to the plaster. John Hyde with Richard and Helen Blackmur in Maine, gardening, putting in bulbs, a silver pitcher of something set in their midst. Nathaniel recognized the Piazza Navona, in Rome, from Art History 211, a chorus kick-line of skinny young men, arms draped over one another's shoulders. My God! That was Lowell and Berryman with Hyde and someone and someone else. And look here, Nathaniel's teacher and adviser, telling Thomas Stearns Eliot a thing Eliot seems to want to know. Teaching Eliot, you might say, advising him.

Later that junior year, one April night already gone to morning, Nathaniel emerged to find himself alone with Professor Hyde and a young teacher, like himself an acolyte. Nathaniel had a race against Columbia in—what?—ten hours, and he knew he needed sleep, but he had walked in on the young teacher's question, and this was a question Nathaniel himself had wanted to ask, and while he listened John Hyde made him a gin and tonic, which the oarsman didn't want, which he took, which he immediately began to drink. The young teacher had asked how it was John Hyde had wanted to be Professor Hyde. This was understood to be a personal inquiry, and was asked with pumped-up bravado.

Professor Hyde took a long pull on his drink, and wordlessly urged his guests to drink deep, and they did. Professor Hyde suggested that, the night being spring-silky, the stars giving a clear show of themselves, perhaps they three might take themselves—with gin, ice, tonic and lime—to his little garden out back. Nathaniel wanted to look hard at his wristwatch, but he didn't. Later—as long later as the time when he reached Professor Hyde's age that soft, happy night—Nathaniel was grateful for whatever instinct had kept his eyes off his wristwatch, for whatever led him to accept Professor Hyde's offer of yet another drink.

Outside, settled in Adirondack chairs under a magnolia whose pale blossoms now and then floated down, Professor Hyde talked of his calling: "When my son was six or so, I heard his friend ask him when was Christ born? My son said, 'A couple of weeks before finals.' Now that is an academic's child!"

Son? Nathaniel didn't know there was a son, *had been* a son? But why should he know? This man he so studiously . . . studied? What did he know about him? Nathaniel knew that he loved Professor Hyde, but what did he know about how Hyde repaired a leaky faucet or selected an automobile (or clubmates during Hyde's upperclass years in Colonial Club)? Did Professor Hyde sweat a date for Houseparties, or fret whether he was destined to be fatally ordinary after Princeton? Did Professor Hyde wish he didn't want yet another drink, right now, before this one was done? Had Professor Hyde ever taught Nathaniel's father? Flunked him? Fleg-negged him? How did this drinker become Professor Hyde, and that one bloody dead behind a bar at the Knickerbocker Club? Nathaniel wondered these wonders, weighed these weights, and if the young teacher hadn't been there, maybe would have—who knows?—asked.

But *son?* Nathaniel knew there had been a Mrs. Hyde. He had believed—*why* he couldn't say—that Mrs. Hyde was dead. "Is your son alive?" he asked.

The young teacher frowned in such a way as to make Nathaniel ponder how tenure worked. Professor Hyde raised his bushy white eyebrows: "Oh. Yes, indeed. Very much so. Honorable fellow, upright, takes after his mother. Cellist. An honors cellist, B-plus cellist; that's unfair, A-minus. That's fair. *Magna*. That's not as much cellist as the world needs just now. Alas. Lives off his mummy's bounty. Here's to bounty."

Professor Hyde drank deep, and the young teacher drank deep, and Nathaniel asked, "Is Mrs. Hyde alive?"

"What a coroner you are, Mr. Clay! How . . . what would it be? Necrological? Yes, necrological. Never mind, students hear tattles about their teachers. I know. I know. You have the scuttlebutt aslant, have mistaken scandal for tragedy. There was a scandal. My wife survived it. I survived it. Life goes on."

The young teacher gave heartfelt affirmation of this wisdom: "Life *does* go on," he said, nodding.

"No, I mean it goes *on*," Professor Hyde said, drinking. "On and around. Cycles. I'm trained in cycles. You asked how I came to be what I believe I am, a teacher. Cycles. I honor the ends of things: sentences, paragraphs, chapters, drafts, books. I honor the completion of things, give and grade *finals*. It's a pleasant sensation to fulfill the curriculum, tilt back in the office chair, put your feet on the desk, say, 'That's done. Might have been done better, but we began at a beginning and came to an end.' Sounds linear, isn't. Because it begins again. The cry is still 'They come!' " Professor Hyde looked at Nathaniel, wagged the gin bottle at Nathaniel's half-filled glass, seemed disappointed when Nathaniel shook his head. "I've taught thousands of you. It's all I ever wanted to do. Not a bad thing to have done. I didn't shift the earth on its axis, but the world's no worse for my having taught here. Can't remember all your names, but I know your name, Mr. Clay, and I'll probably remember it."

Professor Hyde looked at the young teacher, seemed to be on the point of asking him a question; the young teacher was asleep, his mouth opened as wide as his eyes, his pale face bathed in starlight. A magnolia petal had settled on his forehead, and for the first time that night the young teacher had taken a recess from his struggle to make a mark, shinny the greasy pole of faculty rank, seem wised up. Now he was just a kid at peace.

Professor Hyde stared at the young teacher, but directed his words elsewhere. "Don't let the bogeyman get you, Nathaniel. Don't go longing for a doctorate, whoring off to Yale."

"I'll try not to, sir." Nathaniel, awake to the vacuity of his response, struggled to his feet to leave. Professor Hyde worked to convince him to linger for another drink, more talk perhaps, at least another bitty drink. Nathaniel said no; he also said he felt honored to have heard why Professor Hyde valued teaching. Johnny Hyde bowed too deeply, too sardonically.

Then he stood erect and composed himself, straightened his bow tie. "I must seem like Gatsby imploring, beseeching, whining, begging his party guests to stay past the time they wish to leave. You want to go now . . ."

"I have to . . ."

Professor Hyde did not invite the completion of young Nathaniel's reason. "Come inside a moment," he commanded. "I have something for you. I think you should abandon Gatsby now, and I want to give you a send-off gift."

Professor Hyde took from a high shelf a thin volume, Hemingway, *Men Without Women*. That this was a first edition Nathaniel knew by the light of a streetlamp a block down Library Place. What the story collection was meant to teach him—in the narrow sense, as in the broad—he would forever wonder.

The legend of Alexander Hall among Princeton students had it that the edifice had been endowed by an architecture major who failed his senior thesis; Alexander Hall was the thesis. This was a fairy tale, of course, as Nathaniel suspected on no further evidence than his affection for the sprawling Romanesque building where President Dodd had greeted him and his fellow-frosh almost three school years ago. The flunked senior thesis raised like a middle finger from the University's fair campus had the force of parable, telling much about the tellers of the tale: alums (or their dollars) were limitlessly powerful, and cuts suffered at Princeton never ceased to bleed, and to avenge them might make a decent life's work.

Alexander Hall (alone with Palmer Stadium and the under-employed University Chapel) had space sufficient to seat what seemed to be the whole universe of Princeton. Here Ray Charles and the Rayettes sang to the boys and their dates at Junior Prom, the Modern Jazz Quartet played "No Sun in

Venice," Dave Brubeck and Paul Desmond fugued "Balcony Rock," Auden recited, and now, to a packed house, the Beats—that loose confederation of poets, hitchhikers and junkies—had come bearing their hip news.

This was not a hip audience. Oh, was Princeton Charlie unhip! Once upon a time at an Edenic seat of learning in the Garden State, no one smoked reefer. And what the devil was acid? This was that time, and tonight, sitting beside his roommates to experience the Beats' wandering scandal show—Corso, Ginsberg, Kerouac, Ferlinghetti—Nathaniel thought his schoolmates were at once too young too late and too old too soon. Mandarins in white bucks. No: he'd speak for himself; *he* was twenty going on sixty. If he could magic himself into a faithful replica of Professor Hyde, he would, unto acute attacks of gout. He was a kid of high seriousness: he wore (like John Hyde) suspenders and a three-piece tweed suit—and damn, it was hot hot *hot* in here! Nathaniel had even affected a snap-front pocket watch till Booth made an issue of the damned thing. (The watch at least was honestly come by, his great-grandfather's, by way of Gander.) Nathaniel's taste in literature, like Booth's in painting ("Art for graduation's sake" was Booth's major), ran to the vested canon, the sacred and endorsed texts, together with such established alien—us versus them—fiction as *The Catcher in the Rye* and *The Ginger Man*.

For the life of him Nathaniel couldn't reconcile Princeton's pell-mell rush to be grown-up—to be ripe, to be just this side of dead—with its opposing impulse, relentless childishness. To the co-eds of Vassar and the pre-debs of Foxcroft, the ladies of Smith and the scholars of Radcliffe, Nathaniel's fellows were Princeton *boys*. How could he deny the justice of the ridicule? Boyishness was highly prized here: stealing the bell-clapper from Nassau Hall, playing a wicked game of ping-pong, tossing a Frisbee, walking the dog with a yo-yo. Nathaniel imagined he was too old to be a Princeton boy; hadn't he made it beyond tonight's monkey business?

"Don't be such a gravedigger," Booth said.

Nathaniel, scowling, was uncomfortable, not least with himself. He felt like a prig: Corso was reading with more gusto than his verse empowered; Nathaniel's schoolmates were hectoring. How common they were. Really. Nathaniel had been assured, oaths had been sworn, that he was here among the best of the best, natural selection, tiny tippy top of a heap of football captains and valedictorians and student council presidents. He looked over the edge of the balcony to a crowd of . . . just plain Americans. The full run of the country, really: lounge lizards and slickers and hicks and grinds and dullards and loudmouths. No women, of course. No Negroes.

The crowd was shouting down the poets. This wasn't an aesthetic position, mind, just an excuse to be rowdy.

"Plebes!" a scholar shouted.

"Greasers!"

"High-schoolers!"

Jesus. These were to have been Nathaniel's ilk. Chosen to lead the charge. He watched and tried to hear Kerouac (an Ivy League footballer, after all, even if it was just Columbia, even if he was raised in a mill town) reading above the hubbub, welcoming the rough surface to shove against. Nathaniel asked himself to whom the future belonged, who was getting left in the dust, who was a boat-length up here, and pulling away? Nathaniel wanted out of Alexander Hall, right now. He pushed past Booth's knees. Booth, slouched in his front-row balcony seat, seemed as disengaged from the ruckus as from the performance that had licensed it.

"Don't be such a gravedigger, Nathaniel. This might be interesting. Historic. Stick around, Nathaniel. For the love of Pete, don't be such a crosspatch. You're so serious these days."

It was difficult to make out Booth's complaint above the din of insults exchanged between the guests and their hosts. It seemed to Nathaniel, looking back from the aisle, that Booth's sneer was general, a rictus utterly and damningly defining, an expression of voice, diction and physiognomy that located exactly the intersection between juvenile Tigertown and moss-backed Old Nassau.

Booth left the hurly-burly of Alexander Hall with his roommate. Back in the Blair Tower suite they found Pownall asleep on the Brewster green Chesterfield sofa of cracked leather. Handsome piece of furniture; Nathaniel had learned to detest it. He stuck to the damned leather in the heat, and it chilled him in winter. He slid off it, as Pownall was now sliding, glacially.

"Least bit faced," Pownall said, and sank back into a sot's sleep.

Nathaniel picked a fight with Booth about the leather sofa, which like everything in the room was Booth's. This was a one-fighter fight. Booth listened, with his head cocked. "Quizzically" was the fitting modifier. The attitude of Booth's cocked head inflamed Nathaniel.

"Why are you so smug?" Nathaniel asked. Before Booth could shrug, the asker answered: "You know what you know. You're shut to everything new."

"Ah," Booth said, "I've offended an admirer of Beat geek poetry. I didn't realize—"

"Fuck you, Booth!"

This roused Pownall, who suggested his roommates drink to whatever dispute was disturbing his peace, and why not, while they were up, bring him a beverage? He was asleep again before they could respond. Two years ago Nathaniel and Booth would have looked at the body curled on the offending leather sofa, and at each other, and laughed. Now they looked away, from Pownall and each other.

"Look," Booth said. "I don't know what I've done I'd want to do differently—"

"That's it! That's my point—"

"Please. Let me go on. I'm who I am—"

"My point exactly, you won't learn—"

"Learn what?"

"That there are actually people out there who don't live as you live," Nathaniel said. "Who wouldn't know a waiting club from a Tap Day and wouldn't want to know. That there's a world out there that isn't this world."

"Tell me about it. No, don't tell me about it. Sebastian Dangerfield has told me about it: 'I think we are the natural aristocrats of the race. Come before our time. Born to be abused by—' "

Nathaniel finished off the passage: " 'Born to be abused by them out there with the eyes and the mouths.' Wait a minute. Who? Out where? What eyes? What did the mouths say? Did they speak with a foreign accent? The wrong foreign accent? Like my great-grandfather's?"

"Wait a minute." Booth was alert, leaning forward, coiled with anger. "Time out! Hold it right there."

"Hold it? Says who? Fucking Sebastian fucking Danger-field? Fucking looking at them with the eyes? What, looking, did the eyes see? A pouting twenty-year-old sportsman and coupon clipper, perfect blond hair, drooping eyelids and a tight smile below a thin curved blade of Yankee nose? For us to be *us* must they be *them*? Says who? Is this what we were chosen for, to winnow the chaff? You: I wasn't chosen. Say *chosen people* and I swear I'll—"

"Fuck you," said Booth.

"Where's my drinkie?" asked Pownall.

"I'm sorry, Booth. I'm going weird on you. I don't know. I hate this *us* and *them* crap. How did *we* get so special? In your eyes? Who has 'the eyes and the mouths'? Little chaps, wogs, slaveys, weenies?"

"I don't use those words."

"You think them. I can feel you thinking them. You think you're different from the rest."

"I am! So are you. So are we all. There's nothing to choose between my way of life and another? Don't you want to be . . . *better*? I mean better than everyone, at everything. I don't mean a star, of course. A striver or a straight-arrow Little Jesus. I mean to know, privately, that you are . . . Come on, you make me say it: superior. Don't you want to be superior?"

Something about Booth's question, uncharacteristically engaged, made Nathaniel smile reminiscently. He remembered the freshman he had been, writing to Diana at Briarcliff about those all-night bull sessions he romanticized: What Does Life Mean? Does A Cosmic Other Guide Our Destiny? Why Are We Here?

"Superior? To my previous self? To others? To 'them out there'? Depends on who's defining superior, Booth. You're like Pangloss, for God's sake! Whatever is is right, because what is is you've got more money than them, and that's *all* there is to it."

Booth's neck reddened. He stared at his hands. He spoke quietly. "I thought we were friends."

"I think we are."

"I thought you were different. An outsider."

"Jesus, Booth! I was kicked outside."

"You're coarse," Booth said, looking his roommate full in the eyes, "and you're a quitter."

"A what?" Nathaniel knew what. Booth meant Ivy. When Bicker had come along that winter, he couldn't do it. He'd managed not to think about it till it was on him, but he couldn't do it. Wouldn't. Preferred not to. His clubmates had begged him to reconsider: he could scout passionate oddballs with oddball hobbies and theories, the very sophomores they might otherwise miss as valued clubmates, ham-radio enthusiasts, snake-lovers, stargazers, his kinds of guys; his judgment had weight; on geek patrol he could do his club much good. *His* club? No way. So he'd quit, joined Woodrow Wilson Lodge, unfortunately called The Alternate Facility. The Alternate Facility took all comers: paramount weenies, and students so far out of it that they'd never heard what Bicker was, and the heir apparent to the throne of Albania or the Holy Roman Empire, who regarded all clubs as beneath him, even though Albania (or the Holy Roman Empire) didn't have a throne anymore. The Alternate Facility also had as members students simply content to eat with other students, whoever they chanced to be. So while Nathaniel's former clubmates courted and cut, he'd spent Bicker skiing, and thinking he should be thinking through his choice. He'd imagined it would give him much to consider and reconsider, quitting Ivy Club. It gave him nothing to consider. Joining The Alternate Facility gave Nathaniel new friends to add to older friends, and a shorter walk to dinner. Like Ivy, The Alternate Facility had a pool table. Like Ivy, a Ping-Pong table. The same bad food. Nathaniel had no political or moral investment in The Alternate Facility, and when he was given a club necktie— black bananas, turkeys, wieners and bats on an orange field— he no more wished to wear it than he had wished to wear Ivy's. "I'm not a joiner, Booth. And I'm not a quitter. You have to belong to quit."

"I thought you were an outlaw," Booth said.

"Outlaw? Who do you think we are? We're just institutional kids. Outlaws! Is that what you think the Ginger Man is? Open *your* eyes! He's just a squalid, grown-up Penrod. Remember Penrod Schofield? Cobbled up by Princeton's favorite writer? Booth Tarkington, '93? Is that the class—'93? Booth! Look at our friend there. Look at Pownall. Bullyboy? No way, not even naughty, merely drunk. A quitter, you might say."

"This is really about Diana," Booth Tarkington Griggs said.

"I hope not. By the way, it's 'Dee-ah-nah.' "

"Not to me it isn't."

"To her then."

"Not anymore it isn't."

Rowing could not be said to be a useful enterprise. No utility, in the sense Jeremy Bentham regarded utility. "Deep play" was Bentham's term for an exercise like rowing, an endeavor whose expense of energy and risk so grotesquely overrode any possible advantage that to persevere in the venture was stupid. Nathaniel had heard a British poet, drinking at Johnny Hyde's, apply Bentham's dictum to mountain climbing, and it made Nathaniel think of those young climbers' graves in Zermatt, where all that learning at Winchester and Balliol lay buried, all that hope had been interred. A few weeks after his skirmish with Booth, Nathaniel watched a friend who had just sprinted two thousand meters against three faster boats, through the agony of a ruined back, get lifted unconscious from his number four seat by a crane set beside the dock of Harvard's Newell Boathouse, and Nathaniel reckoned he'd just had a glimpse of deep play, a *folie des huits,* if you didn't count the cox, which you wouldn't.

But Nathaniel—thinking much those spring days— thought also of an offhand remark by another literary man (sometimes it seemed to Nathaniel that everything he experienced was slowed or deflected by a scrim of text—everything, that is, but rowing): that young people of Nathaniel's age would likely ripen to old age without ever being obliged (by war?) to learn whether they were brave. Maybe. Maybe to row through pain might give a hint of courage?

Pownall quit. He'd missed a practice, and then a few days later another. He wasn't well, he said. General fatigue: anyone could see the fatigue. Mono, maybe. His lower back. Much was not right with Pownall. The loss of Pownall came at a bad time for Nathaniel, who was seat racing for a place in the First Boat. In the event, Nathaniel moved up, but not before noticing, imagining just maybe he had noticed, a change in Booth's stroke. It was difficult to articulate: Nathaniel, rowing in the seven seat, right behind his dear friend, thought he saw Booth's back and shoulders relent when the blade dug in. He thought he felt Booth ease off pulling before the end of his stroke. He thought he felt the shell relax its motive power, slog. It was an unhappy feeling.

Team rowers are indistinguishable from their crewmates except to eyes practiced in the reading of eight turbulent eddies the sweeps leave to mark where the moving shell was and how it moved away. Each swirl has a signature, and Booth's signature was prettier and less fierce every day. This didn't seem to bother Booth, to Nathaniel's surprise. What must have bothered Booth was his place on the Princeton heavyweight crew's Great Chain of Being.

Oarsmen from different institutions define themselves and recognize one another by a shorthand: "Meet Nathaniel. Princeton. Starboard. Seven seat. First heavies. Runner-up in the Eastern Sprints."

"Here's Booth. Princeton. Stroked the third heavies."

Booth must have said, *Well, screw that.* Nathaniel knew his friend resented rowing with beefy novices, football and basketball rejects, bruisers who beat the water with their oars. "Scaring the fish," Booth called it. Booth was such a pretty rower. But then the oafs got better, acing out the Choaties and Grotties. A few of the new brutes got good, like Nathaniel, not as good as Booth; no one could row as exquisitely as Booth. Nathaniel knew this. Booth for sure knew it. If he'd been willing to sweat off ten pounds, Booth could have stroked the first lightweight boat. The lightweights were Princeton's best crews, hard-charging artists who went to Henley and cleaned everyone's clock.

But boat against boat, the first heavies would beat the first lights. That was fact number one: physics. *Ergo,* to row light was out of the question. For Booth Tarkington Griggs. Fact number two: the first heavies would beat the third heavies. Fact number three: the first lights would also beat the third heavies. Booth was supposed to hurt himself day after day to stroke the third heavies. Fact number four: biography. By late spring of junior year Booth Tarkington Griggs wanted so dearly not to do any more what he had been doing every spring since third-form year at St. Paul's School that he quit doing it to plan his wedding. To Diana, née Dee-ah-nah Carr, of Darien, Briarcliff, Saint Meg's. Uh-huh.

Six

Coherences

Nathaniel had bumped into her in Newport nine months ago and eight months after their dismal parting under the Biltmore clock. He saw her, and changed course toward her; she was looking beyond him, at Booth, and walked bang into Nathaniel. Nathaniel laughed at the little accident and so, to Nathaniel's surprise, did she.

"Diana!" Nathaniel said.

"Booth!" she said.

"Pardon?" Booth said.

This was no moment for small talk, the Newport Jazz Festival, Thelonious Monk playing. At the piano up on the bandstand Monk's goateed face was expressionless; behind his flamboyant gold-framed shades he gave off a potent message: *noli me tangere.* Nathaniel admired unreservedly Monk's indifference to the conventions of a planet he had been temporarily obliged to visit. Nathaniel listened to "Ruby, My Dear" attentively, and just when he recognized that his squinty concentration was affected, it wasn't affected. The three young patrons sat in the front row of stands erected over the grass courts of the Newport Casino listening, Nathaniel on one side of the handsome woman, Booth on the other.

"Still think Jamie Hill is America's paramount pianist?" Nathaniel asked her.

"Huh?" Diana said.

Diana had not deteriorated: her face promised even finer character, deeper intelligence than before. Her dark copper hair (had it always been so rich?) was managed simply, held back from her broad forehead with tortoiseshell barrettes. The high cheekbones, pouty lips, these were as Nathaniel remembered them; let's assume he remembered her in passably accurate detail. Her skin had a fair blush, but no vulgar suntan. Her legs! If Diana's goofy Bermuda shorts were difficult to take seriously, her legs were effortless to take seriously. If her appearance had a fault, it was in the eye department, windows into the soul, blah-blah-blah. Her eyes were as dead as emeralds. Her unplucked eyebrows, however, were wide and full, no shaping, no slutty eye shadow. She looked wonderful.

Monk finished. Stood. Directed an uncomfortable bow of acknowledgment at the audience, split.

She wore a short-sleeved white cotton blouse, with a single strand of pearls. Saddle shoes. Her teeth were perfectly white. Amazing teeth.

"I knew I'd run into you," she said.

Nathaniel was trying to decide what to make of this declaration when Booth said, "Well, why not? I live here."

"I know," she said.

Now the penny dropped; now Nathaniel got it.

"What are you doing here?" Diana asked Nathaniel. "In Newport."

"Well . . ." Nathaniel said.

"Well," Booth said, "what do you say, Nathaniel? Time to mosey home?"

"I guess," Nathaniel said.

"Will I see you here tonight?" Diana asked.

"Sure," Nathaniel said to the back of Diana's head.

"Maybe," Booth said to her face.

"I hope I see you here tonight," Diana said; guess to whom.

Booth drove a '49 station wagon, green Pontiac woody, standard issue in Newport. At the corner of Bellevue and Memorial Boulevard they were passed by a goliath open Bentley touring car packed with a Dixieland band—Yalies, Eli's Chosen Six—playing "Maryland, My Maryland." The trumpet player recognized Booth and, seeing him, wagged his horn, and the Bentley pulled away wah-wahing a boisterous performance of "Hold That Tiger." It was possible to imagine that the world, or as much of it as Nathaniel could see, was his roommate's, free and clear.

The Griggs place did not belong precisely to Newport. It sat on a Middletown bluff facing east beside the Sakonnet River, north of Third Beach and the towering chapel steeple of St. George's School. The boys made their approach along a gravel drive twisting beneath the overarching limbs of lindens. The twined branches were in such abundant leaf that they blocked the sun, save for stroby flashes blinking against the station wagon's polished hood. Beyond the trees, on both sides of the half-mile drive, stretched horse pastures, bordered with white fences. A brick circular drive dead-ended at the back porticoed entrance of a great gray-shingled house, imposing enough to qualify in Newport terms as a "cottage." Behind this was a five-car garage where the Griggses' ecru 1942 Packard phaeton (forget the twelve-cylinder model; eight cylinders were plenty, thanks) shared space with the station wagon and a late-model Daimler sedan, two-tone, burgundy and cream. Beside the garage was a fieldstone stable, larger than the garage; here Booth kept what he called, with what Nathaniel suspected was affected modesty, his "buggies." A white-columned open porch bordered three sides of the main house, with views north up the river, south to the open sea, east toward Little Compton.

The Griggses' house had no name. Look at that copper beech, that cut-leaf beech, that weeping beech and you might say, "Hey, The Beeches." But not if you knew there was a Newport cottage named The Astors' Beechwood Mansion, not to be confused with The Breakers, to which the Vanderbilts felt no need to append their possessive proper noun. Not for the Griggses a show-off Château-sur-Mer or—worse—Clarendon Court. How about Belcourt Castle? No names carved on walnut plates were fastened with bunged bronze screws to the doors of the Griggses' Pontiac or stenciled in gold on the front doors of the Packard.

She was standing in the foyer, dressed in blue jeans. She'd been riding, and her face was dirty, sweat and dust. Her blonde hair was covered with a Thai silk bandanna with colors like sherbet. She kissed Nathaniel, then Booth; she glanced at a man's gold watch with a dark calf band. What a becomingly modest touch. This was not a Patek-Philippe or Vacheron-Constantin: it was an Elgin.

"What constructive thing have you done today, boys?"

"Jazz festival," Booth said, thumbing the day's mail.

"It was excellent, Mrs. Griggs. You should come tonight. Louis Armstrong's going to play."

"I'd love to, dear. Can't. Tedious dinner."

"Tedious dinners are your dinners of choice, Mother."

"Don't be a difficult brat. Nathaniel, be an angel and bring me a g. and t."

"Lime?"

"You have the best ideas, Nathaniel. Lime would be—"

" 'Divine,' Mother. I have a hunch 'divine' is the word you were seeking."

"You're a pest, Booth. I wasn't seeking it; I was just on the point of saying a squeeze of lime would be divine when you blurted it out."

"I try to be of use, Mother."

"Isn't he a beast, Nathaniel? How can you bear boarding with him?"

"*Rooming,* Mother. We're not boarders, we're college students. We're roommates."

"But of course you are!"

Mrs. Griggs grinned at Nathaniel. They spent much of their time together grinning at each other. That Nathaniel had a crush on Mrs. Griggs was so predictable to him and to her that it provoked no wonder, or discomfort, or levity. Every man and boy within sight of Mrs. Griggs and within sound of her Louisville-accented husky voice had a crush on Kate Griggs. Except Booth; Booth did not have a crush on his mother. Not that he lacked affection for her or was incapable of laughing with her; he was proof against her erotic energy was all, and energy was her design. Booth had seen, as he told Nathaniel, his mother's act.

Nathaniel had seen no act like Mrs. Griggs's act. Begin with warmth. She had kidnapped him, made him feel that to spend the summer with her son ("Please, Nathaniel? For me? A favor? Booth so needs a better influence at home than mine") was akin to doing the Lord's work for lepers.

The arrangement had begun mid-spring of sophomore year, when Booth noticed a letter from an alumnus on the Ivy message board, addressed to "My Undergraduate Clubmates." It was a want-ad. The would-be employer, writing from a Wall Street law firm, required the services of a "sensible young man, handy with boats," to teach his twelve-year-old son to sail and speak French. The sensible young man would have the use of an automobile, a comfortable room in a house "near the water," and would be treated "not as an employee but as a member of the family." More: a "suitable financial consideration" was "to be arranged." Booth urged Nathaniel to apply.

Nathaniel was tempted; his previous summer in Seattle had been humdrum. His grandparents had aged ten years in nine months; Gander had quit going to the department store every working day, and Nathaniel's grandmother had lost interest in books. Alarming: they had developed a passion for television quiz shows that could be diverted only by canasta. Nathaniel's mother was not improved enough to benefit from his weekend visits to the sanatorium on Orcas Island; if she recognized her son, she seemed not to care that she knew him. Nathaniel's work in Auerbach's Sporting Goods Department was slow and dull; his Laurelhurst friends seemed uncomfortable—even defensive—around the Princeton boy. He had made another overture to his Lake Forest grandparents at the end of the summer: perhaps he might visit sometime soon? He had written them, maybe melodramatically: Life is uncertain; it would be tragic for one of them to be "snatched away" before they had come to know and "love" one another.

This letter from Seattle was answered promptly by Grandmother Clay: "Sorry we must deny your proposal that we put you up here. Your father's father is exhausted from the summer's activities. He sends his regards."

In short, Nathaniel—who gave his home address as Holder Hall, Princeton University—was master of his time. So he wrote the New York lawyer (at Booth's urging, on Ivy Club letterhead), and a meeting was arranged in New York during spring vacation.

The interview with the father of Nathaniel's prospective charge was in New York, at the Racquet and Tennis Club; Nathaniel, on time for his appointment, waited in the ground-floor Strangers' Room while the senior partner of Hollingsworth, Coverdale & Quint, who meant to treat his summer employee "not as an employee but as a member of the household," ate his lunch. Nathaniel, waiting, had reason to suspect this was a lunch of many courses, with a cigar and cordial after; at length he was sent for, and conveyed to an upstairs lounge where remittance men worked off their hangovers, backgam-

mon losses and bond-yield anxieties in overstuffed chairs, raising the roof with stentorian snores. The senior partner of
Hollingsworth, Coverdale & Quint, portly and florid, in a
pink button-down shirt and Ivy tie, with a honking and un-
compromisingly inappropriate laugh, audacious Long Island
lockjaw, a highball glass more than half full of Jack Daniels
black, neat, seemed uninterested in Nathaniel's modest bona
fides as a sailing and French tutor. The gentleman inquired
into Nathaniel's provenance. Right away: was Nathaniel, *by
any chance,* kin to the Lake Forest Clays? *Aha, yes, well done.* No
sooner had his bloodline been determined than Nathaniel was
offered the job, and a stiff drink to celebrate. More questions
were asked, *just dotting the i's and crossing the t's.*

"You Clays are Choate men, right?"

"I went to public school."

"All the way through? Twelve grades of public school? In
Lake Forest?"

"Seattle."

"I thought you claimed to come from Lake Forest."

"My father's parents are from Lake Forest."

"What took your father to Seattle?"

"He's dead, sir."

"I see," the man said. "Well, how's your section at Ivy?
Good crop this year, I understand. How many?"

"Twenty-eight regular members. Twenty-nine sophomores
in all."

"Meaning?"

"An extra member was . . . after Bicker another sophomore . . ."

"Never mind," said the senior partner of Hollingsworth,
Coverdale & Quint. "Never mind. Well, I've got to scoot
upstairs to take some steam and a nap. I'll be in touch."

In fact he was as good as his word, the senior partner of
Hollingsworth, Coverdale & Quint. The job offer was with-

drawn. A reason was given: "On further inquiry, with reference to your references, I have been obliged to have second thoughts."

References? Nathaniel had given none. So he telephoned the senior partner at Hollingsworth, Coverdale & Quint, who was at a meeting, out of town, at another meeting, busy, at lunch, at a meeting, in conference, at another meeting, unavailable. So Nathaniel wrote, inquiring his own inquiry, and got a response:

> My mother taught me always to answer my mail, so I am answering your inquisitive letter. I owe you neither an apology nor an explanation in so personal a matter as the choice of a paid summer companion to my only child. However, since you push for an explanation, I'll oblige:
>
> The terms of the job description made it clear that such a companion would be for practical purposes a member of our family. Would, that is, play tennis where my family plays, sail from the yacht club where our boat is moored, dine with our dinner guests . . .

Et cetera, etc., et al., et seq. and whatnot and what have you. The letter was so stale that Nathaniel didn't even think to destroy it in rage. He didn't blush with shame or look at himself anew. Looking at himself anew was old now, a disremembered reflex. No more looking at himself anew. He caught the letter's drift, and catching it he quit reading at the words "yacht club." Pity: in the closing paragraph the senior partner of Hollingsworth, Coverdale & Quint—under full sail—hit full speed:

> Need I say more? I would have thought a bright, ambitious young man like yourself would understand

these things without requiring small-print clarification. As I learned at Harvard Law school from the opinion of your co-religionist Mr. Justice Brandeis, decent people enjoy the "right to be left alone," to select their summer companions, just as we are entitled, or so I had always believed, to select our clubmates.

Why did he put himself, again and again, in harm's way? Why did he put himself in orbit with bullies whose principal power was the power of *no*? Mean people—what did Thackeray say of their kind?—who meanly admire mean things. Nathaniel remembered his sorry life lesson from the senior partner of Hollingsworth, Coverdale & Quint because it marked the moment when he ceased to be confused about his place in worlds contiguous to and overlapping his world at Princeton. In one of those overlapping worlds, Booth learned as quickly as Nathaniel knew (but not from Nathaniel) how it had gone with his roommate's unoffered summer job offer in Newport. And no sooner had Booth heard whatever message his tribe's drums had beaten than Mrs. Griggs materialized at the Princeton Inn, and over dinner with Booth and Pownall and Nathaniel said, "Please, Nathaniel? For me? A favor? Booth so needs a better influence at home than mine."

And that was how Nathaniel came to spend the summer of 1958 playing tennis on grass, watching *Columbia* defend the America's Cup, listening to jazz, dancing under tents and washing down scrambled eggs and sausage with champagne at four in the morning. He and Booth had as their summer employment the caretaking of *Snow Owl,* the Griggses' Concordia yawl. Their employer, Kate Griggs, treated the boys "not as employees but as members of the household."

Some house. Begin with money. Although hanging him by his thumbs couldn't have induced him to confess it, Nathaniel had always thought of his grandparents' lakeside house in

Seattle as a "mansion": it had a billiard room, for example, and a library with no function other than to shelve books and provide a quiet place to read them. Edward Curtis's photographs of Northwest Indians and oil paintings of Plains Indians hung in the halls and the drawing room; a bronze Remington cowboy was displayed in the dining room; a few Oriental rugs lay here and there. In the Griggses' place, displayed helter-skelter, hung paintings Nathaniel recognized from Art II: Masterpieces of Western Painting from the Middle Ages to Mondrian. The rugs. It was one thing to cut remnants from a worn kilim prayer rug into pieces for throw-cushion covers; Mrs. Griggs had cut up an unworn kilim to this end. The flowers. The house looked every day as though it were to be the site of a wedding reception, as though Booth weren't the most aggressively unmarried man in the Ocean State.

Booth was a playboy, precisely. Young, game, sporty, tricky. His serious toys were his horse-drawn rigs: carriages and shays and surreys and chariots. But everything he owned was the right thing of its kind: Kästle Combi skis with Marker long-thong bindings, a Jack Kramer autograph Wilson tennis racket (he disdained the Feron his mother had had made especially for his grip). Everything of Booth's, everything in that house was perfect. Just perfect. The least little thing. Perfect.

For a time Booth had been just a degree too condescending about the senior partner of Hollingsworth et al. He mused early in Nathaniel's summer visit that the S. P. of H., C. & Q. was an "Ocean Drive bootlick. Can't bathe at Bailey's Beach or parse the news in the Reading Room. Lucky to rent a mooring at Ida Lewis."

"Don't talk that way on my account, Booth. It doesn't do a thing for me. If one toplofty asshole's one too many, who needs two?"

Nathaniel's mathematics seemed to make no sense to Booth. Booth figured he was one of a kind rather than half a sum; he was a prototype, apart. *Toplofty?* Sure: the first verb he had understood was *to climb.* Newport was loaded to the gunwales with social mountaineers toting new money in new Mark Cross bags. They'd show up one summer with a Texas accent and an Alden cutter they could see from the cottage they'd bought from a Gilded-Ager fresh out of interest and principal; they'd call Bailey's "The Beach" because they'd heard the previous owner call Bailey's "The Beach." The better half would tell Mrs. Griggs, "Oh, we love to swim in the ocean. We just hate tacky pools. But it's so pleasant to have a place to change out of our nasty swimsuits and take a freshwater shower at the beach. Is there, perhaps, a private facility nearby? A beach club, perchance?" Then what? Then the Sunbelt duchess would invite Mrs. Griggs and her cronies to a "tedious dinner," and command waiters in livery to serve them a first course of creamed soup, and that would be that. Put that cottage on the market again. Pack up those new moneybags. Booth'd been sucked up to as a suckling baby. He knew how to read the social score. He didn't think of climbers as climbing a parapet he owned—nothing so coarse. He simply looked down at the climbers climbing and saw a miserable avocation.

"Toplofty? Ma says a Clay signed the D. of I. Says a Clay hung out at the Constitutional Convention. Says they couldn't get the convention going without your ancestor. Says we'd be the Crown's wogs absent the Clay dynasty. Says the radio was invented by a Clay, and sound waves by a Clay before that Clay. Says the Clay imperium has quite the grandest lakeside lawn north of Chicago and west of the lawn upon which we stand as I speak."

"First: the Clays are broke. They made radios; remember television? Second: I'm not a Clay."

"You're not Nathaniel Clay?"

"Just a name, Booth."

"*Just* a name? Oh, Nathaniel. Oh, Nathaniel!"

Diana had asked "What are you doing here?" Better than she knew, it was a good question.

The late afternoon of the final session of the 1958 Jazz Festival, Nathaniel knocked off early: he put away sandpaper, tack rag, varnish brush and left to Booth what Booth called "work." (Nathaniel had finally asked Booth that morning to leave off alluding to himself and Nathaniel as "boat niggers," and Booth, with a shrug, had agreed to retire the locution.) Now Nathaniel caught a ride ashore on the Ida Lewis club launch. It gave him the creeps to be moored right off the finger pier of the yacht club that the senior partner of Hollingsworth, Coverdale & Quint had taken measures to protect against infiltration by the publicly educated grandson of the Seattle Auerbachs. It gave him worse creeps to come and go in the launch like a member; chugging in that afternoon with a schooner full of authentic members, he imagined he knew how Jonah felt a few seconds before he got deep-sixed. Tonight was Nathaniel's final shot at Diana, he reckoned, and to prepare for it he spent a good portion of his summer's earnings on charcoal-gray tropical worsted trousers, a white crash linen jacket (whatever "crash" linen was meant to be) and a sporty blue canvas belt spruced up with sailboats and anchors. He asked one of the Griggses' housekeepers to iron his best broadcloth shirt, and she gave him the business, laughed and asked who was the lucky lady? He waxed and buffed his Bass Weejuns. He chose a skinny bleeding madras tie (he knew what "bleeding" was, and would soon know better) from Booth's collection. How could the tie be wrong? Preparing for the final scouring and perfuming, he asked to borrow Booth's Rolls, a complex British shaving machine, a patented safety razor in a nickel-plated box with its own stropping mechanism.

Booth, distracted by his own bedizenment, gave over The Rolls-Royce of Razors, as Hoffritz called it, with an offhand caution: "Takes a little getting used to."

Nathaniel let the shower run hot to steam up the room, soften the beard. Scrubbed with loofah. Lathered with badger brush and shaving soap. Stropped the Rolls. Went at it. Smoothest shave he'd ever felt. Nothing like it. Resolved to buy his own. Lifetime investment. Oh, to put this slick cheek against Diana's. *Tonight. Yes!* A close look in the steamed mirror: what was bubbling rosy through the lather? Oh! Good God! Oh! Oh no!

"Booth!"

It didn't hurt till days later, when his skinned face scabbed. Then it hurt plenty. Now he lay on the bathroom floor while Booth dabbed at the mess with a damp facecloth, and gave periodic reports.

"I'd take that face to bed, compadre. That is not a face to take out of this house."

"I'm going. Want to hear the music."

"Of course you do."

Bandages were applied. Quite a few bandages. Hold that bay rum! Soothing unguents gave greasy comfort. Nathaniel dressed gingerly, and he and Booth descended to the east terrace to try themselves out on Mrs. Griggs, waiting to be picked up by a tedious widower who would convey her to her tedious dinner.

"Nathaniel. What a lovely new jacket!"

"Notice anything else, Mother?"

"New trousers. And the belt. The belt is brand new."

"Anything else?"

"I've never seen shinier shoes."

"And—?"

"That tie is not right. Nathaniel, you would be the spiffiest boy in Newport if you replaced that banal madras necktie."

"Thank you, Mrs. Griggs."

"That's *my* banal necktie," said Booth.

"Why, so it is, dear. You couldn't be righter."

The three paused to take mint juleps from the houseman. They regarded the soft light on the saffron meadows across the Sakonnet River. They spied *Columbia* flashing white way to the south, well heeled and reaching, beating the sails off *Sceptre* in the third race of the America's Cup.

"Nathaniel, dearie; I think your . . . sunburn? Your *sunburn* is leaking just the teensiest bit on your gorgeous new jacket."

This was so. The lapels of Nathaniel's crash linen jacket— not to mention the breast of his broadcloth shirt, not to mention Booth's bleeding madras necktie—were carmine.

"Let's go," Nathaniel said. "I want to hear some music."

"What happened to you?" Diana said. Of course she said "what happened to you." Whoever would have thought she wouldn't say "what happened to you"?

"What happened what?" Nathaniel said.

"I don't know," she said. "The bandages?"

"I don't know what you're talking about," Nathaniel said. "Let's listen."

Booth wore a seersucker jacket with grass-stained white flannels and paint-stained blue Top-Siders, no socks. Why did grass and paint stains on his clothes look so great? Bloodstains on Nathaniel's kit didn't look so great. He had hoped maybe he'd look like a battered but unbowed soldier, on leave from the front: romantic. That's what he'd sort of hoped.

What was romantic: full moon. A fine democratic stew of college kids in navy-blue crew-neck sweaters, over-jeweled Newporters, photo-hounds with Leica necklaces, sandaled bohemians silently snapping their fingers to the beat, black musicians hanging easy, cool behind their Monkish shades. Anita

O'Day—all teeth and a huge disc of floppy hat—scatted "Tea for Two." Louis Armstrong (also toothy) and Jack Teagarden did their sweet star-turn duet on "Rockin' Chair." Teagarden, with a white dinner jacket and slicked-back black pomaded hair and hoarse whiskey baritone, looked wonderfully unhealthy; his sallow night pallor made him purely glow. Gerry Mulligan, freckles, flattop crew cut, seeming too young . . . too young to . . . too young to shave, delivered the west coast jazz message through his baritone sax, a heftier thing than its player.

The kids listened. While the Jimmy Giuffre trio free-formed sexy tight pulsing ensemble jazz ("Pick'n' 'em Up 'n' Layin' 'em Down"), Diana looked hard at Booth, and rested her head on his shoulder. He stared straight ahead; he didn't move toward her; he didn't move away. Nathaniel wanted to say, *It's okay; I'm here to listen.* He knew this should hurt, and he wondered if it was a mark of his weakness that he felt no anger. Truth was, just now he was interested in the music and the jumble of people and the moon and the bright future. Maybe later, he thought, maybe later he'd coulda-shoulda, dream of Diana. And later, of course, he dreamed such dreams, time out of mind, later in life than he should have dreamed them. But now: how could he be sore, here and now? Well, sure: *sore.* And even in this he had double vision, realizing as he glanced at his awful new jacket, gory and rust-smutched, that this would make a good story long after his scaled face quit burning.

Then Chuck Berry came on rocking and rolling, and the night went wild. "Maybellene" and "Sweet Little Sixteen" and "School Days" and "Roll Over, Beethoven," and now Diana was on her feet dancing. She was good. Who would have thought it? Look at her; root for her. Let 'er rip, Diana. Booth did his damnedest, but that girl was way out of his league. And Booth had up-to-the-minute moves. Everyone in town said it: Booth was the best dancer (and oarsman, sailor, bass fisherman, doubles partner . . .) in Newport. Look at that girl go! When the clasp of her pearl necklace let loose, did she quit? She did not: let Nathaniel scramble for the bijoux.

That tore it. It didn't even matter later when Mahalia Jackson sang "The Lord's Prayer" that Diana made a remark about the gospel singer Nathaniel would neither forget nor forgive. Booth was hooked.

A couple of days later his mother had heard: "It is on the grapevine, Booth dear, that the pretty little Carr girl from Connecticut has set her cap for you."

"Says who?"

"*Tout le monde;* it's the *on dit* this week."

"Mother, I'm going to give you English lessons. In *les États-Unis* we say 'has a crush on'; we say 'everyone,' we say 'says.' "

"Is she quite . . . suitable for my darling boy?" She was smiling at Nathaniel. He didn't think she was serious.

"Well, Mrs. Griggs, let me put it this way. Didn't I hear you refer once to someone at one of your tedious dinner parties—I don't mean *your* party that *you* gave; I mean a party you went to—that she was the kind of person who spends a summer on the Grand Tour and crosses her sevens for the rest of her life?"

"Oh God. Did I say anything so vile? Nathaniel, is this young lady all right?"

"Yes, Mother," said Booth. "She knows her forks."

The summer was almost done. Pownall came up for a New York Yacht Club cruise to Martha's Vineyard and the Elizabeth Islands on *Snow Owl*. The boys drew a twenty-knot nor'-wester leaving Newport at dawn and caught a favorable tide off Buzzards Bay Tower and blew everyone's doors off reaching through Vineyard Sound, laughing for no reason at all other than the best reason of all: they were young, and old enough to know it. A dance was planned at the Edgartown Yacht Club, and they dressed for it; time passed, and they meant to call for the launch, but Booth and Pownall got interested in teaching Nathaniel knots he already knew how to tie: sheet bend, clove hitch, fisherman's bend, rolling hitch. The teachers squabbled about how best to teach the bowline; Pownall wondered whether *The rabbit goes up through the hole, around the tree, and back down the hole* wasn't just the least bit youngish for a Princeton student to teach a Princeton student. Booth said there was no other way to describe the knot to a lubber; Nathaniel asked which was the rabbit, which the tree, which loop the hole? Then, teaching their friend to splice line, Booth and Pownall lost interest in the party ashore. The sun set behind the clubhouse, and they cooked up a can of spaghetti and a can of pork and beans. Music and laughter drifted out to them. It was a clear night; they sipped beers, and way up along the continent's edge Pownall spotted northern lights. The roommates sat silent on sail bags in the bow looking at something wonderful, till Nathaniel said, "Thank you." They slept on deck, and next morning they reached southwest down the Sound till the tide turned on them off Pasque Island, and they beat through Quick's Hole to Buzzards Bay and led the fleet to Cuttyhunk, where Pownall started slow, poured faster, and drank the liquor locker dry. The friends ate ashore at Bosworth House, and when Pownall discovered Cuttyhunk was a dry island he got cranky. He tried to buy wine from a family at the next table, and when they let him have a glass he forgot to thank them. That cloudy night, while Booth and Nathaniel slept below, Pownall made a scandal, went aboard the Commodore's boat uninvited, looking for liquor. They had a miserable passage back to Newport, pounding into lumpy seas against a foul tide. Pownall—some crew—bunked below in the forecastle while Nathaniel reefed and wrestled headsails.

Home on the mooring, Nathaniel told Booth the time had come, they had to talk to their friend, this wasn't right, he was their friend, they owed him help. Booth said it wasn't their place to meddle, which Nathaniel misunderstood to mean it wasn't *his* place. Nathaniel might have sulked at the misimagined slight had he not seen their mission as an urgent rescue. He insisted; Booth shrugged.

"You do the talking," Booth said.

Pownall had puked in his berth. Nathaniel shook him awake, and gave him a wet facecloth and a glass of iced ginger ale. Nathaniel gave his friend a few minutes to remember where he was.

"Pownall," he said, "we've got to talk."

"Don't start in on me," Pownall said.

"You've got to throttle back," Nathaniel said.

"Booth?" Pownall said. Booth shrugged. "Was this your idea?"

"Yes," Booth said. "I guess it was my idea. It was our idea. Your friends'."

"What the hell," Pownall said. "This is a hell of a thing. Friends don't talk this way to friends. This is just the damnedest outrage. This isn't on, Booth. You should know better than this. This is just one hell of a thing to do to an old friend. This isn't right."

"You're not right," Nathaniel said.

"You be quiet you," Pownall said. "You've got no right! No standing!"

"I've seen you row," Nathaniel said. "Try to row."

"For Christ's sake," Pownall said. *"We* taught *you* to row!"

"That's not fair," Booth said. "It's also not true. What is true, this is out of hand."

"You've got to dry out," Nathaniel said.

"You've got to button your lip," Pownall said.

"You can't behave this way and keep friends," Booth said.

"Is this an either/or?" Pownall said, draining his ginger ale. "Let's have a pop."

"Choose us or choose it," Nathaniel said.

Pownall snapped open the blade of his rigging knife. He snapped it shut. He snapped it open. Shut. Open. More of this. More. "Okay," he said. "It."

"There's nothing aboard," Booth said. "You drank the boat dry last night."

"Then let's get ashore," Pownall said.

"What will you do?" Nathaniel said.

"Do?" his friend said. "Get a drinkie-poo."

Booth hailed the club launch.

In the dog days of that Newport summer the roommates got up for a fuss of coming-out parties; their hearts weren't in fun; Pownall got solemnly finger-wagged (let-me-give-you-some-good-advice-young-man) by debs' dads. Nathaniel got a nickname: "The Face Man." Later, his face healing, he danced a time or two with Diana, who was just a bit too cordial to him. Nathaniel thought he knew why, but he was probably wrong. Her indifference to Booth's roommate and friend was no matter to Booth as long as she was civil.

No, she wanted to roll the dice once more in Nathaniel's direction, just to be confident forever they'd always come up seven, first toss. This happened at Newport's passion pit, the Starlite Drive-In. It was Labor Day dusk, hottest and stillest night of the summer. Booth drove the Daimler, with Diana and Nathaniel in the back seat. This was meant to be a lark; car air-conditioning was a novelty, and the kollege kutups wore winter clothes, scarves, pomponned wool caps, earmuffs and mittens. Booth dangled a bill from his frosted driver's window, opened a crack, from the wrong side—British side—of the car. The ticket seller, having to walk around to remove it from Booth's mittened hand, got a teasing blast of arctic chill. Diana seemed to find this altogether the drollest of hijinx, and she buried her giggles in Nathaniel's chest. Nathaniel tensed. The movie was *Cat on a Hot Tin Roof,* and he didn't want to watch that movie with Diana. He didn't want to wear mittens and a wool mobcap and earmuffs, and he didn't want to oblige a sweating ticket taker to work extra for his wage, and he didn't want Diana to bury her perfumed head in his chest here in the back seat with Booth up front, and he didn't want Booth to know all the things he didn't want to be doing that he was doing anyway.

If Diana was trying to make Booth jealous, she was trying in vain. Booth had read "The Rich Boy," and so had Nathaniel; Diana had probably not read "The Rich Boy," and if she had she would have made no connection between her situation and Dolly Karger's, between Booth's and Anson Hunter's: "He was not jealous—she meant nothing to him—but at her pathetic ruse everything stubborn and self-indulgent in him came to the surface."

When they'd parked and taken aboard the speaker, Nathaniel caught Booth's eye in the rearview mirror. Booth's lids were droopy with indifference; it was an expression Nathaniel knew and did not admire.

"Excuse me," Booth said. "I'm going to walk around a bit. Want anything from the concession?"

Diana wanted something. Diana always wanted something; whatever they were giving out, whatever the other kids had a little of Diana wanted a lot of.

By now enough time had passed that the tasseled caps and mittens and earmuffs had outworn their novelty, and Big Daddy, monstrous on the monumental screen, had had a say about mendacity, and Liz Taylor was hugely slippery with lubricious humidity beneath her slippery slip.

"Is she sexy?" Diana asked.

"Yes," Nathaniel said.

"She make you horny?"

"Look, Diana—"

"Can't look. I've got a lash in my eye."

It was so; her eye had teared.

"Take it out?" she said.

"How?"

"There's a way."

"What do you want me to do?"

"Lick it out."

"Look, Diana—"

"Oh, come on!" She stamped her foot. In the back seat of a car. In a large automobile it can be done; in the back seat of a Daimler sedan a young lady can stamp her silk-stockinged leg. "Don't be such a wet blanket! Just lick the lash out of my eye." Her voice dropped to a pitch she must have thought was seductive: "I'd do it for you."

So he did it. And while he leaned down to her upturned face and licked the salt of her eye, she put her hand behind his head, as though they were kissing, as though they were kissing again (if she remembered), rocking sunward on the Empire Builder.

Whether Booth saw them Nathaniel couldn't say. Nathaniel knew beyond a doubt only that Diana joined her new boyfriend Booth in the front seat and that their affectation of rapt attention to the screen and its busy drama was meant to disguise, sort of, whatever they were up with their dexterous, busy hands. Save for the little loudspeaker's tinny cries of mendacity, greed, infamy and lust, the automobile was silent. Unless you'd register as noise the furious throbbing rising beat of Nathaniel's hurt heart.

A stand-up comic called it The Great Pussy Drought of the Fifties. No joke, all stand-up. Sometimes it seemed to Nathaniel that blue balls were the only color balls made. Nathaniel liked to think of himself as respectful of women, which meant he believed in the binary, madonna or whore. Which meant also that he kept his mouth shut in the boathouse locker room when his crewmates carried on about nooky, snatch, the man in the boat—which Princeton boys called the Yale guy in the boat—peach fish, pointers, huggers, hogans, hooters, tipis, bodacious ta-tas. Which meant also that he didn't refer to drive-in movie theaters as finger bowls.

Now Nathaniel tried to look beyond his preoccupied comrades in the front seat, through the windshield, to Liz Taylor, whose temperature continued to rise. Nathaniel couldn't see past Diana's hair. He made a list in his mind of every girl he'd ever kissed, and it was almost as short a list as his list of the girls who'd said they loved him, which was a longer list than his list of the girl who might have meant it.

Not that Nathaniel was a virgin. He'd lost his cherry (depending how you defined "lost" and "cherry") freshman year at the Scott Hotel, and corked an amateur last summer in Seattle. Talk about *An American Tragedy*. She had worked with him at Auerbach's, in Sporting Goods, and knew Nathaniel was the owner's grandson, because a time came when he made it his business to be sure she knew. She was a Deedee, and had red hair. "You can call me 'Red,' " Deedee told him shyly. "I've got a real mean temper," she confessed sweetly.

Oh, the forlorn slapstick of that siege. He'd take her to a movie and they'd neck, and she'd whisper "Don't" over and over, so reflexively she'd whisper the same whisper while he was doing nothing, eating popcorn, sliding past her knees to go to the bathroom. "Don't." He read Red *Ulysses,* the useful part, and Red read him the Riot Act, gave him the flip side of Molly Bloom's soliloquy *and then he asked me would I say* [no] *to say* [no] *my mountain flower and first I put my arms around him* [nope] *and drew him down to me so he could feel my breasts all perfume* [stop, Nathaniel!] *and his heart was going like mad and* [not on your life] *I said* [uh-uh] *I* [won't. No!]. "Don't, doan, what're doin'? Doan."

But he did. At her mom's little walk-up shotgun apartment with its back to Elliott Bay, on her mom's davenport. Three hands: he was at her everywhere, everywhere at her. He applied ratiocination: "Look, let me feel you up and I promise I won't ever try to feel you up again." Tried ambush: "What's your favorite ice cream? How about that! Mine too. What do you mean we have nothing in common? Let me just lie here beside you." Giving what he thought was a snow-job to get what he thought was a hand-job that might lead by codified and inexorable degrees to a blow-job. "Job" says it all.

And her saying, "How can it be fun if you know I doan wannit?"

And him saying, "You supply the pussy, let me worry about the fun." Where did the idiom come from? What taught him the speed of response, the sharp wits and dull vision? What gave his voice that low-octave rasp?

And him having her ready, worn-down, plumb out of "no"s. Bra removed, one-handed. Well, not *off* exactly— unsnapped. Pants around her ankles. The young lovers sweated under a quilt. He thought, This is it; here's the place; now's the time. Took time out to slip on his Trojan ready-roll in the can, do a prudent piss. Came back bold, skivvies in his hand. Slipped under the quilt. Touched. Touched bra, resnapped; touched panties, in place. She'd been rattled by the insolent racket of his waste rattling against the bowl, drilling the water. He shouldn't have taken that piss; next time he'd know better.

But she let him after all, this time. Bang her. Get it. Get in. More or less. This was his soliloquy ("Oh boy yeah jesus yeah yeah yeah"), his one-man show. The unconnected self, even with its plug (more or less) in a socket, was a poor useless thing. He banged with a rubber club. Mitey Mouse. The killer worm. He was Doin' the Do with the Great Undoer. Nathaniel the pussy-hound, treed by his prey. This was what he'd wanted. Done! He'd scored. His first free piece notched on the stock, he rolled off her. This was it? It was as though he'd traveled far, at great cost and risk, climbing a final range of snake-infested mountains to find spread in the valley at his feet . . . Trenton. Nathaniel's stand-up comic was a lie-down comedian, a curled-up joker. The gig was a gag.

Booth and Diana weren't kidding. She gave a prim little cough to cover her heavy breathing while Booth—like a matador who spits before the toro comes thundering from the bullring's dark tunnel, to show his mouth's not dry with dread—pretended to sufficient composure (while Diana did *what* to him?) to look beyond himself, to consider others, to say, "You know, Burl Ives is a pretty decent actor; what do you think, Nathaniel?"

Nathaniel said what he thought: "I think I want to be driven home, right now."

Three seasons later, two weeks after junior-year finals, the gorgeous betrothed were wed. This was a big deal. So big a deal that the Carrs said to hell with convention, yielded their prerogative to pay for the reception in Newport, surrendered to Booth's people the fun of popping for that monumental green-and-yellow canvas pavilion out of *The Arabian Nights,* the fifty cases of Veuve Clicquot, the truckloads of flowers, the incidentals. Ask yourself, would Duke Ellington have brought his band to Darien to play the Wee Burn Country Club?

The Tigertones and the Nassoons sang. The Princetonians who were invited to that wedding—and Booth invited everyone at Princeton whose name he knew, maybe twenty percent of his classmates, ten percent of the rest—would remember it as a radiant flare of glamour, brilliant as a nova, a defining event, a promise that all would pan out. Girls would mean it when they said they loved you, wouldn't hold it against you when you said—after you'd said you loved them too—sorry, you'd changed your mind. There'd be an exciting, dignified, adventuresome, secure job—great pay and quick promotion—and you'd never kiss ass. The stock market would climb and climb; tires would roll twenty thousand miles—forever. The cure for heart disease was right around the corner. When Duke Ellington broke, Joe Bushkin played piano with Red Norvo on vibes, "I've Got the World on a String." Bet your life they did. Go to the bank on it. Rain had been forecast. The night was clear. The moon shone on the Sakonnet River as the astronomical tables had pledged it would. Why have a wedding reception with some half-assed fractional moon when a full moon was available?

Was the night perfect? Depended on your point of view. Pownall Hamm, for example, seemed to think he was having a great time standing square in the riverside entrance to the tent, pissing. Word got around that he said something awful to Booth's grandmother when she scolded him, and then someone took the drunk college boy by the elbow, and Pownall took offense, and high words were exchanged, and Pownall tangled himself in the tent's guy wires, and threw a chair toward the bandstand, and the music stopped while Pownall was subdued. Nathaniel saw none of this, but he heard about it later, how one of Booth's couple of million cousins locked Pownall in a windowless maid's room, and he tore the place apart, like a squirrel trapped in a summerhouse, dying of thirst. So from Pownall's point of view, not perfect.

Not perfect from Nathaniel's, either. He was an usher, too visible, and it got to be a drag answering that tight noose of interrogatories:

Are you a friend of the bride's?

Are you a friend of Booth's?

Did you go to St. Paul's with him?

Then where do you know him from?

The senior partner of Hollingsworth, Coverdale & Quint was a wedding guest. He and Nathaniel moved around the reception like a couple of magnetic toy dogs, negative to negative, avoidance polarity. It puzzled Nathaniel that the S. P. of H., C. & Q. had been invited, and he was tempted to cock a quizzical eye at his old roomie and pal the bridegroom, but this after all was Booth's night, and it should have been his perfect night.

Should have been, but maybe wasn't perfect from Booth's point of view, either. The wedding fell on the Saturday after Princeton's final pre-Henley American race on Lake Carnegie. Two boats' worth of heavy and lightweight oarsmen, coxes, backups, coaches and trainers were hanging around the eastern seaboard waiting to hop the *Queen Mary* to Southampton. Excepting Nathaniel, no rower came to watch Booth splice into Diana. Pownall didn't count; he'd quit too. Quit the whole game, you might say, and not just the part rowed up a two-thousand-meter course. He'd been a sightseer, you might say, and traveling light; now Pownall was off the world tour. Not even the Ivy rowers came to that grand wedding, especially not the Ivy rowers. When Booth deserted his third heavyweight shell—that rowboat going nowhere in particular, that shell propelled by seven anonymous guys who nevertheless liked to row, and worked hard to row as fast as they could, which wasn't all that fast—when the not at all anonymous Booth Griggs jumped ship, he cut many a line to many a friend. Come watch him tie the knot? Maybe not.

And how did Booth feel to be cut dead by his crew? To have his closest fellows—think of a wing commander's flyboy formation—deny him, peel off, pass up a night of champers and Duke Ellington and blondes with ideal bone structure, beneath this palace of a tent, didn't it smart? Nah. Booth was bulletproof: Nathaniel could testify to the magic properties of the boy's armor. Chain-mail self-esteem. Unbruisable. Which was fine, if to be untouchable were a young man's very purpose.

You might wonder about Diana here, how it was to fasten herself to a young man aspiring to untouchability. It was swell was how it was. From Diana's point of view this celebrated fusion was consummate—top drawer, even—above the salt, a jackpot. The girl was purely blissed out of her mind after the wedding and before the reception; why otherwise cry to Nathaniel from her bedroom across the Griggses' hall from his, "Nat, please come here; I need you." Huh? where did the nickname come from? She was what she called tipsy, knocking back champagne. Nathaniel suggested she ease off the drinks and she said, "Close the door. Please. You got mad at me under the clock that night when I forgot to say please." She asked Nathaniel if he thought she was a nice girl, and he said that nice wasn't a word he found appropriate to his thoughts about her. "Don't be such a stuffed shirt," Diana said. She was wearing high-heeled shoes and a slip. She began to weep.

"Don't worry," Nathaniel said. "Everyone cries at these times. At least in the movies."

"You're so sweet," she said. "I want a cig."

"I'll get you one."

"No. He made me stop. He says he wants me to live forever—"

"That's romantic."

"—but it's really 'cause he hates the smell. Also 'cause he's an athlete."

"That's true," Nathaniel said. "I guess."

"Am I as sexy as Liz Taylor?"

"To me."

"Do I make you horny?"

"Diana—"

"I'm wearing a half-bra kind of thing. It's lacy and—"

"Diana—"

"And I'm wearing red panties."

"Why are you telling me this?"

"Aren't you interested?"

"I guess."

"When I was dressing for the movies tonight, I slipped into white underpants but then I thought, Nathaniel's coming, so I changed into my sexy red panties—"

"Diana—"

"Because that night in New York, at the Biltmore? When you were so mean to me? Under the clock? I was wearing these red panties."

"I hate that."

"Hate?"

"That word," Nathaniel said. " 'Panties.' "

"I should have married you."

Hadn't he read "Winter Dreams"? What fool did she think he was? "You know, I can't remember the brand you smoked. I remember those black gold-tipped Russian jobs you had at the Biltmore, but I can't remember what you smoked on the Empire Builder. Benson & Hedges."

"Pall Malls. I should have married *you*."

"I didn't propose."

Diana made a dismissing gesture, as though Nathaniel's failure to propose were a surmountable technicality, which it was. "Remember when you licked the lash out of my eye?"

"Of course."

"Do you want to kiss me?"

"Of course, but—"

"Well, you can't. I'm a married woman."

"I noticed."

She struggled charmingly into a green silk dress, and turned her perfect back to Nathaniel. "Zip me up, darling."

And so he did.

From some of the guests' vantage, that night seemed ideal. Booth had sure married one honey of a girl. He heard a gang of people assure him he'd married one *peach* of a girl. Prettiest girl in America! Her skin. Her hair. Luscious! Stunning! Looks that improved with age. Booth had heard these rave reviews at the previous evening's bridal dinner, which was given not at the Newport Casino, or Ida Lewis or the Spouting Rock Beach Association: these couldn't accommodate such a wealth and ruck of guests; the get-together was at home, where quality control was up to scratch. He'd heard how lucky he was in toasts by all kinds of Carrs, Connecticut gentry who had their hair cut just a little too often, had their nails manicured, wore ducks on their belts and neckties and braces and skirts. From un-Carrs he was toasted with ball-and-chain japes: Jiggs and Maggie, Dagwood and Blondie, you've-done-it-now stuff. Had he been listening attentively, Booth might have picked up a subtext here: that his *honey* of a gal had tracked and bagged him; he was antlers above a Fairfield County mantle. What he didn't hear was the verso on the bygone Dee-ah-nah: *Jesus, she's dumb as a box of rocks . . . What? Did he blow her up? . . . Why did he marry her? She's just a suburban social climber.* Someone who knew her from Darien, taking exception to the slur "suburban," mentioned that in Greenwich the Carrs counted for nothing. They lived in an air-conditioned phony colonial with a heated asphalt driveway and Toby jugs in a corner cupboard and chrome andirons in the den fireplace.

"So he married her to get it steady," said a Dartmouth boy who'd dated her. "Let me tell you, getting it unsteady is the best way to get it from Diana Carr. Hey, no offense to your friends, friend."

"No offense taken," said Nathaniel.

"Well, I take offense," said a tall girl standing just behind

Nathaniel. She had copper hair and coffee eyes, wide open. "You jerks should be ashamed."

The Dartmouth guy shrugged, and wigwagged his empty glass, and made for the bar. The other jerks drifted away.

"You're right," Nathaniel said. "We should be ashamed. She's a nice girl. You're her friend?"

"Cousin. And she's a nitwit."

Her name was Polly Brownell, and her mother was a Carr. She wore bangs and looked where she looked with a frank stare. Polly was between her third and last years at Smith that wedding summer when Nathaniel asked her to dance.

"What's your favorite thing in the whole world?" was her response to his bid.

"My favorite thing? My single favorite thing?"

"In the whole wide world."

Nathaniel thought the question too much resembled questions he had been asked by other strangers his sophomore year. "What is this, a dance or a job interview?"

"Neither. It's my idiot cousin's wedding party."

"Come on . . . Polly? Polly, come on, dance with me."

"You don't have a favorite thing in the whole world?"

"I guess I have a number of favorite things."

"Name one."

"Come on. Give me a break! You're all *stand and deliver*. I just want to have a good time."

"Then have a good time with someone who just wants to have a good time."

Later that night he saw Polly down by the edge of the bluff, high above the river, dangling her feet, sitting beside a little boy; they were pointing at the sky, at the full moon. The scene was just one freeze-frame from a scene extravaganza that spectacular night. Nathaniel was surprised he couldn't shake it from his memory: Polly at the edge of the visible earth, above

a silver necklace of water, searching the night sky, her hair lit
by moonlight; that scene flashed back at a moment when the
screen of his mind was meant—was willed—to be blank,
three-quarters up the Henley-on-Thames course, dead even
against the Union of Soviet Socialist Republics.

"You lost the Cold War," he told Polly four months later,
October of their senior year, in Northampton, at Rahar's, their
first date. They'd just come from the movies, Bert Stern's *Jazz
on a Summer's Day,* the photographer's collage of occasions from
the 1958 Newport Jazz Festival. There was Diana, dancing to
Chuck Berry. Look! Booth. And just there, on the left edge of
the screen, Nathaniel! This was his first experience of nostalgia, a look at his way-back times, fourteen months ago. Well,
then was a different time, and he'd been a different boy. His
mutations were accelerating now; sometimes it made his head
swim. Last week Professor Hyde had told him Nathaniel was
shy of the midpoint of the *Bildungsroman* or *Künstlerromanette* or
whatchamacallit that would be his finished history. The remark was as offhand as his earlier unstudied obiter dictum that
all the life Nathaniel could expect to matter would be over at
twenty. Neither postulate—that Nathaniel was David Cop-
perfield or that he was Nestor, fucking John of Gaunt—had
much appealed to an undergraduate thesis advisee hoping to be
regarded as formed, hoping equally to be potent with future.

Polly watched the movie with eerie concentration. Whatever she did, that was the thing she was doing. Nathaniel
rested his arm along the back of her seat. Funny: he was almost
twenty-one now and this was the first time ever he'd just rested
that old arm along a date's movie seat without even thinking
through the move, sweating its implications, stewing over her
possible response. (*Hey. What gives? What do you think you're
doing?*) She leaned back against his arm—tenderly, he
thought, casually, *nice headrest* kind of lean-back. During one
vignette, he felt her back stiffen, and she leaned forward from

the edge of her seat. The camera had found a cellist from the Chico Hamilton quintet practicing in a boardinghouse bedroom. A slice of sunlight penetrated the gloomy hot cell; the cellist was uncomely and unkempt, stripped to his briefs, sweating; he'd play, pause to pull on a bottle of Rheingold, play; now he'd put his jazz licks aside and was doing Bach's Suite No. 4 in E Flat Major.

Or that was what Polly told Nathaniel the cellist was playing.

"Wasn't he wonderful?"

Nathaniel thought he was wonderful.

"Wasn't he beautiful?"

Nathaniel saw this through Polly's eyes, saw it was so, saw that the ugly man had been transfigured by the thing he did heart and soul. To see this, Nathaniel realized, was to see something unexpected; to be around this gangly young woman in a plaid kilt, knee socks and a not quite fastidiously clean gray cardigan sweater was to be privileged. She gnawed her short fingernails between opinions, and fiddled with the bangs that peeked from under her wool cap.

"Aren't you hot?" Nathaniel wondered.

"No," she said.

"I was thinking about the wool cap. Inside. In here."

"Does it bother you?"

"No. I'd like to see your hair."

"Okay," she said, and took off her cap. Then she put it on.

"I want to see your hair some more," he said.

She cocked her head. Smiled. Nodded. Put the cap under her chair with her other winter clothes. "Here's my hair."

They talked and they talked and then they talked some more. It seemed she wanted to know everything he knew and believed and hoped. He opened up about his mother. Not about his father. While she listened, she sucked root-beer lollipops, and every time he ordered a beer she got a glass of buttermilk. The waitress didn't need to be asked; she knew Polly, and she brought glasses of buttermilk to wash down cookie treats; the waitress called Polly "hon." Polly had a great laugh, a nonstop, eye-tearing, gasping laugh that drew stares from the Smithies' dates that Saturday night. She was what Gander called a self-panicker; she broke herself up, unpredictably.

"You're a wonder," Nathaniel said.

"Yeah? How so?" She seemed genuinely curious.

"You're not like anybody."

"Who is?"

"Oh, lots of people are like lots of people." Nathaniel reached across the table and took Polly's hand. "I want . . . I'd like to . . . get together with you?"

"We are together. You mean sleep with me?"

"Well . . . *yes.*" He couldn't believe he'd said it. He could believe he'd wanted to say it, but to come right out with it . . . He cleared his throat to apologize.

She said, "Okay. But not in my room. And don't say we could go to a motel. Outside. I've got a big sleeping bag."

So fast. Now Nathaniel didn't know what to say, so he called for the check, and paid, and they went into the chilly night with their arms linked, and they were all the way to Chapin House when she banged her forehead and yelled, "Darn! I forgot my snowsuit."

They backtracked to Rahar's, Polly leading fast and purposefully. The bar was crowded, smoky. A fashionable young lady in a black dress sat with her fashionable date at Polly's table. Polly's parka and wool cap were heaped on a nearby table. She slipped into her parka, donned her cap, stood with her hands on her hips and asked the bar: "Okay. Where the heck are my mittens? Who's got my mittens?"

This was not what Nathaniel was used to. This was new. Later, snuggled in a sleeping bag beside Paradise Pond, Polly returned often and threnodically to the theme of her lost mittens. No, this was definitely not what Nathaniel was used to. But what was? He heard the swans paddling in the dark, and buried his head in Polly's abundant hair.

"Have you done this before?" he asked.

"Done what before?"

"This."

"Do you mean am I a virgin?"

"Not exactly. More, you know, this *kind* of thing."

"What kind of question are you asking?" She'd taken her hand from his hand, and was rigid, propped on her elbow. It was cold outside the bag; her voice steamed.

"You know what I mean. This is our first date. You can ask me."

"Why would I care what you've done before? I don't care."

What a night. Polly, the stars, brooding chestnut branches, swans to beat hell. "This is new for me."

"Boy oh boy, just what I don't need, a tiger cub."

Nathaniel guessed she was sore. He saw her a month later in New Haven, after the Yale game. With a guy from Yale, of course. She was entering Fence Club. Her new wool mittens—dark blue with snowflakes, as Nathaniel, who had bought them, well knew—were attached to her coat sleeves by the double-clip fasteners mommies make their kids use. Seeing this broke Nathaniel's heart.

Otherwise, senior year was a gas. Nathaniel woke up one January morning in 1879 Hall, glanced out his leaded window at the morning sun, looked down Prospect Avenue's long row of clubs and realized he didn't care anymore about being liked. At least that was the lie he told himself, and the lie he believed.

Maybe it was John Hyde's influence, but Nathaniel had lost interest in Fitzgerald and now believed ardently in Hemingway's ways. Later he'd understand that he'd outgrown the Fitzgerald whose reverie of Princeton had so distorted the place for him before he'd grown sharp-eared enough to rise to the music of Fitzgerald's sadness. Maybe it was Professor Hyde's gift of *Men Without Women,* but Nathaniel had traded one romance for another, even up. Now it was taciturnity, tenacity, the old g. under p., the sanctity of scrupulously fit deeds, declarative sentences, one set of spurious values replacing another. He'd once fretted about being outside the window looking in; now he couldn't remember why he'd cared which side of the pane he looked through. Now he'd stand pat with the cards he'd been dealt.

He had friends, and he could row a good race, and he knew that if the day came he couldn't row as good a race as his teammates, he'd row the best race he could in a slower boat. Faulkner had carried on in Stockholm about ding-dongs of recorded time, and man prevailing yakkety-yak; it seemed to this young admirer of Hemingway that to endure was plenty, not to quit was.

Nathaniel knew a quitter: his friend Booth and Mrs. Booth Tarkington Griggs lived north of Princeton in Kingston; he'd rented a fieldstone Federal on lots of land backed along the Millstone River. He had a boathouse surrounded by weeping willows, and Nathaniel heard that his old roommate was rowing his scull two hours every morning and two every evening.

Diana gave sit-down dinner parties and arranged flowers in wedding-present vases and covered a wedding-present mahogany dining-room table with a wedding-present Belgian linen tablecloth set with wedding-present gun-handle silver. Booth carved the roast and commented on the wine. Booth and Diana were the only married couple of his age Nathaniel knew at Princeton; students had to get permission to marry. The question of money, of divided energies—the University had an interest. And Princeton was so resolutely male. Well: it was a

complicated and unusual course to marry before commencement, and to Nathaniel it seemed wonderfully grown-up—
ripe—to set up house, and such a house. Nathaniel envied his
friend, and not only for the obvious night-after-night schnoo-
gle with Diana Carr Griggs.

Booth did not envy Booth. It wasn't just that he felt like a
damned commuter, as he told Nathaniel late one night over a
bottle of Wild Turkey, listening to Billie Holiday: he missed
the boys.

"She won't let Pownall in the house. I can't think of her as
a wife, buckaroo. It's like she's a weekend date."

"What's wrong with that?"

"The weekend's over."

Nathaniel considered his friend's dismay. Nathaniel wondered if his opinion was being recruited. Nathaniel decided
that the thing he burned to tell his dear friend in response to
his dear friend's dismay was this: nothing. Nil. Zip.

"Oh well," said Nathaniel.

"Oh well what?" said Booth.

"Oh well let's have another pop, and listen to Art Tatum."

"Hey, guess what," Booth said.

"What," Nathaniel said.

"She's got a bun in the oven."

"Wow," Nathaniel said, trying to look pleased, forcing a
grin. "How about that? An heir!"

"Yeah," Booth said, not trying to look pleased, not forcing
a grin. "Another Griggs."

Later, Nathaniel would try to remember how in the world
the Final Club came to be. Maybe Booth had seen the fellowship as a way to return his old roommate to Ivy, where he was
so certain Nathaniel belonged. Maybe too the Final Club
evolved from dinners Nathaniel increasingly arranged at The
Alternate Facility for John Hyde and Richard Blackmur, fancy
meals washed down by fancy (appropriate) wine (*videlicet:* red

with meat, white with fish) eaten in fancy pants during fancy talk in an unfancy dining room.

But Nathaniel's best guess was the Final Club's seed got planted sometime about dawn of that session of bourbon and jazz and doleful judgment of the estate of matrimony, after one of Diana's increasingly irritated and irritating appearances on the stairs: "Boys, please turn the victrola down a little. . . . Booth, Jesus, it's after four; I'd like to get my beauty sleep before I get my morning sickness. . . . Come *on,* you guys." It wasn't exactly *Streetcar Named Desire* out there in Kingston, with the Millstone gurgling past water lilies, but Booth wanted what Stanley Kowalski wanted, to gather with the guys. If not to bowl or play seven stud hi-lo roll 'em, then by God to break some serious bread.

The Final Club had a dozen members because that was how many members there happened to be. No officers, exalted purpose, dues, clubhouse, bylaws, whereases or wherefores. No coat of arms or Latin motto. No blazer patch or club tie. No blackball. Especially no blackball. No one could have said how the members found one another, except that they were seniors. It wouldn't have been accurate to say the members were all friends, because disparate constellations intersected in the Final Club, so a precept-mate of Nathaniel's joined with Booth's cousin, and neither knew the other's face and name with certainty. Two facts: Booth was the hub of this small universe, and Nathaniel was the only member from the crew team.

Booth must have named it to cock a snoot at Harvard's final clubs, its zenith societies. Here the name signified the finality of non-perpetuation rather than the finality of summit; there was to be nothing beyond this brotherhood of a single year. No Bickering of new members. The boys met more or less once a month, though no calendar of association was published or even scheduled until a week or so before the dinner was laid on.

Dinner was the presumptive big idea, to gather upstairs at Ivy around a long table that seated twelve, like the table at the Last Supper; this practical limit must have determined the roll of the Final Club. To buck Princeton's down-at-heels army-surplus fashion and put on the dog in black tie, to eat what Booth would have been too wise to agree was "gourmet" food—this was the ticket. The members, from the four corners of America, determined the month's repast turn and turn about; Nathaniel saved the engraved menus: imagine the variety.

LA CARTE: FÉVRIER

Most friendships are formed by caprice or by chance,
mere confederacies in vice or leagues in folly.
—SAMUEL JOHNSON

Quenelles aux Huîtres

·

Vichyssoise

·

Tournedos Rossini
(avec la Purée de Pommes de Terre)

·

Crème Brûlée

The wines were relentlessly appropriate: Pouilly-Fuissé with the early courses, claret with the boeuf, a Château d'Yquem with dessert. As the months rolled by, the boys outdid themselves exploring novel gustatory routes: the quenelles gave way to coquilles St. Jacques à la Parisienne, vichyssoise to potage parmentier, the tournedos to canard à l'orange. Coq au vin got a tasting; the clubmen served one another artichauts au naturel (to see who didn't know you weren't meant to eat the whole damned thing). Filet de sole bonne femme was "et" (the "chaps" had taken to speaking to one another Samuel Johnsonly: a chap had not yet got his steamer ticket for the summer hols; he was behind shed-jule), and pâté. Pots de crème ended mars's dinner, and crêpes Suzette avril's.

The boys assembled for these banquets in the library of Ivy during inclement weather and on Ivy's back terrace come spring; they gathered at six, the earliest moment they could let themselves be seen in black tie. Cocktails were served. Martinis ("Dry, sir, *dry*") were shaken (or was it stirred? which method did not bruise?) and served in a proper martini glass, cold enough to freeze the tongue.

"Well done, sir," someone would say to the martini-maker. "Hear, hear!"

Nathaniel was conscious—how could he be unconscious?—of the conspicuous collective affect of them all. Graceful. Insouciant. He thought later he remembered thinking these words, exactly: We're dashing. A few centuries ago Diana Carr, riding the dining car of the Empire Builder, had said to him across a starched linen table: "You look dashing." He hadn't the vaguest notion then what she was talking about. Now he knew: he and his friends—*dashing*.

During martinis ("clears," "see-throughs," "loudmouth soup"), Nathaniel couldn't unsee the why-not-me? stares of those Ivy clubmen whose company he had quit. The Final Club had not been formed to incite envy or even curiosity. Its proceedings were not secret; the congregation was meant to seem to have gathered offhand, gone unnoticed. The dinner-jacketed boys did not go unnoticed. After martinis the young gents made their way upstairs to the private dining room.

There the first course awaited. The silver had been polished, table waxed, crystal buffed; all had been put in readiness by the Ivy Club steward, Prosper. Nathaniel had unwittingly injured this good man inquiring what his name was, really. Why, it was Prosper, really.

Now the martinis, abetted by the first bottles of Pouilly-Fuissé, or maybe even Pouilly-Fumé, bit into the frontal lobes, and the rhetoric got some serious English put on it, a savage Boswellian spin, and the boys became bawdy diners.

Tonight Nathaniel had made up the menu:

BILL OF FARE: MAY

The man must be so much, that he must make all circumstances indifferent.
—RALPH WALDO EMERSON

Olympia Oysters

·

Ivar's Chowder

·

Broiled Coho Salmon
(with parslied spuds)

·

Royal Butterscotch Pudding

The evening's oratory was under way. At each dinner members were expected to lecture on something they thought they knew. Booth was on his feet, doing Animal Husbandry: he lectured on sheep, a deadpan delivery. Sheep, said Booth, were woolly, manageable, useful: "nature's lawn mowers." They made a pretty impression grazing verdant meadows rolling to the water's edge. They were tasty—

"Buggery!" shouted Roscoe, a Birmingham boy ("the Pittsburgh of the south," he reminded his friends). "You seek companionship in pasture and barn; you speak of buggery!"

"I forgot my audience," said Booth. "I was neglectful of the sensibilities of our hip-booted friends from the benighted Confederacy, where women—according to the Union's biological measure—are scarce, and sheep are scared."

"Only the female sheep are scared in Bumminham," Roscoe said. "In Newport—"

"I remind you, sir: I am two months ago a father."

"Baaaaaa," said the editor of the *Nassau Literary Magazine*.

That kind of dinner address. But there were other kinds of discourse also. Nathaniel invited his dinner-mates to search their souls in the matter of Ezra Pound, languishing anti-Semitically at St. Elizabeth's, where he was visited by John Hyde and every other Amur'kn poet, literary meditator and pilgrim. Nathaniel's address: "Uncle Ez, *Il Miglior Fabbro: Madman or Monster?*" Archibald Barrie, a boyish, passionate student of constitutional and international law, denounced Pound as a "damned traitor. The Jew-baiter should have been put before a firing squad. At the least hanged."

Heavy, what? Conversation could be high-minded or about pussy; manners could be self-consciously exquisite, when there wasn't a food fight. Those nights were supercharged occasions for Nathaniel. Lofty, magnanimous. No opinion, belief, speculation, anxiety, passion was off-limits. Denial was tolerated, doubt encouraged. Over cigars and port, cigars and brandy, lost in talk, they heard Nassau Hall's bells at midnight, and those bells chimed just the beginning of the middle of the friends' meetings. The epigraph on avril's bill o' fare was Callimachus's memory of his chum Heraclitus: "I wept as I remembered how often you and I /

Had tired the sun with talking and sent him down the sky."

Within Nathaniel's limited depth of field, the world beyond Princeton's world was bustling with possibility; the
world beyond this table was a monster buffet, a groaning
board of provender. It was such a blast to be a student. Such
fun. And to be the kind of student who didn't shout during
the Yale game, "Handsome Dan's a pussy!" The kind who
didn't go to Baker Rink hockey games got up in a coonskin
coat and rag the Harvard goalie. In the spring of 1960, Jack
Kennedy was a young pol trying to hustle his party's nomi-
nation, but something was happening out there, and here too,
in Mercer County, at Princeton, at dinner tonight. Lester
Lanin was heard less often than the Hot Nuts at college parties; Chubby Checker was just down the road at the Pepper-
mint Lounge, the privileged and conforming were (whoosh)
on the cusp of reefer, beards and irony, poised to twist. But
that wasn't the real point. Meritocracy was. Oh, a perception
of merit had always driven this institution; in Princeton's
fifties, worth had mattered: worthy tailoring on a genetically
worthy body, without unworthy skin or speech defects. Worthy deportment had counted, especially for those unworthily
bred or schooled.

The '50s boys were gone now. The clean young gentlemen
who had done nothing but games to excess, who had thought
they wanted to be good and believed they were, who wished to
draw no attention to themselves, who had zipped their lips,
who dreamt of . . . *competence*—those circumspect clubmen
who had estimated Nathaniel's net worth low were down the
road, becoming Navy officers, studying torts and contracts,
working for Morgan Guaranty, or maybe even Morgan Stanley. In their place were Nathaniel's Final Clubmates. Excepting Booth, they were above all exhilarated, ardent.
Intoxicated, say—from all those marts, all that Pouilly-
something, all that burgundy and port and cognac, but mostly

from their sense of themselves as poised in the starting blocks. Maybe half of them superficially resembled their counterparts: clothes and haircuts hadn't changed much; only a few members of the Final Club had gone to public schools; Roscoe had caught Princeton's winning touchdown against Dartmouth—last game of the season—in the snow of Palmer Stadium, with six seconds on the clock, and he would be remembered for this. But Nathaniel's friends here were different; if for no other reason they were different because they put a value on being different, distinct. On, that is, distinction. They weren't ashamed to confess they'd read a book to its conclusion, for pleasure. Harry, down there at the other end of the table beside Booth, directed plays for Theatre Intime and didn't worry whether this would make him seem, or maybe even become, a fairy. Nathaniel wrote for the *Nassau Literary Magazine.* At Harvard such extracurriculars would provoke a so-what? At Princeton they were revolutionary. The wind had shifted, and at the Final Club dinners, when the youngsters weren't horsing around as youngsters will, the boys were proving to themselves that they were special—arguing, confessing, questioning, speechifying, challenging, exhorting, declaiming—that they were *just now* thinking thoughts never before thunk.

Great Ideas? Unconventional wisdoms? Fooey. Later, Nathaniel would see his friends' post-midnight aperçus for what they were: homiletic platitudes, what oft was thought and oft as well expressed. Alas. But now? Tonight? They knew a thing or two. They knew they'd be pals forever; some discussed living communally, in an agreeable place like Oyster Bay or Marin County or Far Hills or Bridgehampton; this arrangement—a housing development for the well-educated well-off—would someday, after all the fun had been squeezed out of being just guys together, include wives; no need to ask Booth why his hangdog look during

this brainstorming session. Something else they all knew—
and this was glue that bound them: in years to come they
would never have to explain away why they'd gone to college
where they went to college. Nathaniel didn't know what he
wanted to be when he grew up or what he was growing away
from or who he had really been. But Hundred Percenter or
not, he would never have to wonder how it would have been
to get into the college he'd wanted to get into. His classmates
would never have to say where they *almost got in,* or lie about
where they got in but chose not to go.

At the final dinner of the Final Club, in May, Nathaniel's
Pacific Northwest feast, the members rose in turn to say toasts.
Pete, a West Virginia high-schooler, ferociously bright, theatrically seedy, Balliol-bound on a Rhodes, said, "I'll miss
Princeton more than most of my biographers will believe."
Nathaniel, Trinity College (Cambridge)-bound, believed.
Gin, wine, Madeira, Armagnac and the occasion had turned
him maudlin, and he found himself on his feet reciting his
favorite valediction, lines he'd tried on Polly in her sleeping
bag with less success than Milton's periodic verse enjoyed
tonight among the lads:

> *The world was all before them, where to choose*
> *Their place of rest, and Providence their guide:*
> *They hand in hand with wand'ring steps and slow*
> *Through Eden took their solitary way.*

Now the young men were quiet, contemplative. Nathaniel
realized he had touched them, that they too felt this place was
Paradise, and now they were to be gone from it. Oh, this was
gorgeously affecting. Melancholy. Their youth was spent.
How pathetic the long littleness of others' lives. Not their
lives. The world awaited them: hushed, expectant, fertile, in
estrus. Here they came!

Before they parted that night, they made a pact: they would gather again, in this very room, ten years hence, during their class reunion. To bind the pact, each wrote for each of his fellows a prediction, and sealed this gross of handwritten (unsigned) prophecies in a manila envelope, and entrusted it to Booth. Then they drank deep of the port's dregs and, like Russian noblemen or something, cast their empty glasses into the fireplace's robust blaze, which had raised the warm May air several notches past the discomfort level, melting the damned Brie. Then they loosened their ties and made their way into the pinkish gray of dawn, arms around one another's shoulders, five or six abreast, taking over Prospect altogether, singing corny Princeton songs, singing "Jerusalem," swooning crazy lovestruck with fellow-love and self-love.

Nathaniel graduated well; Professor Hyde saw to it. Professor Hyde also urged his avid student to be a man of letters, reach for the stars—that is: *write*. Professor Hyde also said of a novella Nathaniel had written (delicate boy as hero, mountain-climbing mentor-dad dead on Matterhorn after fall or jump from Hörnli Ridge): "I hope you don't try to publish it. If you do try, you should hope that no publisher accepts it."

Mixed signals from Johnny Hyde. Mixed signals too from Seattle; none from the Auerbach clan could come to Princeton commencement: "Gander's doing better," Nathaniel's grandmother reported. "Don't fret about us." Nathaniel hadn't been told anyone out there was doing badly, or worse than usual.

Unmixed signals from Lake Forest: "We wish to acknowledge receipt of your invitation. We cannot attend your graduation. Your father's father is unwell." In amelioration of Nathaniel's loss, the Clays bestowed a graduation gift, a photograph of the extended family at Christmas, gathered beside the tree in a large room, presumably north of Chicago, a Clay console radio shining front and center; recessive-chinned kin smiled glumly; two of the men wore Ivy bow ties. Mrs. Clay's letter uncharacteristically continued past its repudiating purpose:

As you'll see by the family portrait, the Clays have made a good showing at Ivy Club. We have been told you are a member. We trust you did not use your connection to the Clays, via your late father, to thrust yourself forward at Ivy Club.

By the by: you tell us you are to row at Henly this summer. I believe you are entitled to complimentary tickets on that account. Your father's father and I plan to be in England during the time of Henly and Wimbildun and would like tickets to the rowing events, on the day you perform or any other day. We would entertain you in return during our stay in England, but we can't.

To Nathaniel's surprise, he answered this letter:

I'd get you tickets to Henley, but a congenital illness, principal symptom terminal indifference, renders me unable. As my other grandfather liked to say to shitweasels, "Piss up a rope." The both of you.

Your very own,
Nate

P.S. "Shit in yore hats." My maternal great-granddad, one of the Auerbach clan, liked to say that, probably because the immigrant could pronounce, and almost spell, its monosyllabic components: "Shit in yore hats."

Nathaniel was at Henley, the day before the first heat, when Gander died. Mrs. Auerbach's telegram said to stay put, row a good race. He flew home that night on Icelandic, an interminable odyssey via Prestwick, Reykjavik, Goose Bay and—how about this?—Gander. That old man had never crisscrossed Nathaniel's life without making Nathaniel feel better. It occurred to Nathaniel, seated behind the violent, fumy prop wash, beside a hugely pregnant young woman who occupied herself moving her lips and weeping as she read the New Testament, that he was now fundamentally alone in the world without that old man. Bulling westward in a Lockheed Constellation with the grim cargo of his fellow-passengers, the engines' exhaust flaming orange, Nathaniel thought that of the things he had learned during his *Bildungsroman,* Gander's lessons were fundamental. The doctor's vow—what was it? To do no harm? Well, that would be Nathaniel's purpose, he thought.

His grandmother was at the funeral, but she didn't know it. The Henley telegram hadn't come from her after all. She had had a stroke, was as dead as Gander but didn't know that either. Nathaniel's mother had sent the telegram. She was home from Orcas Island, to stay. She was like Rip van Winkle awake after more winks than a person needed, Dorothy home from Oz. Bright, zippy, well rested indeed. She might have said to her son, "Hi, honey, what's up?" But she was too nicely repaired not to appreciate how odd her ordinariness would seem to Nathaniel, so she took it easy with him, let him accustom himself in his own sweet time to her fine new health.

He tried to adjust to his mom. He did try. How could he know that what he saw now was what would be? The mother before the windblown mad night with the handgun? How could Nathaniel know his widowed mom would now live an implacably reasonable and serene and sociable life? That she'd take an interest in the Laurelhurst school board, and plant a tree on Arbor Day? That she'd awaken every morning for a swim in the lake, eat a sensible breakfast, putter in her garden, eat a light lunch, read the newspaper, treat herself to a nap, feed and pat the pets, write a few letters, look in on her failing mom. What about that night, the Colt .45, the offered choice? What about it?

He asked her. How was he supposed to think now about that night less than six years ago?

"Oh," she said. "Consider it the way your father would have considered it."

They were sitting at the end of the dock Nathaniel had seen from the kitchen window that busy night. He dangled his feet, staring at the water: "And how would he have considered it, Mother?"

She sat cross-legged, looking directly at her son. "You used to call me 'Mom.' "

"And how would Dad have considered that night? If he were here, say."

Nathaniel's mother sighed. "Oh, I guess it took him about a minute to forget I wanted to kill him or die. And would have taken him about a year to remember it, if you put a gun to his head to make him remember it."

Nathaniel didn't know what to think about his mother now or his father then. He thought he'd known that his father married an Auerbach for Auerbach money because Clay money had been spent. That might have been a reductive version of events and motives, but true at its core. Nathaniel could comprehend such a version of events.

But—as his mother insisted he understand—he understood wrong. "It wasn't like that at all." She explained that the Clays had been drowning in money when she married Nathaniel's father. They were still drowning in the stuff. The only injury done the Clay radio family by television was the worst injury available: it had sapped them of purpose.

Nathaniel's father had married for love, such as he understood love, and he understood it superficially.

"He said the word often enough, heaven knows: he *loved* his M.G., till he *loved* his Jaguar better; he *loved* his Jaguar better than any car ever made anywhere in the whole history of creation, till he saw his first Aston Martin. And he loved me. Oh, let him count the ways. He *did* love me, too, in a Hallmark-card kind of way. The same way he loved other—"

"Mother, please. This isn't easy for me."

"Oh. Oh, sure. I should be more sensitive to your feelings, Nathaniel. You always were a dreamy boy. So sweet. This kind of biography—so intimate—must be difficult for you."

"Mom. Please. Don't be sarcastic. You stink at it."

His mother smiled. Nathaniel recalled that smile from a sea-trench of memory; his connecting line to his mother's smile had sunk that winter night in the kitchen, and now he fished it from his darkest deep, toward the light of recognition. Nathaniel smiled.

"He was an odd man," his mother said. "Odd boy, I guess."

"The fireman?"

"Oh, the fire hobby was adorable. Everyone should have a silly passion." Nathaniel's mother touched his arm: "Do you?"

"Do I what?"

"Have a silly passion?"

Nathaniel shrugged.

"Is there something," his mother asked, "that matters to you more than anything else in the whole wide world? Your favorite thing?"

"I got asked that recently by someone else."

"A girl?"

"A girl."

"A good girl."

"Yes. A good girl."

"That's what I said. I wasn't asking; I was saying. Good girls ask good questions."

The house was bordered on one side by Lake Washington, on the other by Union Bay. A novice Husky eight was being rowed with comic imprecision and spendthrift energy along an erratic course more or less toward the dock where Nathaniel sat with his mother.

Nathaniel called out, "Hey! Wane off, you guys." The cox gave Nathaniel the finger and resumed shouting in a pip-squeak voice his contradictory directions. Nathaniel waved, and cheered, "Get the swing! Go for it! Whip those pussy U. Cal. Bears!" He said to his mother, "I like to row."

"You're good at it."

"I think so."

"I know so. I wasn't asking; I was telling. Like before. You think I don't know things, because I've been gone. Because of where I've been. But despite having been gone, because of where I've been, I know things."

Nathaniel thought this was bullshit. What he really believed: he believed it was too easy for his mother to decide that sickness had marked her special. Nathaniel thought he wanted to change the subject. "Do you miss Gander?"

"What an odd question. What do you think? What else do you like, besides rowing?"

"Reading. Writing. Friends. Laughing. Train travel."

"Gosh. You sound like Miss Mississippi telling her hobbies to the Miss America judge. How about that good girl?"

"Pauline?"

"Is that her name?"

"Polly."

"Do you like Polly?"

"Yes."

After the silence had endured too long, his mother told more about his father. How irresponsible he was, how bone-idle, how negligent, how much fun, how courageous, how cowardly, how chivalrous. His father's virtues and vices had been for Nathaniel a confused mess; for his mother—she said—they made a complicated and delicate alloy. He preferred to have people regard him as a gold digger than to have them know his family were bigots.

"He gave up his claim to their money to marry me."

"But he lived off Gander."

"Yes," his mother said. "Gander didn't care. My mother didn't. I didn't. It's difficult to explain. It just didn't matter. I suppose it should have mattered, but it didn't. Especially after our trip to Santa Barbara."

"Santa Barbara?"

Nathaniel's mother explained that soon after Nathaniel was born his father decided to break out of Seattle. "He hated the rain, he said. In fact, he didn't like living in that little lakeside cottage Gander built us. Your father grew up in a lakeside house *very* much grander than Mom's and Dad's."

"Have you ever seen it?" Nathaniel asked.

"Snapshots." She had settled beside him, and dangled her bare feet toward the water. She had rolled up her khaki pants, and Nathaniel saw how thin his mother's legs were, how paper-white was her skin. He thought he understood that his mother was still frail, and he wanted to shelter her from her future's storms. "Anyway," she said, "your father had this big idea that there was an enterprise to be exploited in Santa Barbara. Your father called it"—she did a fair approximation of his voice—" 'an enterprise of some little interest.' A Choate friend was manufacturing fancy record players—what are they called, high something?"

"Hi-fi."

"What does it mean?"

"High fidelity."

"Oh. Fi-del-i-ty. That's a nice word. Loyalty. Devotion.

Steadfastness. High fidelity would've been a nice business to have been in. Except it didn't work out. In fact, we never got to Montecito, where the Choate hi-fi man lived. On the outskirts of Santa Barbara we drove past these restricted motels. One of them had a sign, 'No Catholics, Children, Jews, Dogs.' Your father tried to register us under the name Cohenbergstein. Have you ever! Such a name! Anyway, we found a place with a six-pointed star in front, and we stayed there. Your father registered us as Commodore and Lady Vanderlip von Vanderbilt. I remember he asked the night manager did they take parrots. The poor night manager was so bewildered. Your father said that some of his best friends were parrots, but he preferred not to sleep near them. Their hooked noses, raucous voices. It was just a preference of his to sleep apart from parrots. That's what he told the night manager."

Nathaniel's mother was laughing. Her laughter—the heaving chest, gasp for air—worried Nathaniel. "Are you okay? Mom?"

She nodded. Explained that Santa Barbara seemed like a place they wanted not to know better, so next morning they turned north, and went home, and stayed home.

"Until Dad left."

"Until I made him leave," said Nathaniel's mother.

Nathaniel shifted a fraction. Toward her. Their bare arms, warmed by the noon sun, touched. He wanted to tell his mother a simple thing, that he wasn't ashamed of her. Anymore. He would have told her this if he hadn't had to tell also how ashamed he had been of his mother and father's squalid mismanagement of their marriage. He would have told her it was all right now, she had returned from the dead. He didn't want her to know that the death he had in mind was a death he had caused, for in his shame he had killed her off, so that nobody could ask him where she was, and why, and how he felt about all that. He had killed her recently, while he lay in the arms of that good girl Polly, beside Paradise Pond, after she grilled him about his history. He mistook her questions for the kind prospective in-laws ask. He'd hedged, dodged, told the plaintive story of his dad's woeful fall from a great height. And then, to his amazement, he had told Polly his mother too was dead, and Polly had comforted him, and he had much enjoyed that comfort. Nathaniel, who hadn't told Polly a single importantly true thing, could not now tell his mother why she was coming alive for him.

"Do you miss Gander?"

"I miss what he was before he was what he was just before he died. I miss my mother, because she's supposed to be alive."

"I think I understand," Nathaniel said.

"Of course you do. You're as bright as a new penny."

And then his mother stood, unbelted her khakis, peeled off her blouse and dove in, slipped as silver as a fish into the soft water of the lake, and swam underwater offshore, and Nathaniel could just make out her scissoring legs. And when she came up for air, way out there, she didn't have to beg him in, or tell him how fine it was in there. He dove right in too, and he knew diving that here was his wish for himself hereafter: to dive headlong.

Gander remembered Nathaniel in his will. Of course. He left Nathaniel his library. Left him enough to pay for Cambridge, some travel, a used car. The interest from the estate was to be administered by Nathaniel's mother on behalf of her mother and then on her own behalf. The principal, in the form of the department store, Gander left to the store's employees, in proportion to the years they had worked there. In addition, the owner of that bazaar invited each of its employees to accept as a gift whatever item, never mind its list price, had caught that employee's eye, "a fancy from your wish-list," as the bequest had it. This last will and testament was thought to be scandalous, capricious, evidence of stone senility. Except by Nathaniel's mother, her mother and by Nathaniel, who had had the advantage—the beneficial interest—of his grandfather's bountiful company, Gander's companionship, Mr. Auerbach's life. The giver's gift was A-OK by his grandson. Oh, and the employees of Auerbach's had no beef with their employer's will. It seemed the entire department store—customers as well as staff—came to Gander's memorial service. All those strangers who cared whether Nathaniel's grandparents lived or died. That was something, wasn't it? To leave so many with such an urge for you?

Gander's memorial service was celebrated in the fusty lunchroom and tea parlor of Auerbach's, a big room overcrowded with people who knew what he'd been, and wished he still was. Nathaniel stood at the far end of a dark-paneled room whose walls were hung with photographs from Seattle's glory days, pictures of lumbermen and stevedores; of Boeing test pilots posed beside the nose of a Flying Fortress and riveters on the assembly line; of importers whose ships had pushed east to the Orient and seamen casting off for Alaska. Nathaniel stood in front of a copper samovar Gander had imported from Vienna, where it had been the centerpiece of a bombed-out coffeehouse near the Sacher. Above this polished samovar hung a photograph of Gander's father, beside a locomotive, shaking hands with James Hill at the Pacific-most limit of the Empire Builder.

"Too many of you asked to pipe up your memories of Gander, so my mom asked me to figure out a ceremony, and what I figured out was to hog the whole thing for myself. Forgive me. Like most of you, I've eaten many a meal in this room. Gander's gone, and my grandmother's not up to this occasion, so let's share a secret: I've eaten better food. No offense to the cooks. The cooks cooked the way Gander wished them to cook:

nothing show-offy, or overdone, or too rare. Nothing you'd have to ask your lunch partner, 'What's *béchamel* mean?' The only hoity-toityness on the menu were scones and those damned finger sandwiches, those tubes of crustless white bread stuffed with spread: cream cheese and pimento? I was with him when he fell for scones and finger sandwiches in Victoria, at the Empress Hotel. High tea. He said his customers needed high tea. His customers got high tea.

"Customers didn't always get what they wanted. I'm thinking of the Appliance Department. 'Third Floor: Housewares, Bedding and Appliances'—Darlene, you've got the best elevator-caller's voice in the Northwest, according to Gander; according to Gander, Frederick & Nelson wanted to hire you away, and when they couldn't, they went to escalators. Anyway, the Appliance Department featured Clay radios, till the Clay company shut down. Customers didn't stand in line to buy Clay radios, but Gander wanted to sell Clay radios, and when Clay went out of business, our salespeople were told to boost top-of-the-line television sets by saying, 'If Clay made a television set, this is the set they'd make.' That was how Gander wanted it, the way it was. I assumed he was loyal to that radio because it had my dad's name on it, and Gander was loyal; sometimes he was indiscriminately loyal. Thinking I knew how he'd answer, I asked Gander why he insisted on selling Clay radios long after customers' verdicts came in on Clay radios. I thought he'd wink at me. Remember his wink? Gander said, 'I sell the Clay because I listen to a Clay, and I like what I hear, and what's the point of owning a store if you can't sell a Clay radio in that store?'

"What was the point of running a store? I thought I already knew the answer to that one. Remember? We all heard it often enough: 'It's a living. I buy at one price, sell at another.' There was more to it than that, wasn't there? Solid, stodgy, durable goods, mostly. But also a display of

our country's fashions and fads and angles, its wit and ingenuity, its profits and losses, your whims and needs, our
big ideas and little dreams. Plus it was fun, the emporium
was. The horn of plenty, cornucopia . . .

"Oh boy, I see my mom flinching. I think she thinks 'cornucopia' is pretty fancy. Not too fancy for Gander to
understand—he understood everything I understand—but too
fancy for him to use. You know how he loved plain speech.
Maybe from loyalty to his dad, who wouldn't have known a
cornucopia from a metaphysical poet. Did you know Gander
liked to read Elizabethan and Jacobean poetry?"

Nathaniel heard the rustle of mourners shifting in their
seats. He imagined himself shifting in his own seat, checking
out the room, stealing a peek at his wristwatch. But so what?
He had more to say.

"He paid for my education, and in return expected me to
correspond with him, share what I had so expensively learned.
I think that's how he found John Donne, though Gander was
a slyboots: he might have pretended to learn about Donne's
'First Anniversary' from me. I don't know how many of you
know Donne's 'First Anniversary' . . ."

Nathaniel heard a significant rustle; he heard murmurs; he
saw someone reach under her chair for her umbrella.

"Wait a sec; time out. I think I *do* know how many of you
are familiar with Donne's 'First Anniversary'; distinguishing
between what's nice to say and what's true to tell is a way to
begin spending my legacy from my grandfather. Donne's 'First
Anniversary' is an elegy on the death of Elizabeth Drury, the
young daughter of the poet's friend. It was composed at a time
when the world, when the cosmos itself, seemed to have tumbled upside down. Whatever good-willed people had known
was now in doubt. Astronomy, natural law, degree, proportion, God's plan and mortal order—it was all open to debate.
Gander loved debate. He didn't fear contingency. But boy oh

boy oh boy was he a sucker for a sad elegy to a dead child. So here are some lines by John Donne that Gander asked me to read aloud to him. They are about the world's mutability and about the aftermath of a gentle person's death:

> 'Nor in ought more this world's decay appeares,
> Then that her influence the heav'n forbeares,
> Or that the elements doe not feele this,
> The father, or the mother barren is.
> The cloudes conceive not raine, or do not powre,
> In the due birth-time, downe the balmy showre;
> Th' Ayre doth not motherly sit on the earth,
> To hatch her seasons, and give all things birth;
> Spring-times were common cradles, but are tombes;
> And false conceptions fill the generall wombes;
> Th' Ayre showes such Meteors, as none can see,
> Not only what they mean, but what they bee.'

"I said earlier that Gander's father wouldn't have shared Gander's appreciation of metaphysical poetry. I probably sell that grand old pirate short. Maybe my grandfather's father didn't know poetry, but he sure as shooting knew this samovar. He used to drink tea and eat tortes and read newspapers in the Vienna café where this samovar came from. My great-grandfather was a pioneer along the Great Northern line. He was in for the long haul. He kept a diary, and Gander gave that diary to me. I've always thought of my great-grandfather as first a writer, because that's how I know him, by the sound of his voice:

> '. . . but I cant figger what the damhell hapened. Used to be Id tell myself lookee here lets say I buy that chunk of timber cheep out by Ponderay on the Priest River and howl I get the dough? Well lets say I sell that chunk for plenty

I got down next to Tumtum on the Spokane River. Thatll be dam good. Thatll be dam good fun. I kin make out dam good on that deal. Before Im done me and Jim Hill will have the hole dam thing. Then lets say I buy out Jim and pritty soon Ill own the hole dam country. Hoo Ray! Used to be like that. What the damhell hapened? The winters aint as cold and the snow aint as deep or as white and the rivers are weak as piss from a chikadees pecker. Now its lookee here be careful Nathan Auerbach dont get big for yore britches you got plenty of trezure you better save it. You got a wife and a bran new kid. You better go home and take care of the trezure you got. You got enuff dough. You had plenty of fun. You showed them pissant skonks you got plenty of brains. Now you better use yore brains to be frends with them skonks. Im a furriner so I got to be nice to them skonks so my kid can be American. Now no more fun. Im thurty now Ill dress nice. And then Ill croak but my bran new kid will live happy ever after. The End.'

No, not happy ever after; and no, not the end. I'm the end, for now. But I won't be the end forever. I promise you, Gander. You were my best teacher, and what good teachers teach stays out there in the world. Now: my mom's hungry. I see more than a few of you eyeballing the snacks; let's eat finger sand-wiches, and tell Gander stories to one another, and fill this room with noise. This room was built to be filled with noise. And after I've eaten my fill, and talked your ears off, and you've talked mine off, after we've traded stories I'm going shopping; I'm going to browse this trading post for a fancy from my wish-list. How about you?"

A front-page story in the *Post-Intelligencer* told of Gander's unremitting generosities, but that was just the obvious part of the old man's legacy. His passion was the thing, the hunger for yet another experience. During Nathaniel's freshman year, while the boy was portaging into the new frontiers of Tuxedo Park and Bala-Cynwyd, Gander had treated himself to flying lessons. Until his body quit on him. If it quit on Gander, it would quit on anyone.

Even on Grandfather Clay. Nathaniel called him Grandfather Clay from pleasurable spite, since the old fart had never acknowledged kinship with Nathaniel save through the evasions of syntactical roundabout: *As your late father's father I write to advise you regretfully . . .* Now three weeks after Gander's pump went, so went that old customer's scarab-hard heart. They were the same age, the two granddads. How could it be—a couple of fellow-citizens, breathing the same republic's air, westerners, entrepreneurs, fathers of two Americans who chose from all other Americans each other—utter strangers? Who would choose to deny community so ruthlessly, choose to banish his son's son?

Thinking these thoughts flying east to Chicago, Nathaniel began to laugh aloud at himself. He heard how sappy his inner voice sounded. *Oh, woe is me! I've been denied! I'm a poor lost abandoned child! Oooo, my grandfather is a meanie!*

"What's so funny?" asked Nathaniel's seatmate, a Navy officer who'd been garrulous since takeoff, crying up the advantages of a career in "Uncle Sam's neatest service."

"You'll have to pardon me," said Nathaniel, wiping from his cheeks the weepy residue of weird laughter at his own expense. "I'm not fit for talk. I've had a family tragedy."

Silence followed this sad news. Who, even Uncle Sam's Warrior, needed this hassle? Tragedy? You could catch tragedy. Gander would have handled this differently. He would have pumped the sailor dry. Where had he voyaged? What had he seen? What was his favorite duty? Favorite port? What was the difference—in displacement and length, firepower and speed—between a destroyer and a destroyer escort? Had he ever been in battle? Had he been afraid? Well, Nathaniel wasn't Gander, more was the pity.

Nathaniel remembered. Rolling into Chicago on the Empire Builder with his heart full of Dee-ah-nah seemed as far back now as Nick Carraway had seemed then. Another time, that is, but parallel to this time, as vivid times will be. Nathaniel was beginning to recognize the destiny he must guard against, the habit of living in time past and time to come, the habit of history.

Nathaniel's late father's late father, history for sure, was remembered by the Chicago *Tribune,* which had reason to appreciate the armadillo's politics, as a Lake Forest clubman who oversaw the decline of his father's radio company and retired young. Nathaniel read the obituary riding by taxi from Midway Airport the day after Mr. Clay had been planted in a Presbyterian cemetery. Why had Nathaniel been summoned here? Long ago—hell, a year ago—he might have tricked himself into some appropriately bittersweet sentiment: return of the exile, acceptance of the denied, reconciliation, blood mingling again with blood. Now he felt inquisitive.

His mother hadn't exaggerated: it was a big house. It was grotesque, insanely fake, like that billionaire Texas cornpone's replica of the White House at a scale of two to one. Turrets, spires, Nathaniel half expected to cross, or be barred from crossing, a goddamned moat. The trees were many, but too small for majestic trees that wished to imply they'd been around a couple of centuries. These trees had been around since the heyday of radio.

He was delivered to Grandmother Clay. She sat straight-backed in a straight-backed unupholstered chair, in very firm control of her grief.

Nathaniel bent past her wispy orange hair to kiss her powdery, parchment cheek, and she recoiled.

"No! Don't! What on earth have you been eating?"

What a tough hide! It almost made Nathaniel proud to come from such stiff stock. Maybe, if a time came when he needed not to bend, he'd give himself a shot of this biddy's unyielding genes.

"Eating?"

"I didn't receive your hateful letter responding to my late husband's request for Henley tickets."

"Must have gone astray in the mail. I sent it, believe me."

She stared at him. The gentlemen standing attendance around her stared at him. Nathaniel flashed to gangster movie scenes, to war movie scenes of the good guy fallen into enemy hands. He wondered if he'd walk out of this ludicrously high-ceilinged drawing room alive. It was a good question. Grandfather Clay had let himself die intestate. Dying slowly of congestive heart disease, he'd made no will. His logic was brutally available to Nathaniel: when Grandfather Clay died, the world died. But why was Nathaniel here? What had any of this to do with him?

"We will of course repay those expenses you have incurred on your detour to Lake Forest. You are to renounce your portion of the estate."

"Oh," said Nathaniel. "How much is my portion of the estate?"

"That is none of your affair."

"I think I've asked an interesting question."

"Your late father's late father disowned your late father."

"Evidently not," Nathaniel said.

"He hated the very idea of your mother and her family. You will release your portion of the estate."

"Jeepers, I think not."

"Don't talk like your mother's tribe. It was not Mr. Clay's will to leave money to an Auerbach."

"Mrs. Clay: if you had got the letter that went astray in the mail, it wouldn't have said to piss up a rope, or to shit in your hat; it would have said, 'Grampa, thanks for making me rich.' Now, will you direct one of these gents—what are you guys? cousins? lawyers?—to call me a cab?''

So much for money. The time was down the road when Nathaniel would doubt the good luck of good money, when he'd wonder *if only:* if only he'd been needier, if only he hadn't had the illusion of a net beneath the tightrope. For now—for a young man full of beans, out on the Cam with his Cambridge crew, set up in Trinity College digs with a sovereign view of the Bridge of Sighs, set up period—a sweet chunk of Clay seemed just divine.

Nathaniel sailed through his first term at Cambridge. He was older than the English boys, and that mattered. To him. He could afford *noblesse oblige,* to let them patronize what quite a number of his college-mates called "our distant colony." The oarsmen recollected with counterfeit rue the regrettable exclusion from Henley in bygone days of chaps who had worked with their hands, manual laborers; English boys *loved* to say "manual laborers." They were ferocious snobs, these tykes from Winchester and Eton, expert at delicately signaled condescension, the feint and jab of slight. Watch them shake hands, or watch a boy from a second-rank public school try to shake hands with a little lord from Harrow: friendly party uncertainly extends hand; superior fails to acknowledge extended hand until extended hand is in process of injured withdrawal; superior hand is thrust, if a limp wrist may be *thrust* forward; friendly hand is puzzled; friendly boy, off-balance, is humiliated; superior boy sneers, just as he thought, second-rank public school produces second-rate, maladroit, fumbling proles. Nathaniel, not three years beyond his experience of Bicker, was amused by the inexorable classifications on British society's Great Chain of Being. Had he forgotten pain? Or was a certain kind of pain now simply beneath interest? Now, to watch two boys not shake hands was vaudeville, nothing more. Of course Nathaniel was a wog, and that made all the difference. He was like a Mohawk or an Iroquois brought to the court of George III; he was a novelty. Not that he was regarded as some monkey freakishly taught to row a shell and parse Pope's *Dunciad*. He was more than a mascot but less than kith, and this was just fine with him. Call him a spectator; call him an outsider looking in, without the least wish to enter. Call Nathaniel, by his lights, grown-up.

He spent Christmas in the Arlberg, skiing at St. Anton with a fellow-American rowing for Cambridge. This was an okay life, no? This wasn't so bad. This was getting to be a lot of fun, being a man of letters.

You did your scholarship on the night train from Paris, and drank some good beer, and woke up in the mountains, and found yourself at noon in a hut perched beside the top of the Galzig lift, drinking *Glühwein*, hearing across the dark room a not unfamiliar voice: "Okay, you guys. Where the dickens are my mittens? Who's hiding Polly's mittens?"

That afternoon they tea-danced in ski boots at the Post Hotel, where Nathaniel was booked. Then they ate dinner at the railroad station, at a long table, a league of nations of young skiers: Americans, Europeans, New Zealanders, Canadians. A bunch from Cambridge, King's College boys, shaking hands with anyone and everyone. No surnames allowed. That was the rule here in the depot. The wood stove pumped heat; their voices rose good-willed. They ate *Gulash-suppe* and the Farmer's Platter; they drank beer and joked about the little horned chamois mounted above the ticket window ("the baggage-handler's first sweetheart"). They laughed and drank more beer and laid plans: to drink more beer and lay plans for the next day: to ski, eat lunch on top of the Galzig lift, tea-dance at the Post, eat dinner at the railroad station.

Polly was installed in a farmhouse on the outskirts of town, dug in (a dollar a night) for the winter. She was a wonderful skier, wonderful. She had come to get better. An Olympic hopeful, someone said of her. She called herself an "Olympic hopeless," and seemed satisfied to be what she said she was. "I was a whizbang in Vermont and—gee—I must have been the fastest skier at Smith College. Now I'm just plain Polly."

She worked at it. At skiing fast, getting stronger, being just plain Polly. The third night she invited Nathaniel to "sleep over" with her, as though they were throwing a pajama party for each other. In bed, huddled under a goose-down cover, looking through rimed panes at a silver moon disappearing now and then in clouds, hearing cows thump against the walls of the barn next door, running their fingers through each other's hair, they talked. Nathaniel knew this was it, the final couple of hundred meters of a win-all lose-all race. He knew this wasn't the night to think too hard, conserve, think the thing through. She wanted to know everything: his mother, his father; she got more than she asked for: Gander, his grandmothers, the accidentally generous Clay. She got the truth, this time. Nathaniel reckoned it was fair, all these questions. Young women needed to know things. It all counted; nothing was casual; he was her prospect; she needed to know where this was leading.

So Nathaniel believed. But Polly didn't seem to require his résumé; she seemed to have no interest in his Dun & Bradstreet. She wanted him to tell her something else, more, always more than he could give. In the milky moonlight she shut her eyes, and touched his eyes with her fingertips. "I'm blind. I can't see you. Tell me what you're like. Everything about you. What you look like. Whether you're handsome, the way a blind person would understand handsome."

"Polly, come on!"

"Shhh," she said. "Just do it."

So he told her, exasperated now, what he thought. That she was true to a type they used to joke about at Princeton, The Sophomore at Smith. Short hair and Big Questions.

Polly thought about this. She said: "What's with your funny way of talking?"

"What funny way?"

"Your dialect. You sound like a truck driver or something. A dock worker. A—"

"Manual laborer?"

"Yeah. It's new on you. Where did you get the voice? Dis inflection id different den duh inflection you usa have."

Polly had a point there. Nathaniel had been marching in London with Ban-the-Bombers. All his resolutions about no more joining, and there he'd gone and joined again, herding with Bertrand Russell's flock in front of the American and the Soviet embassies. And once again his bona fides had been examined by the faithful; just how radical was he? Where had he gone to school? (Cambridge was acceptable to the Brits, but for the one-true-cross American zealots Princeton was the wrong answer: Madison was wanted, C.C.N.Y. would do, Berkeley carried water.) What had been his contribution to the Montgomery bus boycott? Protesting the Nassau Street Woolworth's didn't cut the mustard. This was like Bicker again. Knowing this, Nathaniel had nevertheless begun talking like a grease monkey, a bricklayer, a ventriloquist's dummy.

"My accent is phony," Nathaniel said. "How about yours?"

"Now your accent is gone. Now you sound regular. Like me. I don't have a funny way of talking."

"That *is* your funny way of talking, Polly."

"You're an oddball," she said. "I can't figure you out."

"For instance?"

Polly said she didn't get it with his friends.

Nathaniel told how it was with his friends in the Final Club. How much they meant to him. "My family," he called them. He told all they'd done for him. He even told how he'd come to row, how he'd first rowed the night he was taken in by Ivy, how he happened to be taken in by Ivy, who he was, what Princeton (and *The New York Times*) had considered him to be on the final night of Bicker.

"I just don't get it," she said. "What am I missing here? How have I gone through life till now never hearing the phrase Hundred Percenter? Tell me why I should feel bad not knowing what a Hundred Percenter is, why I should have had strong feelings about Ivy Club. And if you can't tell me those things, tell me the picture you'd draw if a blind girl told you she loved you."

"Marry me," Nathaniel said.

"Say what?" Polly said.

"Let me marry you."

"What?" Polly said.

"Let's marry each other," Nathaniel said.

"Okay. Dandy."

So that was that. Cambridge beat Oxford and later at Henley—ultimate seat race—Princeton. Booth came to that Henley, but not to row. Nathaniel somehow missed hooking up with his friend after the races. Booth was at the wedding, though. Polly and Nathaniel married in Vermont. Her father, a freethinking Vermont lawyer and justice of the peace, married them. He'd been a political oddball in Vermont, a Democratic congressman; he'd run for governor, lost, and during Truman's final year in office the President appointed him Ambassador to Switzerland. Now he was a dairy farmer in Plainfield. Pownall Hamm couldn't come, but that was a story too bleak for a wedding. Nathaniel's mom couldn't come: her doctor wouldn't let her; she sent a telegram, said her doctor was just a sissy, she'd come to his next wedding. Booth was best man, and Mrs. Griggs came, and milked a cow. She explained she'd been raised on a Kentucky farm, but Booth and Nathaniel knew that Mrs. Griggs could do any pleasurable thing; milking a cow was the particular fun thing Polly's farm offered. Mrs. Griggs commanded Polly to take *extremely* good care of her sweetest sweetheart Nathaniel. Diana came, and after the simple ceremony, at the simple reception, Polly told Diana she was sorry she'd always thought of her as a nitwit.

"Nathaniel loves you," Polly said. "He loves you too," she told Booth. "That's good enough for me."

What did Polly mean by "love"? Now here was a subject crying out for study, and Nathaniel was ready, finally, to become a student.

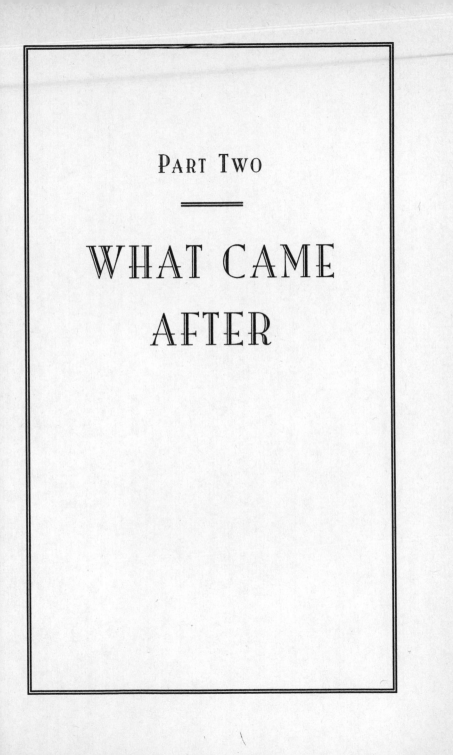

PART TWO

WHAT CAME
AFTER

Seven

Five Years Out: '60 in 1965

NATHANIEL AUERBACH CLAY
("The Face Man")

Residence: Star Route 6, Mad River, Vermont
Occupation: Apprentice writer
Married: Pauline Carr Brownell (1961)
Children: Jacob (3); Ginger (almost 2)
Education Since Princeton: Uncompleted graduate study

We moved up here from New York after Kennedy was murdered. It must be a common story: the whole country seemed to tear up roots last year; farmers moved downtown, urban guerrillas ran to the woods. I picked up a hitchhiker this morning, young woman in buckskins carrying a papoose on her back, hailed from Scarsdale. Is that a dime-a-dozen irony, or what? She asked me what crafts I was into. I said Booth Griggs's Concordia yawl. I was being a dime-a-dozen wise-ass, a Princeton Charlie, a Tiger. The craft I'm really into is being crafty, putting an open look on my face and averting my face. My wife's an aspiring teacher, and she's trying to teach me to speak as openly as I seem to look. So here, five years out, is maybe more candor than she bargained for:

You want me to say how I feel now about Princeton, and I can't. Would I want my kids there? One, being a girl, isn't eligible. Jake? I don't know. Feelings (we've sure been hearing about *them* lately!) shifted when Polly met some of my best Princeton friends. She didn't feel the gratitude I hoped she'd feel on my behalf. "What am I missing here?" she kept saying. What she's missing is my power to articulate fierce emotions. Sometimes I catch a whiff of Princeton on a spring zephyr, perfume. You know. Then I'll catch myself checking the Montpelier *Times-Argus* for football scores, and I'll feel good all Sunday if *we* won. I read the *Alumni Weekly* back-to-front, necrology first. I'm relieved to know none of us have been wasted by that damned war, but I also wonder why. Does this make sense? Then I remember my friend Archibald Barrie. Archie's a cog in the Lyndon machine, and I wish he weren't. But then I remember what kind of cog he is, prosecuting bigots for the Attorney General. I don't like his boss's boss, but Archie's a smart and decent man. Boy, I mean. We're still kids, no? Booth? Pownall? Didn't we laugh? Boy, didn't we laugh!

Seriously, I don't want to be hard on people. I was hard on my mom and my dad. Now their shortfalls seem everyday, what happens to people insufficiently protective of their fortunes, goods, health, reputations.

Here's what I've got to figure out for me and Jake and Ginger (Polly's got it figured on her own): how to protect fortune, goods, health, reputation and also go full blast. I'm trying to write work that I'd like to read, and until I puzzle out this homework—how to secure what I know while I dare what I don't know—I'll have no voice, and I sure don't want to carry apprenticeship to the nursing home, so I'm pulling some fierce all-nighters up here. So I'll have to pass on yet another Reunion; I've got some serious brush to clear.

See you, future willing, at our Tenth, up the P-rade!

BOOTH TARKINGTON GRIGGS
("Booth")

Residence: "The Beeches," Middletown, Rhode Island
Occupation: Self-sustaining buggy nut (called a "Whip")
Married: Diana Carr (1959)
Children: Benjamin Tarkington Griggs (5)
Education Since Princeton: Not Applicable

Not much to tell, really. Few complaints, actually. Like-minded wife and robust son. Keep myself busy with my hobby: horse-drawn rigs. I guess I never progressed past the horse and buggy days. Just now I'm putting the finishing touches on a restoration of a Brewster basket vis-à-vis, with willow basket-work woven over an iron frame. Quite a beauty. I've redone dogcarts, sulkies, shooting breaks—a hearse, even. Oh well, it keeps me off the streets. I also putter with boats, sail rather than self-propelled. Was at Henley June of '61, as a spectator rather than participant. Nat Clay did a wizard job pulling for Cambridge, as I suspect many of you know. For my own part, after graduation I moved my family to Philadelphia, smack on the Schuylkill, Boathouse Row. Gave sculling the old college try with an eye to Henley and beyond. Olympic gold was not to be mined by yrs. trly. Got good enough to be mentioned in any list of twelve American scullers, not good enough to be mentioned if the list were cut to six. There you have it. See you in June at Reunions!

P.S. Where the hell is Pownall Hamm?

(P.P.S. If anyone out there knows of a Thomas Goddard brougham, with or without original accessories, I'd be interested in making an offer.)

POWNALL HAMM
("?")

Residence: Platinum Mountain Retreat, Silver Valley, Conn.
Education Since Princeton: You don't want to know.

Eight

A Lovely Father

Jake Clay
June 1, 1970
Ms. Brownell-Clay
Revision

Once upon a time this little squirt hid in the shower bawling. If somebody called that kid a crybaby somebody'd eat a knuckle sandwich and I'm not kidding. This was long ago, more than a year, and on the day I'm telling about he was crying because he didn't know what to do.

The trouble was school, a tough guy in school whose real name probably wasn't Rudy, but I'm calling him Rudy. By the way, I'm not telling about Rudy Camp, in case someone thinks I'm trying to get Rudy Camp in trouble for what he did to me that fall we were in fourth grade at Mad River Alternative Elementary School. This assignment is a Personal Essay or a Fiction Story, and let's pretend I chose Fiction Stories, which are made up. And this also isn't Rudy Camp's story, because the assignment is to tell about some person who made a Lasting Impression on Your Lives and Why, and I have almost forgotten Rudy Camp, but for sure I remember my dad.

Okay, the person who made a Lasting Impression on this

kid is his dad. My title calls him A Lovely Father because he loved his son to death, and when he heard his son bawling and found him in the shower with the curtain shut he said, "What's the matter, Sweetie?" He was the kind of lovely dad who'd say some goofy word instead of his son's name. Sometimes it was embarrassing, "pumpkin," "hon," "lamb," "snookums," "angel," "precious," you know. And sometimes it sounded phony, especially when he wanted his son to do something: "Sweetums, will you take out the garbage?" "Honeypie, would you fetch me a brewski?" "Pet, how about feeding the goldfish?"

But I'm not ready to talk about pets. To get back to when he found this kid crying in the shower, all hunched down and curled up, cold and not knowing what to do, the dad was worried.

"What's up, Chickadee?"

And the kid told him how Rudy had said if he was nice to Molly any more he (Rudy) would hammer the living *s*-word out of him (the kid crying in the shower).

"Does Rudy like Molly?" this kid's dad goes.

"What do you mean?"

"Have a crush on her, a thing for her."

Oh, boy. This is why you can never tell a man or dad what it's like at school. I mean, they always ask, "What happened at school today, Pookie?" Suppose you *wanted* to tell them the truth. No way! Even a mom who teaches at a school doesn't know thing one about kids. How can a mom, who is a girl, really understand a boy, even if that boy is her property?

Maybe I'd better tell you about Molly. By the way, these names are made up. And something else, I don't want some teacher saying "Here's an excellent paper. Jake, why don't you read your paper out loud. Class, pay close attention to Jake's paper. He's a child prodigy. He's so mature. His voice is so wise. His typing is almost perfect. He's such a freak."

The first thing you've got to realize about Molly is that

when she was a baby she fell on her head. She wasn't dumb, exactly, but she talked slow, and she blinked a lot when people talked to her.

Let's say you asked her to catch fastballs for you. Here's what would happen: "I don't know." Blink. "What do you mean by catch?" Blink.

To tell the truth, it got easier not to ask, just to blast a tennis ball against the side of the house by yourself, or wait till Dan or Greg stopped over, and said, "Your ass, fastball. Put one in here, pussy." (That's the way kids talk, in case somebody is wondering about the vocabulary in my Person Who Made a Lasting Impression paper.)

Maybe Molly blinked, and I'll admit she wasn't what you'd call pretty. Still, she wasn't mean to people, and she washed her hair, and she wasn't obnoxious on the schoolbus, and she never told teachers or her parents that most of the kids in fourth grade teased her. In fact, the only way you teachers found out how Molly felt about herself was because you made us do Strokes and Pullups.

We didn't complain, we didn't know we had a right to complain, but some of us were totally grossed out by Strokes and Pullups. Sometimes I forget which was good and which was bad, whether a Stroke was good, like petting somebody, or a Pullup was good, like somebody helping somebody get to his feet after he got knocked down by somebody. I hope I forget I ever heard those words. But now I remember, Stroke = Good and Pullup = Bad. We couldn't say how we felt about them because they were invented by Stevie's dad, who got lots of money for telling businesses how to talk and feel about how to make lots more money, and how to feel about talking about their feelings about money. It was amazing that he came to Vermont to raise sheep, till his sheep died again, but he got tired of the rat-race I guess. Stevie said his dad made eleventy zillion dollars off Strokes and Pullups in big companies in big cities, and I guess Stevie knew, and wouldn't b.s. about something like that, but as far as I'm concerned, Strokes and Pullups weren't worth zip, even if Stevie's dad was on the School Board, and I've heard some adults say some amazing stuff about Stevie's dad. Still, the same adults, and this is just a fiction story, made us do Strokes and Pullups every Monday morning in Homeroom, and that's how the teachers found out about Molly's Problem.

Here's how they worked. Everybody in the class had to give every other kid one Stroke and one Pullup.

"I think Rudy was brave to fight back when Clyde Greensleeve called him a rich-bitch, and that's my Stroke. But I think he takes too many chances, and that's my Pullup."

"I think Jake is real sensitive, which is my Stroke. But he takes things too seriously, can that be my Pullup?"

And then one of the Alternative School teachers would rub her chin, and look like she'd never heard anything that deep before, even though it was what somebody just said about April before they said it about Jake, which is my hero of this story's kid's name.

Anyway, the teacher would say, "What do you mean by 'too seriously,' Stevie?"

I knew what he meant. He meant I didn't laugh at Molly, and they did. I didn't get some girl to write Molly a note— "Oh, M., I love you so much! Won't you hug and kiss me? xoxo"—and sign it *R.* for Rudy, who was in on it, who even thought it up. And then get five or six of the most popular kids—Stevie, April, Lauren, Mike, Babe and someone else— to hide in a closet while he told Molly he'd let her kiss him on the mouth for a quarter. And when she thought it over and decided to buy him for a quarter, Rudy yelled, "Gross! You got to be kidding!" Maybe I didn't think that was funny, so that was what Stevie meant by "too seriously."

From then on, Molly was out of luck. I used to see her

dad wandering around the woods near our house, with his monster Santa Claus beard and those red suspenders on those itchy wool pants Dad called "bullet-proof," and his chain saw. You better believe that if Molly had told her dad about Rudy, and the way him and his friends would say back to her in her funny voice the sweet things Molly said to Rudy after she read his "love note," all the words sounding the same—like when my sister Ginger does piano practice and hits the C-note over and over until someone hollers at her to quit, and she says, "Have I practiced long enough?"—if Molly's dad knew about that he'd come after Rudy, and a few other kids I could name, with his chain saw. There was a movie about someone who had a chain saw, and got pissed off, and that's how Molly's dad would have felt if he'd known about Rudy and his daughter. It's how my dad would have felt, and how I would have felt, and I used to think about me and a chain saw and Rudy, which is maybe what Stevie meant by "too sensitive."

Molly kept it inside. When Strokes and Pullups came up, she'd be the only one who wouldn't do it, and that made me like her. I don't mean "like her" the way you and Dad mean it, or the way Rudy meant it. Let me put it this way: Ginger didn't tease me about how I felt about Molly. She just didn't screw around with that subject.

You could see Molly couldn't figure out why I didn't jump on her every time she opened her mouth, or every time I saw her coming down the hall. She'd look at me and blink and maybe wonder was I like her. But I wasn't even unpopular, till Rudy decided to make a big deal out of people who were mean to Molly versus people who weren't mean to her.

What made Rudy make such a big deal out of Mean to Molly versus Not So Mean was the smart idea certain teachers had when they figured out some kids were more popular than other kids. Come on. Where did those teachers grow up? Someone's always more popular than someone.

Anyway, the Great Idea the teachers got was The Circle. Remember The Circle? How it worked was every kid in fourth grade was supposed to go to the gym, and use center court as the middle of everything, and sit in a circle as close to the center as we wanted, or as far away, depending on "how we felt about ourselves."

Mom, I know it wasn't your idea, but couldn't you have stopped it?

I'm sorry, I'll get back to this paper. Rudy and April and Stevie, the in-group, laughed and shoved their way to the center. I couldn't believe it. They knew where they belonged; how did they know? Some kids got closer to the middle than they belonged. Others—Joanie and some goody-goody girls— sat on the foul line, farther away than they should have sat. Don't worry, everyone knew where those girls belonged, in- cluding those girls. I didn't know where to go, who to sit with. I'd fished with those kids, played ball with them, shot the bull with them, rid bikes with them, camped overnight with some of them, and I didn't know where I fit in with them.

Molly knew. Boy, did she know. She went to Homeroom, got her book-bag, and her mittens, and her snow-jacket, and walked right through the school doors.

Remember? My favorite teacher asked, "Where are you go- ing, Molly?"

Molly blinked. "Out there."

That was when the laughing started.

"Out where?"

"Where we fit in the group," Molly said.

"Don't be fresh, young lady," another teacher said.

But Molly was gone. And who would have guessed she was that fast? Holy smoke, by the time you guys got parkas on and scraped the ice off your windshields, she was history, halfway home. She was safe with her mom and dad and they didn't make her feel like a piece of crap just because she had freckles and blinked a lot because she fell out of her crib a long time ago and thought Rudy Camp was "cute," which she wouldn't have thought if she hadn't of fallen out of her crib.

And still she wouldn't tell her dad, which is all that saved some sorry shitbird's ass, and I'm sorry I have to talk this way, but when you told us about writing you said, "Find your own voices, boys and girls, and you'll do just fine." And that's my voice. Rudy Camp—not because he wrote a fake love note but because he laughed when Molly walked out the school door, because she couldn't find a place to sit in the game you guys called Circle—is just one sorry sack of shit.

All this happened before My Lovely Father found the kid in the shower bawling. He said, "What's the matter, Sweetie?" That wasn't the best name to call this kid right then, and I went, "Nothing." So he said he knew something had to be the matter, so I said I didn't like to be called "Sweetie." So my dad went, "Look, I called you 'Sweetie' *after* I heard you in here, so I know something is troubling you."

I just looked at my dad, and quit blubbering, and rubbed my eyes. The reason the kid quit was I'd never heard this dad say "troubling you" before, so I figured he figured it was serious. So when he hugged me, which he did at least twice a day and I didn't mind, *that* day I tried to figure was it *really* serious?

It was. We went to his office up in the crows' nest to talk about it. That's another thing I better say about My Lovely Father, how he gave names to everything, like calling his office "the crows' nest" and our lawn "the back forty feet," and how he said Stevie's dad was Number One Asshole in Vermont and Seeded Nationally, which he said even before Strokes and Pullups. Anyway, that night we went upstairs through the kitchen where my mom was cooking dinner. That was when she still cooked dinner for my dad, because he was still around to eat with us, and she said, "What's up?"

"My office. Jake and I are climbing together to have a talk," my dad said.

"What's cooking, Jake?"

Before I could say "nothing" (which must of been my favorite word that night) my dad said, like he was sniffing food, "That's what we were wondering, Polly." My dad answers questions people ask me. He always says something smart, too, but he's a writer, as you know.

Anyway, I sat in Dad's desk chair and he sat on the floor. I guess he wanted me to feel important. Pretty soon he had that you're-driving-me-out-of-my-tree look on his face, because you know me and my hands. First I stapled things to other things, and he pretended not to notice. Then I stamped his rubber stamp on scrap paper, and he just said, "Please, Sweetums."

So I asked him something I'd wondered: "Had they invented toilet paper when you were a kid?"

I don't blame him for laughing, but I didn't ask to get a laugh. I was curious was all. But pretty soon he quit laughing because I was trying out the keys of his typewriter. I don't mean I was writing stuff, but I was tapping them. I loved that typewriter. It was big and old-fashioned, round black keys with gold letters on them, and it didn't jump around the desk like this thing I'm trying to type on now. It wasn't what they call a "portable," which means you can't carry it around with you, but it got carried away anyway, didn't it? I guess though that part's not supposed to be part of this revision assignment.

"Don't play with my typewriter, Jake. Please. Tell me what's the matter. And don't tell me nothing's the matter.

I just found you in the shower, crying, and if you cry, something's wrong, and I want to know what's wrong."

What Dad meant was no more horsing around.

Okay. I told him. The whole thing, what Dad calls "the whole nine yards" or "the whole ball of wax," most of it. How Rudy Camp said if I was nice to Molly any more I was out of the gang, and besides he might even have to climb into my face and eat my lunch, whip my ass. Dad didn't even flinch, but his ears got red, and that made me feel two ways, like it would be a hoot to see what my dad would do to Rudy if my dad caught him whaling on me, and it wouldn't be a hoot. It would be pretty bad news, if you want to know the truth, because after Dad did to Rudy what he'd do, there'd still be Rudy, and there'd be me, and oh boy is all I can say.

I figured Dad would say something like he says when something bad happens to me or Ginger: "Well, screw um, excuse my French." Or he'd just wave the back of his hand, like he was out by the pond brushing off a fly. But instead he said, "That's tough, Jake. That's a tough spot to be in."

This surprised me, and it made me realize that it was a tough spot, and I was in it. So I explained about Strokes and Pullups, and Dad listened, and he said what he said all the time those days, "Goddamned fruit-and-nut-eaters."

Something made me say something uncool. "I don't want to be mean to anyone."

I knew those were the wrong words when I saw Dad swallow hard and dip his head so I wouldn't see his eyes, and I thought oh-oh here he comes, and sure enough, he's on his feet, leaning over the desk chair and hugging me, but he can't get a good grip on me because the chair's spinning around, and he's kissing my neck, and pretty soon I think I ought to be bawling again. But I didn't, because all I'm thinking about is how am

I going to get Rudy Camp off my a-- and still not act mean to Molly, which I don't want to.

And Dad said, "Stay the way you are." That was a nice thing to say, but it didn't help me much with my problem. So I went, "What am I supposed to do in school tomorrow?" And Dad said, "Just what you did today."

Now that made me want to boo-hoo again, because "today" was gone forever; if the Wishwitch was real she'd give me back today, and everything would be the way it was before Strokes and Pullups, except maybe kids would lay off Molly. Then I could be normal to her, maybe even laugh at her when she did something weird. I could hang out with the gang, fish for trout in Kids' Brook and watch Rudy catch suckers all day, and beat the bejabbers (another word I learned from a Writer) out of worms, banging them against the water, while I fished upstream, where the brookies couldn't hear Rudy holler *shit-fuck* because the fish didn't want him to catch them. I may not know it all, but I'm not a moron, so I don't blame the fish for being careful, and I fish close enough to Rudy to have some company but far enough away to catch some dinner.

So Dad's hugging me, and telling me to stay the way I am, there's no need to "come down to their level," and Molly isn't mean, and that makes her better than Rudy. Well, better-than-Rudy is frankly b.s., because if you saw the two of them standing with a bat at home plate in Little League, I don't think you'd say she was better than he was. I don't want to be nasty about this, but when the ball comes toward Molly she BLINKS. And even if the ball accidentally hit her bat, which accidentally poked the pill over the pasture fence (I got "pill" from who I'm calling Rudy, who I'm going to pretend chews tobacco), halfway to the Mad River, she'd still get thrown out at first.

Then Dad gives me more advice. What he says is all I have to do is whack Rudy once in the *face,* and he'll never bother me again. Dad says nobody likes to get one in the "kisser," and it makes them pick on someone else. I'm thinking maybe this is good advice to give Molly, that maybe she should give Rudy a poke in the kisser. (In case you think I'm being sarcastic, dear little precious Ginger has popped a couple of guys, in case you didn't know, but I *am* being sarcastic about Molly.) So Dad is telling me about playground bullies when he was a kid, and how he learned to stand up to them when they hit him in the arm, and if he hit them just once in the face, they'd leave him alone, even if they "beat the stuffing" out of him first. Wow! "Beat the stuffing" out of him. When was the last time someone didn't hear Dad say "beat the shit"? I figured it was time to go to bed and take my problem with me.

"Thanks, Dad. I feel a lot better. I'm kind of tired."

And he smiled that huge smile. And he hugged me, and looked into my eyes, and I guess what he saw made him quit smiling.

"This all sounds like bee-ess, doesn't it?"

"No, Dad. It's just my problem."

"But I want to help. Why don't we talk to your mom?"

"No."

"Well let's at least scarf a little chow."

Dad wouldn't miss his chow if the War was on, right? But I wasn't hungry, so I just sat at the table eating Cheerios and wanting Golden Grahams, listening to Ginger rag on people, listening to Mom tell her not to be so anti, and hearing Dad tell about something that happened to him when he was my age. It wasn't exactly like what was happening to me, but maybe it was sort of like what was happening to me. While he talked Mom pulled at strands of her hair, and looked out the window a lot, or at the food, or at her spider plant to see if it was dry, and behind Dad's back Ginger made a humungous yawning face, like she does, like whatever someone else was saying was the most boring thing that had ever been said in the history of the world.

I went to bed. Mom didn't make me practice the piano, because she knew something was up. Maybe Dad whispered something to her. Ginger didn't hassle me. Mom came to my room to say goodnight, and Dad came to my room to say goodnight. He brushed my hair out of my eyes, and that was great in the dark, and he hugged me hard, and I hugged Dad back, and we both meant our hugs. Not like the hugs in the office, because down in my room he shut up.

The next morning Ginger woke me up, of course. It's like she has to prove something. Like look-at-me-I'm-up-first. She throws a pillow at me. She can be a pain.

As soon as I was awake I knew I wouldn't go. School was out. No Rudy. No Molly. Forget Strokes and Pullups. I didn't know much, but I knew I'd taken my last Stroke and given my last Pullup.

Mom came down and saw me sitting in bed, looking out my window at our favorite tree, what Dad calls the "electric birch," because it's colorful, I guess. I've never told anyone this, but for a whole summer after he gave it that name I was scared to touch it, like it was an electric eel?

"Jake? Do you want to tell me what's going on?"

I knew Ginger was in the hall, listening. Why does she always listen? She doesn't care what anyone says. She hears something, it doesn't matter what, and pretends she's yawning. I didn't care if she was listening: "This is my worst year ever in school."

"You've only had less than five, including kindergarten." Ginger, of course.

"Shut up, Ginger," Mom said. "What's going on?" Mom asked.

"It's just not a very nice day is all," I said.

"Better than no day at all," Ginger said. But she didn't say it snotty. She sounded kind of scared, and one thing about this kid's little sister, better believe it, you can't *scare* her. I know. I've tried.

Mom said she had to go to school, "and so do you, Young Lady," and I should stay home and take it easy, and maybe tomorrow I'd feel better.

Sure.

A Lovely Father said, "Let's drive up to African Park Safari." He said the theme park's name in American to make it easier for me, but I'd heard its real name about a million times on TV in Canadian, Parc Safari Africain; it was this place on the way to Montreal, about three hours from our house. Molly had been there, and she said there were giraffes and lions running around, and I think elephants, and also animals that would be freaked to see a lion, black bears, for example. I'd wanted to see that place from the minute I heard about it, but I never told Mom or Dad I wanted to, so it's just another example of this dad's ESP that he knew exactly what would make this kid happy.

I guess I'm the only person in our family who believes in ESP. I don't like to say what I believe, because every time I try to talk about it some mother or father tells the story of that time Ginger heard me looking for my mittens, when I guess I must have been talking to myself, which is not exactly maybe a crime. Ginger told everyone what she says I said: "God gave me ESP, but he took away my findability. God," I guess I yelled pretty loud, so I could be heard, "take back the ESP and let me find my mittens." This story breaks up my Mom and Dad. I mean it makes them laugh. It used to.

Whenever something makes me sad, my dad takes me to see animals. When I was really little, and Ginger and I were fighting, or maybe I was mean to her before she was old enough to be mean to me, which she is old enough to be now. Dad would take me to some barnyard to buy an apple and cider and look over the fence at the "critters," which is what he called them.

Jeezum crow, I watched a lot of cows and sheep when I was little. And it isn't like my lovely dad is a vet, or even an expert on "varmints," which he also calls them.

He's the guy who called the Greensleeves and told Claude Greensleeve, who's a farmer and cuts our hayfield and already thought we're "flatlanders" or "leaf peepers," or "snowbirds" (because we ski sometimes), or "shitbirds" (because we drove a Volvo with a weird-looking humpy back . . .) anyway, Dad told Mr. Greensleeve: "I hate to bare sad tidings, Claude, but I believe your horse is dead."

After Dad explained he hadn't shot the "beast," or hit it with our Volvo, he told Mr. Greensleeve his horse was dead because it was lying down. Mr. Greensleeve told my dad it was lying down because it was sleeping. "Oh," I heard my dad say. I wish he'd stopped talking, but of course he didn't. "Oh, well good for it. I hope Old Dobbin has sweet dreams of hay and sugar lumps." Mr. Greensleeve told Clyde Greensleeve, who of course told Rudy on the schoolbus, so what Dad said to Mr. Greensleeve wasn't exactly a secret from the kids.

The other reason I can't figure out why Dad always takes me to animals to cheer me up is how he feels about them. Everytime the subject gets around to buying a cat or a dog or a gerbil, count on Dad to say that thing he heard our first year up here, "The only good pet is the pet in your freezer." He sure thinks that is funny.

The other reason I couldn't figure Dad and animals is the business that happened with the Worths up the hill from us. My lovely father read in the Montpelier paper how coyotes were making a comeback in Vermont. "It seems some sheep have been killed," Dad told us at dinner, as though we should hide our sheep, if we had any, or Stevie's dad, the Strokes and Pullups inventor, should guard his sheep, if they hadn't already been killed by Stevie's dad's "terminal assholery," as some kid's dad called Stevie's dad's problem. Anyway, remember how we heard howling every night that winter and Dad went ape? He came down and sat on our beds and said, "Jake, Ginger, listen to that! Pure wildness! That's a coyote," except he said it "ky-oat," like in cowboy movies. It sure was loud. Dad said it was beautiful noise, untamed, "absolute assertion," whatever that is.

Dad was excited, and I think he wrote a piece about it, about wildness versus tameness. So was he pissed when he found out that it wasn't a ky-oat making all that noise. It was Mr. Worth's Irish setter Tim, who was freezing his buns tied to a tree while Mr. Worth tended bar at Little John's after Mrs. Worth moved back to Hartford. So now Dad got excited in a different way, and called Trooper Winooski, and complained every night, and said it wasn't fair to the neighbors or the "poor animal," and Dad likes to be teased, but for sure not about Tim, the ky-oat.

Driving up to Parc Safari Africain Dad asked me if I wanted to talk about Rudy and Molly, and I said no. Well, he said, what do you hanker after for your birthday? I told him something that wasn't wooden, something plastic, that ran on batteries and made noise. I'd never told Mom and Dad that wooden toys were boring, because The Vermont Toyman builds them right near us in the Mad River Valley, so every kid who wasn't born in the Mad River Valley, every kid whose Mom and Dad "didn't need the rat-race," every kid like Ginger and me has a whole box filled with wooden cars with wheels that are too big, and don't look like any car you've ever seen, and aren't even painted, and with unpainted train engines that you wouldn't want in a nursery school, and unpainted wood airplanes that you'd never want to make an airplane noise with but you wouldn't mind watching it fly off the roof, if you get what I'm driving at. Maybe I'm being rude about wood toys, maybe I feel this way because my cars and trains and airplanes are what's called "factory seconds," but as far as I'm concerned, if I still liked toys, I'd prefer styrofoam, I'm sorry.

We were on this back road north of Burlington, and Dad was talking. The leaves were gone, and it was coming on deer season, and Dad was telling about how the "herd" in Vermont was bigger than anytime in the century, and he was going on about "herd management" and "overbrowse," and how a hunter had brought a cow into a weigh station, which I'd heard him tell before, as you know. He was saying how the reason we didn't have a dog was because hunters would "drop it, sure as shooting," which was b.s. in my opinion, because the reason we didn't have a dog was dogs tangle with porcupines and skunks, and I remember Dad watching Mr. Worth when Mr. Worth was still his friend wash Tim off with V-8 juice after Tim got skunked, and I remember how I knew then, watching my lovely father watch Mr. Worth and Tim, that one thing I'd never have was a dog.

We were talking about dogs, or Dad was, when it happened. I remember the noise: *slap-slap*. To tell you the truth, I heard it—something like the noise when you got really pee-ohed at me when I shoved Ginger off the piano bench, and you whacked me with my slipper—but I didn't see it. I knew it was bad because Dad said, "Oh, wow!" He stood on the brakes, and we swerved off the road, and hit the fencepost, and the radiator went *hissssss*.

Dad jumped out, and I thought he'd look at the car and say, "This piece of shit of a Volvo B-18," the way he used to, but instead he headed back toward home, running, and I couldn't figure it out, even when I saw him bending over.

He didn't want me to follow him, but I did anyway. Okay. Well, I guess we were on Route 7, near a town called Georgia Plains. *What My Lovely Father Was Looking At:* Okay. Two dogs. I know you said that on this revision you want us to "concentrate on details and be specific and try to describe instead of just tell." But I don't want to be specific. One of the dogs was gray, kind of fuzzy like a sheepdog in a kids' book, but smaller. That one was dead. That's it for Dog #1. Dog #2 was yellow, part collie, and it had been chasing Dog #1, sort of grab-assing I guess, when they headed across Route 7, paying attention to each other instead of traffic, which there wasn't any of anyway, except us, or the geeky looking Volvo with the humpy back, which was up around seventy I think, even though Dad said forty, which I know he believes, but I've got to go with seventy.

About Dog #2: It was all crooked, and blood was coming out of its ear, and that's all I want to say about Dog #2, except it was still alive, and looking up at us, like *what the hell?*

Dad had stopped saying "oh, boy," and was petting Dog #2 between its ears, which was the only place he could pet it without maybe hurting it worse, and Dog #2 was sort of trying to bite my lovely father, who didn't seem to notice he was almost getting bitten.

There was a farm down a driveway, and Dad told me to go there, and find somebody. I was scared. Mostly I was scared they'd send Dad to prison for what he'd done, and all I could think was how fast it had happened, and how it was so weird that you could do something that made your whole life different, and all you heard was *slap-slap.*

"Go," Dad yelled. "Move!"

I hauled ass. I wanted to get there, and I didn't want to get there. I started hollering when I passed the silo, but no one hollered back. Pretty soon I heard a noise, a car going sort of *barooom-barooom*. The car was in the barn, with a number on it, like the stock cars that race at Thunder Road in Barre, which as you know Dad calls "gay Bear-ee," for some reason.

I had to yell for them to hear. There was a guy bent over the engine, and another inside the car. The guy inside was older than Dad, and the guy fiddling with the engine was younger than Dad. I said, "Help, my dad's hit a couple of dogs." I was right next to the younger farmer when I said it, but he didn't look up at first.

He said: "You're on private property."

I said: "Two dogs need help."

He said: "Two what dogs?"

I said: "Please."

By this time the old guy in the car had shut off the engine. He heard about the dogs, but he just said the *s*-word, and said to the young guy who looked like him: "That's three since spring."

"That's a hat trick," the young guy said, and I didn't know what he meant by that, but I know now, of course, but then I have to admit I thought they were talking about some kind of magic, and I even thought that maybe those dogs were playing a trick on us, and they'd be okay, even though I also couldn't see how that would work.

"You'd best git," the old guy said. He said it quiet, but it scared me the way he said it, and when he turned the engine back on, and raced the motor, I knew I'd better get out of there, and I did.

When I got back to the road, there was my dad, standing next to You Know Who from my first draft.

She was bent over Dog #2, and touching it all over, and talking to it, so I didn't see then how pretty she was. I saw how the other dog, #1, was sort of stiff now, and how its tongue was out and gray as its fur. I knew Dad was going to jail for this, and I also knew it wasn't his fault, and I felt like bawling, which was exactly what got us to this back road in Georgia Plains: bawling.

She turned around. Boy, was she pretty. I'm sorry, but she was, and that's just the truth. She looked at my dad, and said: "He's got to be destroyed."

I knew what that meant.

Dad said, "Are you sure?" She nodded. Dad said, "This nice person knows a lot about animals." I'll say she *looked* like she knew a lot about animals. She had long yellow hair, and a soft face, a big face, if that makes any sense. I know you said in my revision I should cut some of the characters, how this is way too long, how the woman is "incidental to the action," but that's wrong.

The pretty girl was smiling. She never quit smiling. It was like she had been told that the minute she quit smiling she'd get sent to her room without her supper.

Dad told the pretty girl, "This is Jake." I would have shook hands, but she was busy with Dog #2, and it didn't seem important to be polite.

"And who are you?" she asked my dad.

"I'm Jake's father. Is the pup going to make it?"

She shook her head. "Howdeedo, Jake's father." Then she said her name.

Then Dad said his name, *Nathaniel.*

"Nat, or Nate?" the pretty girl said.

Dad gave her a hard look, and kind of cocked his head at her.

"Let's get a gun," the pretty girl said.

I didn't like the sound of that.

"Who's at the farm, Jake? This is my son, Jake. Did I introduce my boy, Jake? Jake, who's there?"

"Two men. They aren't nice."

"Do they own the dogs?" the pretty girl asked.

I shook my head, but I wasn't really sure they didn't own the dogs. It was something about them. I just wasn't sure.

"We can probably get a gun there," my dad said.

"I don't think they'll help us," I said.

"I'll stay here," the pretty girl said. She was holding Dog #2's head in her lap, and it wasn't trying to bite her, maybe because it liked her better than it liked my dad, or maybe because it was too tired to care about biting anyone. "Take my car," the pretty girl said. "The keys are in it."

Her car was a Bug. The front seat was a mess. Candy wrappers, and Hostess Twinkie wrappers and in the back seat was a big, fat, gray cat. I sat on top of the wrappers, and Dad got the Beetle going, and we drove straight to the barn where the stock car was with 83 painted on its doors. #83 had humungous rear wheels, and was way up in back, like a slot-car. It wasn't painted any color, just what's called a primer coat, I think. I was afraid, but I noticed these details. I hope the details help you like this Revision.

Dad told the two farmers what had happened, and asked if they would put #2 "out of its misery."

"I'll tell you about misery, mister. I'll *show* you some misery if you don't get off my land."

"The dogs—" the dad said.

"I don't care squat about dogs," the older man said.

"Won't you please shoot the dog," the dad said. "Please."

The younger guy laughed.

"May I borrow a shotgun?" the dad asked.

"No one uses my weapon," the younger man said.

My lovely father looked at them, and I was afraid he was going to do something awful to them, hurt them, or say something dangerous to them. "If that's the way you feel about it," the dad said. "Could you direct me to a vet, or perhaps a sheriff?"

When the farmers didn't even look at the lovely father, but studied #83's engine, we got back in the Beetle, or Bug, or whatever it's called, and drove back to the Scene of the Accident.

Dad explained to the pretty girl, who said, "They're just ignorant, suspicious Green Mountain Boys." I didn't like to hear that, because the club me and Stevie and Rudy started before the Molly problem was called the Green Mountain Boys.

The pretty girl was from St. Albans, not far from Georgia Plains, and she knew a vet there. The dumb Volvo wasn't going anywhere, so we all piled into the Bug. She drove, and the dad sat beside her holding the fat, gray cat in his lap. I don't like to remember the rest, but I was in the back seat, with Dog #2 sort of in my lap. The dog was twitching, and bleeding, but not bleeding a lot. The cat was doing what a cat does when she's near a dog, and my lovely father was trying to hang on to it, and all I can say is there was a lot going on in the car.

At first Dad kept looking back at the poor dog, and at me, and he was saying: "Oh boy, oh boy, boy oh boy, I'm so sorry, I'm just so sorry," and the pretty girl was sorry too, and she must have felt sorry for my lovely father, because she started stroking him the way she had stroked the dog beside the road, gently, saying soft things I couldn't understand, because in a Bug the engine is in the back right behind me and Dog #2.

Then the lovely father began talking to the pretty girl, and looking more at her. The pretty girl was dressed regular, but she was pretty. It was what you'd notice first about her. My lovely father got the cat to settle down, and I could hear it purr even though the engine was so loud, and Dog #2 was making noises too.

"She's been a naughty girl with some old tomcat," I heard the pretty girl say. "She's heavy with child. I guess it's just human nature."

I didn't think this then, but I think this now, one word for what the pretty girl said about her cat and human nature: *dee-you-em-bee*.

Things speeded up when we got to the vet. He was closed. It was Wednesday, and on Wednesday he was closed. His sign said GONE HUNTING.

"We've got to do something," I said. Dog #2 was gasping, and shaking all over, and its eyes were wide open, and I was amazed at everything that had happened to me and to Dog #2 and to this dad.

The pretty girl had an idea. I said, "no!" Dad said "no" too. But it happened. I guess there was no choice. The girl put Dog #2 in front of the wheel, and I was supposed to look around to see if anyone was looking, I guess so they wouldn't have to go to prison, and the lovely father drove the car forward, and did it, and I heard the noise, and I'm sorry I remember it.

And then they took Dog #2 to the Vet's back door, and left him there on the mat, and then they drove to the pretty girl's apartment, where the dad called Triple-A about the humpback Volvo murderer, and then Dad and the pretty girl cooked coffee, and drank beer, and talked about whose idea it had been to put that dog out of its misery, and then they got bored talking about the dead dog. I could hear them talking, even though I was watching TV in the bedroom and they were listening to the Beatles—who this Lovely Father usually hated. Sgt. Pepper. Lucy in the sky. Let It Be. Dad was telling about the bunnies, and I don't care if that's a little kid's word for rabbits, because they weren't rabbits yet.

The Bunnies. Maybe you remember. Dad was mowing the "back forty feet," and he looked down at a place he had already cut and saw these three little things that moved. He called me and Ginger. They were bunnies. You could tell by the shape of their ears, even though they were as big as a thumb. There had been four. The ones that weren't mangled were blind, with their eyes shut tight, and I tried to think how scared they must be. Maybe they had been lying in the sun next to their mom's fur, and then here comes the Lawn Boy, and Mom's down the road. A Lovely Father said, "Gentle, gentle," when we put them in a shoe box, how people will with little animals. I put some lettuce in there, and a carrot, which Ginger explained (and how) was *extremely* stupid, which I saw right away it was. We took turns trying to get the bunnies to lick milk off our fingers, all day and night; me or Ginger guarded them while me or Ginger slept, and we talked to lots of people about how to help the survivors eat, but no luck, and Mom and Dad finally said their time was up.

That was true, too. Me and Ginger knew it, in case someone thinks we hold it against the grownups. It was decided someone had to "do them in." Dad decided to drown them. He put the box with the bunnies we hadn't even named yet because Mom and Dad said it was a bad idea to give them names and get too attached to them inside a white "Medium" garbage bag. He also put a stone in the plastic bag, and we brang everything to the Covered Bridge, where Dad said he'd "do the honors." The thing was, the stone fell out when he dropped the bag, and somehow the shoe box and the white bag stayed on top of the water, and we could see one of the bunnies in the box, blind, floating down the busy Mad River toward the Ocean, and I thought, What am I supposed to think about this?

I heard Dad tell about the bunnies, and I thought I heard him *laugh*. I thought maybe it was the Beatles laughing, so this kid pretended he wanted another Pop Tart so he could see if his lovely father had laughed about what happened to the bunnies, and maybe he hadn't, because the pretty girl looked mad, like maybe she'd never smile again, and they were both quiet when they saw me, but they "popped another brewski" and started telling each other about their lives, and then drank more beer, and some of what I heard from the bedroom while they listened to Janis Joplin and the Buffalo Springfield was true, and some wasn't, but none of it had a thing to do with Rudy and Molly, or with me, or with the lovely father's wife.

This kid isn't ashamed to say that kid felt like bawling. I'm not ashamed. I feel like crying right now, even if me and Ginger are going to the P-rade Saturday with a lovely father we haven't seen recently because some teacher can't tell the difference between a fiction story and true facts. If I cry I sure won't crawl behind a shower curtain to do it. Whether I'm crying now or not crying now, that's for me to know and you to find out.

Nine
Going Back: 1970

Squalls rolled in on the home front, trouble following trouble like sullen heaps of black cloud. Polly stormed; Nathaniel was scared. A week before his tenth reunion he called his mommy.

Sarah Clay came through, and so it was that on a fine June morning Nathaniel sat eating creamed chicken hash in the Plaza Hotel dining room with his son and mother and daughter.

"Isn't this nice?" he said. "Here we are. All together."

"Except for Mom," Jake said.

"Except for Mom," Nathaniel said. "Those are pretty flowers in that vase, don't you think?"

"I guess," Ginger said.

"Polly should be here," Nathaniel's mother said. Nathaniel thought his mother's sentiment was ironic; his mother would not, given Polly's torts, have been here. More precisely, she would not have been here unarmed.

"Well," Nathaniel said, "she didn't want to come, I think."

"Think?" Ginger said.

"Know," Nathaniel said.

"Ginger," Mrs. Clay said. "I showed you Seattle, and I showed you Vancouver. I want you to show me New York this morning." She looked out the Plaza's high window at the open carriages lining Central Park South. "I want to ride in one of those buggies. Ginger, will you do that for me? Will you take me for a buggy ride?"

"I'm broke," Ginger said.

"I'll loan you some money," Jake said. "I'll take us for a ride."

The waiter came with the check, and gave it to Mrs. Clay, who slid it across the table to her son. "We'll get the money from your old man," Mrs. Clay said to Ginger. "Let's leave these guys to their own mischief. Let's beg some money from Nathaniel. He's loaded."

"Mother, don't start in on me. I don't like to talk about money in front of the kids."

"I do," his mother said. "Crazy me, I'll talk about anything."

"Mother!"

"Your dad is loaded," Mrs. Clay told Jake. "Your father has deep pockets," Mrs. Clay told Ginger. "Let's get some dough from him, ride in a carriage and go shopping. Let's buy out the town. Let's"—she grasped Ginger's wrist—"buy clothes!"

"Okay," Ginger said. "Great," Ginger said. "Great!"

"How about me?" Jake said.

"You get the surprise," Mrs. Clay said. "We get the fun of buying you a surprise, and you get the fun of getting a surprise."

Nathaniel said, "It's all surprise in this life."

"Oh, my," Mrs. Clay said. "Hea-*vee*. Deep."

"Mother? Please?"

Mrs. Clay kissed her son on his cheek. She said, "Life is a surprise. That's okay. Surprise is okay. You'll be okay. Polly will. Jake will be okay. Ginger, you'll be okay."

"Promise?" Ginger said.

Now there was a new one. Nathaniel had never never

never heard Ginger ask for a promise. Ginger didn't believe in promises.

"Promise," Mrs. Clay said.

Next day, coming down from New York with Jake and Ginger that hot Friday afternoon, Nathaniel saw a fight on the train. The Pennsy was going tits up, and rumor had it the railroad discouraged passengers so it could haul nothing but freight, a more gainful cargo. For sure there were fewer seats than riders this early June day, and these rush-hour commuters seemed to be deliberating why they were hostage to a train air-conditioned in winter and heated in summer; not a few of the hunter-gatherers might even be speculating whether early retirement might not be just the ticket, whether the moment might not be ripe to cash in the inflated homestead, whether the time was not propitious for a lifelong vacation in the Society Islands on a Hinckley yawl, or on Ramrod Key with a cute teen.

Standing sweat-soaked in the aisle above his seated children (this was supposed to be a treat, fun for all), waiting to depart Penn Station, Nathaniel watched a man in a chalk-striped worsted suit try to sit beside a man in a chalk-striped worsted suit. The man in a chalk-striped worsted suit seated ahead of Jake and Ginger said, without looking up from his *Post,* "Saved."

"You can't save a seat on this train."

"Well, you can't sit in this seat." To prove this was so, the speaker slid to the aisle, leaving the window seat empty. The other gentleman tried to force past him, and they began to shove at each other.

Ginger nudged Jake. Nathaniel shook his head, the eternal gesture of parental warning—*Behave, kids*—in a public place, on a public conveyance. Moms shook their heads this way at little Cabots on the *Mayflower;* caveman dads shook their heads at their litter huddled around the first communal fire.

Nathaniel saw that just when he thought he'd seen it all, he still hadn't seen it all. A carload of commuters reading their closing-market reports decided not to notice a man, early forties, who wanted to sit down, sobbing and wheezing. His face was red, and he was swatting an older man with a *Wall Street Journal,* whacking at the older man's panama hat. The older man batted his attacker with the *Post,* till they both stopped. The train jerked and groaned, and entered the tunnel to the Jersey Flats; his spunk spent, the seated man said, "I guess my companion missed the train." He slid to the window, the other man in a chalk-striped worsted suit sat beside him, and they read their mangled papers, just like everybody. Never happened.

Jake was looking up at him: "Is this train the train you rode to Princeton when you were a kid?"

Ginger rolled her eyes: "Does this train have a sleeping car, Jake? Does it? Because *if* it does, I'm going to sleep, and wake me up when we're home in Vermont."

"Don't be such a priss," Nathaniel said. "Jake's right; I did ride a train from New York to Princeton my first day there. But no, this isn't it. Or like it."

Bet on that. This was not even a clumsy counterfeit. This was a jail cell on wheels, what they were calling these days a people-mover. It dead-ended in glum Trenton (beside the tracks a sign complained: "Trenton Makes; the World Takes") and passed through a hellscape so often and so floridly narrated that Nathaniel couldn't see it plain. Newark, Bayonne, Elizabeth, the Secaucus Flats: these were wastelands of legend, right up there with the valley of ashes over which the eyes of Dr. T. J. Eckleburg keep watch. To the right Esso's refineries were belching sulphur.

"Peee-yew," said Ginger.

"That stands for Princeton University," Jake said.

"Smarty-pants," Ginger said, smiling.

Debarking at Princeton Junction, Nathaniel guided his children into a menacing, piss-soaked tunnel; the humorless graffiti glistened with sweat. On the other side of the tracks they emerged blinking into bright sunlight, and Nathaniel saw he had been disoriented; his memory had played a trick on him, because now they were on the northbound track, beside a grim parking lot, and back there, just where they had entered the tunnel, waited the two-car train, humming on a siding spurred off the main line: the Dinky.

"I just wanted to show you both sides of the track," Nathaniel said.

"Thanks, Dad," Jake said.

"Sure," said Ginger.

"You're getting on my nerves, precious."

"Dad," Ginger said, alarmed, "puh-leeze don't call me the *p*-word."

"Maybe I won't and maybe I will. Watch your step. I mean watch it getting on the Dinky. Preciousest."

"Dad."

"You be courteous to your brother—"

"I'm going to throw up."

"—and sweet as pie to your daddy."

"Tell Jake to quit giggling. It's immature."

"Jake, your puh-*rice*-less little sister requests a show of maturity from you."

Jake laughed. The Dinky pulled out with a squeak, like a ride at an amusement park.

"Okay, kids, look sharp. There's Walker-Gordon Dairy. Let me tell you, when the wind blew wrong we used to get a hairy blast of cowness downwind at Pyne Hall. Where I roomed freshman year?" Ginger was staring at him, a remarkable likeness of rapt attention. "Have you kids heard of Athens?"

"Sure," said Jake. "Athens, Greece: it's famous. The Cradle of Democracy."

"Right. Well, they call Princeton the Athens of New Jersey."

"Because it's a cradle of democracy?"

Nathaniel pondered the question. He might have invoked James Madison and Woodrow Wilson. John Foster and Allen Dulles. Princeton in the Nation's Service. Wasn't a Continental Congress held in Nassau Hall? Wasn't Princeton—for a day, maybe a week, maybe even longer—the Nation's Capital? Modern times: wasn't crew an entirely democratic endeavor? Row fast, first boat; row slower, second. Wasn't the democratic reality of crew precisely why Booth Tarkington Griggs had quit crew? Wasn't the Final Club an association open to all (within the bounds of merit and fellowship and dinner-jacket ownership)? No, the Final Club wasn't. Nathaniel said: "No, Jake. Princeton is not a cradle of democracy. They call it the Athens of New Jersey because it's got a lot of culture going for it."

"Do they call Athens the Princeton of Greece?"

"I guess they must, precious."

Nathaniel felt anxious coming back here with his kids. Proprietary, avid to have them proud to have a father who lived here four years. But why should his children take pride in such a thing? Their hearts should beat fast because their dad had rest-stopped at an oasis? Because that was Princeton's most telling reality: oasis. Despite discord high and low this year, the past half-decade, Princeton had endured few insults to its tranquility. It would be nice to imagine the University's civility could be thanked, but Nathaniel knew better. This place was governed by smugness, the self-assurance of oasis-dwellers who can just barely see the god-awful desert beyond these date palms and fig trees, who are sure that by the authority vested in having rested here four years their children are obliged to feel pulse-racing pride.

On the other hand: ease up. At such a time in such a world, repose could be a virtue. Nathaniel, quondam Vermonter, could get behind repose. Didn't the entire country, if only it knew it, yearn to hole up in safe ports like Princeton, and watch the sun rise and go down?

"Look!" Jake said. "We're here!"

Nathaniel thought the commuters filing out looked like the guys the guys in the Final Club had sworn they'd never look like. The commuters didn't look so hot. Okay: *hot* they looked, but not so great. Mature, but unsecured . . . floating. Dizzy. Today, greener than he knew, he thought he recognized who was a commuter and who was not. But he didn't know a thing about these men—and they were all men—wearing suits and carrying briefcases. He didn't know this one had made a victory of his perennial beds (*mano a mano* against aphids, bulb mites, slugs, thrips, scab, leaf blight, scorch, crown rot, tulip fire, hares and voles), or this other forgave his daughter for stealing from his wallet, or this one here took pride in his work and at home played the mandolin like a trouper. Nathaniel knew nothing of the mineral collection of that perfect stranger yonder, of another's passion for birds.

That gangly fellow up the platform, last off, an object of puzzled attention carrying his effects in a shopping bag, dressed for Christ's sake on an afternoon train in an ancient double-breasted dinner jacket, was no commuter. Pownall ducked unnecessarily stepping from the Dinky to the platform. Tall, he wasn't that tall. Pownall was even skinnier now, slope-shouldered, loose, graceful and goofy. His short hair was untamed: sprigs stood straight up. He greeted Nathaniel with a wave and a loopy grin.

Nathaniel hugged him, introduced him to the kids. Ginger tried a curtsy. This was a move Nathaniel had not seen Ginger attempt till now.

"They shrank your poplin suit," Pownall said.

Nathaniel, feeling the weight on him, sucked in his gut. "They sure didn't shrink your tux," he said. Pownall's dinner jacket hung on him like a poncho, and great folds of his pleated trousers were gathered by a worn khaki belt, Marine Corps issue, cinched tight. "I feel like a bozo," Nathaniel said, without knowing why.

"We are bozos," Pownall said, taking in with a sweep of his hand the crowd milling purposefully around the toy depot for a toy train with a silly whistle, the grinning students busting out of town after exams, the bankers and brokers and editors and academics searching for their crosspatch wives seated distracted in prudent Volvos. Pownall said, "We are," and ran his hand through Jake's hair. "But so what if we are?" Jake grinned. Ginger seemed to be thinking.

Nathaniel hefted his sturdy plastic suitcase toward a taxi. "Sensible grip," Pownall said.

When they were students, and Nathaniel learned from Pownall that a full boat didn't always win a pot but a player must bet as though it would, Pownall used "sensible" to describe fellows with "teensy sets," belt-and-suspenders boys who balanced their checkbooks, sent their laundry out in plenty of time to get it back before vacation, holed up in Firestone Library carrels ("weenie bins") from September to February to leave time for a revision of the thesis (due in April) prepared by a professional typist. "Sensible grip" would have stung back then, but now there was no death sentence in Pownall's verdict. Down on his luck, looking hard at his own hole cards, Pownall had merely noticed the defining feature of a dun, damage-resistant suitcase.

"Pownall. Pownall. My God, it's been ten years."

"So it has."

"I'm glad to see you," Nathaniel said.

"I know you are," Pownall said.

After a campus tour, and a supper for the kids at the Annex
(a basement bar and grill across Nassau Street from the library
and a sanctuary from learning), Nathaniel took Jake and Ginger
to their room at the Nassau Tavern, and settled them in front
of a television screen. The big story was a trial of black militants
up in New Haven, and the fallout on Yale was heavy. Pickets,
placards, upraised fists, slogans, reflexive fury: rancor was general over America that night, as on many a recent night before,
and it puzzled Nathaniel to watch his children watch this and
that riot with sleepy lids and sweet faces; Ginger pulled at her
hair, a habit taken from her mother, and Jake scratched a bug
bite and guys from Yale threw rocks at cops.

Nathaniel dressed, and sat at the foot of the bed. He caught
Ginger's eye, and nodded her to him, and she sat in his lap.
She was wearing soft flannel pajamas, and her hair smelled of
soap.

"Be nice to your brother tonight."

"Why?" she asked. There was no energy in the question, no
edge to it.

"What am I going to do with you?" Nathaniel said. "You're
smart, but you've also got a smart mouth on you—"

"—young lady."

"Ginger!"

"Sorry."

"Why do you have to be such a wise-ass?"

Ginger shrugged.

"I love you."

Ginger didn't shrug. Ginger said: "Then why did you make
Mom so mad?"

Nathaniel shrugged. "I was stupid. Your mother thinks I
was stupid."

"Is she going to let you come home?"

"She hasn't kicked me out yet."

"She has too! She said she'd rather if you didn't come home after the parade tomorrow. We heard her say it. We were listening. It's our business."

"Yes, it is your business."

"Is she ever going to let you come home?"

Nathaniel was on the point of lying—*Sure, sure, it'll pass*—when he didn't: "I don't know. That's all the more reason for us to do the tighten-up—"

"I hate that song," Ginger said. "It's dumb."

"You're wrong there. It's the most brilliant song since 'Roll Over, Beethoven.' But you've got to take it easy on your brother. I can take the smart mouth: I'm tough—"

"You are not!"

"—as nails. Jake's a softie—"

"What are you guys saying about me?" Jake said.

"Dad said you are the most talented person he has ever known anywhere in the United States of America."

"Ginger."

"Why are you dressed fancy?" Jake said.

(Oh, why indeed? Three weeks ago, the day after Nathaniel finished his second novel, the day before Jake submitted the first draft of "A Lovely Father" to his lovely teacher, Nathaniel got a phone call from Booth: "Well, old boy, ten years have passed."

"Ten what years?"

"It is time for the reunion."

"Princeton's? Not Princeton's? Surely you don't propose we march shoulder to shoulder in the P-rade? In a beer jacket emblazoned with tigers, behind a Dixieland band, in front of an orange-and-black fire engine?"

"That too, incidentally. But I speak of the reunion of our club we promised ourselves. Our Final Club reunion."

The memory was dim: final meeting senior year . . . after

the Parker House rolls had been pitched at one another . . .
during the cheese course . . . Yes, they had sworn to meet ten
years out to reckon themselves, had written prophecies of one
another to be read at their tenth reunion.

"I can see the fun in it," Nathaniel said. "Question is, is it
worth it?"

"*Worth it* is not the question. We swore to do this. I've
already phoned Tony—"

"Who the hell is Tony?"

"One of your fellow-members."

"Of the Final Club?"

"Of course of the Final Club."

"I don't remember him. Never heard the name."

"You've never heard the name *Tony* before?"

"Tony Conigliaro."

"Don't be a weenie," Booth said. "Do you remember a
fellow named Pownall Hamm?"

"Don't be a weenie," Nathaniel said.

"Well, you call Pownall and I'll call the others."

"Was Pownall a member?"

"Come on, Nathaniel. This isn't some damned joke. This is
what we did then, who we were."

"I was serious about Pownall. My memory's discharged;
can't get five watts into the light bulb in my head. Listen, we
can't ask Pownall to spend money . . . how much, by the
way?"

"Fifty apiece should cover it."

"Pownall hasn't got fifty dollars, from what I hear. Besides,
we can't invite him to watch us drink. To give an account of
himself. To confess to us. We don't have—what do you call
it?—*standing*? I haven't seen him since we left."

"I saw him once," Booth said. "In Philadelphia. He was not
a pretty sight."

"See? We can't ask him to put on a geek show for us."

"Who said he was a geek?" Booth said. "He was our room-mate, clubmate, crewmate."

"Till he quit," Nathaniel said. "It's not right."

"Why not? We swore we'd do it. I'll front him the dough."

"I don't think Pownall would like to come on a Booth Tarkington Griggs Scholarship."

"You call or I'll call him."

"I'll call Pownall," Nathaniel said. "I know his address. He wrote me."

"Did you answer?"

"Jesus, Booth. As you said, he was my friend."

"So there you have it," Booth said. "He must be there. In a dinner jacket. Wear a dinner jacket."

"Say what? I don't think I have one."

"Find one. We always wore dinner jackets."

So Nathaniel had tracked down the new Pownall, who sounded at the distance from Vermont to New York just like the old Pownall. Nathaniel said it would cost his old roommate just fifty dollars to eat dinner and watch his Final Clubmates drink upstairs at Ivy. Pownall had said he didn't recollect eating fancy food upstairs at Ivy, or eating anything upstairs. However, he didn't recollect much of anything from his Princeton years; any-thing was possible; he'd honor his marker. Dinner jacket? "Je-sus," he'd said, "you gents know how to show a guy a great time. Wouldn't miss it for the world.")

"Why I am dressed fancy, Jake, is I have to eat dinner tonight with my old friends."

"Is it going to be fun?" Jake asked.

"I think it is," Nathaniel said. "These are people I loved. Some of them I love. I've missed them. I walked out of their lives without much of a backward glance. Yes, it should be fun."

"Can we come?" Jake asked.

"I'm afraid not, sweetums. It's private. Members only."

"All boys?" Jake said.

"Wow, Jake, you're so subtle," Ginger said.

"Men only," Nathaniel said. "All boys. Just boys. I'll be home early, I promise."

"Maybe you will and maybe you won't," Jake said.

"What does that mean?" Nathaniel said.

"Maybe you'll come back tonight, and maybe you won't."

"Where would I go?"

"Away," Jake said. "You'd walk away. Out of our lives."

"Leave me out of this," Ginger said.

"Why would I walk out of your lives?"

"Who knows?" Jake said cheerfully.

"But I'd be a monster if I ran off and left you both."

"Leave me out of this," said Ginger.

"Yes, you would be," Jake said.

"Have I acted like a monster?"

"No way," Jake said. "You'd have to fool us. That'd be part of the trick."

"Jake, this is some weird conversation," Nathaniel said.

Jake shrugged. "I'm just saying what I think is true. You and Mom said always say the truth."

"I've got to say you've got a crackerjack record in the truth-telling department," Nathaniel said. "I've got to admit you deliver the goods, Jake. The truth, nothing but the truth, the whole truth."

"You've got it mixed up," Ginger said. "It's the truth, the whole truth and nothing but the truth."

"Whatever," Nathaniel said. "I've got to go now."

"Sure," Jake said.

"See you soon, kids."

"Maybe," Jake said. "Maybe not."

———

Waiting at six-fifteen on the back terrace of Ivy were Booth and Pownall, Roscoe, Archibald Barrie and a fellow these fellows were calling Tony. Nathaniel shook Tony's hand, and was greeted with companion ignorance; neither, it seemed, recalled the other. Ten years wasn't *that* long ago, was it? Six of twelve had made it back. Of the other six, four were scattered to the four winds and seven seas, in the service of First National City Bank (London), the Peace Corps (Turkey and Nepal), the Muse (Tangiers) and the Central Intelligence Agency (who knew where?). Two had fallen off the edge of the earth.

"To absent friends," said Archibald, raising his martini glass. A federal judge, Archie had formal properties; wearing his bespoke dinner clothes, holding his glass just so, with the other hand folded behind his back, he spoke in periodic sentences of each "absent friend," ruminating with deliberation the fate of "colleagues," muttering "ahem," thrusting out his lower lip in distress, clucking censure at those "dinner companions" who had "departed these shores" leaving with Booth no forwarding addresses. Archie said "Well done" at good that was perceived to have been done: the mixing of the see-throughs.

The mysterious Tony grinned and grimaced, happy and sad, at Archie's toasts. Pownall, drinking lemonade from a martini glass, looked Nathaniel's way, but past him, at the kids watching the half-dozen old grads.

These spiffy Final Clubbers were not alone with their narratives and aperitifs. Nathaniel felt like a specimen in a bell jar being examined by Ivy's tanned revolutionaries; these tame naysayers got up in peasant shirts from India or Haiti observed Nathaniel's companions pretend to be even older than the Final Clubmen in fact were, while the undergraduate Marxist-Leninists aspired, like most Americans, to be fourteen. Ivy's rigorously uniform iconoclasts looked that night to Nathaniel like hanging judges. Exclusive. Blackballers. He hoped that Jake and Ginger could find it in their hearts to trust at least two people who had hit thirty.

These sourpuss observers were difficult to love, easy to leave when Prosper announced—mercifully—that all was in readiness upstairs. Lining the second-floor hall were group portraits of Ivy members, and Nathaniel paused to examine them. Till 1967 the club sections were photographed indoors, in the billiard room; dress was uniform—dark suits, white shirts, Ivy ties. In 1967 a white suit was added here, an open collar there. In 1968 the insolent, smirking group moved outside, and was tricked out in zippered paramilitary kit, paratroop boots, tie-dye shirts, shoulder-length locks, not a necktie in view. Last year's section had favored an agricultural affect: bib overalls, Diamond Feed caps. For the first time since he'd found his dinner clothes in the attic trunk, Nathaniel—as right-thinking a dove as you'd care to meet—was pleased to be dressed up.

Prosper, accustomed now to the macrobiotic appetites of rice, sprout and tofu eaters, had pulled out all the stops for these adult carnivores. The long mahogany table had been buffed to a fine luster; the silver and crystal gleamed. Booth had specified place settings for twelve, and place cards for the missing. Booth sat at the head of the table, Pownall to his right and Archie Barrie to his left. Nathaniel was seated at the table's far end; Roscoe, to his left, faced the unremembered Tony.

Egg rolls and steamed dumplings awaited the diners' pleasure (sufficient for six, Nathaniel was pleased to note, rather than twelve; one never knew with Booth), and champagne: good label, good year, Archie's contribution. Booth had at first proposed—à la mode—nouvelle cuisine. Roscoe had put a cap on that caprice: "No dainty crap for me, Buster. Leave the celery and carrots in Newport. Ole Roscoe wants a slab of red meat, and a potato as big as a shoe." So Booth had had a nouvelle notion: the gentlemen's food had been sent in from a Chinese restaurant located in a Texaco station south of New Brunswick on Route 1. Word had leaked out about the place, and a few days after Booth placed his order for Peking duck and Hunan this and Szechuan that *The New York Times* called the little joint, straight out of *The Postman Always Rings Twice,* "the best Oriental cookery east of San Francisco and south of New York." Booth, as ever, was ahead of the wave. The youngish Sons of Old Nassau picked patiently at their food, and toasted one another, and Pownall drank iced tea and seemed distracted. Wine followed wine, course followed course. A groaning board for trenchermen, a feast fit for tigers.

As they ate—and, God knows, drank—Archibald Barrie insisted they give accounts of themselves. It seemed to Nathaniel that Judge Barrie and Roscoe were eager, Archie and Roscoe couldn't wait another second to give accounts of themselves. Booth said it was premature, that their self-summings needed more oil, that he'd prefer to wait a little. Booth proposed that they try out their memories telling the very worst thing each had done since graduation; he got the mass confessional under way by telling about an adventure on the Ivory Coast, where Archie had briefly served the International Court of Justice. Booth, visiting his old pal, had rented a Hertz Land-Rover and run it in a forty-eight-hour jungle rally. When the axle broke, after Booth had driven a distance on the rims, Booth asked Hertz for a replacement, taught Abidjan's Hertz representative an American idiom, "piece of shit." "That vehicle was a hurting unit when I returned it. I was in a pickle, let me tell you. Our legalizer here bailed me out."

Archie shook his head vigorously, chuckling. "Rum job," he said. "Rum job."

It seemed to Nathaniel that Booth's Worst Thing I Ever

Did These Ten Years Past had a shopworn sheen to it, an apocryphal atmosphere.

Judge Barrie stood to tell his worst. He had a belly on him, true enough, and his hair had thinned, but Nathaniel had never seen a fellow look better in dinner clothes. His manners were impeccable; he spoke in complete sentences. He was a moderator, a grown-up. He meditated First Principle questions in various languages. To think that Archibald Barrie was alive in the Age of Bell-Bottoms, co-existing with classmates wearing wife-swapper mustaches . . . this was unimaginable. What was the worst thing Archie could confess? "During the brief period after I left the A. G.'s office as a civil rights litigator, and before I joined the White House team, I put myself to my own uses, spent my energies on a comfortable career at Covington & Burling. I will say tonight—for your ears only—I'm ashamed to have taken my eye off my goal."

"Which is?" Nathaniel asked.

"To serve, of course."

It was Tony's turn: "Booth there put me in mind of an action of mine I'm none too proud of. It was in the car-rental line, like Booth's bad deed. The way it happened . . . I don't know what got into me. I rented this Avis car . . . it was a sedan, Ford or Chevrolet, I believe, but it might have been a Plymouth. My Friday plane from New York to Bar Harbor got grounded in Boston. Fog in Maine. So I was stuck, you see. I had to rent a car. I was surprised how expensive it was. They charged for every mile, quite a lot of money. That doesn't excuse what I did, but I think their fees are on the high side. Well, I drove this Avis sedan to Northeast Harbor . . . Roscoe knows the place. Roscoe visited Sandy and me there last summer." Roscoe—nodding, beaming—affirmed this. "Anyway, I'd racked up quite a fair number of miles on the odometer, and it got me to wondering how odometers work. Well, the way they work is they go backward if the car goes backward. I don't know what got into me; I'd never done such a thing. But Saturday morning I raised the car up on jacks, and put it in reverse, and let it idle off those expensive miles. It works! You can drive to your destination backward and make Avis pay you. You can't be in a rush, of course. Anyway, I did that. I wish I hadn't."

Nathaniel stared at Tony. What planet had he come from? Was he Roscoe's friend? Had Tony been one of the brightest, one of the best? He had a pointy nose and the palest skin. His fine, fine hair was parted in the middle. He brought to Nathaniel's mind Savage's savage eighteenth-century portrait of one who displayed a played-out gene pool: the "tenth transmitter of a foolish face." His fingers were bitten bloody.

Booth said, "Nathaniel, you're up."

Nathaniel didn't like this. The room was spinning. Had he drunk enough to have the whirlies already? He felt dislocated. The room was familiar, the scene too. Why did he feel out of place, as though he didn't belong here? Of course he belonged. These were his friends. His brothers. Back then they had known they'd never not be as tight as a Scout knot. One for all and all that jazz. They had sworn this. Except maybe Pownall, who had wandered off the reservation, but here he was, back where he belonged. There was nothing he wouldn't have confided in his friends. Nothing! But this? The worst thing he had done these past ten years? This wasn't sharing a grief; this was a parlor game, a frat's initiation prank. Why this was like a Bicker question!

Nathaniel gave a Bicker answer, the kind that would have done him good service twelve years back: "I'll tell you truth," he said.

"Don't reassure us," said Booth. "Please. For a friend to assure his friends he'll tell the truth is redundant, or tautological. Which? You got the *summa:* redundant or—"

"I'll tell you the truth," Nathaniel said. "Back in the spring of my Cambridge year, Pete came down from Oxford—"

"Balliol," Archie said.

"Yup," Nathaniel said. "So we entrained together for Rome. Pete was more Pete than Pete. Gauloise, talking a kilometer a minute about Juvenal and Horace, Plautus and Propertius, Martial and Virgil, Catullus . . . oh, how he carried on about Catullus. 'The evening is come; rise up, ye youths.' But in Latin. Of course. Down in West Virginia, Latin was all the rage when Pete was growing up. Anyway, like the rest of us, I was in awe of Pete."

"Hear, hear!" cried Judge Barrie. "To absent friends! Huzzah!"

"Hip, hip, hooray," said Tony, beaming.

Nathaniel drank, and refilled his glass. "Okay. Let's cut to Rome. In Rome I removed Pete's commonplace book from his bedside table while he was in the shower. And looked it over."

"Bad form," said the Honorable Archibald Barrie. "That's like reading a chap's mail."

"I thought we were confessing," Nathaniel said.

"Get on with it," Roscoe said.

"Nevertheless," Archie said, "to read a friend's private papers . . . Gentlemen do not read gentlemen's mail."

"Unless they're OSS gentlemen," Nathaniel said. "Unless they're CIA gentlemen. MI5 gentlemen. In-the-service-of-their-nation gentlemen. Wiretap-authorizing gentlemen."

"Gentlemen!" Booth said.

"You're right, Archie. I wasn't a gentleman. I thought we settled that twelve years ago. Look: I peeked at what our genius clubmate had written in his notebook. He'd copied something about Rome from a guidebook, maybe Fielding's *Travel Guide to Europe.* Or *Europe on Five Dollars a Day.* He'd put a little star next to the quote, so he wouldn't forget it, headed the passage 'Things to Do.' I'm quoting from memory, of course, but trust my memory on this: 'Go to Piazza Navona. Read a newspaper. Sit in the sun at a café and stare at the girls. Order a gelato. This will be the highlight of your trip.' I wrote under this passage: 'In Greece visit the House of Atreus.' I guess Pete didn't think what I wrote was funny. Or maybe he thought I was being helpful. Anyway, he never mentioned my addition to his commonplace book."

"Get real," Booth said. "You're horsing around. This dinner isn't a joke."

Nathaniel blushed; he noticed his friend had pouches beneath his eyes. His old roommate looked soft, dissolute. "Booth, don't tell me what is what. Okay? Okay, the worst thing I did since graduation? I went outside the marriage."

"Don't be flip," Judge Barrie said.

"Flip?" Nathaniel said. "Perhaps I spoke casually, but I'm not being sardonic."

"But everyone 'goes outside the marriage,' " Booth said.

"Hear, hear!" Roscoe said.

"What a quaint way of phrasing it," Archie said. " 'Went outside the marriage.' Is that a Pacific Northwestism?"

"It's a damned shame," Nathaniel said. "Just a shame. Roscoe?"

Roscoe said: "I blackballed a nice man applying for membership at the Mountain Brook Country Club because I didn't share his clothes sense and hadn't heard of the place that educated him. I'm sorry."

"Sorry?" Pownall said. Nathaniel realized this was Pownall's first word since the Final Club had sat for dinner. "Sorry? Did you tell the ill-dressed and obscurely educated fellow, the would-be golf player, that you were sorry?"

"See here," Roscoe said. "None of your damned business . . ." Roscoe wore a black velvet dinner jacket. It didn't look right to Nathaniel, a black velvet tux on the guy who caught a game-winning pass in the snow. Roscoe looked to have been out in all weathers, sure enough. He was too tan.

"That's it?" said Tony. "What you just said, blackballing somebody, *that's* your worst?"

"Gentlemen," said Booth. "Gentlemen! Be at peace. Quaff from the cup."

Pownall sipped his iced tea. Cleared his throat. "I'm sorry too. I caused hurt. But I think what you'll think was the worst thing I did during the past ten years—and you'll have to give me a couple of weeks on this one, give me, say, ten years and ten days—I cheated on my final exams."

"That's not humorous," said Archibald.

"Not a good joke," said Booth.

"We are not amused," said Roscoe.

"Sorry about that," said Pownall. "But it's the honest truth. Word of honor."

This was a sticky wicket. Nathaniel's tenderest memory of institutional Princeton was of its honor code. He could see by the faces turned to face Pownall that his was a shared regard. To be trusted in matters of consequence had been everything to Nathaniel. It had allowed him, by a simple willingness not to do a forbidden thing, to trust himself to bear up. The system worked. Friends flunked out rather than violate that system.

"What do we do now?" Judge Barrie said.

"Pour another drink," Roscoe said, "get on with our autobiographies."

Tony cleared his throat: "I believe Archie's speaking of the thing Pownall just told us."

"Oh, for sweet Jesus Christ's sake," said Booth. "Come off it! That was ten bloody years ago."

"Still and all," said Archibald.

"Let's ask Pownall what he thinks we should do," said Roscoe.

"Let's not and say we did," said Nathaniel. "Let's drop this subject pronto or let's call this meeting closed."

Pownall sipped his iced tea, watching his friends. Nathaniel waited for Pownall to grin a conspirator's grin (*I'm pulling your chains, chums*), the jokey grin he had grinned the first night of Bicker, when Nathaniel was scared witless waiting for the first knock on the door. Tonight Pownall didn't grin, but something in his unblinking gaze told Nathaniel that whatever evil Pownall Hamm might have done ten years ago, he didn't cheat on his final exams.

The memoirs began when smokes were lit. Pete, a spook somewhere in the Middle East, had sent a box of Cuban cigars with a return address APO New York. Pownall passed on tobacco. He had given up iced tea for iced water. If he had been Pownall, Nathaniel thought, he'd spend his time staring at his fingernails. Pownall spent his time staring at eyes, looking perhaps to learn something. Tony lit a pipe, held it with cupped hands, smoked it inverted, as though he were in the cockpit of a Friendship sloop, beating up Eggemoggin Reach into a nor'wester. Roscoe reached into his inside pocket for a silver cigarette case, curved like a hip flask: "Yo! Let's spark up a bone, boys."

Booth glanced at Pownall.

"Not for me," Pownall said. "Suit yourselves."

"I'd be more . . . comfortable," Judge Barrie said, "if you'd save drugs for another occasion, when I'm not present."

Roscoe lit up.

Nathaniel saw that the Honorable Archibald Barrie was drunk. Archie was on his feet, telling in clearly enunciated sentences the history of his career. The words were formal, stiff, correct. He wanted wholeheartedly to be an adult. Adults had treated the student Archie as a man of parts; he had welcomed their high expectations with undisguised relish. But he also had a schoolboy's robust fondness for horseplay and rough games. Archie played by rules: he played rugby, bridge, chess, hearts, roles. Dressed as he was, in a plain-fronted Hawes & Curtis dinner shirt of sheer cotton, mother-of-pearl buttons rather than jeweled studs, buttoned cuffs rather than jeweled cuff links, delicate platinum pocket watch on a delicate platinum chain threaded through his waistcoat's buttonhole, Archibald was laboring to bring alive traditions dead before he was born. He cleared his throat, just as an unsubtle character actor playing a First Lord of the Admiralty would clear his throat. Nathaniel wondered if it was false to play a part. He thought of Jake, walking the sidelines during Little League games the year before he was old enough to play, tossing a ball in the air and making a spectacular diving catch, as though he were rescuing his pitcher from a home run, then rising from the dust, brushing off his cap, and spitting, as though he'd loaded up a chaw. Archie had finished clearing his throat. He looked now like the bright young kid Nathaniel remembered. Archie smiled, and then he put on his serious face again, and there he went, speaking as though Oliver Wendell Holmes had chosen him as the instrument through which to enunciate matters of the profoundest consequence to the Republic.

The Honorable Archibald Barrie was lecturing on the proper balance to be struck between freedom of speech and freedom of assembly. He had adjudicated a case, United States v. Milofsky *et al.,* in which a classroom building had been taken by war protesters, and then liberated by the National Guard. This was a most uninteresting case. Well, uninteresting to Nathaniel; to young Judge Barrie—rookie of the year, a very baby of a federal judge, a federal judge owed a heavy debt by Lyndon Johnson the President's last year in office—a mesmerizing case.

Nathaniel remembered—how could he forget?—a 1967 letter to Archie. His friend was a counsel to President Johnson, and Nathaniel had written him at the White House, accusing his Final Clubmate of crimes against humanity, beseeching him "in the name of God" to "force sense upon the murderer for whom you work." Mutual friends had told Nathaniel his letter was silly enough to have merited responsive readings in the White House mess and at the Federal City Club. Now Nathaniel thought he was wrong to have written a friend such a letter; now Nathaniel thought Archie was wrong to have made public fun of such a letter.

"Summing up," Archie said, "I feel, on balance, I have served my country with discipline and energy. Much remains to be done; many miles remain to be traveled before I sleep." He took a deep pull on his cigar. The ash was impossibly long, a defiance of physics. Nathaniel suspected that Archie was concentrating ferociously on his cigar's miraculous discretion. Archie brought the cigar to his lips contemplatively; the least unsteadiness of hand, the merest zephyr, would tumble the ash on Judge Barrie's shirtfront. The room was still, poised: "I shall conclude," Archie continued, "with a saying of the great Lao-tse in the matter of rulers." Saying the inscrutable saying, a ragout of inscrutable banalities, Archie angled his cigar delicately, and its ash tumbled a foot through space into the bull's-eye of an Ivy Club ashtray.

"Your turn," the Honorable Archibald Barrie said to Tony.

"Boys? Your Honor?" Booth said. "Ahem. Aren't you forgetting old Boothy here?"

"It's Booth's turn," Tony said.

"I stand corrected," Archie said. "It is indeed Booth's turn. I give you our esteemed and estimable classmate Booth Tarkington Griggs, father, husband, husbandman."

"Is a collector of horse-drawn conveyances accurately called a 'husbandman'?" Booth asked. "Nathaniel, what do you say?"

"I believe *farmer* is what I would say for 'husbandman,' " Nathaniel said.

"Well, I'm not a farmer. Sorry about that, Arch."

Archibald made a charming gesture of surrender. Had they always been this silly? Nathaniel resisted believing it.

"Where to begin," Booth began. "After graduation, Diana and I took the infant Ben to Ireland, where my dear ma was married in even more spectacular circumstances than her only son. Shopped in Dublin, played in Cork. Rode to hounds. Hunted castles. Tasted wine. Designed and purchased in quantity engraved calling cards. Visited Nathaniel—solo trip—at Cambridge; punted on the Cam; crawled pubs; charmed rosy-cheeked chickadees. Used a walking stick. You might think there was a goatee; you'd be wrong to think it. My aspiration? Then? To be a man of the world. Now? To maintain the local life I lead, on the little patch of world where I lead it. I have a beautiful wife and healthy son. I am comfortable. I want only to keep in touch with you old friends, who are all the friends I wish. And to be informed of any carriages I might appropriately add to my quite extensive collection."

How had Booth got here in ten years? From whippersnapper to codger in a decade. What had happened to him? Was this waiting for Nathaniel too? Waiting bullshit: it was here. Nathaniel was afraid he was about to weep, like a cartoon bar drunk. Where were his dreams? He had wanted . . . everything. And just when . . . everything—Polly, Jake, Ginger, a calling he wasn't great at but could get better at—just when *everything* decided to jump in his lap, he had got restless, stood up, scratched his nuts, dumped the treasures out of his lap, alley-catted off to some dumb alley. . . . Oh, Nathaniel, Nathaniel cried to himself, you're so careless! So bad! So blotto!

Tony was talking: "I sell stocks and shares. It's not world-shaking, what I do, but it shakes my world. Sometimes. Sometimes it's been rewarding, making money for other people, for myself. Much of the time it hasn't been. Rewarding. I don't know what a Princeton education has to do with what I do.

Sometimes it can wear you down, the work I do. I'd sit at breakfast sometimes with my wife, Sandy, and the kids, and think to myself, What the hell's the point? Who cares? Is this *it?* But I try not to let it get me down. I know everyone worries about these things. I guess they do. Anyway, it's what I do. I don't have the wisdom of Solomon" (he looked at Archie) "and I'm not a gentleman of leisure" (at Booth) "or a writer" (Nathaniel). "I don't know what you do, Pownall. But I know what Roscoe does, part-time anyway. His hobby, I guess you'd call it. What's the word, Nathaniel? Avocation?"

"I don't know what you're trying to say," said Nathaniel.

"I'm sure I don't either," said Roscoe, with calculated indifference.

"Here's what I'm trying to say. I'm just a white-collar working stiff. I'm not a goddamned adulterer like Roscoe."

"See here," said Roscoe.

"Don't worry. I'm not here to make a scene," said Tony.

"I believe you have already made a scene," said Archie.

"Judge Barrie's point is nicely taken," said Booth.

"What a trip," said Pownall.

"I knew as soon as it happened," Tony said to Roscoe. "I don't blame Sandy. You're an appealing man, Roscoe. That's why you were my best friend. I looked up to you. I guess you seduced me, too. But why did you have to do it in Maine? Where Sandy and I had been so happy. In my house? Down the hall from my kids? I'm just curious is all."

"You're a world-class asshole is what you are," Roscoe said. Roscoe rose. Roscoe took a deep hit off his toke. Roscoe did an exit.

"Gee," said Tony.

"Gosh," said Pownall.

"Go on," said Nathaniel, to be kind (he thought), and because he was interested.

"Well, Sandy left me a couple of weeks ago. Not because of

my old roommate and Cottage-mate and Final Clubmate Roscoe. More because the stock market's down, as I guess you all
know—"

"I didn't know," said Pownall.

"—and I lost about five million dollars in four working
days. April 28th the Dow dropped to 724. Tony sucked maximum pipe. Sandy left me because I couldn't quit bawling
about my losses. My mother flew to New York to keep me
company and, coming in from LaGuardia in the fog, I plowed
the Peugeot—the bank's Peugeot—into some road machinery
and killed my mom. Bernie Cornfeld ran off with his pockets
full of my money, and my clients'. But I try not to let it get
me down. Sandy's got the kids and the house in Maine—the
bank's house in Maine. I think there will be changes in my
life."

Drinks were poured. Throats were cleared. Tony wanted
them to wait for Roscoe; he might come back, Tony said. He
actually seemed to believe that slammed door would open, and
Roscoe would come through it, blushing, muttering how sorry
he was to have blown his top, explaining to Tony just why
he'd chosen to cork Tony's own Sandy in Maine, in the guest
bedroom that shared a bathroom with Tony's little ones. Tony
seemed truly to have hope that Roscoe would come back,
extending the hand of friendship, saying, "Hey, ole buddy,
don't be cross with ole Roscoe, let's shake on it, let bygones be
bygones."

"Tony," Nathaniel said, "your friend is not coming back
tonight."

"Gee," Tony said, "what's Roscoe so sore about? It's just
the truth is all."

"Tony," Nathaniel said, "I'm going to begin. Landmarks:
first, I finally got laid by somebody who liked me."

"Get with the program," Booth said. "We're opening our
hearts here. Try to be serious."

"I told you before, Boothy: I don't want you telling me how to be. I don't want you interrupting me."

Pownall grinned at Nathaniel.

"I learned the habit of love from the person I'm speaking about. I love this person's sunny disposition. She's got great values, gives great value. I never had a better friend, no offense. She's got a great laugh. I learned from her to take myself seriously by laughing at myself. Maybe laughter became a vice, maybe irony became a vice. Booth is right about one thing—and I mean *one* thing—it's possible to turn just about anything into a joke. I got some of the messages scrambled. I look at myself plain—I *try* to look at myself plain—and I see a guy too sharp for his own good. Too quick to judge. I look back at what used to snow me and I . . . snicker. Why do I find it necessary to look down on every girl who ever looked up at the Biltmore clock? Booth, speaking of looking up, did Diana ever tell you about the girl who jumped out her Biltmore window through the skylight of the Palm Court?"

"Yes, she did. Never book an—"

"—inside room. I remember," said Nathaniel.

"I remember you remember," said Booth.

"Speaking again of looking up," said Nathaniel. "You all might look up some of the things I wrote. Archie sent me a sweet note about my novel, but as far as I know, none of my old friends have found leisure to read deeply in the *oeuvre* of Nathaniel Clay. It's risky, writing. She taught me to run risks. I wanted to write, but it seemed such a quixotic, self-important, doomed ambition. She didn't see it that way. She said, 'Let's do it!' I'll never be able to repay her for that."

Nathaniel paused. It was as though there had been a time-delay fault in his speech-audition mechanisms. It was as though he were in a huge, oppressive audience, listening to a bad ballad singer whose lips had been moving fifteen minutes before the singer's sticky, molasses lyrics invaded Nathaniel's ears:

> *I love you, more than I can say;*
> *I owe you, more than I can pay;*
> *I'll hold you, till our dying day;*
> *And this is no shit!*

This was dreadful. He was just a fool. Or maybe he was just drunk? He was drunk, definitely. But was he a drunk fool, or just a foolish drunk? Or was this a distinction? He had come here believing that these old friends and this Tony stranger could understand, would rescue him, haul him back aboard where he belonged. He had come here to tell what was what with him, tell what he had done to Polly and himself. He hadn't come here to tell how he'd fallen in love with twenty-year-olds. But he'd thought that here, tonight, he could say: *I think I've lost my wife, and I feel gut-shot. Tell me what to do, friends; bind up my wounds, dear comrades. Succor me!* Now he could tell them nothing. What he'd done was personal. As Gatsby said, "It was just personal."

"Let me try again," Nathaniel said. "I've written two novels. One got published. A few people liked it, a lot of people chose not to have an opinion about it. It was about two sets of grandparents, a bad set and a good set. I put them in collision. Professor Hyde always said a novel ran on heat, friction. I had lots of friction in my first novel. My second, *What Teiresias Saw,* was meant to run on the heat of the sun. To be a sunny story. Instead, it got complex. It's out there now, looking for a home. The publisher of my first passed on it. This is not a great sign."

"What's it about?" Pownall asked.

"About? Heisenberg's Uncertainty Principle, vision and re-vision, distinctions between *making* poems and *taking* pictures.

Huh? What the hell am I talking about? A crucial passage in *What Teiresias Saw* turns on the notorious war photograph of a Chinese baby abandoned on railroad tracks, crying miserably during a Japanese aerial bombardment of Nanking. A character in my novel asks, in a great many words, how such a photograph could have been taken. Why didn't the photographer put down his camera and pick up the baby? Or did he pick up and comfort the baby *after* he took the picture? Or did he take the picture so that the world would tolerate no more scenes like this? Or did he— But you get the drift."

"Not absolutely entirely," Tony said.

"Well, it's about lifeboats. We sink or swim together. Think of crew. How we're all in this together. How deeds count. How the ideal of the American loner, outsider, alien, Adam in Eden—claptrap. Gatsby's 'Platonic ideal of himself'—claptrap. What 'fresh green breast' of what 'New World'?"

"I'm afraid you've lost me," Booth said.

"When I'm not losing listeners and readers, I make my way as a journalist," Nathaniel said. "Like Tony here, I sometimes wonder what I'm doing, what I've done. I keep putting myself in the way of rejection. I don't know why that is, but it's an old story with me, as Pownall can tell you, as Booth can. Maybe I'm like Fitzgerald, longing to go through the shut doors. I don't mean I write like Fitzgerald. I don't just mean I don't write like him; I also know I don't write as well. When my first novel was published, I lived with Polly—that's her name, Pauline, Polly—and the kids in Seattle. On Bainbridge Island, to be exact. I was coming across on the ferry on publication date and it was damp on deck and I was inside the main cabin and this really pretty girl was sitting on an aisle seat reading the *Post-Intelligencer* and had turned to the page that had a review—good review, too—of my book, with a picture of me. Can you imagine how that felt? So this pretty girl looked at the picture, and looked at me sitting across the aisle, and looked again at the picture, then at me, and folded shut the paper and leaned her head back on the seat and closed her eyes and fell asleep. Soon after that we came east, to New York. I told Polly I had to be closer to the red-hot center. She said, 'Great, let's do it.' Then we moved to Vermont. Vermont's not that close, I guess. But I can get to New York when I must, and that's helped me find jobs free-lancing essays. Book reviews, what they call think pieces, some reporting. Let me put it this way: I don't have to worry anymore about being famous before I hit thirty. I hit and bounced. Hit and grounded out. Hit bottom and went aground. I'm three sheets to the wind, so I've got to wind this down. But to tell you the plain truth, I'm skidding through an icy patch just now. Things are not correct at home. I met somebody. Come on, fellas, don't look at me like that. You know me. I have a fear of depths, true. But that's not so weird. There's this lake in Formosa, beautiful lake, clear water. No one will swim in it. Why is this? 'Too deep,' the Chinese say. I understand. What happened that I understand? I hold seriousness to me like a secret. If I'm reading Conrad in public, *The Secret Agent,* I wrap the book in Hardy Boys covers, *The Secret of the Old Mill.* What is it about Princeton that turned us out like this? Not you, Archie. I'm thinking, say, of Booth. Booth? What do you think? Why do tigers want to be such cubs, jokers, playboys? Back home I should have been more serious. Back home, what happened, my own son accidentally spilled some serious beans on me just recently, and I'm having to pack some suitcases. So that's how it is with me."

And before Nathaniel sat down, Pownall stood up. "My name is Pownall H. and I'm an alcoholic."

"You don't have to do this," Nathaniel said.

(Oh, Nathaniel hated that word. "Alcoholic" was like "melanomic," "cirrhotic." The word weighed; it wasn't like pie-

eyed or tipsy or faced or stewed or plastered or smashed or
bombed or lit or fried or loaded or skunk-drunk or stinking or
three sheets to the wind. What Pownall had been summoned
to tell these clubby eaters was no less than the tale he regularly
told members of a real fellowship, and Nathaniel was ashamed
to be part of a design that had as its end Pownall Hamm's
casual confession—at a time not of his choosing—to people
who had decided by apathy to have no stake in his destiny. It
would be nice, Nathaniel thought, to have come all by himself
to his understanding of the culpability of lassitude. But he had
had help from Pownall's father, Dr. Hamm, who had driven
all night from Philadelphia to Newport to retrieve his son
from the guest bedroom in which Pownall had been locked
during Booth and Diana's wedding reception. It was dawn,
eleven years ago, when the doctor had arrived; Nathaniel
was—what?—"crocked" and trying to sing "When Sunny
Gets Blue" to a girl trying to play "Sunny Side of the Street"
on what she might have thought was a ukulele but was in
reality a banjo. The doctor had come right up to Nathaniel,
who'd been cared for by the Hamms. Dr. Hamm had iced
Nathaniel's sprained ankle at Stowe, and asked after the
health of Nathaniel's mother, and Mrs. Hamm had called
Nathaniel "dear." At Booth's wedding reception the doctor
had his black bag, just like a movie doctor. He was dressed
in black brogans, suit trousers, no socks and a pajama top.
"Where's my boy?" No pleasantries. Nathaniel told the doctor that Pownall had merely had a wee bit too much to
drink, had merely created a sort of scene was all, had merely
gone an inch or two too far, had merely done a little damage
to a guest bedroom. The doctor had said: "What is wrong
with you people? I don't get you. Don't you know how to
be friends? You aren't friends to your friends. You don't take
care of them. You don't care about them. You don't care
about anyone. You're cool. You're cold. You're ice men. I'm

freezing to death just talking to you." Nathaniel could have defended himself, sort of. He could have offered as evidence in his defense that little talking-to—what did they call it now? *intervention?*—the previous summer on *Snow Owl.* Instead, Nathaniel said he'd find Booth; Booth had the key to Pownall's room. He'd return with Booth. "Don't bring that boy back to me," the doctor had said. "I've seen as much of him as I want to see. I've been seeing boys named Booth Tarkington Griggs since I was a baby. I've watched them smirk and whisper in chapel and study hall, at ball games and dances. I've seen all I want to see of my son's roommate. Get the key to my son's room, and take me to the room, and return to your party, and then I won't have to feel the chill coming off you, and I'll keep out of your way, and that's a promise.")

"I don't have to do this? Of course I don't," Pownall said. "I do it all the time, several times a week."

So he did it again, told how he'd quit crew when he got so drunk so often he had reason to believe he might go out on the water and drown a boatload of scholar-oarsmen. How he'd gone into the Marines for six months to straighten out while Nathaniel was at Cambridge and St. Anton and Henley-on-Thames, while Booth was castle-hunting.

"I went into the Marines knowing how to drink, came out knowing how to fight drunk. Came home. Promised Ma and Pa I'd straighten out. Tearful family meeting when that promise was promised. Didn't straighten out. Got a position as assistant to a private investigator. Nice hours. No time clock. Expense account. I must have got canned. Can't really say how it ended. Half-drunk half the time, all drunk the rest. Mum got me a job as a floorwalker at Strawbridge & Clothier. Wore a carnation in my buttonhole while I scouted for shoplifters and boosters. Never caught a criminal. Eyesight imperfect. Attention elsewhere. Ran a gaming concession at the department store's elevator banks, betting on the elevator races. Perhaps you boys know the game?"

Nathaniel nodded; he knew the game.

"Got fired. That was July. Hot in Philadelphia. Applied late to graduate school in San Francisco. Berkeley or the other place that's not Stanford; memory's foggy on the details. Got in graduate school at Berkeley or the other place. San Francisco State. San Francisco State University! Removed tuition money from Ma and Pa on their condition that I live with my aunt and uncle on Nob Hill while I went to school. They'd keep an eye on me. You're wondering, graduate school in what subject? Good question. Darned if I know. I'd leave Nob Hill every morning with my books, and head over to the North Beach tenderloin, and duck into a saloon, and sit there till dinner doing what you do in a saloon. After dinner I'd go back to the saloon to do what you do in a saloon. Slipped this slider past my aunt and uncle a few weeks into spring term. They wanted to believe I was getting together with classmates for a pop or two, and after dinner hitting the books at the libe. I spent money conservatively. Dad caught me. Wrote a letter to the graduate school I had never enrolled in, never set eyes on. Wrote a letter or phoned—it doesn't matter. Sent my uncle airfare to Philadelphia. Uncle made the mistake of giving me that money to buy my ticket home. Bought a bus ticket to Mexico, Mazatlán. Sailed through a fogbank of tequila and mescal, teaching bus travelers to play hearts for money, to shoot the moon."

(Now Nathaniel remembered how the Final Club got named. Hearts. During the early days and nights of Bicker, waiting for knocks on the door, Booth and Pownall had distracted Nathaniel with the card game. It was good news in that game to get the jack of diamonds, bad news to pick up a trick of hearts, worst news to get stuck with the queen of spades. Unless the player could get all the hearts, and the Dark

Lady and the Diamond Jake. To go for broke—shoot the moon—was very heaven, and a sucker's game. It required luck, nerve, a memory firing on all cylinders. Pownall loved to go for the moon. Nathaniel played a teensy-setted game, giving trouble a wide berth; he learned to avoid taking tricks, but still he seemed to get stuck with the Evil Queen, thirteen points in the hole, a mighty hurt. It was Booth who explained the trick of it: watch out for clubs. He or Pownall would void himself in clubs, and Nathaniel would lead a club, and bingo one or the other would drop the bad news on him. "Keep count," Booth had taught Nathaniel, "keep your eye on the final club.")

"I journeyed as far as Huatabampo, where they threw me off the bus for shitting in my pants. Got a broken hand that night. I had boils in my armpits; I guess I forgot to rinse the salt off after I went swimming. Something went wrong with my pecker; it must have been the clap, but I hadn't had a hard-on for a couple of years, so how would that work? I do recollect a rendezvous on the beach near Punta Rosa three or four afternoons running with a youngster who'd suck my dick but wouldn't let me kiss her. How could I blame her? My lips were chapped raw from sun. My gums bled, and let's assume my breath was unwelcoming. Anyway, she wasn't a she, it turned out. You hear about this kind of thing every day now, but it was new to me then. I wore sandals, and split my toe on a road sign hitching inland to Navojoa, where the cost of living was said to be lower. Sometime that night or the next I got beat up, and then I got beat up again by the police. *Muy mejicano—¿verdad?* Dad came for me. Driving up to San Diego, my dad let me suck vodka from a baby bottle; he said it was dangerous to quit cold. Also my toe was infected, and it hurt where I'd lost these lower teeth. I guess in the fight in jail; they'd been loose. See, these are China clippers: they come right out. See, Booth? Don't look so depressed, Nathaniel; I'm alive, don't you think? What happened when I got home happened over and over. Got sent to the Hartford Institute, and ran away after a couple of years. Put Princeton on my line of march hitching home to mater and pater. Did a horror show here, downstairs, Harvard Weekend. Pissed on people. I mean *pissed* on people. When I woke up at home in my room with sailboats on the wallpaper, and class pictures from Chestnut Hill Academy and SPS and the photos from Princeton of our freshman crew—remember, Booth? How we were going to tear up the water?—and our Ivy section . . . Nathaniel, you were the most dignified-looking guy in the bunch; too classy for us; no wonder you bailed out. There was no group photo from—what was the place?—San Francisco State. I guess I flipped. Scared my mother. Took Dad's Princeton sweep off the wall and swept the house with it. Told my ma that everything in the house was too high off the ground, that I'd reduce things for her, cut them down to size, cut her right down to size. So they shipped me to a locked ward. And when that was done—I don't remember its doing—Platinum Mountain Retreat. Almost six years ago. I had my last drink two thousand eighty-one days ago. I've been looking for work in New York for four years. I tell prospective employers I'm an alcoholic, and this makes them antsy. That's okay, because that's what I am. Monday I'll be back on the street job-hunting. Something's bound to turn up. And there you have it from Tranquility Base here; this eagle has landed; that brings me right up to date."

Nathaniel was afraid someone would applaud. Because he wanted to. But of course the others knew even better than he that hearing the plain truth was like hearing a good sermon in church: one didn't put hands together at such times. Trust the chaps to appreciate the proprieties.

"What can we do to help, Pownall?" Archie wasn't kidding;

Archie was ready to roll up his sleeves and adjudicate this case. "What kind of work are you looking for?"

"I'd like to be chief of litigation at Covington & Burling, and a partner," Pownall said. "Nothing less."

"Oh, Pownall," Archie said. "Don't talk to me that way. That's not right. I don't deserve that. What earns you the right to talk to me that way? Tell me."

"Prophecies," Tony said. "I want to hear those prophecies!"

"Yes," said Booth. "Prophecies."

He had with him a manila envelope signed along the seal by The Chaps. Seeing this, remembering it, Nathaniel was puzzled how it was that such honorable friends, so constrained by so exact a system of honor, would feel it prudent to devise a stratagem to prevent their honorable clubmate Booth Tarkington Griggs from peeking into that envelope wherein were one gross foretellings of twelve futures, written by well-fed drunks on ecru stock with green letterhead, *The Ivy Club*. Nathaniel was ready for this. He wanted to know now what his friends had thought would become of him. He suspected he might learn something about himself, about the self he was then. He felt a rush of gratitude to these boys, to those absent friends, too, who had troubled to take a few minutes to puzzle out Nathaniel Clay's future. Nathaniel drank deep of the Remy and felt another rush to his head, if not of gratitude then surely of warmth.

"I'd like Archibald to read," Booth said. "He's got the better voice."

While Archibald poured champagne, while Archibald removed from his black silk vest a silver pipe cleaner and penknife with which he slit open the envelope, while Archibald cleared his throat, Nathaniel looked quizzically at his ole pal Boothy through candlelight bouncing off silver; did Booth know something? He was a slyboots, Booth; what did he know that had caused him to open distance between himself and those prophecies?

He knew his clubmates was what he knew. A clubman knows his clubmates. Judge Barrie began reading in an Academy Awards voice. The prophecies were worse than awful, merely cautious, merely inoffensive. One unsigned seer looked into the future and saw that Archibald Barrie would "probably become a legal eagle, given his aptitude for the fine points of law." Booth, according to that anonymous prophet, would "likely continue his keen interest in our equine friends." Eleven pals, distinct one from another, hunched that Booth and horses had a future together. Nathaniel, eating fortune cookies, began to confuse those prophecies with these. ("Inspiration is eighty percent perspiration"; "Journey of million miles begins with single footstep"; "Tomorrow is your looky day.") Nathaniel learned that his Final Clubmates were willing to venture he'd probably be an "avid reader." At least one of the boys with whom he had shared four years of his life was willing to venture that bookish Nathaniel might "do something practical with his love of The Word: teach, perchance, or write poems and plays." They saw for Tony "business on the horizon"; he might dare become a "captain of industry or of commerce." Roscoe: "Good might come to him if he behaves himself, but if he behaves too well he'll lose his spirit."

Pownall? Nathaniel noticed before Archie but after Booth that there were no prophecies in that envelope for Pownall Hamm, who was first to notice. Pownall's memory, with heaven knows how many synapses crisped by tequila and rum and fortified wine, had served him well enough to recollect with accuracy the people he had chosen not to dine with, wearing a dinner jacket, ten years ago. Pownall had just honored a marker that wasn't his to honor. Or maybe he'd never been asked to join the Final Club. He'd been barred by Diana—Nathaniel recollected—from the young marrieds'

Kingston love nest. That would have given Booth cause to organize a Final Club, to get together with his dear old pal. Could Pownall have been excluded from such an association? Wouldn't Booth recall such an exclusion? Booth above all people? Wouldn't Nathaniel, of all people, recall such an exclusion? Nathaniel caught Pownall's eye. Pownall shrugged. *Why not?* he used to say, shrugging, whatever the proposition.

"I'm sorry," Nathaniel said.

Pownall shrugged. "It was a good feedbag," he said.

"I for one," the Honorable Archibald Barrie said, "am here to say if Pownall Hamm was not a member, he most surely should have been. I would like to propose honorary membership in the Final Club for our courageous friend, Pownall Hamm."

Nathaniel stood, swayed, cautiously lurched to the bathroom. He stood at the urinal reading cultural graffiti he didn't quite comprehend, and a slogan he did comprehend:

FRIENDSHIP YES, BICKER NO!

PROSPECT STREET HAS GOT TO GO!

The dinner was finished. In the hall Nathaniel saw Archie bending over, studying his feet, manipulating his silver pipe cleaner. Leaning against a doorjamb, Nathaniel watched Judge Barrie pick vomit from the lace holes of his Lobb dress shoes; even bent over this way, the Chief Justice looked very good in a dinner jacket. Of course he wasn't Chief Justice yet, not quite. When Princeton boasted of sending its sons to the Nation's Service, this was the son they spoke of. Nathaniel couldn't recall ever having seen Archie drunk before. Not that this was "drunk" as Pownall meant the word.

"Where's Pownall?" Booth asked Archie.

"Dunno," said Archie, almost finished with his meticulous work. "Left before Nathaniel got back to make the vote unanimous."

"Where's he sleeping?" Booth said.

"In my room," Nathaniel said. "He's got a key."

"He didn't even say goodnight," Booth said.

"He must have been tired," Tony said.

They were all out there in the hall now. All the clubmen, all four of the original dozen.

"The reunion can't have been much use to him," Tony said. "He's on the water wagon, and we're all potted."

"Really?" said Nathaniel.

"You know," Booth said, "we roomed together in the ninth grade. Before. Shared a bunk at camp in New Hampshire. What was it? Fifth grade. Fourth."

"Damned pity if he cheated after all those advantages he enjoyed. Can't abide a cheat. You know, Tony, you may be right," Archie said, "I may just possibly be lit."

Never mind. This was a drunk a fellow could live with. Judge Barrie would have to send his gear to the cleaners, but he wouldn't have to write letters to people saying he was sorry. Archie straightened. Smiled. Belched wetly. Cleaned the tip of his pipe cleaner between two fingers. Said, "G'night, we did it, g'night, we kept our promise, g'night," and slowly climbed the stairs to his third-floor bedroom, without using the bannister, a class act all the way.

"What became of Pownall?" Booth said. "What became of Booth?" Booth said.

"See you tomorrow," Tony said. "At the P-rade."

"Tomorrow," Booth said.

"Tomorrow," Nathaniel said.

"Promise?" Booth said. "Tomorrow?"

"Tomorrow," Nathaniel said.

Ten

P-rade: 1970

Going back, going back,
Going back to Nassau Hall.
Going back, going back,
To the best old place of all.
Going back, going back,
From all this earthly ball,
We'll clear the track as we go back,
Going back to Nassau Hall.

Next day on the button of noon, in steambath June heat, the assembled Tigers departed Nassau Hall and passed beneath FitzRandolph Gateway. Tradition held that any undergraduate who exited the campus by FitzRandolph before his commencement would get the boot before he got his diploma. So potent was this taboo that the gate from the campus to Nassau Street used to be chained and locked except on days, like today, of big magic.

The procession hooked a right on Nassau Street, marched to Washington Road, went right again, past Woodie Wilson's reflecting pool (where show-off co-eds in wet-look hot-pants frolicked and splashed). Left on Prospect, The Street. From the caravan's midst, rolling high on Booth Tarkington Griggs's carriage, Nathaniel checked out his old roommate's get-up: a black hacking jacket and orange breeches. The orange-and-black carriage, a defiance of sumptuary law, finished with twenty coats of rottenstone-rubbed copal varnish, was adorned by lamps of black japanned tin with silver-plated reflectors. The springs were Swedish steel, the spokes hickory (painted alternately orange and black), and that ubiquitous heraldic device, the University Seal (DEI SVB NVMINE VIGET), had been inlaid, orange and ebony, in the side slats of this preposterously elegant dray drawn by two brace of black Flanders mares. Booth reined them in, "Whoa." The horse nearest Nathaniel lifted its tail and shat.

In the hierarchy that is a P-rade, front-of-line pride of place went to the twenty-fifth reunion class, in the blossom of its fiduciary virility, fruitful with children of college age, givers, boosters. Every reunion class had a uniform, and these uniforms borrowed single-mindedly from the college mascot's vivid palette. For a wonder, the quarter-century-out class of '45's costume was neither orange nor black but dun: lederhosen. This was the next to last of the flaky W.W. II classes, unstable in demographics, accelerated through a curriculum of relaxed expectation, a little unawed by Princeton after an experience of Sicily or North Africa, Tarawa or the Bulge. Nathaniel saw, way up ahead, a member of '45 carrying with his remaining arm a placard: "WE BOMBED IN BERLIN!"

Showing the colors were more than five thousand, but the extended family was twice that, and add to them professionals: tuba players, drummers, twirlers, mummers, mimes, men and women paid to walk on stilts, to walk on their hands. Following '45 came the classes in order of seniority: a lone survivor of '99, walking beside an orange-and-black golf cart, tapping the tiger-handled cane bestowed each year on the oldest of the Old Guard. His wispy yellow hair had been painstakingly combed, his rheumy eyes were fixed on the place he would put foot after foot, until he got where he meant to go.

The Old Guard—Naughty-Niner followed by the Double Zip followed by '01 followed by . . . the rest—were applauded for their grit; these were salty gaffers who had slipped past the damned necrologists; their funerals would be well attended by kin and kind; they would be air-expressed to Heaven with a Presbyterian prayer, and "In Praise of Old Nassau" ("Tune every heart and every voice, / Bid every care withdraw; / Let all with one accord rejoice / In praise of old Nassau. / In praise of old Nassau, my boys, / Hurrah! Hurrah! Hurrah! / Her sons shall give, while they shall live, / Three cheers for old Nassau."), all the verses. They were followed by graduates merely old, grim Depressioneers stoop-shouldered beneath the burden of a scruffy banner proclaiming, on behalf of '32, "THERE'S NO BUSINESS LIKE NO BUSINESS." Regard the bandoleered graybeard granddad from '37, carrying the placard "¡VENGA!"—a premature anti-Fascist from the Abraham Lincoln Brigade. Seeing "¡VENGA!" Nathaniel grinned with affectionate pride; he nudged his old roommate.

Driving his team along The Street, Booth wheeled past Campus and Tower, columned Colonial, dread Cannon Club. This progress was according to the inexorable ceremony of Princeton men reunited, P-rading the route they had P-raded time out of mind. Booth saw the old coot from the Abraham Lincoln Brigade being cheered that shrill summer of Cambodia by Sons of '70 holding aloft their own exhortation: "REMEMBER KENT STATE," as though anyone was likely soon to forget. The graduating class was all imperative: *remember!* and *gimme!* They'd even bullied the administration—*we demand!*—into leaving FitzRandolph Gateway eternally unchained and unlocked, a symbolic approach to and from the town and world beyond the narrow opening. On the gate's right-hand pier, going out, was engraved "1970 Together for Community," with a peace symbol.

Nathaniel saw "REMEMBER KENT STATE." It wasn't a month old: Nixon's Protective Reaction; the Parrot's Beak; the fury of protesting children; the children of the Ohio National Guard moving forward, firing through the smoke. That photograph: a child stretching out her arms—*What is this?*—above a dead child.

Booth saw another slogan, carried by a student, a sandwich man, sandwich gal: "Male Chauvinists BEWARE!" Wasn't this parade meant to be fun? Here, wearing tiger stripes, cowboy hats, leis, togas, terrycloth caveman skins, boaters, dunce caps, the Sons of Old Nassau had come to mend the divisions of the world. Here was a community of memory and affection, undergraduate wounds mostly scarred over by now, except by the sourpusses too hurt or self-important to make a showing, give an accounting, let their classmates remark how well or ill their form and speed in life's race had been predicted. Sometimes it was difficult for Booth to measure how it had come out for his classmates. After all, any fool could paste a cocky smile on his mug, and hide his hurt in an orange-and-black costume. At West Point and Annapolis reunions the history was right up front: this classmate outranked that one. There it was. Plain as day. Booth wondered, What were the wives like at a West Point reunion? Diana would love it. If Booth had rank, that is. Which he would have, if it mattered. Which it would, at a service academy.

Booth was struck by something he'd long noticed but never articulated: the reunion of Princetonians was a fellowship of shitface, for this too brought Booth's friends together. (Where the hell *was* Pownall?) Beer was drunk at Reunions from custom cans; some variation of a tiger, passed out atop a keg, quaffing suds, lifting a mug with his playful tail, was the common logo. The memories, the memories: of garbage cans

brimming with passion punch at a Right Wing Club party, of
a few too many at the Peacock or the 'Nex, of the Final Club,
of the stuff in a cooler hauled with a blanket to the shores of
Lake Carnegie to dull the pain of watching Yale win by a
length.

Well, fuck Yale. Such a solemn crew of bond salesmen
and Community Chesters. Princeton was less popular with
the serious girls, but more fun. Princeton dads initiated
their sons into the brotherhood of blotto. At Reunions, say,
or at home, on a back terrace in Grosse Pointe or Sewickley,
in Far Hills or Louisville or Newport (of course), with fire-
flies lighting the wisteria growing sweet tangles out there in
the dusk, with juleps iced in the rumbling spare fridge, this
bridged the split.

Which had been a good thing, Booth believed. Now the
times were rotten. Booth, clicking instructions at his horses'
asses, saw right and left wispy beards and ponytails, took the
measure of the scholars' uniform tatters (pre-washed, pre-torn
jeans), observed tanned Top-Sidered naysayers got up in peasant shirts from Haiti or Bangladesh and those goddamned bib
overalls. It made Booth mad. The dumb axioms about vegetables, and rice, and raw fish, kiddies with culinary convic-
tions, getting in touch with their cells. Planning to call their
daughters Autumn, Moonbeam, Sunshine, Mist, like pretty
names for ugly boats. Oh, boats: Booth had watched a race this
morning, and the stroke of the first heavyweight eight wore an
Afro and—Booth could swear—an earring. Booth, riding
high, remembered the good old days, May of senior year down
at the lake with Pownall and Pownall's date. (Truth to tell,
Booth was there that long-off day to essay a little bird-
dogging. Who could blame him? Diana-the-Hausfrau was in
use by The Infant.) Ten years later, maneuvering his rig
through the crowd, Booth recalled Pownall's date. A pretty
thing, and quite a tease belly-down on the grass, lazily cross-

ing and uncrossing her pale legs, giving him a peek at the gleaming pale flesh where her stockings quit. The three companions were meant to be watching Nathaniel's boat, the flashy Pocock pulled through the water by tall, short-haired boys in orange-and-black jerseys. Booth knew she was dreaming of one of them while Pownall calculated her, but Pownall was out of it, per usual. (Where the hell *was* Pownall?) Pownall had taken on a load from the cooler, and Booth noticed her scowl. It was her business to be sober, to think how this day might lead six years down the road to Mrs. Pownall Hamm. Not likely. Christ: girls were born mature. She had sat up straight and pulled down her skirt and asked after Diana. Pownall poured himself another, and Yale won by a length.

This morning, just ten years gone, it was Syracuse kicking Tiger ass. Seriously: *Syracuse!* And down by Lake Carnegie the hairy-legged co-eds in granny glasses were fretting different frets: *Suppose he sells stocks; what if he eats meat; maybe he won't turn against his parents.* Stolen by gypsies, Booth reckoned. And worst of all, the blasted drugs. To disagree about music and politics, this could be abided. But who fathomed drugs? The tribal elders were suddenly the young. Dads were at their kids' knees, and the kids didn't do what they once did on the screened porch, listening to Pa legendize Hobey Baker, or brag about stealing the clapper from Nassau Hall, or about welding the wheels of the Dinky to the track, or scaling the University Chapel. The kids were elsewhere, hiding their devil's work, inhaling and snorting, screwing up their faces, furtive and solitary, lolling on water beds, toking dynamite weed, setting off the smoke alarms and sprinklers in 1879 Hall. And what did dads know about coke, X-roads and hash, or want to know about speed? Drugs—the whole horseshit culture that the P-rade meant to defy: hip repudiation, communal solitude, broken bonds—all that was *terra incognita*. Booze was what Tiger grads knew, as Inuits knew seals, and Blackfeet

bison. And so it was with mounting anxiety that Booth
watched the dazed, stoned sobriety of the graduates of more
recent classes and wondered (where the hell was Pownall?)
where it had all gone.

Nathaniel had taken Jake and Ginger to breakfast this morning with Professor Hyde, who led the kids to the library,
showed them his Clay console radio, snazzy ash cabinet,
radium-green dial, massive flywheel on the 78-rpm record
changer.

"I bet you've seen a few of these," he said.

"Not really," Nathaniel said.

"Your ancestors were responsible for this beauty," Professor
Hyde told Ginger.

"How so?" asked Ginger.

"They don't know much about the Clay side of the family,"
Nathaniel said.

"Pity," Professor Hyde said. "They should know everything
you know. Be a teacher, Nathaniel. Ah well, ah well, neither
here nor there." Professor Hyde removed a book from an eye-
level shelf. A novel. Shelved between Paul Claudel and Samuel
Taylor Coleridge. By Nathaniel Clay. "And your father's responsible for this."

"I wasn't sure you'd read it," Nathaniel said.

"Wasn't sure I'd read it? How queer of you. What an odd
thing not to be sure of. I'm sure I thanked you for the inscription."

"You did. I wasn't sure you'd read it."

"Well, Nathaniel, that puts the shoe on the other foot. All
those precepts where I wasn't sure you'd read your Dryden,
and now you're not sure about me."

"I read my Dryden," Nathaniel said.

"Just so," Professor Hyde said.

"What did you think?"

"I think we should eat breakfast," Professor Hyde said.

"Of the novel," Nathaniel said.

"Which novel?" Professor Hyde said.

"My novel."

"Oh, your novel. Oh, Nathaniel, for charity's sake, don't put on such a long, injured face. Can't I tease you?"

"Dad has great teasability," Jake said.

"No such word," Ginger said.

"Of course he does," Professor Hyde said. " 'Teasability': I like it; the mother tongue has just evolved, again."

Then they sat out back in the little garden, eating strawberries and cream, scones and lime marmalade.

"Where's the magnolia?" Nathaniel asked.

"It died," Professor Hyde said.

Johnny didn't look a day older. Teachers seemed timeless; time rubbed teachers as smooth as sea stones, while students grew bumps on their faces, went thick through the middle, puff-faced, puff-eyed, hoarse, thin-haired, jowly, red-faced, coarse.

"Time's a bitch," Nathaniel said, conscious as he said it that he was trying out a forward idiom, that he was saying: *I'll speak to you now as I speak.*

"Is it ever," Professor Hyde said. "I miss you all. You were my best students. Now they give an honorary degree to Bob Dylan. What's blowing in the wind, yes? Now——"

"Did Bob Dylan go to Princeton?"

"No, Jake," Nathaniel said. "Don't interrupt Professor Hyde."

"I'm sorry. But is he here now?"

"On campus? Now? Probably. Your father was——"

"Will he sing 'Mr. Tambourine Man'?"

"I doubt it," Professor Hyde said. "Oh, Nathaniel, you and your classmates were state-of-the-art students: civil, malleable, eager to please. Nowadays . . ." Nathaniel, unsure how he felt about those old-time virtues, had heard about *nowadays*. "Did you know I was dean of students in '68?"

"I heard something."

"It was a piquant experiment. I got tetchier and tetchier with those paramilitary younglings demanding to know the relevance of King (Just Another Old Fart) Lear. I spoke up. From the sanctuary of faculty meetings, where young untenured lecturers and assistant professors with hair and beads and bells had the nerve—I mean nerve, it was difficult not to respect their nerve, but I managed to resist respecting their nerve—to hiss and boo. Children were one thing, dreaming of the Revolution and demanding course credit for the dream; deans were meant to know better. I was . . . irritated with the deans. They couldn't distinguish between a political prisoner and a sophomore on probation. Anyway, put up or shut up, I guess. They made me a damned dean. *The* damned Dean. The experiment lasted a semester."

Nathaniel had heard. Dean Hyde had been mounting the footworn limestone steps of Nassau Hall to his second-floor office; the way was blocked by protesters protesting who remembered what? They hadn't occupied the building: nothing so bold. They were scowling, muttering imprecations, another ultimatum on R.O.T.C., Princeton's Fascism, the usual. Shouting at the Dean, a skinny youngster with a greasy beard spit on Johnny. It might have been an accidental expectoration, or incidental to the youth's rhetoric. No matter. Day was done. After an adult life loving Princeton, Professor Hyde would make a life elsewhere and otherwise. He'd teach at Princeton, punch the clock, take the paychecks. But he lived somewhere else now, apart from his colleagues.

These had been Professor Hyde's friends. It hurt Nathaniel to hear Johnny Hyde speak with the furious heat of a betrayed lover. Dr. Hyde would never forgive his colleagues for whoring after the young, smoking grass, inviting babies to first-name them. How could such a believer, such a child of the academy, go on here, missing the Good Old Dull Old Days? Hectoring lifelong friends with references to the *trahison des clercs*? Now he rallied at Mr. Tambourine Man's honorary degree. "Next'll be the Fab Four. They'll make Janis Joplin a trustee." Jake looked interested. Ginger studied her fingernails; night before last Mrs. Clay had polished them red. "I hate kids," Johnny Hyde said.

Ginger said, "We're kids."

"Oh!" Johnny Hyde said. "Forgive me! I didn't mean what I said. I didn't know what I was saying. It was just a verb."

Say what? Professor Hyde didn't know what words meant? Didn't know that verbs count? Then who did?

Riding on the open carriage bed behind the old roommates was Booth's son Benjamin T. Griggs, firstborn of the class of '60, the Class Baby. The Class Baby wore diapers. Ben Griggs's diapers had been custom-tailored by a Newport seamstress who had taken her work to heart: the diapers fit without chafe or bag; they were velvet, orange and black, the colors of that Bengal tiger caged behind Ben, roaring in outraged bewilderment. The rig was a buckboard, but for young Ben it was a tumbrel. What could the smile hardened on the face of the Class Baby suggest? At ten his voice had just begun to shift register unpredictably; he had raised a modest boner when that pre-teen on the sidewalk in front of Ivy raised her bare arm to adjust a barrette. Her fingernails were red. She flashed her teeth; Ben Griggs fell in love.

Leaning against the wall outside Ivy, Jake nudged Ginger: "Look! It's Dad in the wagon! Look, Ginger, a tiger!"

"So what?" said Ginger, wondering why her father was dressed like a footman, trim in silk hat and top boots, wearing the grim grin of her piano teacher encouraging Ginger to learn a new number.

Jake smiled, awed by the P-rade and his dad's part in it, awed too by Ben, by the horses and other beasts. Jake was amazed by all the different bands playing all the different Princeton songs. And the hats. Orange-and-black cowboy hats, orange-and-black baseball caps, straw hats (skimmers and panamas, if Jake had known their names), canvas hats, sailors' caps . . . Jake smiled too at his little sister, the girl who had just caught Ben Griggs's eye and heart. Ginger was smiling. Wasn't Ginger having a neat time? Jake thought, This is the berries. Count us in.

Alexander's funeral phaeton, bearing his corpse out of Babylon, carried no sadder load than Ben Griggs, facing backward, rolling toward Palmer Stadium in the company of a hired circus tiger. It had not escaped the Class Baby's notice that the big cat's trainer was even more frightened by the Sons of Old Nassau, got up in implausible beer jackets and chimerical hats, than were the old grads by the predator. It was then, shortly after noon, June, 1970, that Ben Griggs began to study the art of nonchalance, of negligence. He might as well profit from his perception that he was not to be like other boys, that he was a Class Baby, that he rode familiarly with Bengal tigers, that Newport was not America, Tigertown was not, that his father was not a regular American dad, that the Boy Scouts (whatever they were) were not for him, that Little League wasn't, that a long-haired blonde girl adjusting her barrette, the daughter of a gentleman regarding the Class Baby's father with must have been (if only the Class Baby could see) frank respect . . . undisguised deference . . . *veneration* . . . might be just for him.

Ah, if Ben had been facing otherwise than arsy-turvy he could have seen Ginger's dazzling show of teeth for what it was, no complicit smile of welcome but a smirk, a young girl's perfectly heartless response to a sight she knew to be simply foolish. Her father was ridiculous tricked out in that high hat, and his friend driving the wagon was, and her brother Jake didn't know any better than to enjoy a parade. But the crewcut boy in diapers: he was a fool, period.

The Class Baby, facing backward, sweating in his velvet diapers, a quarter ton of animated Bengal tiger inches from his neck, was no sociologist, but a few blocks beyond his father's eating club he knew for sure that his father's ways were not the world's. There and then—just as he saw the girl with the hair and arms and fingernails stick out her tongue, at him, at Ben Griggs, at the Princeton University Class of 1960 Baby—he resolved to by George have it no other way. At Princeton. As a Princeton Tiger. *Hold that tiger?* Fat chance.

Eleven

Knock-Knocking at
the Door of Paradise

PART I: THE APPLICATION PACKET

PRINCETON UNIVERSITY

Personal Application for Admission to the Class of 1982

BIOGRAPHICAL INFORMATION

Legal Name: <u>Griggs</u> <u>Benjamin</u> <u>Tarkington</u>
   Last   First   Middle   Jr., etc.

Usually Called (nickname): <u>Benjamin</u> *Sex:* <u>Once, at Beavertail</u>

Permanent Home Address: <u>"The Beeches," Newport, Rhode Island</u>

Birthdate: <u>July</u> <u>4,</u> <u>1960</u> *Place of Birth:* <u>"The Beeches"</u>
   Month Day Year

The following item is optional:

How would you describe yourself? (Please check one)

American Indian, Eskimo, or Aleut —— Black, Negro, or Afro-American ——
Asian/Oriental American —— Spanish American (including Puerto Rican) or Chicano ——
White, Caucasian American __X__ Other (specify) ————————————

FAMILY INFORMATION

Father's Name: <u>Booth Tarkington Griggs</u> *Living? (Yes* __x__ *No* ___)

Father's Address (if different from yours): <u>17354 Ash Street, Trenton, New Jersey</u>

Father's Occupation: <u>Paramedic</u>

Business Address: Trenton Free Hospice, Trenton, New Jersey

Father's College (if any): Princeton University   *Year:* 1960

Graduate School (if any): N.J. College School of Public Health   *Year:* 1975

Mother's Name: Diana Carr Griggs

Mother's Occupation: Home Maker

Business Address: "The Beeches," Newport, Rhode Island

Mother's College (if any): Briarcliff Junior College   *Year:* N.A.

Mother's Graduate School (if any): Not applicable   *Year:* _____

Parents are: Separated ____ *Divorced* x

Please give the names and ages of your brothers and sisters:

I am an only child.

Please list any Princeton relatives, their relationship to you, and their year of graduation:

Booth Tarkington and Booth Tarkington Griggs and Booth T. Griggs II and
Booth T. Griggs III and everyone on my grandmother's side of my family
and no end of cousins.

How did you first learn about Princeton?

Whatever was my first message unit of datum, it was of Princeton University.
I am The Class Baby of the Class of 1960, for instance.

EDUCATION

Please list secondary schools you have attended, grades 9-12.

Name of School	Location	Public or Private	Grades
Shrewsbury	England	Public*	P.G.
St. Paul's	Concord, NH	Boarding	9-12
Fay	Southborough, MA	Boarding	5-8

*"Public" in the British sense: a boarding school, actually.

Possible area(s) of academic concentration:

History, History of Art, Music.

Possible career or professional plans:

Law, Investment Banking, Foreign Service, Rock Musician.

EXTRACURRICULAR AND PERSONAL ACTIVITIES

Athletics:

CREW (I expect to row on the varsity eight at Shrewsbury; I was Captain at
SPS, 1977, on the varsity crew, 1975-76, junior varsity, 1974.)
ICE HOCKEY (Captain and goalie, 1976-77; varsity goalie, 1975)
(I ski, sail and play court tennis.)

School Activities:

CHAIRMAN: Dance Committee. LEAD GUITAR: "Dow Jones & The Industrials" (Rock
'n' Roll Band)

SUMMER EXPERIENCES

I've devoted my summers to improving my athletic skills. I've also helped
around the house with chores, such as assisting my mother in various
refinishing projects, mulching my mother's garden at "The Beeches," clipping
hedges the landscape people neglected to trim (I'm six feet four, which
helps me reach the high boxwood on our place). I raced Etchells sloops
(captain) at local regattas. Living by the water I like to share our place,
"The Beeches," with classmates and friends, and I'm kept pretty busy
arranging beach parties and so on, trying to give everyone who comes to
visit a good time.
    In the travel department I've visited my grandmother at her Irish castle
(before she died a slow death from cancer), and branched out from there
throughout Western Europe. This broadened my horizons. Seeing how the
French and British live has made me prouder than ever to be an American.
(My mother told me to say this; I hope you like it!)

PERSONAL ESSAY

Please type on 8½ x 11 inch paper an essay responding to <u>one</u> of the following questions:

> 1. *What dead person from history would you most like to meet, and what questions would you ask him or her?*
>
> 2. *Tell us about a teacher who has had a significant impact on your intellectual growth. How?*
>
> 3. *What is the most life-changing event in your personal history? Why?*
>
> 4. *Tell us all about yourself (in five hundred words or less).*
>
> 5. *What do you hope to gain from a Princeton education?*

SUPPLEMENTAL MATERIAL

Please feel free to submit supplemental material—tapes of music composed or performed, slides of your artwork, photographs, stories, essays—in support of your application.

If you are submitting supplemental material, please check here: __x_

If you are submitting supplemental material, please describe below:

I'm sending you a tape of "Dow Jones & The Industrials" doing a few of my songs, as well as the Bob Dylan classic "Knockin' on Heaven's Door." Hope you dig 'em.

The Dead Person I'd Like to Meet
Benjamin Tarkington Griggs

Studying at Shrewsbury this year I've become familiar with
the works of William Shakespeare in preparation for the
ordeal of Oxford-Cambridge "A" Level Examinations in English. We've read many other English authors in great
depth, such as Geoffrey Chaucer, Edmund Spenser, John
Milton, Alexander Pope (he's one of my favorites), John
Dryden, William Wordsworth (he's not one of my favorites), Samuel Taylor Coleridge, John Keats, Alfred Lord
Tennyson and many others. Shakespeare is the winner and
still champ, in my book. I've been reading *Henry IV, Part
One* in great depth, and I'd like to know Hotspur, because
he's such a kick-ass war hero and because my grandfather
died flying fighters to protect England in World War Two.
I've also deeply explored *Hamlet,* and I'd like to be friends
with the Great Dane so I could advise him to get off his
behind and act like the Prince he is. It's time for him to
take responsibility for his family and the people who depend
on him. After all, even *The Bible* says Put Away Childish
Toys, as we learned all the time at St. Paul's, in Chapel.

But the Dead Person I'd Like Most to Meet is F. Scott
Fitzgerald, '17. I'd like to meet him first of all because he
went to the college where my family has sunk deep roots.
And because he must have known the great World War
One hero and Princeton hockey star, Hobey Baker, about
whom F. Scott Fitzgerald had written. Even though I've
been having a great time at Shrewsbury, which is one of
England's great Public Schools even if it isn't as well known
in America as Eton, Harrow and Winchester, let's face it:
I'm an American!

F. Scott Fitzgerald, '17, traveled extensively through
Western Europe, settling in Paris with his crazy wife Zelda
and visiting the Murphys who owned Mark Cross at their

fabulous villa in the South of France. Wherever he went, F. Scott Fitzgerald was an American, like me. I remember reading in one of the many biographies of F. Scott Fitzgerald I have read during my life that one night when he was asleep in Asheville, North Carolina, a town I have visited with my mother, two college boys in raccoon coats, having a good time with their flasks, came to his hotel and threw rocks at his window and woke F. Scott Fitzgerald up. They yelled up at him to come down and have some fun, that they'd learned how to have fun reading his books.

I know what brought them to his window that night. I feel the same way. However, there is more to college life than fun! It's great to dance the Charleston at Spring Houseparties Weekend, or take a hip flask to the Yale Game, or whoop it up on The Street. I say there's more to college life! There's reading profound books, and helping your teammates win at crew and hockey, and being loyal to friends, and above all working to make my American Dream come true! Because nobody in the history of the world understood the American Dream better than F. Scott Fitzgerald. Just read his novel, *The Great Gatsby*. F. Scott Fitzgerald, '17, is the Dead Person I Would Most Like to Meet!

PRINCETON UNIVERSITY

Personal Application for Admission to the Class of 1982

BIOGRAPHICAL INFORMATION

Legal Name: Clay   Jacob   Auerbach

      Last   First   Middle   Jr., etc.

Usually Called (nickname): "Jake"   *Sex:* Boy

Permanent Home Address: Star Route 6: Mad River, Vermont

Birthdate: April Fool's Day, 1962   *Place of Birth:* Seattle, WA

      Month   Day   Year

The following item is optional:

How would you describe yourself? (Please check one)

American Indian, Eskimo, or Aleut —— Black, Negro, or Afro-American ——

Asian/Oriental American —— Spanish American (including Puerto Rican) or Chicano ——

White, Caucasian American _?_ Other (specify) ————————————

I guess I'm just regular White, Caucasian American, but I wish I could be an Abnaki Brave.

FAMILY INFORMATION

Father's Name: Nathaniel Auerbach Clay   *Living? (Yes* _x_ *No* ——_)_

Father's Address (if different from yours): Princeton Club, NYC (For now),

Father's Occupation: Writer and Philosopher

Business Address: Wherever there's something to write about

Father's College (if any): Princeton University   *Year:* 1960

Graduate School (if any): I don't know   *Year:* ????

Mother's Name: Pauline (Polly) Brownell-Clay

Mother's Occupation: School Teacher

Business Address: Mad River Elementary School: Classroom 5

Mother's College (if any): Smith College   *Year:* 1960

Mother's Graduate School (if any): I don't know   *Year:* ????

Parents are: Separated _x_ *Divorced* ——

Please give the names and ages of your brothers and sisters:

My little sister Ginger is just barely fifteen.

Please list any Princeton relatives, their relationship to you, and their year of graduation:

My dad went to Princeton with the class of 1960. His dad went to Princeton,
but I don't know when. I'll ask my dad when I talk to him, and I'll let
you know what he says.

How did you first learn about Princeton?

From my dad, and when I was a little kid during a visit to the Princeton
P-rade in 1970.

EDUCATION

Please list secondary schools you have attended, grades 9-12.

Name of School	Location	Public or Private	Grades
Mad River High School	Mad River, Vermont	Public	9-12
Mad River Alternative School	Mad River, Vermont	Public	6-9
Mad River Elementary School	Mad River, Vermont	Public	1-6

Possible area(s) of academic concentration:

English and American literature, Comparative Literature, Classics,
Philosophy

Possible career or professional plans:

Writer and Philosopher

EXTRACURRICULAR AND PERSONAL ACTIVITIES

Athletics:

Little League catcher for Mad River Dodgers, League CHAMPS in 1972! Also
volleyball and hockey games with kids and grownups. Also fly-fishing.
Also softball and hiking and mountain (really hills) climbing. Also Ski
Team Captain and Eastern Regional Junior Champion in slalom and giant
slalom.

School Activities:

Editor of Parchment & Quill Literary Magazine. Editor of Bugle Newspaper.
Piano player in The Hep Cats school jazz band. Member of Los Amigos y Las
Amigas School Spanish Club. Member of Model Railroad Club. Member of
Friends of Critters Animal Rescue Association.

SUMMER EXPERIENCES

I've played a lot of baseball and caught a lot of trout. In fact, no trout
is safe when I'm around. This is bragging, but I think the first thing a
mother trout tells her small fry is: "Remember kids, look sharp for Jake
Clay. He's a killer. He'll catch you before you know you've been caught,
and if he doesn't eat you he'll throw you back and catch you again, and
then he'll eat you." Other things I've done with my summers is go camping
with my friends and sometimes with Ginger, who is my little sister. I've
also put in some hours lying in a hammock and reading books. And of course
like every kid I've had jobs. I've painted houses, planted trees and the
last three summers I've worked for Doctor McGraw, Doctor of Veterinary
Medicine, who is our local Veterinarian. I clean up, calm the animals, try
to make them happy, and do what Doctor McGraw says to do. I also even get
paid.

PERSONAL ESSAY

Please type on 8½ x 11 inch paper an essay responding to one of the following questions:

1. *What dead person from history would you most like to meet, and what questions would you ask him or her?*

2. *Tell us about a teacher who has had a significant impact on your intellectual growth. How?*

3. *What is the most life-changing event in your personal history? Why?*

4. *Tell us all about yourself (in five hundred words or less).*

5. *What do you hope to gain from a Princeton education?*

SUPPLEMENTAL MATERIAL

Please feel free to submit supplemental material—tapes of music composed or performed, slides of your artwork, photographs, stories, essays—in support of your application.

If you are submitting supplemental material, please check here: _X_

If you are submitting supplemental material, please describe below:

I am submitting the supplemental material called "A Lovely [sic]
Father," an essay I wrote when I was a quote Child Prodigy unquote.

Jake Clay
New Year's Eve, 1977

*A Teacher Who Had a Significant Impact
(And My Life-Changing Event)*

I can't answer Essay #2 without answering Essay #3, and I
can't answer Essay #3 without answering Essay #2. I tried
to figure out a way of writing just one of them, but it
didn't work, and I hope it's okay to do this the way I have
to do it.

This is the whole point of why I want to go to Princeton
University. I want to write things that are true and important, like my dad writes. He always says he learned to write
at Princeton University. I don't mean he says it every day; I
don't even see him every day, or every week, but I've heard
him say it a couple of times. What Dad *does* say all the time
is "never say never" and "never say always," so now I'm
never going to say "always" again.

I wouldn't mind writing about the Man from History,
who would be my granddad, but I don't know anything
about him, because my dad and my grandmother won't
talk about him. My dad told me once, when he had had
what he calls a "snootful," that his dad died falling. He
was a mountain climber, and he died falling off a mountain. I'd like to know more about him, and ask him
about my dad when my dad was a kid.

Anyway, here goes: The Most Life-Changing Event in My
Personal History was writing about my dad in a paper for
The Teacher Who Has Had a Significant Impact on My
Intellectual Growth, who is my mom. That paper is the
Supplemental Material called "A Lovely [sic] Father." Back
when I wrote it I thought "lovely" meant "loving." My
mom asked my dad to leave home after she read it. She
didn't want me to think it was my fault that he had to pack

his bags and go away, so she sent him away on a vacation for a little while before she gave him the axe, but my paper did it, and I know it.

"A Lovely Father" was about a lot of things on my mind when I was a kid, and one of those things was a problem my dad was having then. My mom says my dad's problem was pretty much a Pretty Girl Problem, and that the paper I wrote just brought what she calls "the realities" into focus.

Maybe. All I know is he lived with us before I wrote the essay, and didn't after. If you ask me What I Hope to Gain from a Princeton Education I'll say: to write clearly, without ever again saying *anything* that can be misunderstood.

I just read "A Lovely Father" and I think it gives a false impression of what kind of kid I was. While I was reading it I felt this lump in my throat I feel at the end of a sad movie, and I got to thinking "Oh poor Jake, boo-hoo, what a sweet little boy, how ghastly for poor little Jake."

There's this word in French, *jejeune*. We learned it cramming for French Achievement or Advanced Placement. I heard that word and my ears turned red. It means naïve (*naïf*) or innocent (*innocent*), and it makes me regret the false impression I gave in "A Lovely Father" about how a dying bunny rabbit dropped off a bridge changed my life.

I don't mean I wrote that essay to leave a lie. But my real life is hidden in that essay, and hidden on purpose. For example, you'd think reading my Supplemental Material that all I wanted was never to be mean to Molly or to any other child. This isn't true. For instance, after school some of the gang tied a kid named Happy to a tree. First we made him be naked, and then we tied him to a tree and shot a few arrows at him. We missed him on purpose, but we could have missed missing him, if you see what I mean; we weren't what you'd call *archers* in eighth grade. Then we gave him the good news we'd decided not to scalp him, but we rubbed honey on his face and said by morning a bear would find him, and what the bear left of him the ants would "pick clean, pardner."

Why did we do this? Because Happy was a boy with what we decided was a girl's name, and because we'd decided to name our gang which we had first called The Green Mountain Boys "The Abnakis," which were Vermont Indians. We changed the name because I read a book called *Bury My Heart at Wounded Knee* which made me angry at The White Man. Happy was a White Man, or at least a White Boy.

Dad called our gang a "confederation of Merry Andrews," but what did Dad know about it? He was gone then, in New York. The Abnakis was just a club: people we liked got in and people we didn't like didn't get in. We used to hang around the woods in our clubhouse (which we called a "wigwam") and smoke weeds and talk big about what we were going to do when we grew up, which meant Get Our License. Here's what I was going to do: I was going to get me a pickup and swing by The Blue Tooth and drink a couple of beers and pick up a "lady." I wasn't old enough to shave and I was saying "pick up a *lady*." We talked about having a toga party, and Eric said when he grew up he was going to be a "sexist," which he thought meant *Playboy* photographer. We ragged him for that one. Lots of us knew from our moms what "sexist" meant.

If my little sister Ginger had heard Eric say he wanted to be a *Playboy* photographer, she would have bored him a new one, as we sometimes say. I know I'm taking a chance writing this way in this essay which is so important to me, but I want to write what's so, and these things I'm writing are so. My mom's a great teacher. She taught me to tell the truth, but I know she'd edit this essay if I showed it to her.

She turns me on to books. Not just *Catcher in the Rye,*

but Mary McCarthy's *Memories of a Catholic Girlhood* and Frank Conroy's *Stop-Time* and Frederick Exley's *A Fan's Notes*. And then she talks to me and Ginger about them. She's getting us to read these books she reads so she'll have someone to talk to about them. I think she's lonely sometimes without Dad. But there's more to our reading together than passing time. When we talk about books, and argue about what they mean, it's as though who we are doesn't matter anymore. Talking about what Nick Adams saw in "Indian Camp" or how Huck felt about Jim or why did Iago do it, we forget ourselves. We're too busy thinking and talking to remember that I'm sore at Ginger or Ginger thinks I'm a geek. We read alone and talk together in my family. I'm proud of this. Ginger is too, if she'd admit it, which she wouldn't.

Oh, Ginger! Really and truly. Have you ever played the game of Battleships? She can blow all your ships out of the water, and that's what she loves to do, almost as much as killing me at chess. But what she really loves is to gross out boys. My friends think she looks really cute, and I guess they must know what they're talking about. They never say anything about Ginger that I'd call improper, or I don't know what I'd do. But the kind of thing Ginger likes to do, besides using a prissy voice to say terrible words, is hawk up snot (I know I'm taking a chance writing this) in the lunchroom and mix it up with her food and eat it. I guess you could say Ginger likes to show off. I hope if she ever applies to Princeton University you won't use this against her, because the way she does it is actually rather amusing.

Here's another thing Ginger did. This was long ago when we were walking down to the elementary school to play the last game of baseball before winter. (I tell stories from long ago because I think now I can make sense of them. Or maybe I like who I think I was then better than I like who

I think I am now. Is this unusual?) It was late October, but snow was supposed to fall that night, and as usual there was a frost warning. Along the way we bumped into Mr. Greensleeve's son. (See "A Lovely Father," the man whose horse Dad thought was dead because it was taking a nap.) He was fiddling with a brand new Caterpillar Road Grader at this garage near the school where the town of Mad River's highway machinery is kept. Ginger said hey, what do you think you're doing? She can be fresh sometimes. Mr. Greensleeve's son said he was preparing the Road Grader for winter. He said it was a tricky job, and expensive. He said how much antifreeze do you think I've got to put in this bear? Ginger said, with her priss accent, I wouldn't have the vaguest notion. Mr. Greensleeve's son said seventy "dollar" worth. It wasn't only that Mr. Greensleeve's son isn't exactly a candidate for admission to Princeton University, it's the way lots of Vermont natives say "dollars," without the "s."

"You don't need to spend that money," Ginger said. "You can keep it for yourself."

"What do you know about it?" said Mr. Greensleeve's son.

"I know you can put spring water in there instead of antifreeze," Ginger said.

This was getting interesting.

"Get with the program," said Mr. Greensleeve's son. "Water freezes. That's why I got to put in *anti*freeze."

"Have you ever seen a spring?" Ginger said.

"Sure," Mr. Greensleeve's son said.

"Have you ever seen a spring freeze up?" Ginger said.

And that's how it was that the Town of Mad River had a big extra line item in the Town Budget come Town Meeting first Tuesday in March. I know all about this because we discussed it in Civics next day in school. A citizen of the Town of Mad River asked Mr. Greensleeve, who was the Commissioner of Roads, how come there was this thing called Miscellaneous Repairs that cost thousands of dollars. Mr. Greensleeve said "that's for me to know and you to find out."

I know I'm way off the subject. I know this is too long. You probably think this is a first draft, and I just dashed it off. But the truth is that it started short, and every time I work on it it gets longer. I can't seem to flat out say why my mom is a great teacher or why writing an essay for her changed my life, and how. I keep circling around what I mean to say: Nobody's perfect. It's not just that this is complicated, which it is. It's that it's confusing. If you've gotten this far you can say you should have thought of that before you decided to write about it. You should have written about something that wasn't confusing. But I don't want to write about things I already understand. My mom taught me to write about things I don't understand yet.

Here's what I understand now and didn't understand when I wrote "A Lovely Father": Nobody's perfect. I'm sure not, as I hope I've shown. Ginger's not. Maybe my mom was quite perfect, before she got mad. But my dad made her mad, so it's hard to know what's what in the perfect mom department. Here's another thing I don't understand yet. I don't understand why my dad decided to have a Pretty Girl Problem. I don't understand why he became so sad even though my mom was ALWAYS nice to him. He said he was "restless," and I guess he was. Sometimes he'd drive me and Ginger to Waterbury to watch the loonies in the State Mental Hospital turn out to watch the Montrealer come in on its way to New York. This sounds insensitive, but we liked to do it because the loonies had such a great time yelling "choo-choo" and making train horn noises that it really cheered you up. And once, the November before he got kicked out of the house, he got bored reading the Sunday *New York Times* and took me and Ginger to Burlington, which is sixty miles distant, to watch a matinee of *Smokey and the Bandit.* It was raining, and Dad was unusually quiet in the Volvo, and when we got there we were hungry. The movie theater was downtown and there weren't any fast food places and we didn't have time to go into a restaurant. There was this deli next door, and we went there and ordered grinders and Dad ordered a meatball grinder with cheese. We started eating and the woman who gave us our food and took our money said you can't eat those in here. And my dad went on eating, and said please. This made the woman furious and she said I want you *people* to leave immediately, and Dad got red in the face, and I thought he was going to flip out. Instead he left the deli and Ginger and I were just glad there wasn't a fight. So we tried to stand under the movie awning or whatever it's called. But there were all these people waiting in line, and it was *really* hard to hold a wet grinder together and also eat it. Dad tried to eat his too fast and got it all over him and we didn't have any napkins and Ginger and I started giggling it was so gross and we thought Dad was giggling too but he was crying. I mean crying!

I started my Supplemental Material essay with me crying and now this essay's ending with Dad crying. You must think we're a sad family. We're not. Why? I don't know yet. It's confusing.

PART II: THE LEGACY ROUND

The admissions committee met in a high-ceilinged, walnut-paneled West College conference room decorated with gloomy oil portraits of President Wilson (robed), President Madison (wigged) and President Bowen (robed). The past hung like a goad or a reproof. The room and portraits insisted this was for the ages. Offsetting the gravity of the architecture and interior decoration was a cork bulletin board to which were thumbtacked notably risible snapshots and Bachrachish portraits of those young hopefuls who had judged their likenesses would weigh favorably in their balance come the moment of thumbs-up/thumbs-down. Add to these photographic novelties an atmosphere of calculated good will and chumminess among the three New England regional admissions officers offering to the Dean of Admissions their judgments of certain alumni sons and daughters who had survived Princeton's first cut. The three had brought to the conference room that February morning their own coffee mugs; doughnuts had been set out at the table; it was difficult to rise to solemnity wearing a powdered-sugar mustache and jelly on the chin.

The students under discussion could be voted in at this session, or put on the waiting list to be considered at the final general admissions round, or rejected. Like minority students and athletes wanted by coaches, legacies had the advantage of an assumption of welcome. Unless there were good reason to cast them out, they would be taken. This policy was neither cynical nor secret; admission to Princeton was not for sale, although it was true that money-raisers in the Development Office were apprised which of the children of Old Nassau had been cast out, so a Princeton daddy wouldn't be rubbed up for a cool million a couple of days after his Missy or Reggie got the thin envelope. One applicant in five from the general population was invited to Princeton; half her legacies got the bid.

Everyone in this room had gone here. The Regional Director was the eldest, class of '50. His two assistants were recent graduates: she was class of '74, as was he. (Office buzz gave them a history, had them down as an on-again off-again—off *now*—hot item.) The Dean had been a freshman Nathaniel's senior year. They were discussing Benjamin Tarkington Griggs.

"Why are we talking about this boy at all?" the young man asked. "He's a solid Academic Two; he's got good scores, he's got okay grades from St. Paul's, he's got hockey and crew, he's a legacy a zillion times over."

"Is that *the* Booth Tarkington?" the Dean wondered. "Booth *Penrod* Tarkington?"

"Got to be," said the Regional Director. "But that would be *N.* Booth Tarkington, '93. One of the reasons we're talking about him is I—how can I put this unprejudicially?—don't like him."

"Did you interview him?" said the Dean.

"I did," said the Regional Director. "The boy crossed the Atlantic Ocean to be personally witnessed; I asked him if he had questions I could answer and he said, 'Please: tell me all about yourself in a few well-reasoned paragraphs, five hundred words or less.' He laughed charmingly, but give me a break!"

"Was he arrogant?" asked the young woman. "I wasn't wild about the sex-once-at-Beavertail response."

"Come on," said her classmate, who wore muttonchop whiskers. "Don't go fem on us so early in the morning. It was a funny answer. Lighten up. Can somebody tell me: what's a Beavertail?"

"I'm counting about a thousand references to 'The Beeches' of Newport, Rhode Island," said his classmate, fiddling with her pigtails.

"It's where he lives," said the Dean.

"Fair enough," said the Regional Director. "Let's look at his essay."

"It's ghastly," said the Dean.

"Awful," said the young man. "But say this for it: no Emerson or Thoreau."

"No *cogito ergo sum*," said the young woman.

"No proper study of mankind is man," said the Regional Director. "And we're talking here about a boy who's studied his Pope—"

"In great depth," said the young woman.

"—in great depth, at an English public school—"

"Which is not to be confused with a publicly funded school," said the young woman's classmate.

"There's a great run-on halfway down page 2," said the young woman. "The essay's about a quarter inch deep. Where did he get those values? I mean, tell us about your summer vacation. Well, I walked among the poor, read to the blind and arranged beach parties for visitors to The Beeches."

"Tell me about his father," the Dean said. "I vaguely remember him. Lank. Golden boy. Great sculler, I think. What's he doing in Trenton?"

The Regional Director said he didn't know what Booth Tarkington Griggs was doing in Trenton, and noted that whatever it was, it didn't seem much to interest his son.

"Do the recs say?" asked the Dean.

The Regional Director examined the young man's letters of recommendation. There were many, invariably articulate. They spoke to Benjamin's self-assurance and determination. St. Paul's college counselor assured Princeton that Benjamin had had no discipline problems at the school. That the boy had remained seemingly "unruffled," even when his father "went off the deep end" during Benjamin's fourth-form year.

"What do they mean 'deep end'?" asked the Dean.

"Doesn't say," said the Regional Director. "Discreet. Puts the matter in the larger context of Griggs family tradition and stability, 'generations of distinguished St. Paul's and Princeton graduates—' "

"Blah, blah, blah," said the young woman.

"The crew coach writes that the boy has a lovely natural stroke," said the Regional Director.

"Is the boy tall?" the young man asked.

"Do you mean will he row heavyweight? No. Too skinny," said the Regional Director. "Also, our crew coach doesn't want to recruit him. Says he rowed with his father, and doesn't want to recruit the boy."

"Isn't that a little visiting-the-sins-of-the-fatherish?" said the Dean.

"Coach didn't say he'd bar the boy from the boathouse. Just doesn't want to recruit him. But Griggs is evidently a first-rate hockey goalie."

"My older brother dated his mother a couple of times," said the Dean. "Had her up to our summer place in Rolling Rock. The plain fact of the matter is I never saw a better-looking girl before or since."

"Present company excepted?" said the young woman. "Did he explain his ambition to be a rock star? I like Dow Jones & The Industrials."

"You listened to the tape?" the Regional Director asked.

"God no! The group's name's funny is all."

"He is more than a bit wise-ass," said the young man.

"He's a legacy," said the Dean. "He has an honors average, has taken difficult courses at St. Paul's—"

"Please: 'S.P.S.,' " said the Regional Director.

"—he has more than respectable Board scores," continued the Dean, "keeps a puck out of a net—"

"And don't forget that he has 'broadened' his 'horizons' traveling through Western Europe," said the Regional Director.

"—and I'd like to admit him," said the Dean. "Are there insurmountable obstacles to my wish?"

There were none.

They broke for lunch, had an afternoon meeting during which one candidate sent to the Dean a Balloongram, "so you'll remember me." Done and done: unforgotten. Last week there had been a smoked salmon and a Tapdancegram. "If this trend continues," said the Regional Director, "the children'll someday be sending videotapes of themselves." A cake with orange and chocolate icing from a candidate's mother was delivered (and eaten). The committee broke for dinner. Now, thirteen or so hours after they began, Jake Clay was in the batter's box. The standardized tests were mezzo-mezzo, low six hundreds verbal, mid-fives math. Grades were good, but not perfect. Mirth was spent on the boy's course selection: in addition to Advanced Placement French (B +) there was Animal Behavior, Vermont Literature, Frontier Literature, Practical Architecture, Asian Philosophy, College Algebra—"Bonehead Math," the Dean called it.

"Where would *I* be without Bonehead Math?" said the Regional Director.

"Regional Director of Admissions for New England, Princeton University," said the Dean.

The young man said, "I'm turned off by the way the kid takes the high ground about what he writes in his essay and why he writes it, all that here-I-stand-I-can-do-no-other malarkey. I think our little Jake's too good to be true. All that Holden Caulfieldish sentiment. Wanting to be an Abnaki Brave is just too cute for words."

"He means it," said the young woman.

"How do you know?" said the young man.

"I interviewed him," said the young woman.

"Is 'jejune' spelled the way he spells it in his essay?" asked the Dean, looking at Jake's essay.

"No," said the Regional Director. "And it isn't French. And it doesn't mean 'naïve.' It means underfed. Undernourishing, actually."

"I looked it up," said the young woman. "It also means unsophisticated."

"I stand corrected," said the Regional Director.

"If 'jejune' isn't French," said the young man, "the kid lied on his essay about where he learned it. You see what I'm driving at? Read this essay a certain way, it can seem kind of calculated. Ingratiating. Kind of sweaty to get in."

"Oh, no!" said the young woman. "That's not fair! It's a wonderful essay. Straight from the heart!"

"On first glance it seems like an awfully young essay," said the Regional Director.

"He won't be sixteen till April," said the young woman.

"Yeah," said the young man. "April Fool's Day. Darling."

"Maybe a P.-G. year would make sense," said the Dean.

"Look at the essay," said the young woman. "It's a heartfelt, wise essay. It needs no defending. I've read hundreds and hundreds, I've read thousands of these damned things. I can't remember one of them. I can't even remember the drivel I wrote to get in here. All I remember is how smart I felt psyching out what you"—looking at the Dean—"and you"—looking at the Regional Director—"wanted to hear. I applied to this place celebrated for its honor system with a strategic lie of about five hundred words, cut to order. This boy applies with the best truth he knows how to say, and—"

"Maybe he had help with it," said the Regional Director. "His father's a writer, mother's a teacher."

"Come on!" said the young woman. "First, I can't believe either of them would let him put this story in the mail. I mean, calculating is one thing, but to use a story of the father roostering around, cheating on the mother: not on your life!"

"That's my point," said the young man. "It gives me the creeps. Too raw. Too . . . personal."

"No fair," said the young woman. "Essay 3 tells these kids to open a vein, and Jake Clay opened a vein."

"I'm a bit in the dark on this one," said the Regional Director. "The Supplemental Material essay is interminable, and the boy paid no attention to our space requirements on Essay 3. To which, I notice, he added Essay 2."

"Okay," said the young woman. "So sue him. But he's a great kid."

The Dean wondered about the boy's accomplishments as a skier. The young woman read a letter from Jake's ski coach at Mad River, saying Jake skied flat-out, recklessly, also saying the captain was "the most unique captain I've ever coached in my three years as a coach." Also saying that in U.S. History, which the coach taught, Jake "read too much for his own good" and didn't know how to keep his mouth shut: "At college someone should teach him to button his lip!" The young woman said she'd asked Jake about his Eastern Regional ski championship, and he'd shrugged it off.

"He told me he's probably peaked. Too tall. Has other interests. The athletic accomplishment that raced his motor was a Little League championship game—"

"Is he varsity material?" the Dean wondered.

"No, no," the young woman said. "But he gave me this great blow-by-blow of a Padres-Dodgers game when he was eleven. The ball's hit sharply toward him at third base, he lunges to his left, snares it, pegs across to first, nips the Dodger at first . . . that kind of thing. Oh, fly-fishing. I asked him what he'd read recently and he told me about—I mean *all* about—Norman Maclean's *A River Runs Through It*. I had to beg Jake to stop listing the fish he'd snagged, and how he'd snagged them, and where he was when he snagged them, and what he snagged them with, and how big they were, and how they tasted, and who ate them."

"So the kid's a bore," said the young man.

"No," said the Regional Director. "He's a trout fisherman."

"He's not a bore," said the young woman. "For one thing, the way he talked about Norman Maclean got me to read *A River Runs Through It*. For another, he's a sweetie pie."

"O-*kay*," said the young man. "Yo, Julie! Go for it!"

Julie laughed. "Cut me some slack."

"This isn't all that bad," said the Dean, reading through half-glasses. "He's got pep, a voice."

"Raw, maybe," said the Regional Director. "An uncut diamond, perhaps?"

"Not really," said the young woman. "Someone, probably his father, dressed him up in tweeds and flannels—cuffed—for the interview. Timberland boat shoes. The etceteras."

"Tie?" asked the young man.

"No," said the young woman.

"Perfect," said the young man.

"Such a sweetie," she said. "Had notes written all over his hands. Appointments. Addresses. He came down in the spring. Stopped to see Amherst on the way."

"Amherst is perfect for him," said the Regional Director.

"Grades aren't good enough for a non-legacy," said the Dean. "Middlebury, maybe. Definitely Middlebury, with the skiing?"

"I don't know," said the young woman. "The Amherst interviewer told Jake to go home till winter. That if he saw Princeton in the spring we'd steal him away, no contest."

"Sounds as if Amherst wants him," said the Regional Director. "His mother's Smith connection might be a factor."

"How do we know Amherst tried to head him off?" asked the young man. "We know because *he* told us."

"Oh, cut it out!" said the young woman. "He told me because he was knocked out by the orange tulips in Prospect Gardens."

"Was he knocked out by the black tulips in Prospect Gardens?" said the young man.

"It's late," said the Dean. "We're tired, we haven't met our quota of fly-fishermen, I want him. Okay?"

"Great!" said the young woman.

"Okay by me," said the Regional Director.

"It's worth something that his mother's a teacher," said the young man. "But, wow! All those dead-pet stories!"

"Plus his father writes," said the young woman.

"What *does* he write?" said the Regional Director. "Anything I should have read?"

The young man shrugged, didn't know.

The young woman shrugged, never heard of Nathaniel Clay.

The Dean said, "He writes for *Gentry*. He's the guy who does the ethics column."

"The *what* column?" asked the Regional Director.

"Ethics," said the Dean. "As in morals, principles, codes of conduct, values."

"Oh," said the young man and the young woman.

"I see," said the Regional Director, turning the pages of "A Lovely Father."

Twelve

The Man Who Wrote
the Ethics Column

It had been almost ten years since Polly sent Nathaniel away. Forever? That wasn't Polly's way, to *forever* someone she'd held in her arms and whispered secrets to. She'd exiled him, she said, until he learned to want to be happy and to behave better. Until she longed to eat breakfast with him more than she longed to punch him in the snoot. Then, maybe, she'd send for him. Given the terms of return, Nathaniel had assumed he'd been heave-ho'd for good. Nevertheless, he had lived all this time in a room at the Princeton Club, to trick himself into hoping his expulsion was temporary, that nothing but an unpacked suitcase stood in the way of homecoming.

Nathaniel's first year alone—oh, *very* alone!—in New York he had bulled through revisions of a second novel and dashed off celebrity profiles and cultural meditations for magazines. As his second novel moved ever deeper into fens more tangled and murky than the swamp at the end of "Big Two-Hearted River," he became handier, slicker, trimmer as an occasional journalist. By the time of Watergate, he was a pro, a writer to whom editors assigned Big Ideas.

The ethics column was his Big Idea. His novel had been respectfully rejected by half a dozen of the dozen or so publishers who had earlier rejected an earlier version. He rolled up his sleeves to have at the thing again, and the more he read of it the less he understood. To read *What Teiresias Saw* was to glimpse a penumbra of unfamiliar shapes obscured in the dim owl-light before blindness. As he reread the chaotically amended manuscript of that second novel, Nathaniel labored to remember what he'd forgotten since he wrote his first. To remind himself of the nature of the mission he had launched himself upon, he spent an afternoon in the Princeton Club library with *The Great Gatsby*, the very narrative whose purity had made him, thundering east on the Empire Builder, want to make up stories. But no sooner had he embarked on his refresher course in the art of clarity than he saw, clearly, that all this time he had mistaken his calling. It was not make-believe the lover had wanted to make; the adulterous Nathaniel had wanted to make judgments.

Nathaniel, wishing to go easy on himself, liked to recollect Nick Carraway's page 1 recollection of his father's advice to go easy on people who may not have "had the advantages that you've had." Right off, Nick brings to aphoristic judgment his habit of withholding judgment: "Reserving judgments is a matter of infinite hope. I am still a little afraid of missing something if I forget that, as my father snobbishly suggested, and I snobbishly repeat, a sense of the fundamental decencies is parcelled out unequally at birth."

But overleaf Nick reveals an opposing habit of character, and it was this tic of discrimination that caught Nathaniel's eye with the force of revelation that afternoon in the Princeton Club library: "And, after boasting this way of my tolerance, I come to the admission that it has a limit. Conduct may be founded on the hard rock or the wet marshes, but after a certain point I don't care what it's founded on."

Eureka. In that summer of Watergate, Nathaniel would write about conduct! Nathaniel's misbegotten second novel had been rejected with delicacy and good will, without condescension, by a fellow who had now left book publishing to become the new editor of the venerable *Gentry,* a magazine divided against itself: in the near corner—consumer guidance; in the far corner—hip, anti-bourgeois journalism. Tape decks and bell-bottoms were winning the bout on points; the new editor was hired to fix the fight for literature. Nathaniel pitched his Big Idea for an ethics column to the new editor. All due respect, the editor of *Gentry* had said (with all due respect), "Why you?" Nathaniel had explained, beginning with Princeton's honor code. He knew right from wrong, by God, and believed he could find words to tell the difference. The country was going to hell in a handcart, and someone should preach the verities: why it was wrong to cheat, connive, abuse power, read others' mail, break promises, betray trust, betray friends, betray your wife. Oh, and lie: one thing for sure, he'd never tell (his readers) a lie. He would be a compass adjuster, take on Hemingway's burden of showing (except— big *except*—he would tell rather than show) why a life can be said to be well or ill led according to the smallest decisions, made serially, accumulating into the personal history of a Good Man or a Bad Man.

Well and good, the new editor of *Gentry* had said, that summer of Watergate. Would Nathaniel please specify? What ethical question, for example, would his first essay ask? Nathaniel said he'd like to write about reliability. What kinds of men could men trust to come through? In a hunting blind, say, or in combat, or during a showdown meeting with a client, or if money were needed, or in an underdog eight-oared shell leading a better boat by a seat, with two hundred meters to go. The bid was a go, a modest hit on the newsstands, an entire issue devoted to the question posed on its cover: WHEN THE GOING GETS TOUGH, WHO'S IN SEVEN SEAT? Literary personages weighed in with uplifting celebrations of Friends Who Were There in the Crunch, or downcasting revelations of Ex-Friends Who Were Not There When the Cards Were Down.

Nathaniel, using the pen name "Nick Carraway," wrote the summary essay; he had found his profession. In months to come he meditated upon hypotheses:

• Being told by a college roommate, ten years after graduation, that the teller had cheated on a final exam.

• Being subtly seduced by a friend's wife (kin by marriage).

• A friend, down on his luck, owes one money. How does one negotiate the shoals?

• Hearing from the mouth of an otherwise decent fellow the word "kike."

• Getting caught in an adulterous relationship because a son taught to tell only the truth told only the truth to his mother.

. . . etcetera, etcetera, etcetera, unto some dozens of hypothetical etceteras, until he no longer felt comfortable trading on the name Nick Carraway and changed his byline to "Polonius," whereupon he wrote about:

• Whether and how long a writer might hide from his loyal and helpful employer the writer's eagerness to shop his talents to a rival magazine.

• Why it's a mistake to borrow from or loan money to a friend.

• What to say when a friend asks about a woman you cannot abide: "What do you really think of my wife? I'm going to leave her. Do you have a problem with that?"

• *If* a university's trustees—call the place P.—got a phone call from a Wall Street friend, and *if* the friend said "sell Penn Central right now, this morning, before lunch," and *if* P. were the largest single stockholder of Pennsy, and *if* P.'s endowment were a National Trust in the Nation's Service, was it wrong to sell Pennsy?

. . . etcetera, etcetera, etcetera, etcetera, until he came out from behind the arras where Polonius had hid before he got run through, and called himself "Nathaniel Clay," and then dropped the arched eyebrows of the quotation marks. Irony. Irony's a bitch. When Nathaniel heard his voice go skittish and laconic, when he caught himself kite-tailing to a heart-lifted declarative sentence a clause of deadweight dragdown, when he grafted a parenthetical (ironical) modification onto every clean expository line, when he retracted, held out, smirked, sneered, let the air out, said *Says who?* . . . Who instructed him? Johnny Hyde didn't teach Nathaniel Clay that to be wise was to be a wise guy. Where had Nathaniel learned to feel such terror at the prospect of being fooled, of seeming a fool?

This sunny spring morning a few months before his twentieth reunion, a few days after Ginger had been admitted to Princeton midway through Jake's second semester of his second year, a couple of hours before he was to meet Ginger and Polly for dinner, Nathaniel was walking Forty-third Street west toward *Gentry*'s offices on the Avenue of the Americas. He was cobbling up material for his next column. Boy, was he short of material. Had been, he knew now, since he began the damned ethics column. Still, wasn't it now a little late in the day to question his standing to scold and map the high ground and pontificate on Generosity, Honor, Loyalty, Ambition, Courage, Masculinity, Monogamy? "Nick Carraway" and "Polonius" and "Nathaniel Clay" and Nathaniel Clay had sounded off on owning up to responsibility for acts and running around outside the marriage and self-indulgence and he didn't know what all. Oh, on lies: little white, charcoal gray and midnight black. Who did he think he was?

Never mind. *Carpe diem!* So bright and clear a day, such promise in it, he was whistling despite himself—"Lush Life"—when a young guy snatched a shopping bag. Nathaniel saw it, not six feet away. The woman shrieked—exact quote—

"Stop; thief!" Just like that; with the medial caesura. So Nathaniel lit off after him. He was fast, but Nathaniel was fast too. Nathaniel surprised himself. He didn't think then about not thinking through the ramifications, but he did think, Okay, here it is, the final heat, you're going for the gold. Nathaniel was gaining on him, truly. The crowd was cheering, and then Nathaniel was down. Someone threw an elbow under his chin, right in the neck, directly across the street from the Princeton Club, and he went down. And then, breathless and hurting, Nathaniel heard the victim again: "No, no, no! Not that asshole! It was the nigger!" He felt so bad. Worn out. So he sat where he was sitting, on the sidewalk, thinking he'd better stay right there, because where was there to go? A memory stole into his consciousness. A black kid riding the Pennsy south from New York, dressed in a clean white T-shirt, circling the want-ads, smiling, sitting alone by the window in a seat for two on an overcrowded coach, finally not smiling. How old would he be now? Older than the young fellow Nathaniel had just chased after. As old as Nathaniel. Nathaniel wished he were back twenty-four years, riding the Dinky that first time, going to meet Pownall Hamm for the first time, to see Princeton for the first time.

"Let me get this straight," said the editor of *Gentry*. "You want to write a column for our magazine about a practice called Bicker? Is that what you just told me? What in the lovva Mike's a Bicker?"

Nathaniel knew this editor was a good editor, and Nathaniel knew why. He'd been raised and schooled in Nebraska, and he wore a bolo necktie with a turquoise cinch, and seemed not to have heard of bell-bottoms. On his walls were furious letters to the editor, some of which had amused the editor and some of which had chastened him. It was to the editor's credit, Nathaniel believed, that Nathaniel couldn't figure out which had entertained, which instructed. Model airplanes hung by threads above the editor's desk: Lightning, Mustang, Corsair, Thunderbolt. He had debated their merits with Jake, who didn't care if the Thunderbolt had a top-speed advantage, he was a Mustang man all the way. The editor told Jake this was a kidlike opinion, and kept on his desk toy cars and a pea-shooter, which he used to shoot spitballs at copy editors. The editor's desk also had the advantage of a little flagpole up which he ran—for the benefit of his writers—signal pennants: a question mark for a puzzling proposal, an exclamation mark for a good idea, a period for an exhausted idea, a white flag to cave in.

This rumpled editor, no dope, was less interested in what he knew than in what he didn't know. His signature gesture was raised eyebrows, widened eyes. "You don't say," he'd say. "Tell me about it!" About the wide world's plenty this editor was inquisitive, so long as pieces of the world's plenty could be cut to usable length and made to catch a subscriber's eye.

"Bicker's what other colleges call 'rush,' " Nathaniel said.

"So?" the editor said. "Who cares about rush anymore? Who joins fraternities?"

"Eating clubs," Nathaniel said.

"I don't get it," the editor said. "What's to say?"

"Plenty," Nathaniel said, and then he explained the occasion for such a piece. That he'd been asked by his college alumni officer to bring his *vitae* up to date for his twentieth-reunion book, that his classmates required an essay of a couple of hundred words on The Meaning of Life, on what Nathaniel thought now about what he thought then, on what he'd learned. "They want me to own up to what's been fatter than I dreamed, what's been leaner. Maybe they want a nut of wisdom—"

"The futures market's going south?"

"No: more like 'What I Learned Walking Through the Fire of My Divorce.' "

"What did you learn?"

"Don't start on that again," Nathaniel said. "Besides, I'm not divorced."

"Ten years isn't divorced?" the editor said gently. "That's a long separation, Nathaniel; that would make one hell of a good column, how a ten-year separation works, what it's like."

"It's like personal, is what it's like."

"I thought *personal* was your vocation," said the editor of *Gentry*.

"I want to write an open column responding to a questionnaire from my Princeton classmates. I want to treat their little inquiry seriously, as though they don't expect taproom wiseassery, or a confession to feed their appetite for *Schadenfreude*. I'd like to write a column as though I believed they hope for a few words that can make a difference, a bite to chew on, a glimpse—nothing to excite envy, mind—of an old friend modestly prospering."

"I've known you how long?" said the editor.

"Ten years, a bit less."

"A long time," said the editor of *Gentry*. "Now's the first time I heard you talk like a cynic. What's eating you?"

"I'm not cynical! I'm not."

"How old are you?" the editor asked.

"I was '60."

"You're no sixty!"

"I am," Nathaniel said.

"Sixty years old?"

"Class of '60. You know?"

"I don't know. That's the problem here. I don't count by college classes. Cornhuskers don't. People don't."

"I do," Nathaniel said.

"Well," said the editor of *Gentry*. "Well . . ."

So Nathaniel told what was eating him. He wanted to be tested. He wanted to be given a binary—right answer, wrong answer—examination of his decency and courage.

"Listen," he told his editor, "I've daydreamed of the moment when a surgeon calls me into his office: 'Your son, to lead a normal life, must have a kidney transplant.' Would I come through? Would I ever! Is it wrong to test-drive the imagination with such a fancy?"

"I don't think so," said the editor. "I think you've got a piece there."

"I'm not talking about that kind of piece," Nathaniel said. "Thinking about giving away a piece of myself—a kidney, let's say . . . it's a way of setting up as a base camp the question I know I can answer, using it as a push-off point to grope toward the questions I can't answer, which are most of the questions I've asked in this column, and pretended to answer."

"You've done a pretty good job," said the editor of *Gentry*. "We're satisfied."

Nathaniel didn't like the sound of "satisfied." Was he about to be canned? Jumping was one thing, getting pushed another. But he knew what he couldn't say right. He had had no business setting up in this business. In what voice may one discuss conduct? He hadn't wished to hector, to scowl, to scoff, to proselytize, to deplore. Loud pedal or soft? What was the octave, tempo, key?

Nathaniel said, "I'm tugging at this, tugging at that, please be patient. I'm trying to lever a load off my heart, and I don't know where to place the crowbar. Let me try indisputable failure, how I believed at college events would fall out, and how they in fact fell out. First of all, I haven't written any *Great Gatsby*, and I'm not apt to."

"Give us a break!" said the editor of *Gentry*, running up a signal pennant, black dot on a white field. "Not Fitzgerald again? When was it? Three issues ago? Your column on 'The Rich Boy'? The opening passage: 'Begin with an individual, and before you know it you find that you have created a type; begin with a type, and you find that you have created— nothing.' "

"You quote accurately from memory," Nathaniel said. "How do you do that?"

"Frankly?"

"Sure."

"Because I had to edit that column through so many drafts. That was one jumbled piece of thinking."

" 'Tortured' was the word you used at the time," Nathaniel said. The editor shrugged. "There's a difference between jumbled and tortured."

"You're a good writer," the editor said. "I'll take your word for it. What was your point?"

"That Americans can't not typecast. It's our destiny. Even Fitzgerald, one paragraph after he wrote that 'there are no types, no plurals,' wrote: 'Let me tell you about the very rich. They are different from you and me. They—' "

"No," said the editor of *Gentry*, "I mean the point today, for the June issue."

"That I'm no Fitzgerald."

"So what?"

"So what exactly! I'm not tugging my forelock, scuffing the rug. This isn't some damned sprint I'm in. This is a long-distance event, and stamina counts, and I can train myself for stamina. What's wrong with this country, it's all finals. Final exams, final heats, final matches, sets, games, points, final words. . . ."

"I'm sorry," said the editor of *Gentry*. "You're losing me here. Going back to types: you mean to tell me the French don't type the Krauts? The Brits don't type the Frogs? You mean to tell me 'finals' is an American word, American idea?

Heard of the Olympics? Henley? You used to see things so clearly, Nathaniel. What's knotted you up? You're all loops, grays, byways. Why don't you do me a piece on your little drama coming over here? Crime, the good samaritan, bigotry, you in the middle. That could be a barn-burner."

"I want to write about Bicker—"

The editor of *Gentry* groaned.

"—about being a student. What I learned. How I learned not to be a fool. My classmates taught me to value above all things not being anyone's fool. From my classmates I learned how to dig down inside myself, way deep where my truth hides, below my heart, below my belly laugh, to scheme profoundly for . . . a wisecrack. Who would want to learn such a thing? Have you ever seen a Bicker committeeman's face while he talks to someone he thinks is a fool? The smirk is not a pretty sight, and it will not do for a Bickered boy to be anyone's fool. What in the lovva Mike is Bicker, you asked. It's an institution's way of telling some people they're assholes and telling other people they're not. Why should you care what involuntary reflex played across the puss of a Bicker committeeman? Good question. It's a question that my classmates have asked in their fucking questionnaire: 'Do you feel Bicker and the selective club system should be abolished?' If I say yes or no, I'm supposed to say whether I feel what I feel *not very strongly* or *fairly strongly* or *very strongly*. I feel what I feel very strongly. But why? It's not as though I was shanghaied freshman year by pocket patricians and cut to fit a cult of condescension. I assume that my classmate friends valued me—and they did value me—precisely for those foolish, unstudied qualities from which I fled pell-mell. I was, I think, a decent man."

"Safe to say," said the editor of *Gentry*. "But there's more to it than that."

"You think I don't know that?" said Nathaniel. "I'm compressing the complications, a bad habit that comes of writing to length. Remember how college was at its best between Thursday midnight and dawn of a classless Friday? There seemed to be all the time in the world to tell stories painstakingly, doubling back on them, testing them for the quality of their ore."

Then Nathaniel tried to tell the editor of *Gentry*, who seemed to listen carefully, why Nathaniel believed Bicker was not an interesting use of a great institution. Nathaniel told of coming east from the aboriginal northwest to sit in lecture halls and at round tables in preceptorials to learn tolerance, grace under pressure, the best that had been done and thought, what had been what, what should have been what, what might be what. Nathaniel told of coming east, dreaming these dreams of fundamental apprehensions that would be reached, at his college, with his fellows, together. With his comrades he would study, reason, exhort, distinguish.

"And so you did," said the editor of *Gentry*. "Did you not?"

"Jesus," said Nathaniel. "Where did you go to college?"

"I didn't," said the editor of *Gentry*. "I thought you'd never ask. So what did you do together?"

"Some of us rowed boats together, but to the end of eliminating another boy from his seat, another crew from the race. We shared tall tales and lore with roommates, sometimes late at night in the no-man's-land of a dark room, usually after loosening up with beer or tequila. We told how a second cousin had a friend whose dad was a curator at the Smithsonian who had seen—with his own eyes!—John Dillinger's dick, fourteen inches pickled in alcohol, doubled back on itself in a mason jar."

"Do you believe that story?" asked the editor of *Gentry*, raising his eyebrows, widening his eyes.

"Of course!" said Nathaniel.

"Good," said the editor of *Gentry*. "So do I."

"What did we do together? We argued ideas together—if

hunches and prejudices can pass for ideas, which they can—
but almost always exclusively—*exclusively*—in the controlled
laboratory of a classroom. Passion for learning was not unusual, but it was judged excessive, as shameful as wearing my
heart on my sleeve. So my passion was solitary, I snuck off solo
to Firestone Library, down to a basement carrel, a weenie bin
on dank C floor where light did not reach. In the sunlight of
a Saturday afternoon we cheered Princeton against Yale together, and laughed together at the uncool sound of our cheers,
and then cheered the Princeton marching band because it
couldn't keep time, or stay in step. We weren't black and
white together. The single black man in our class wrote a
sociology thesis titled 'A Study of White Adulation of Negro
Jazz Musicians.' Did we love music? We sang together, some
of us, after drinking together, most of us. At Junior Prom we
made a conga line, danced the bunny hop together, but this
too was for irony, to laugh at our foolishness. We laughed
together. We did surely laugh together, and I miss our laughter. I've lost the gift of foolishness. I'm unfooled. Too wise to
my act. I'd like to be a fool again."

"Sounds doable," said the editor of *Gentry*.

"I mean dreamy. Literal. A b'gosh and b'golly fool."

"Innocent?" said the editor of *Gentry*.

"Innocent," said Nathaniel. "We did surely laugh, back
then. I wish I didn't remember how much of that laughter was
charged to the account of others, reserved for outsiders, fools,
weenies."

"It sounds to me," said the editor of *Gentry*, "collegial."

"What was collegial about our college? What yoked us?
Booze and Bicker. We drank purple passion together from a
common garbage can, and together, like members of some
damn-fool country club, we excluded one another. I came to
Princeton to learn to discriminate between what was generous
and what was awful. Instead, the principal principle of dis-

crimination I had drummed into me was between the weenie and the non-weenie. What was a weenie? A Jew, a high-schooler, a greaser, a boy wearing a two-button jacket, a boy with an 'exotic' accent, a boy with garlic on his breath, a boy with a father with garlic on his breath. In the spirit of candor let me say I was a weenie."

"What a word!" said the editor of *Gentry*. "It's kind of private, though. Particular to a time and place. Sort of a microcosm kind of thing, a microcosm of a microcosm. I don't want your piece to need a goddamned glossary. Do you really want to write about being a weenie?"

"Listen," said Nathaniel. "I was hurt by a cohort of tweeded strangers. To admit this isn't cheap. It will cost me to tell readers, strangers, that strangers had such power over me, but they had power over me, and that was wrong, and even if I can't write *The Great Gatsby* I can maybe tell how it felt and why it was wrong."

"You can't be trying to tell me you became a writer to shove it up the pipe of some kid in a striped tie who was—once upon a time—mean to you?"

"In part, by God. In part. It's more complicated than that, but no more noble. I became a writer to send love letters to a girl I loved in seventh grade, who didn't love me back. And on the off chance that another girl whose father's lawn I mowed would read me and say, 'Nathaniel Clay. Wasn't he the guy who mowed Daddy's lawn?' And because if I don't mean it, I don't want to say it. And to license myself to tell lies—"

"That could be an interesting piece," said the editor of *Gentry*.

"And to correct with truths on the page the lies I've told with my mouth."

"Now *there's* your piece for June!" (And up went the excla-mation signal.)

And so it was. It came to be that Nathaniel Clay, who had

known if he knew anything that he would never lie to his children, used the unfathomable indulgence of *Gentry* to right a wrong, correct a deceit, fuse a time bomb set to go off the week before Princeton's reunions. The published column was a letter, addressed to Jake and Ginger. *About your grandfather?* the ethics column asked. *My father? Who died? He didn't, in fact, die climbing. The Matterhorn or any other summit. He died falling in a men's club bar. That's how he died. And not how I said he died. I'm sorry. Now you're unfooled. Be fools.*

And that was all. Nathaniel used to deliver the goods, open his veins. The damnedest aspect of Nathaniel's ethics column: to write so close to the heart was seedy, utterly incongruent with the ethical precepts of his teachers at his college, professors and classmates. For their distinct purposes his teachers had favored reticence over candor: professors professed inference, renounced authorial intrusion; friends valued restraint, oblique discourse. Understatement and good taste were synonyms, to Nathaniel's old friends. So how did he get here, bare-ass naked to the weather, spilling his guts? What he wouldn't confess out loud to his kids, he'd sell strangers. But not a word more than he meant. Nathaniel used to write to length. The editor of *Gentry*, running up the white flag, opined that forty-five words made for a mighty terse ethics column. Nathaniel could see the editor's point of view, but he didn't have another word to add, and so it was that the man who writes the ethics column became the man who wrote the ethics column.

Thirteen
The Final Club

By sunset he'd whistled at springtime, chased a thief, been called an asshole, and talked himself out of a job; now he was deep in a leather chair, in the lobby of the Princeton Club, trying to look as casual as he'd tried to look twenty-two years ago. Under the Clock. Nathaniel was waiting for Polly and Ginger, waiting to celebrate. They were due at six; the clock said six; they were here.

Ginger had got the thick envelope yesterday. So how did he feel about that? Having his college be their college? Dandy, he thought. It wasn't his college, after all. Wasn't anyone's. It was some buildings and ideas. Buildings change; ideas change.

Polly hadn't changed. Her face was flushed; her hair was in her eyes, blown there by breakneck walking. She moved fast, Polly.

Now she was standing over him, running her fingers through his hair: "God almighty! Who cut it?"

"Club barber," he said. "Ginger, baby. Are you proud?"

Ginger shrugged; Ginger grinned.

"I always cut your hair," Polly said. "No one else knows how to cut your hair."

Nathaniel stared at her. Was his wife asking him a question? When Polly had invited him to go away, Nathaniel had set himself an exercise. He'd be loyal. Who'd care? That was the point. Maybe he'd never be asked, "Are you seeing any-one?" Probably he wouldn't. He'd never been asked before. It wasn't the kind of question Polly asked or had to ask. But if he was asked, he reckoned he could answer any way at all— "What do you mean, seeing?" or "No, I'm not seeing and have not seen" or "Nope"—and it would sound true, uttered off-hand or an octave too deep: *no*. So she had never asked, until— maybe—now.

How had it happened? How had he let it happen? He'd worked up answers, had had time aplenty to calculate answers. For instance, when he hit thirty the snow didn't fall as thick and white, and a New York Checker cab didn't smell as though it had just given a ride to the Deb of the Year. It wasn't just snow that had petered out dingy. Illusion was leaking out of him. Could there be an older story? When he wasn't writing, which was most of the time, he was leading himself around by his heart, hunting for one girl who would remind him for a week or a night the way he felt once—*one* time!—riding east on the Empire Builder. He wanted to smell her perfume again. He could have made it easier on people who cared what became of him; he could have picked up a telephone, dialed a number he knew, asked Diana straight out, "What brand of perfume did you wear when you were eighteen?" It would have been a better thing if he'd been dumb enough not to understand how pathetic an enterprise he'd chosen, chasing (his) tail. The fool he did *not* wish to be was the sort of fool he was, a stooge of the boudoir. No more. For now. Day at a time, as Pownall would have it. Day at a time.

Ginger had never seen the Princeton Club. It was comfort-able: too clean, too quiet, but comfortable. Crossing the threshold from the lobby to the Princeton Bar, Ginger looked down and read an inscription cut in a stone floor plaque: "Where women cease from troubling and the wicked are at rest."

"What does that mean?" Ginger said.

"I never noticed it before," Nathaniel said.

"What does it mean, Mom?"

"It means your father has lived too long in this joint."

Thus he was returned from exile.

A couple of months later, Nathaniel drove his mother and Polly and Ginger from Vermont. On the New Jersey side of the George Washington Bridge a gray sky began to leak gray rain, and by the time the Clays passed the oil refineries south of Bayonne the rain gusted in sheets. Polly and Ginger said to wait it out in a Ho-Jo, but Nathaniel pressed on. He'd paid through the nose to bring his mother east for his Twentieth Reunion cocktails, Twentieth Reunion dinner, Twentieth Reunion dance to the velvet and satin strains of Peter Duchin. She'd never seen Princeton. The rain hammered the windshield. Jake would meet them in Holder Court in an hour. Nathaniel laid his foot into the Saab, and switched off the radio's dire report of the cold front's progress.

"At least we can't see New Jersey," Polly said.

"At least we can't smell it," Ginger said.

"I think you're both much too mean about New Jersey," Nathaniel's mother said. "It's a very garden of a state."

"Girls," Nathaniel said. "Please?"

"I'm having a great time," Polly said.

"I've never had a better time than this," Ginger said.

"Ninety-nine bottles of beer on the wall," Polly sang.

"Roll me o-ver, in the clo-ver," Ginger sang.

Nathaniel's mother sang, "I want a gal . . . just like the gal . . . who married dear old Dad."

"Put a sock in it," Nathaniel said, "or you'll get 'I've Got a Lovely Bunch of Coconuts.' "

At Exit 9 off the New Jersey Turnpike the sky was torn by lightning, and they pulled over. Polly covered her ears; it was an awful tempest, and it shook the car. Ginger sat phlegmatic, as though she were with Jake at a horror movie whose purpose was to offer an opportunity to show a poker face. Thunder clapped an inch above their roof, and Polly flinched. Nathaniel and Ginger looked directly at each other, with droopy lids; neither blinked.

"How's the popcorn?" Nathaniel said.

"Nice show of noise," Ginger said. "Remarkably high fidelity."

"I know what high fidelity means," Nathaniel's mother said.

"Jerks," Polly said. "My husband and daughter are just a couple of jerks."

Ginger said, "I'll be taking that remark to my analyst someday: 'Mumsy used to call me a jerk, Doctor.' "

"If the shoe fits," Polly said.

The cloudburst spent itself, and Nathaniel drove Route 1 south of New Brunswick through a feeble drizzle. A few miles short of the Washington Road turnoff, running half an hour behind schedule, they had a blowout. The Saab veered into the high-speed lane; nothing hit them. Nathaniel wrenched the wheel right and manhandled the car onto the shoulder, and for a moment they sat there. Ginger and Polly seemed impassive. Nathaniel trembled.

"What are we doing here?" he said.

"Meeting Jake," his mother said.

"What is he doing here?" Nathaniel said.

"Going to his daddy's college," Ginger said. "Like me."

"Going to your reunion," Polly said.

"Having fun," Ginger said.

"In the meantime, in betweentime, ain't we got fun?" Polly sang.

Nathaniel and Ginger changed the wheel. They had done this before; they didn't have to bargain a division of labor:

Nathaniel dirtied his hands on the spare and Ginger jacked and cranked off the lugs. Passing cars sprayed gouts of water at them, and Ginger hummed "Raindrops Keep Falling on My Head." Nathaniel looked around; the farmland he'd known twenty years back had been clear-cut and bulldozed: the University was building another research park, or shopping center. The landscape was unfamiliar to Nathaniel. There's just one first look at a place; after that there's only review, revision. He could never again see Princeton the way he'd seen it from the Dinky platform, fresh, green, lush, *his*. Wet and dirty, still frightened, he began again to tremble.

"Toss it in the trunk, Dad, and let's blast off."

Behind the wheel again, Nathaniel said, "I'm sorry."

"For what?" Polly said.

"I don't know."

Nathaniel signed in at an orange-and-black canvas pavilion deployed over Holder Court. He was given a program of events. Among those events was a meeting of the Princeton Alumni Gay Alliance. (Nathaniel looked to his right and left: who?) Among these events were twice-daily meetings of A.A. (Nathaniel had no need to look right or left: straight on sufficed.) He was given a necktie, orange-and-black striped tigers rampant on striped fields of orange and black; the tigers bore the legend 60 on their foreheads. The necktie, to be worn tomorrow in the P-rade, completed a class costume whose other component was a jacket. Nathaniel had believed that his college was incapable of surprising him, but this jacket surprised him. A beer jacket wouldn't have surprised him, a safari jacket wouldn't have, a frigging Nehru jacket wouldn't. This was a gray polyester jacket. What Monkey Ward would sell with a two-pants suit. Not banker's gray: banker's mail clerk's gray. Shapeless, hapless, resigned. This was a jacket to wear running up the white flag, stipulating to error, shopping for a used Plymouth ("I'm just hoping for dependable transportation, nothing fancy"), signing the Chapter Eleven agreements. This was a jacket to be buried in.

This was a jacket Nathaniel did not wear. Carrying it slung over his shoulder in a way he had learned in Newport to carry a dinner jacket after the dancing ended and before the sun came up, Nathaniel led Polly and Ginger among his classmates clotted here and there under the tent. The massed effect of gray polyester was oppressive and unsettling. He spied ex-boys who'd written in their twentieth-reunion book about their volunteer work for the Community Chest and Temple Beth Israel, classmate after classmate who'd "had my ups and downs, but on the whole I guess I'm satisfied." He saw fellow-graduates who'd been pictured for their twentieth-reunion book wearing riding boots, or patting a golden retriever. He searched for his college classmate who'd listed in outline form—"I" through "VIII," with sub-rubrics "(a)" through "(c)" under each heading—the reasons he decided to practice ophthalmology in Troy, New York. Who could have guessed the iron predictability? That there was always, everywhere, a classmate who'd navigated the Amazon on a camel and crossed the Sahara in a dugout canoe only to "come home to Procter & Gamble"? How could he have known? But then Nathaniel couldn't have guessed he'd lie to his kids, either, or to anyone.

Ginger had spied Jake, laughing hard.

"He's such a geek," Ginger said. "Listen to that hee-haw! You can't miss him!"

Jake was laughing with Benjamin Griggs. It had to be a Griggs: same hawky blade of a nose, same icy eyes. And there was Pownall; he looked younger than ten years ago, and he seemed to be the cause of Jake's laughter.

"Dad! Mr. Hamm was telling about your run-in with a razor back when you were in college."

Here they all were. Ginger and Jake punching each other in

the arm, Jake kissing his grandmother, Polly running her hand through Jake's hair, hugs here and laughter there. It was confusing to Nathaniel. He had wished to time-travel back to before. Before what? Before it stopped becoming. Before it became. Even before the Dinky. Back to the station platform in Seattle, to that moment when he poised a toe on the steps of the Empire Builder. Not that he wanted to live again back when, a visit was fine.

He was on the point of introducing himself to the haggard stranger wearing a ponytail and a patchy ginger beard when he saw who it was: "Booth! What the hell? Booth?"

"It's only long hair and a beard, Nathaniel. Don't be alarmed. Same old Boothy under the skin. I'm still a meat-eater. Come here and let me get a look at you."

Of course Nathaniel had heard, but nothing could have prepared him for the experience of this Booth Tarkington Griggs. This was not at all the same old Boothy, under the skin or anywhere. Booth had nursed his mother through an ugly, deceitful, patient, determined cancer; Mrs. Griggs's death was slow; Booth's vice versa was sudden and violent. Within weeks post-mortem he had put off his lendings, told Diana he wanted a divorce, moved to Trenton (the worst sinkhole his limited experience of sinkholes could call to mind), and begun to study how to be of use, how to help the dying die and the surviving live with as little pain and as much dignity as circumstance allowed.

"Crikey, Booth! I couldn't have guessed!"

"Oh, Nathaniel. Don't be so theatrical. If you couldn't guess it's either because you sold me short or I sold you long. I guessed that you could have guessed. It's just a job. Novel for a Griggs, I'll grant you, but any job is novel for a Griggs."

Benjamin Griggs said, "I work, Father."

"Of course you do! Mrs. Clay, my son helped raise this very tent."

"With Jake's help," Benjamin said.

Nathaniel remembered: it was a plum job, reserved for jocks. Working reunions paid a fine hourly wage, and gave the workers the run of the place, the best parties, legendary tips, life-changing job offers, seats in poker games at which the drunk old-timers competed to lose significant money. This lucky job made kids feel smarter than they were, the way prizes made prizewinners feel.

Now they were all talking, two by two, and laughing. Now it felt comfortable, and to feel time slip away made Nathaniel feel he was floating. He went woozy, and woozy he welcomed. The women listened while the old friends remembered together, boring Benjamin and Jake and Ginger silly. Benjamin seemed comfortable with his father, and why not? Nathaniel had assumed Benjamin would be embarrassed by the beard and the ponytail. The beard and the ponytail were, after all, ridiculous, but why should Benjamin know this? Nathaniel wondered: was he a snob, too? Nathaniel knew: he was a snob. Nathaniel wondered: had he been taught to be a snob? Nathaniel knew: he had studied hard to be a snob.

But to hell with that. Here they were, together. Polly asked after her cousin, and learned that Diana was arriving tonight, to watch Benjamin row tomorrow morning. Nathaniel said he would be glad to see Diana again, and Polly didn't give Nathaniel a sharp look, and Booth didn't give Nathaniel a sharp look.

Now other classmates, strangers mostly, began to join their group, tentatively at first, then easily. Hijinx were recollected, boat races were, classrooms were. Where they stood now, in Holder Court, they had gathered twenty-two years ago as sophomore cattle at a cattle auction, when they shared the final day of Bicker, when some stood clapping one another's backs, when some slunk hang-doggedly across Holder Court to eat alone in Commons, when Nathaniel hung on a telephone with a reporter from *The New York Times* debating why, exactly, he might have been a Hundred Percenter. But that was done! Nathaniel had put paid to that due bill. Hadn't he?

Nathaniel's classmates jabbered about the past, and slid into now. Months back, when he'd looked ahead to this experience, Nathaniel had expected a congress of extreme people. He'd warned himself to be vigilant, keep a weather eye for bores and fanatics. He'd expected to hear these Sons of Old Nassau deplore the removal of the cross from Chapel during the Opening Exercises of Jake's freshman year. He'd expected to hear middle-aged mossbacks bleat about the admission of too many high-schoolers, how smart-ass crummy the marching band had become, how about those Commies who'd fifth-columned the faculty? What happened to the good old bad old days when . . . He'd expected to hear it said of his son, who held unshaded views of apartheid and of Princeton's investment portfolio, *Wait till those kids have to meet a payroll!*

Nathaniel heard no such thing. Like Pownall, Pownall's classmates seemed to enjoy listening more than talking. They seemed . . . well, they seemed at peace. Not smug. Not even approximately smug. They seemed calmer was all. Maybe fashion had had a hand in their composure. Gone were the wild, wide neckties of ten years ago. Gone the wide lapels, wide bell-bottomed cuffs, wild doped eyes, dilated pupils, muttonchop whiskers. Here was nothing extreme. Jake wore a blue button-down shirt with a frayed collar, khakis, battered loafers. This was what Benjamin wore, with boat shoes, and the shirt was white. This was what Pownall wore. Everyone dressed as everyone used to dress. Regular. The men and boys looked like the men and boys of 1956. Regular.

Some few classmates had traded in wives on newer models, shooting to hold the wife age to mid-twenties, thirty max. These few fellows seemed anxious, overbarbered, on guard against bird-dogs. The few young wives seemed chipper, on the lookout for bird-dogs. Nathaniel would have warned Jake and Benjamin to keep clear of young wives who plan to be twenty-five forever, but what was the use? Tonight was Nathaniel's night to let be what would be. Tonight was Nathaniel's night to be surprised.

There was to be a sit-down dinner at (Hobey) Baker Hockey Rink. President Bowen would ask for money, surprise surprise. Nathaniel and his classmates had been asked for money. They could give one another chapter and verse on the beggar's cup. In 1980 Princeton's endowment came to more than a hundred fifty thousand dollars per student. Brown's was ten thousand. Princeton liked to use its riches as a club to beat greater riches from its get. *We're so rich! Won't you put another thou in the moneybags? Put a nickel on the drum and you'll be saved.* That was Riff Number One: *We're the richest, we're the best, only you can keep us Number One.* Riff Number Two: *We're so needy, we're barely keeping afloat, insurance is so high, fuel oil's through the roof, the janitors—ingrates—are pumping for a raise, help us, oh, it hurts so bad, oh, what are we to do, help!*

(A couple of weeks after Nathaniel finished his final ethics column for *Gentry*, a couple of weeks after Ginger was admitted to Princeton, Nathaniel got a phone call from a classmate who insisted on addressing him as "Nat." This fellow knew not only that Nathaniel had money in the bank, he seemed to know how much and where it had come from. Princeton was wise to market research, of course. But now it had private eyes on retainer. This classmate had confided in "Nat" his opinion that "inheritors of wealth" were under a special obligation to Princeton.

"Princeton counts on us," the classmate had said.

"I've given some," Nathaniel said.

"Nat, you've got kids. Think of their future."

"I've thought of little else. No. I don't know why I'm

telling you this, but this year my wife and I are giving what we give to a couple of local colleges."

"Nat! Stick with a winner!"

Usually the message was delivered in the idiom of High Institutional: *Paying the price of excellence, swim or drown, climb or fall* . . . But it came down in the end to the same old crap: winners beating losers, natural selection, kings of the castle raising the drawbridge to keep the dirty rascals on the other side of the moat.

"Stick it up your ass," Nathaniel had said.

"I'm sorry you feel that way, Nat. Princeton took in your kids. I'd hoped you'd be grateful."

"I'm hanging up now," Nathaniel said.

"Well, won't you reconsider? Our class is poised to top our giving goal. We could go right over the top with a little help. Whatever you could find it in your heart to give—")

Now, discussing whether to eat at Baker Rink, Nathaniel said, "They'll try to pick our pockets."

"Again," Booth said.

Pownall said, "They begged me for any old stocks I might have tucked away in my sock drawer. Tell me, guys, when did 'stock' become short for 'stocking'?"

Ginger said, "Are you serious, Mr. Hamm?"

"Usually," he said. "Too serious, usually."

Booth said, "Listen, why don't we pick up some fast food, wander over to Ivy, kick back upstairs, leave the hockey rink to the weenies in the gray jackets?"

Nathaniel said, "I was hoping to finally meet my class-mates."

Pownall said, "I can't, Booth, I've got to run a meeting."

Jake said, "What kind of meeting, Mr. Hamm?"

"Alcoholics Anonymous," Pownall said.

"But how can you be anonymous if you're telling us about it?" Ginger said.

"Ginger asks questions," Polly said.

"Diana said she'd meet me upstairs at Ivy," Booth said. "I promised you'd be there. I'm using you for bait. Please join us, Mrs. Clay. Come on, Polly."

Nathaniel said count me in; Polly said where he goes I go.

"Should we come?" Benjamin said.

"I can't," Jake said. "I'm not a member."

"You can be my guest," Benjamin said.

"I don't think so," Jake said, "I'll take a pass on eating clubs. Besides, Ginger's a girl—"

"Thanks for noticing," Ginger said.

"They don't let girls in," Jake said.

"She can be my date," Benjamin said.

"No, thanks," Jake said.

Nathaniel asked his children: "Have you read my June column in *Gentry*?"

"No," said Ginger.

He could see Jake thinking whether to lie. Jake hated to hurt his dad's feelings. "Is it a good piece?" Jake said.

Jesus! Why did his kids have to know how to call an essay a *piece*? "It's short," Nathaniel said. "It's a letter to you both."

"Great!" Jake said.

"Tomorrow for sure," Ginger said.

"Run along," Polly said.

A couple of hours later, upstairs at Ivy, munching sandwiches and potato chips, Booth and Nathaniel talked about their kids. How their kids didn't know their friends' last names, or even their full Christian names. They didn't know where their friends went to school, or what their friends' fathers did for a living. Nathaniel raised a glass to what their kids didn't know. Sometimes he wished he were "Polonius" again, telling Ginger and Jake how happy he was rowing at Princeton, urging them to row at Princeton. What was the use? The only way he could get Ginger to row was forbid her. He had reasoned with Jake, began with nobly periodic rhetoric about the majesty of the swing, when eight pull as one. Jake had looked at his old man blankly. Nathaniel had focused on the crew, calling the eight boys a "society of willing men." Jake had said *¡Caramba!* Nathaniel had told him crew would whip him into great shape; Jake had said do I look out of shape? Nathaniel had said rowing would introduce him to the best boys and girls at Princeton, and while Jake cocked his head, trying to puzzle out where *that* was coming from, Nathaniel felt a cold chill cramp his now unmuscled chest, and then his face flushed hot. So Nathaniel had told his son some people believed a seat on the first varsity heavyweight boat was as good for the rower's future as a half-million-dollar stake. Jake, bless him, had said, "Dad, how much is volleyball worth? Volleyball's such a hoot!"

That was last year. This year "Polonius" wanted to advise his younglings about friends and friendship. There'll be nothing like the friendships you'll have in that place where you are, Jake, where you're going, Ginger. Friendship here is a wonder, and a function of wonder. Friends find friends to wonder with; where have we been, where should we go? Friends are those few you dare be fools for. Nathaniel had told stories to friends of such terrifyingly unimpeded frankness that years later, writing personal essays, or an ethics column, he'd wonder what had now blocked his heart, why it wouldn't pump fierce fearless verity anymore.

What *had* happened? No want of aphorism to compress the process of ruin (see Emerson, Twain, Dr. Johnson, Chesterton), but be real: what *happened*? Pownall? Booth? Nathaniel has missed you. What *happened*? Marriage happened, he knew. Wonder relaxed, he guessed. Jake, Ginger: *you* happened. Nothing could have prepared him for you. At Princeton the future oppressed with possibility; if he could imagine it, it could happen. Nathaniel would be an Olympic gold medalist in Rome and Tokyo. His first novel would be eclipsed only by his second. He'd buy the Great Northern and name a train for his great-grandfather. He'd use his inheritance only for the benefit of others, share his royalties with novelists less successful. He'd be friends with his friends forever.

Now Booth raised a glass to the Final Club's absent friends, absent by choice. Tony had made a comeback in the equity markets, and this must have put lead in his pencil: first he forgave Roscoe for that ugly mess with Tony's wife; then he achieved what didn't seem to Roscoe a hostile take-over of Roscoe's textile company; then he put Roscoe out on his ass. Hearing these stories, Polly said the Final Club was like twelve little Indians, and here they were in the afternoon of life, down to two old oars paddling away, the stroke and the guy from the engine room. Polly said she thought it was all sort of sweet, and she smiled when she said it, and Diana, just then coming through the doorway with a bag of groceries to feed the friends, shook her wet hair and said, "What's so funny?"

Across campus, one entry over from his father's rooms sophomore year, Benjamin held court. His roomie Jake wore a headpiece called a "beer helmet," a contrivance made from a baseball batter's hard hat equipped with two brackets for beer cans; from the cans depended plastic tubing so that a boy could sip gravity-fed beer from both cans at once.

"There's a toga party over at '75," Benjamin said. "Frank said they've got Ray Charles there."

"Who's Frank?" said Ginger.

Jake said, "Frank's the guy we ran into at Woody-Woo who was with the humungous girl with cornstalk hair."

"She looked like a fucking Valkyrie," Benjamin said.

Ginger said, "You're speaking of one of my sisters, bub."

"What's Frank see in her?" Jake asked.

Benjamin said, "He's wearing beer goggles is all. When better women are made, Princeton men will make them."

"Jesus," Ginger said. "That old saw. Get out of my face. Besides, no more screwing around for you numbnuts. Screwers get sores all over them. *Time* says, right on the cover, the sexual revolution's over."

"Hey, not so fast!" Jake said. Then Jake sucked beer and went dreamy, recollecting a family visit to Martinique. "There was this monster full moon and me and Ginger lay on the beach under a palm tree in our lingeries—"

"Wow," said Benjamin.

"He means chaise lounges," Ginger said.

"Chaises longues," Benjamin explained.

"Up your *shez-a long-a*," Ginger said.

Their conversation had abrupt transitions. The three talked like party animals, and then they talked like professors. They talked like their parents' kids, and then they talked like their 'rents' 'rents.'

Now, in deference to Ginger's winning envelope, Benjamin was talking about admissions: "I coasted in. I had this old geezer who interviewed me eating out of my hand. No shit. I couldn't believe it. It was a cakewalk. I made a joke to show the common touch. I worked some Shakespeare into my essay, typed it myself so there'd be some typos and misspellings, got my old man up to speed with Annual Giving and kicked back to wait for the good news."

Benjamin Griggs believed admissions was rigged, and it wasn't.

Jake said, "I squeaked in. I figure my dad going here helped me."

Jacob Clay believed admissions was catch-as-catch-can, and it was.

Ginger said, "I think I deserved to get in."

Ginger Clay believed admissions was fair, and it wasn't. What *was* fair?

The three talked about Bicker, and about Ivy Club. Benjamin had opinions about Bicker, and about Ivy Club, and about Jake's failure of ardor for Bicker, and Ivy Club. Jake had had the benefit of Benjamin's opinions before tonight. Now Benjamin told Jake—for Ginger's benefit?—he should have Bickered, because he would have been a shoo-in. Jake said he hadn't wanted to join. Benjamin said, "Why not? The principal reason to join Ivy these days is to quit a few months later, no? Do I lie?" Benjamin said he'd heard Jake's father was some big Ivy gun, "a Hundred Percenter or something." Benjamin might have smirked: honest witnesses might disagree whether a twitch of smirk had adjusted Benjamin's lips. Jake, sucking at the stuff clamped to his beer helmet, said he wouldn't know about that. He said he didn't like how selective clubs told kids they hadn't made the cut, slipping empty envelopes under their doors. He was grossed out that club members trashed their clubs at parties and made the servants clean up the mess. He didn't like it that Ivy Club had waitresses and wouldn't let girls join. He didn't like any place that wouldn't let his sister be a member. The three talked about a lawsuit brought by a recent graduate against Ivy.

"Remember," Benjamin said, "Ivy members always stand when a lady enters the clubhouse."

"Fuck stands!" Ginger said. "Why not let ladies in?"

"Well, gals should have their own clubs. My ma belongs to the Chilton in Boston and the Colony in New York."

Jake said, "I know about the Colony. I went to a tea dance there."

Benjamin said, "Just so. They make a great cup of tea there; they make a small, teensy martini. Ma likes tea better than she likes marts, which is why she's not banging at the door of the Knickerbocker Club."

"Well, the only one I've heard of," said Jake, "is the Colony."

"This is a hundred percent the dumbest conversation I've ever heard," Ginger said. "Who owns all these leather books?"

"Those happen to be my books," Benjamin said. "I brought them back from England the year I studied at Shrewsbury."

Ginger said, with an inapproximate Oxbridge accent, "Well, I'm sorry, your royal high-ass." She took books from the case, turned pages. "Have you read all these books?"

"*Mais oui*," Benjamin said.

"Have you read *A History of Polo in the Punjab*?"

"I have."

"Have you read *The Campaigns of the Coldstream Guards*."

"I said I've read them all."

"All three volumes?"

"Now look," said Benjamin.

"How would that work?" Ginger said. "I mean I'm curious is all: how do you read every page of a book whose pages haven't been cut? I mean do you peek inside, or do you X-ray the pages? Maybe you use a little mirror, like dentists have? Or were these pages cut before, and then you glued them back together?"

"Come on, Ginger," Jake said. "Let's just have fun."

Ginger shrugged.

Then, out of nowhere, Benjamin began to tell them how it had been to be the Class Baby ten years ago. Jake had completely forgotten that his roommate was the goddamned Class Baby. Awesome!

"You remember the tiger on the back of my father's wagon?"

"Sure," Jake said. "My dad rode on the front of the wagon."

"God!" Ginger said. "You looked pathetic. You were wearing diapers! It was so dumb."

"Perhaps it was," Benjamin said. "But the night before,

under a reunion tent, I'd listened to my father tell another man—maybe *your* father—about tigers—"

"What's to tell?" Ginger said. "They're big, they're cats, they have stripes."

Benjamin stared at Ginger. Jake reloaded his beer helmet. Benjamin tilted his head at Ginger; he squinted; he smiled a gorgeous smile, a smile anyone would be pleased to get. "No, Ginger. There's more to the tiger's story than stripes and big." Ginger shrugged. "Well, during a Yale game my dad's freshman year, or—it doesn't matter—maybe his dad's freshman year, they had a Bengal tiger staked to a leash at Palmer Stadium. Sturdy stake, sturdy leash. Princeton men knew their geometry, so no Princetonian was liable to wander within the circumference described by the radius of the sturdy leash. Didn't matter. The crowd noises excited the beast, and then he saw our head cheerleader romping in his tiger suit, made from a real tiger skin, and the sight of that boy twirling his tail like a cane, the audacity of that boy fingering his whiskers and squeaking roars, inflamed the circus tiger, and he flipped out."

"What happened?" Jake said, sitting on his chair's edge, draining both barrels from his beer helmet.

"Tiger just pulled up the sturdy stake and ate the head cheerleader. Or so I heard the night before my father dressed me in a pair of orange-and-black diapers and installed me a few inches from a Bengal tiger. My father—maybe your father, too—thought this was very funny, this tiger, the stake, the cheerleader. 'Best way to go, m'boy, chomped on by alma mater.' It felt, I don't know, odd."

Ginger knew she should shake her head in sorrowful sympathy; she wanted to shrug, but she laughed.

"Is this a funny story?" Benjamin asked.

"Oh, is it ever," said Ginger.

"Ginger! She must be blitzed," said Jake.

Ginger gave them both the finger, and walked to the land-ing, and looked out the window, down on Holder Court, at a gang of old men dressed in gray jackets ladling kamikazes from a garbage can.

"Your sister is a fox. She's one pretty girl."

Jake blushed: "Like a melody, asshole?"

Benjamin said, "Chill out, dude."

Ginger said, from the doorway, "You're a couple of pussies. Let's go find some action."

Mrs. Clay had left Ivy for her room at the Nassau Inn. Diana and Polly were discussing their sons, how times had changed, how Kids Today lived like rock stars, up all night, in bed all morning. Polly was laughing about the oddly timed meals, the mood swings: lassitude now, full-tilt boogie a few minutes from now. Diana worried about drugs, she said. Benjamin kept a copy of the *Physician's Desk Reference* on his bedside table. He knew his Quāālude side effects from his Methedrine contraindications.

"Kids today," Polly said.

"Uh-huh," Diana said, "what can you do?"

Nathaniel thought, here we are, just the four of us. This wasn't what he had expected. What became of the ceremony, the self-importance, the rich food, the cigars? Here they were, munching sandwiches and potato chips like folks at a backyard picnic, talking about their kids. Nathaniel had been anxious when Jake and Benjamin decided to room together. He couldn't have put his finger on why, but there was something Nathaniel feared his son might learn from Diana and Booth's son that Nathaniel didn't wish Jake to know. You wouldn't call it arrogance, exactly; or glamour, exactly: Nathaniel feared recklessness. How cautious Nathaniel had become. And he thought he wouldn't have had it any other way. Because here they were, happy. They were! Nathaniel listened to Booth's voice telling some kids-say-the-darnedest-things tales about his little boy, Benjamin, and try as he might Nathaniel could not time-travel ten years back to the previous night he had been in this room. He could though remember with the most sensually sharp acuity the first night he entered the boathouse, and what Booth told him that night about friendship. Now Nathaniel felt that friendship like an aura in the room; it all added up to a simple sum from a complex calculation. Nathaniel was glad to have shared the world with Booth, in *this* contrived Eden, in *their* time, now, in *this* room.

He remembered his wedding, and he remembered Booth's wedding. He couldn't believe what had happened to Diana. Nothing seemed to have happened. It was as though nothing had happened to Diana. She looked the same. Exactly the same.

"You haven't changed a bit," he told her.

"Thanks a lot. I'd sort of hoped I had."

"Was I really dashing?"

"Huh?"

"On the Empire Builder. You called me dashing?"

"What's the Empire Builder?"

"Our train."

"Oh. Sure. I always liked you, Nathaniel. You're so serious. I wish I'd been more serious. Oh well . . ."

He wanted to take her away somewhere. On a train. He was thinking how this might be, recalling how it was, when Pownall showed up. Pownall looked awful. Nathaniel thought Pownall was drunk, and Nathaniel thought Booth too thought Pownall was drunk.

"Yo, Pownall," Nathaniel said. "What's happening?"

Later, Nathaniel would remember that stupid question, those two dumb words, as the last words he spoke before he graduated from this world into that one. "What's happening?"

"There's been a mistake," Pownall said.

Booth didn't catch the drift. "It's okay Pownall, clear your head. What are you trying to say?"

"There's been an accident."

"Who?" Polly said.

"Everyone," Pownall said.

McCosh Infirmary lay a few blocks south of Ivy, along the route these three boys once walked from their club to their boathouse. Nathaniel had never been through the infirmary doors. Leaving Ivy tonight, all five had begun running, but pretty soon, breathless, they had slowed to a fast walk. How could it be they couldn't run? Pownall tried to tell what he knew, and Nathaniel tried to understand.

At McCosh the nurses were doing triage on dozens of drunk people bewitched, bothered, bewildered, bruised, sick. A young doctor, Indian or Pakistani, told Nathaniel and his friends that their children were "fortunate." Before they could see the children, the doctor explained that the students were very drunk, that this was a very great shame, that it was most reckless of drunk young people to climb the sides of buildings, that they were "fortunate" to be alive.

Pownall told the doctor he suspected these people didn't need to hear just now how drunk were their sons and daughters, how fortunate everyone was.

"Let me see my babies," Polly said.

"Yes," Diana said, "let me see my babies."

The doctor was the cleanest-looking man Nathaniel had ever seen. The doctor's skin shone. Nathaniel shivered, the doctor was so clean. The doctor's robe was blood-spattered. He made a puzzled face, said he had only three students in his emergency room.

"My wife has only one baby," Booth said. "A son. My son. My wife is upset and confused."

"I am not confused," Diana said.

Booth said, "We would like to see my son. Now."

They were alive. Jake sat blinking like a losing fighter waiting for the bell to toll the fourteenth round. He was slumped on the edge of a cot in a makeshift emergency room. A nurse was scolding him, telling him to lie down, she'd restrain him if he didn't lie down.

Benjamin and Ginger lay side by side on ambulance stretchers, their heads strapped motionless. Benjamin's face was stained with blood. Ginger said, "Mommy," and tried a smile. Ginger began to cry, and quit. Facing the fluorescent ceiling lights, she couldn't see Nathaniel. "Don't scare Daddy," she said. "He's such a crybaby."

"What happened to you?" Polly asked them all. "Who did this to you?"

There was a knotty question. The easy answer would have been *them*. Princeton dunnit, or the world; life pushed them off the roof, youth dropped them from a great height. Some facts had been pieced together: the children, blasted on reunion beer, had climbed the face of the Chapel. Jake (whose June issue of *Gentry* was not yet in his mailbox)—like the late grandfather he had been licensed to invent—loved a high climb. He conquered apple trees, Vermont's midget mountains, boulders, the towers of Dillon Gym, the spire of the University Chapel.

"Who had this great idea?" Nathaniel asked.

"Don't raise your voice in here," Diana said. "You must not take that tone with my son."

Benjamin spoke. His forehead was bandaged, and when he opened his mouth Nathaniel saw teeth missing. Diana saw this, and reached for her throat, and then steadied herself. Nathaniel thought he heard Benjamin ask what he owed.

"What did he say?" Nathaniel said.

"He asked," Booth said, "if he'll be able to row tomorrow."

The doctor said they would be all right. Tests would determine the extent of their injuries. Diana demanded the attendance of a real doctor, and the doctor said he was a real doctor, and Diana said she wanted her son removed to New York City immediately, and the doctor said that would not be appropriate or possible, and Booth told his wife to shush, and the doctor left the room.

Then Jake said it all, in a monotone rush: "It was my idea to climb they didn't want to do it we got up coming down I belayed Ben Ben belayed Ginger the rope broke they fell Ben fell on Ginger."

Polly said to her cousin: "My daughter broke your son's fall."

Diana said to her cousin: "It was your son's idea."

Benjamin said: "The rope didn't break. The knot untied."

"Whose knot?" said Nathaniel.

Booth said, "Don't ask questions like these."

"My knot," said Benjamin.

Nathaniel said, "Your knot? You're a Newport yachtie! Didn't they teach knots at Ida Fucking Lewis? Can't the boy tie a simple rolling hitch?"

Ginger, looking dreamy, said nothing.

The doctor returned. The children were to be moved to the Princeton Medical Center right away. "We cannot deal with the insults to their persons."

Ginger said, "Am I going to die? It's okay, I just want to know the truth. Just let me know where we are. Okay?"

Nathaniel said, "Ginger, Ginger! Jake's the one with the imagination for disaster, honey. Just be quiet."

The doctor said the ambulance was here.

There wasn't room for all of them. The children were accompanied by Nathaniel and Diana. That was just the way it happened. The others got a ride with a McCosh nurse.

Diana kept asking the ambulance attendants, "What's this

about? What's happening? I just came down here to watch my little boy row a boat. What is happening? What is happening to me?"

Nathaniel couldn't think of a single useful thing to ask, or to say. He squeezed his children's hands. Ginger squeezed back. Jake's hand was cold, dry, inert, so smooth it could have been skinned.

At Princeton Medical Center the staff moved fast, with a rehearsed choreography. The person on whose behalf they moved so urgently was Ginger. Pownall dealt with the insurance and payment questions.

Jake said, "What, Mom?" Jake said, "Why, Mom?"

She was bleeding inside was what. She fell was why.

While the doctors did their special things to Ginger, people drifted in. Johnny Hyde first, and he sat in a corner of the waiting room talking to Jake, who didn't talk back. The Princeton Borough police came. The police had heard rumors that all was not as it should have been. The police told Pownall they had heard that someone had been pushed off the steeple of the University Chapel. The police had also heard that someone jumped off the steeple of the University Chapel. The campus cops, Princeton proctors, came: the proctors huddled with the Borough police; there was a witness, here he was, he had seen it all. The witness spoke precisely. He was a nerdy kid, what Booth and Pownall and eventually Nathaniel would have thought of as a weenie. He had been leaving the library, chanced to look up, saw them against the gray steeple, way up, almost in the gray sky, and then he saw two of them fall. It was just an accident, he said. He spread his hands when he said "just," a mathematician describing Random Walk Theory.

Nathaniel witnessed these comings and goings, but he comprehended nothing. He watched Jake, and he watched Polly. He knew that whatever he said to them would count forever, so he said nothing. He tried to remember by exactly what mechanism he had cleared his head a quarter century ago in his parents' kitchen while his mother held a handgun and commanded him to choose. All he could remember now about what he sensed then was extraneous to the action: the woodstove had hissed and smoked, sleet had rattled the panes, a weak dirty light had blinked pitifully at the end of their dock. But how had he unsprung his mother's coiled fury, how had he armored them all against furious hurt? Lost. He knew Ginger was bleeding inside. They all knew it. Even Diana knew it and, knowing it, she had managed to quit telling perfect strangers that her son hadn't even graduated yet, this was never supposed to have happened.

Booth sat beside Polly and talked quietly to her. He seemed to understand that Nathaniel would not tolerate Booth's solace. Pownall sat beside Nathaniel reminding him how tough kids were, what terrible injury they could endure, how they bounced back from the damnedest hurts. Nathaniel listened to Pownall's conventional wisdoms; Pownall's conventional wisdoms seemed to bear revolutionary truth.

At dawn a doctor let Polly and Nathaniel see her. She was in a recovery room, intensive care. Nathaniel liked the sound of intensive care; Nathaniel didn't at all like the sound of intensive care. He saw her first, and told Polly to keep Jake away. He didn't want Jake to see this, or suspect what he had not seen. Jake argued; Polly spoke sharply to him; Jake kept coming on toward the room; Nathaniel barred the doorway.

"Go away!"

Jake pushed against his father.

"Please!" Polly said loudly. A nurse shushed her. Jake turned his back.

Ginger was not awake.

———

The sun was hot, the morning bright when Johnny Hyde insisted they eat breakfast. He got them a table at the Nassau Inn: Booth and Diana, Nathaniel and Polly, Johnny Hyde. Pownall had stayed at the hospital with Jake. Mrs. Clay was upstairs. "Let your mother sleep," Polly said. The dining room was cheery with fresh flowers, decorated with tiger motifs. The walls were hung with dated oars and footballs, with group photographs of bygone brave boys. Nathaniel saw outside on Palmer Square a couple of laughing '80 grads wheeling a drunk classmate in a baby carriage. The boy was spread out as still as a corpse on a bed of ice. The P-rade would set off from Nassau Hall in a few hours, and last night's hearties were clearing the track with eggs and bloodies and bullshots. They were got up like jesters for the P-rade, and Nathaniel couldn't unknow the power he had to shut their laughter. There was an iron band of exclusion circling the table where his party sat; he knew that his party, their faces etched with grief, was set apart from the light-heads reviewing last night's fun. Nathaniel felt himself unlearning what time had taught him. He looked at his college-mates and couldn't imagine that they had ever got a bit of bad news. Not one was divorced, an orphan, widower. Not one had been fired from a job; not one had failed a course; not one had suffered a hurt at Mother Princeton.

Pownall brought the news. The waitress was taking their orders. She tried to interrupt Pownall, said, "Let me just write this down so these people can eat." Pownall wouldn't be interrupted. The waitress said, "Other people are waiting for this booth. Please be considerate." Diana spoke to the waitress softly, and the waitress's hand flew to her mouth. She was old enough to be a grandmother, and had painted her cheeks with cheerful rouge. She wouldn't leave until Booth assured her that he understood, that he knew for a positive fact she had not meant to seem unfeeling.

"Oh no," Polly said. "Oh no. Oh, Ginger. Oh no. So this is what it is? Oh no."

Nathaniel behaved badly. He said this can't be right. It should have been Booth's kid. It was the Griggs kid's fault. He fell on her. It was his bloody knot.

Professor Hyde was talking under his breath, as though to himself, staring at his menu, saying what Nick had said about Tom and Daisy: "They were careless people. . . . They smashed up things and creatures and then retreated back into whatever it was that kept them together, and let other people clean up the mess they had made."

Nathaniel knew what Professor Hyde thought he knew. He knew Diana was a careless fool. He knew Booth Tarkington Griggs had bone structure too fine for his beard and ponytail. He knew that Myrtle (and Jay Gatz) and Ginger had been smashed by Tom and Daisy and Benjamin Tarkington Griggs. It made such a pretty literary equation. The habit of metaphor made life so deductible, conclusive. Professor Hyde was not cruel; he was Nathaniel's adviser. Professor Hyde did not mean to wound Booth; he meant to explain to Nathaniel.

"No," Nathaniel said. "It isn't like that. It isn't like that at all. You don't know . . . anything."

Ginger couldn't die. But of course she could. They had their claws out here in Tigertown. She could die after all. *That* was the final club. Everyone was a member, not exclusive in the least, all comers were goers. The final club had been played. They'd dropped the queen of spades on him again; they'd dropped that witchy evil right on his little girl. On his little boy.

"I want my mother," Nathaniel said. "Someone wake her up."

"Where's Jake?" Booth said.

And on the stroke of his friend's question—and this was

hard for Nathaniel to comprehend—the new Nathaniel behaved as though he were still the old Nathaniel. How could he speak now in complete sentences, respond to a friend's question with the old formal artifice of strophe/antistrophe, as though natural law and human civility hadn't been suspended by the inexorable force of gravity? How could some old habit of decency have kicked in now? Nathaniel saw himself looking at himself, and he didn't want to avert his eyes from shame at what he saw. Was this graduation?

"I want my son," he said. He took Diana's face in his hands, and brought her eyes level with his. "Let's rescue our sons." He turned to Booth: "Help me, again." He said to Polly: "Help me help Jake." He said to Pownall: "Thank you." He wanted to tell Johnny Hyde, *It's okay.* He wanted to tell the waitress, *Don't be sad, you did right.* He wanted to tell everyone eating breakfast dressed in funny costumes: *Don't worry, it's just pretend.*

Why did he want these things? Was *this* commencement?

Born in Los Angeles in 1937, Geoffrey Wolff has written a biography of Harry Crosby (*Black Sun*) and *The Duke of Deception: Memories of My Father*. Author of four previous novels—*Bad Debts* (1969), *The Sightseer* (1974), *Inklings* (1979), and *Providence* (1986)—and the forthcoming book of personal recollections *A Day at the Beach*, Mr. Wolff lives in Jamestown, Rhode Island.